CONSEQUENCE OF RESISTANCE

CONSEQUENCE OF RESISTANCE

Book Two

JONATHAN CHANEY

HeWhoSteps Publishing House

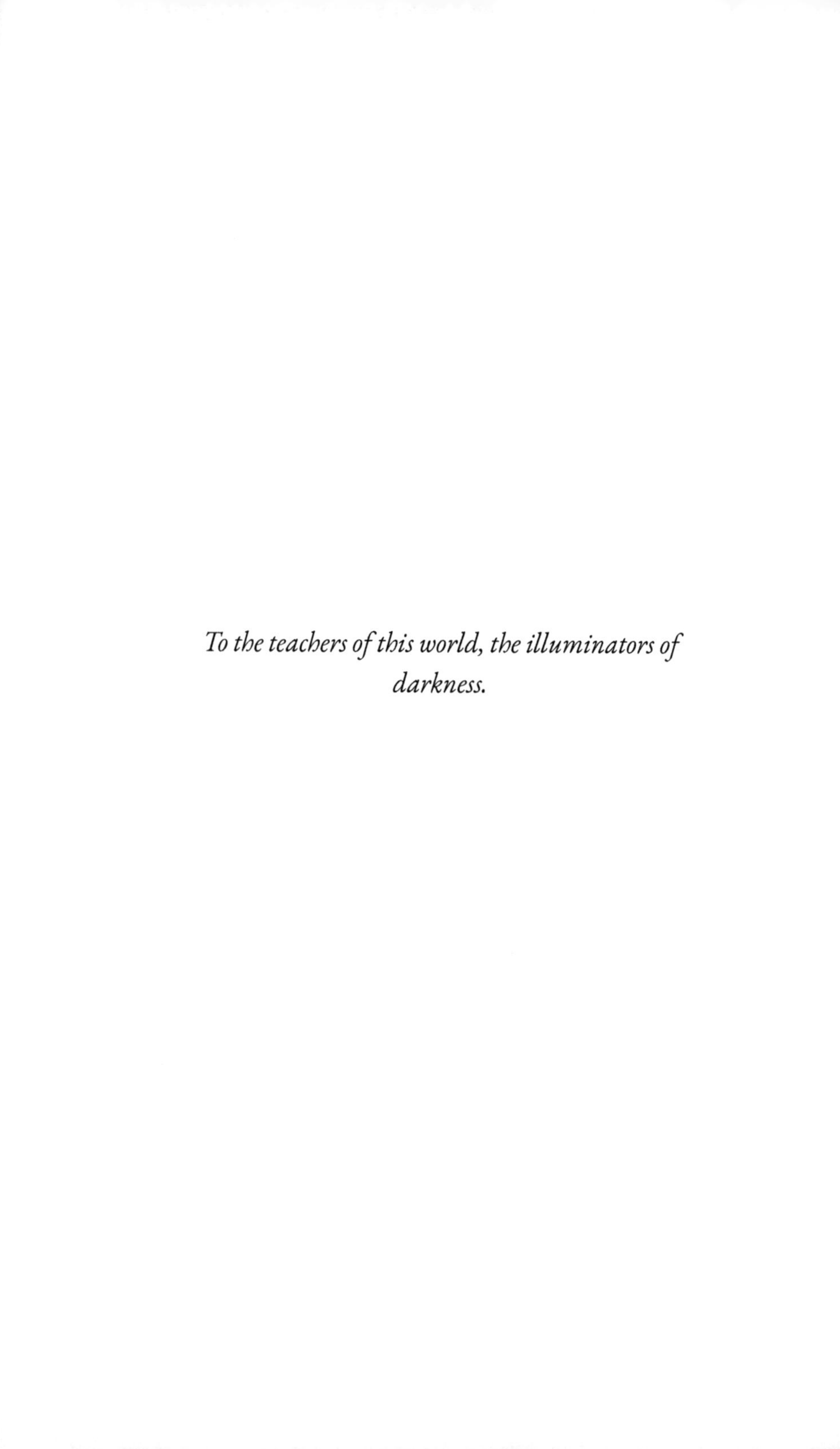

*To the teachers of this world, the illuminators of
darkness.*

Author's Foreword

You could say that the character Remy LeBeau is quite near and dear to my heart. He's not a perfect man but I like him. Will readers sympathize with him? Demonize him? Dismiss it all as a dark fairy tale at best. Time will tell.

Thank you, reader, for your time and attention. Stay frosty and prepare for the unbelievable.

CHAPTER I

USA

The entire pub had dropped their voices to the merest of whispers. The bar -- usually flush with the sounds of drunken agreement, laughter, uproar, and general merriment -- seemed to be collectively holding their breaths, ears pricked. The dining area had grown as quiet as any library. The speaker engaged in the phone call was oblivious to all of this as she plowed onward with her conversation.

"No. No. It's fifty-dollars for thirty minutes. Fifty. Nothing else. Just dancing."

Remy came around the corner, heard that, and stopped everything: all of the tickets he needed to enter into the computer, all of the food orders that might be ready to deliver, the new guests that had just sat, the old guests that undoubtedly wanted something. He halted, dead in his tracks and listened, as had the majority of the pub.

"That's extra. It's two-hundred dollars for that. Yes. Two-hundred. No. Two hundred. What? Oh. Two hours. Two hundred for two hours."

He looked to Nina as she blabbed away on the phone. She was speaking in a relatively normal volume but since the pub had become deathly quiet, her voice carried easily to even the most distant tables. He smiled at her to get her attention. He tried to gesture both the symbol for phone and loud but she wasn't getting any of it. She shook her head distractedly, pivoted away, and continued speaking in the same clear voice that held the entire pub's attention.

"What's the address? Okay. Two hundred. Okay. Bye."

"What'cha doin', Nina?" Remy asked with a smile that clearly said, *I know exactly what you've been doing.*

"Nothing. Taking an order." Oblivious, that one. Mostly stoned out of her mind.

"Really? A food order, was it? To-go?"

"Yep."

"Need any held with that? Sounded like a pretty big order."

"No thanks, I'm okay." And with that, she marched back to the main floor where the volume of the pub was quickly revving back up. It was only then that he realized that the pub had been waiting on bated breath for his words, too. He smiled to himself, enjoying being part of this massive secret, and set to his various tasks.

A half hour later, he confronted her in the kitchen.

"Nina, are you a dancer? A private dancer? Dancing for money, you do what I want you to do?"

"What the f^$# does that mean?"

"It's a song. But it's also you, right? Do you want me to use the real words? Are you a prost---"

"Enough. Okay. I don't want to talk about it. Not here. This isn't the right place."

"Yeah, I was thinking that myself as I and the entire population of this pub listened to your conversation."

"What? Are you f*%&ing serious? You shouldn't spy, Remy." She spun around with hands full of plates of hot food, retreating.

Remy pursued. "You know, ears don't close, right? They aren't eyeballs. They're always open. No one can shut them."

"Well, stop listening."

"Let me guess. I hear too much. I've heard that before."

"Then you should know by now."

"I do and I don't, little one. I do and I don't."

"What does that mean?"

"It means I know what you want me to do, but I won't." Her face was a mix of confusion and displeasure. "I don't cower and I fundamentally oppose immoral behavior so, you know, it leads to conflict. Like this."

She smiled weakly and left the kitchen, hands full of rib dinners.

An hour later, she spoke just as brazenly on the phone again, her voice carrying throughout the building. "Yeah, you are the shit, girl. So hot. Yeah, go there at ten, okay. Yes. He will. No, no. He will. After, okay? If not, call me."

He theorized correctly that the other person was the live-in girlfriend of Nina the bisexual server, their relationship that of pimp and prostitute. *Too sullied for the pure and too virtuous for the wicked. I am truly cursed. My whole life will be this. Fighting. Always fighting. And alone.*

CHINA

CHAPTER II

CHINA

Monica wasn't startled in the least and Remy quickly surmised she would be just fine. His next thought was that of William's safety. He disengaged from her loose embrace and dashed into the adjoining bedroom where William shot up on his feet from within the kennel that he slept in. His reaction time was impressive: he was on his paws and ready to go before the door fully swung open. The shadowy figure on the ledge had apparently raised the hound's hackles, too.

He walked over and opened the cage door. William jogged away and into the bedroom, directly to the window from which Remy had witnessed the shadowy figure pass. On his heels, Remy entered in the bedroom as that same infiltrating humanoid shadow crossed the window and disappeared around the bend of the building. His breath caught in astonishment, his mind failing to make sense of what was happening, while William stoically acted, wedging his muzzle under the curtains to get a better look. Collecting his disjointed thoughts, Remy ran to the kitchen which contained a sliding glass window that if completely opened could easily allow a man to pass in or out. He was tense and in combat mode as he swept his eyes through the apartment, grateful to find it empty. Relaxing from a martial stance, he slid the long window open wide, leaned out and caught a blur of movement at the corner of the building that swiftly disappeared from sight. The danger seemed to have receded.

"What the f&%$ was that, Moni! What the f&%*. What...who....why are you...?"

In response to a barrage of nonsensical half-questions, she entered the living room and sat down heavily, adorned in a sheet that she had draped about her. William trotted to the kitchen behind her, looking edgy and wound-up. Remy crouched eye-level with the hound and patted the top of his wide head. "You caught a little bit of that one, old boy, didn't you? Guess we're under attack now, eh?" He smiled at the joke he made and then realized it wasn't a joke at all. Curious as to if evidence was left behind, he adjoined back to the bedroom. Monica followed and began slipping on panties, trading the makeshift toga for actual clothing.

"Yeah, I guess it's business time now."

"Business time." She repeated, crossing a bra across her chest and affixing a clasp. Her next move was toward her bag, and the phone therein. Remy let that go. The jig was up.

"So, the P.E. teacher, the one you were with after you left me to fend for myself at the police station. You said you'd return to continue the statement, but you didn't. Of course, you didn't. I tracked you down afterward, you know, to find you smiling ear to ear, strolling along with that P.E. teacher. What's her name?" Remy stopped, trying to recall. He'd only met her in passing once or twice.

"You want me tell her name?" She smiled as if that was absurd. Her face hardened as she changed the topic, "You follow me then?"

"How were you unaware of one of the only foreigners in your entire city trailing you? That's what you should be asking yourself."

Remy approached her and playfully poked her exposed stomach. "You suck."

Her smile was cold and wrong, reminding him of the mannequin she had once become at the police station months ago. A mannequin wearing an empty grin where his lover had once stood. The room filled with loathing as they dressed.

"She took that sexy picture of you. Or at least that's what you told me. That's the only thing I'm comfortable thinking about, so let's go with that. You two looked so pleased with each other that I at first confused you for lovers. But perhaps that was no confusion at all." Monica's scowl inspired Remy onward. "She does *dance*. I saw that with my own two eyes." He thought back to a Christmas talent show that the sophomore and junior students had put on at the end of the year. Monica and the P.E. teacher had performed a dance for the crowd, quite erotic in nature, more like strippers than cheerleaders. Remy's face relaxed as a realization came.

"She was one of the girls you learned to dance with. One of the chosen ones. She was recruited by some demon right along with you. She's your lover? Or something else? I can't quite put my finger on it."

She had regained her composure and looked up calmly from scrolling through a long list of Chinese text messages that Remy had no hope of glimpsing any meaning from. "What you mean?" she asked sweetly. "Who you talk about? What you mean dancing?"

"Okay, Monica. Okay. It's like that now, is it? Okay."

He walked over to the bedroom window and flung the curtains open wide.

"I no go near. If I you, I no go near window."

"Well, you're not me. I have a soul, for one thing, so that's an easy way to tell us apart." He turned from her, slid open the window, and leaned his torso out, looking to where the shadow had crept out of view. "Anytime, you pansy! Anytime that you feel like coming in, you do it. You do it and see what happens. Night or day. I don't care if I'm sleeping at the time. Sleeping is the only time you may actually have a chance of landing a blow. You hear me?! Anytime!"

He returned to the bedroom, leaving the window fully open. Cool autumn air blew in as he returned to the living room and sat angrily, staring at a wall brooding for an hour while Monica caught up on her messages, of which she had plenty. The city didn't respond to Remy's challenge that night. Monica furtively typed away on her phone as the minutes passed: sending, receiving, sending again. By three a.m. they had relaxed enough to contemplate sleep. They looked to each other and gave sad smiles. His eyes misted and she came to his side.

"I wish you would just leave with me. Leave this nonsense behind you."

"Shhhh," she hushed, and kissed him. He was saddened and infuriated and ready to fight and pondering what to do about wayward shadows and all that entailed, but when she peeled away her blouse and unclasped her bra, everything else dissolved away.

CHAPTER III

USA

Remy could literally smell the cocaine in the sinus cavity of the hostess. He sniffed her again, this time openly, close and loud, making a show of it. Amusing himself at a job he hated.

"What're you doing?"

"I'm smelling you. What'd you think I was doing?"

"Well, quit it. I don't feel well."

"Sinuses, I imagine. Bobby sounds a little sniffly, too." *And smells like the same batch of coke. I'm more certain now than ever that you two have regular sex with one another. And you, hostess, in a long-term relationship with a hapless bloke. Shame, shame.*

Remy walked off, preparing for the oncoming business that Friday nights delivered. He was one of the few that did such things, the rest of the staff lounging on their laurels, chatting about nothing good and nothing interesting. He held little interest in the personal lives of most of the people he was forced to work with, feeling very much marooned with ne'er-do-wells. He was clearly unemployable in other types of work which had been proven to him by the multitude of applications for employment in higher fields that had led to zilch. Too virtuous for the wicked, too mistrusted by decent folk, and very much on his own.

Later that night, as he awaited drinks to be made far, far too slowly, his peripheral vision captured the bartender slipping a small white packet into the palm of a customer at the bar. The manager, the general manager, the head honcho, had witnessed this, but more importantly, had witnessed Remy's awareness of the situation. At once it was clear that the manager was in the know. Why he still employed him was beyond Remy's ken.

"If you have time, you shouldn't be waiting here. Go to the kitchen and run food."

"Sure, boss." But before he left the bar to go to the kitchen that he knew had no food waiting for him, he simply turned and looked back to the manager, locking eyes but with a pleasant demeanor. *I know that you know,* spoke Remy's eyes. *I know that you know,* spoke the manager's eyes. And with that he pivoted and slowly ambled away.

Three hours later in the parking lot, after a typical grueling shift, he turned the key to his Honda and nothing happened. Even more disheartening was the fact that he could not pull his key out of the ignition. He struggled with the locked key a little more before abandoning the notion that he was able to solve the issue. His gloomy thoughts turned to the path he would need to travel to return home, either a seven-mile hike or a twenty-dollar Uber ride. Accepting failure, he scrutinized the darkened parking lot for potential trouble as he exited the vehicle. Abandoning his vehicle with the key in the ignition, tired strides took him toward the pub as he inwardly prepared to return momentarily and find his prized car missing. In the midst of these morose thoughts, an epiphany emerged: the gear was set in the reverse position somehow. Resetting that to park allowed him to turn the key freely and all trouble dispersed. Jazz played loudly through open windows as he exited the parking lot and merged onto the mostly deserted streets of Orlando.

There wasn't much in his apartment but there was everything needed for creature comforts. A comfortable sofa with spare cushions. A padded chair to sit upon, rarely used. Shelves adorned the walls of the living room holding nothing of importance: an extra video game controller, a collection of moneys from far-away places and even farther away times displayed in a crystal bowl for no one to see. A fifty-inch plasma screen television with all of the best that video games and television streaming had to provide.

Such was the life of Remy LeBeau in the summer of the year 2019. The refrigerator was stocked with food and beverages. His gasoline tank remained pretty full. No repairs were needed for his car in the immediate future. He had little savings each month, and plenty of debt to work on, but it was more or less routine. Stable. Normal. The days had grown indistinguishable. It was that, more than anything, that concerned Remy the most.

CHINA

There was a firm, unspoken rule in China in regards to daytime and nighttime activities. Poker was never played while the sun shone, for example. As the last of the sun's rays peaked and vanished across the bluish-purple sky, a room would open in the back of some pub or another and cards would be shuffled, chips purchased. Conversely, last calls came at dawn in any pub or nightclub that had chosen to remain open so late. On certain side streets, pimps and pushers called another work shift to a close and abandoned their haunts.

When the sun rose, Remy welcomed its arrival. He carefully unwove himself from Monica's resting form, donned some comfortable clothes and took a rather joyful William on a walk around the block. The morning was shaping up nicely. He was exhausted but clearheaded and happy to be walking in the light of day. There was a feeling in the air that everything was going to be alright. A man creeping around the ledge of his bedroom window on the seventeenth floor seemed quite far away indeed. "Olly olly oxen free," Remy sang-song, smiling at the respite from the tension of the previous night. In response William slowed down, thereby weakening the massive pull he generated on the leash and looked back quizzically, head askew, the stereotypical dog expression of trying to figure out what a sound means.

"What're you looking at? I wonder how much English you actually understand at this point, my furry friend. You understand more than just my commands, I'm sure. It means we're fine, boy. For now, I guess. For another eleven hours or so. Man, that does suck, but hey," he bent low and grabbed the gentle beast's face, shaking it back and forth playfully. William brightened. "You are one hundred pounds of tough guy and I've trained a bit. Let them come, I say."

She was boiling water for tea when they returned. William bounded off of his leash, rushed over to her, sniffed her outer thigh, snorted, and bounded off to gnaw on a rope-toy. Remy relaxed on the sofa, enjoying the cozy moment. For all intents and purposes, last night had never happened. He blew along the rim of the mug, rippling the contents with cooling breath. She held her own mug in both hands, warming her palms. Taking the hint, he fished for the AC remote control on the coffee table and turned off the unit. She smiled. He sipped. They drank in silence.

"I don't know what to say to you, Moni. I've offered you every chance to end what you're doing and forge a new path with me. You've definitively rejected the offer. I love you and you say you love me, too, and yet, this." He waved his arms about, gesturing to the windows, to his laptop, his phone, his heart. "Your tale of the dance school saddens me, though the fact that you've resigned yourself to such a life is even worse. Interpol isn't going to fix this. The Chinese police force is apparently obedient to sinister forces so I can't rely on them, and I, well, I'm not making any progress. I've exhausted all the avenues and dark alleyways the black-market merchants inhabit. I've questioned pushers and users, gamblers -- a wide variety of folk that aren't so far removed from those who steal money via bank theft.

I've gotten nowhere. I won't get anywhere. Anyone who is anyone has heard me coming a long way off and they've nothing but distraction, lies, or silence to offer me. Now, I'm able to sort through some of that and find a portion of obscured truth through the occasional lie, but it takes a toll on me. It's grueling and exhausting and at times wholly inaccurate, and at this point, apparently dangerous to boot. Truth be told, recovering my lost finances isn't even a priority at this point."

More silence as they sipped tea.

Remy smiled. "Let's get married today, huh? Just journey down to city hall and get married. What'd'ya say?"

She laughed warmly. Demurely. "In China, friend and family must give money to man and wife. No gifts. No presents, like America do. Just money."

"Yeah, we talked about this the last time you visited. I remember. I spent a little on a friend's wedding last year." He remembered back to a trip to Shanghai, to a New Orleans/Chinese hybrid wedding ceremony. He'd put a couple hundred dollars in an envelope for the new bride and groom, then, as had most of the participants. *Best I don't contact those two any longer. There's a decent chance that my communications are monitored by malignant forces these days. Who knows what I could inadvertently suck that couple into? Would be nice to phone a friend though, but what would I even say? "There was a stranger creeping along my seventeen-story ledge last night." No one's going to believe that.*

He was staring through the wall, stone-faced, as grim as a battlefield soldier. She rose gracefully from her seat and sat down next to him. She set down her mug, leaned over, put her face in front of his, nose-to-nose, bringing him back. He smiled shyly and kissed her, in love and in sorrow.

"I can't marry you," she said.

"You won't marry me. You choose not to, but I get it. Who would even attend the wedding? No one from work, I can promise you that. I'd be relying on you and yours to fill the seats," he chuckled. "Or maybe your father would pay me a dowry to take you off of his hands." The smirk faded quickly as Remy thought of the story of her father, of the dance school that was much more than simply dancing. Of what she must be caught up in. How inextricably ensnared. Of what she had done, of what she was hinting would come. Of the glimmer of goodness that shone through from time to time. Of how futile it all was. *I'm shaking my fists in anger at the wind and it blows all around me without care or concern.*

"Come." She stood and pulled a now teary-eyed Remy onto his feet. "Be happy."

He offered a weak smile and was led into the bedroom where they spent the remainder of the morning and quite a bit of the afternoon in play. Later, they shared a large glass of water, exhausted, out of breath, muscles cramping, yet still hungry for each other. She passed the glass to Remy who drank deeply.

"You no work with us. You different."

"What do you mean, Moni? I do work among you. I teach kids, a few of which are very much spoiled rotten and some of which are sweet kids on their way to doing some good in this terrible world. And there's my detecting. That's work. Loving you. That's work, too." Remy smirked at his own joke.

"You different," she repeated, smiling sadly and looking down. "You like people you work with? At job?" she asked, with a sad smile that made it not a question at all.

"Not at all. There was one, Ez..." Remy trailed off wondering if simply mentioning the man's name would endanger the fellow. "There was one. But I don't see him much anymore. Different teaching schedules, I suppose. Probably for the best. The rest are either bullies, threatening me openly right in the office, bullies beyond reproach in this dreadful place, or Chinese teachers that keep their distance. Yeah, I see what you're saying. Different. I care about protecting the little guy, not taking what I can from him. Fairness. Equality. Justice and whatnot. Putting decent people ahead of myself if their needs are greater. That sort of thing. I'm nothing like that thug that threatened my brother or that mastermind computer-guru. I hate them, actually. I'm proud to call myself an enemy."

"Enemy," she echoed, as if recalling something far away and unclear.

"Enemy." Remy repeated, very clearly, with newfound strength. "It's sad, isn't it?"

She nodded solemn agreement as they embraced. William crashed into the room and stuck his cold wet nose between their embraced bodies, alternately nudging one and then the other. Remy kissed his doggy head and led him out of the room, closing the door solidly behind him. William immediately leapt up and began scratching at the door from the outside though he'd been trained not to years ago, having left that behavior behind in his puppy years, and yet, there he was, jumping and scratching at the closed bedroom door. Remy opened the door and looked down at the agitated German Shepherd gazing up at him. "You know not to do this. Stop." He shut the door and William was immediately at it again.

He shot open the door again, angry now, snatching William by the leash and pulled him off to his kennel, having to drag the hound most of the way. "What has gotten into you, boy? I need you to be cool. Things are getting bad and I don't know what to do next. Don't fall apart on me now."

He latched the kennel gate shut, a large kennel, full of cushions and a toy. He pawed the gate forcefully, uncharacteristically seeking immediate exit. "I don't need this right now, William. In four hours the sun will set and I imagine life will become even worse for us. Get some rest now while you can. You'll need it." But his words went very much unheeded. He shut the door to a hound whining quietly to himself as he rattled the kennel gate.

He returned to the bedroom and found Monica dressed in something provocative and new she had brought over. She stretched out in an inviting manner. Remy accepted the invitation.

They spoke around kisses.

"William is okay? He is good dog." It was the first time she had ever acknowledged that. More than once they had argued over the merits of having feelings for animals. She, like many Chinese, frowned upon caring for animals and believed Remy's love of William was a sign of immaturity.

"He's a very good dog. The best dog I know."

"You are father. You doggy daddy." She rolled with him, opening her mouth and kissing more passionately.

"I am, I suppose. Though I think of him more as a friend."

"He is good dog," she repeated.

They kissed more and rolled and splayed and sweat. Their love-making was intense and cut through the stillness of the ordinary day. Rhythms shifted, increasing speed and velocity, dying down and rushing forward, pausing, and returning hungrily, bodies colliding and separating rhythmically.

"Let me top," she whispered, spinning about and rocking her hips in ways Remy had never experienced before. His need for her grew deeper. He moaned euphorically. And then it happened.

She paused in midstride and in that instant repositioned her hips and, using newly arrived vaginal muscles to lock Remy's member in place, came crashing down in a radically misaligned angle. The attack ruptured the blood-filled internal organs that fortified his erect penis. There was a disturbing popping noise, the same sound as bone tearing free from a joint: muffled and yet piercing. He gasped in pain and hurled her off his hips. Across the mattress she flew before tumbling to the floor. He doubled over, adrenaline coursing through, in trauma-induced shock but knowing that something very bad had just happened. Taking a deep breath to steady his racing mind, he raised himself to a kneeling position and looked down at a penis rapidly losing its rigidity. There was a dark redness and an ominous lump around the midsection. Remy probed the area with fingers. Enduring the pain this caused, he found a strong curving ridge where there had been nothing of the sort before.

"What have you done? What did you just do to me?!"

She had made no move to rise from the floor. She lied there, looking away, distant.

"This hurts so much that it doesn't even hurt. I'm flooded with cold adrenaline." He probed again with diagnosing fingers, removing all doubt that something rather permanent had transpired. "You maimed me! You maimed my penis." He looked down at her. "Well, speak, damn you. Speak!" He bent over and scooped her up off of the floor, dumping her carelessly onto the center of the mattress where she bounced a bit before coming to a resting position.

"I sorry. It accident."

"Accident? No, it most certainly was not! You stopped. You shifted. You came down differently. You attacked me, is what you did. And scored. You landed a blow that maimed me."

Remy leapt atop her, all love and sorrow and pity gone. Only justice. Pain and justice.

Neither fear nor anger shown through her fine features. He shifted his hips to the side, keeping his most vital bits out of striking range. Situating himself defensively, one palm found its way to her back, centering her, the other gently rested on her shoulder, poised, ready but uncertain. "You are this lure. This painful, beautiful lure and a barbed hook all rolled up into one terrible person. You," he tensed, feeling most unlike himself, "are dangerous."

She broke then and began weeping, pausing intermittently to gasp in air between wails. "Do it," she croaked. "Better me. Better you." Another wail shook her. "Do it."

He was overcome. His muscles melted and his grip on her and the situation dissolved. She continued sobbing -- howling really -- mucus pouring out of her nose, face squinted in pain. She rolled away and curled up. He approached the other side of the bed tenderly, crouched low and held her. She sobbed more intensely, making weak moves to push him away while Remy held the embrace, whispering encouragement. In time, her breathing slowed and deepened and became more regular. The tears subsided. Her muscles relaxed.

"Loving you hurts, Monica."

"I know."

He kissed her delicately on the lips. She pulled away, fresh tears streaming through old channels of wetness streaked across rosy cheeks. "I forgive and love you, Monica Hu."

"What?" she spat.

"I don't have a choice. I don't get to decide these things. I just do."

She rolled over and held him and they kissed. Remy brought her close and they pressed firmly against one another, body shifting, a gentle rhythm developing.

"What you doing?" she asked. "You need go hospital."

"A hospital here in Guangzhou? In Guangzhou, China? To be sliced open and operated on? No, I think not. I'm not a fool, Moni, despite what your band of thugs may think of me. If they can permeate a police station, they can control a doctor all the more easily. I'd probably come out of anesthesia a eunuch. No, I think I'll take my chances and heal on my own." He kissed her ardently. "Maybe a little love medicine would help."

"You are crazy person."

"I love you, babe. Do you really find that surprising?"

And with that they returned to what they had been doing most of the night and morning and afternoon. The new erection brought an excruciating pain that Remy gritted his teeth and persevered through. The sex brought very little pleasure to either of them and he went through the motions only to prove to himself that he was still able, as well as to show whoever had ordered such a thing and the one who had implemented it, that he would persevere, to show courage in the face of such a heinous act. Afterward, they detangled, happy to end such a forced, unpleasant act and slept on opposite ends of the bed.

Day turned to night while they slumbered. He awoke once at a late and quiet hour, the sound of a helicopter echoing throughout the bedroom, almost as if such a vehicle was landing on the rooftop a few stories above. It was a new sound, so oddly nearby. He stood and shuffled over to the bedroom window, drew the curtains wide and checked the ledge for signs of someone passing through, finding none. He once again replayed the previous night's incident in his head, weighing doubt against memory and concluding yet again that it had, in fact, happened, evidence or not. Someone had actually been creeping along the ledge of his apartment, seventeen stories high. He then searched the dark sky for that helicopter that had sounded close enough to lower a rescue ladder, finding nothing save dark emptiness. *Wishful thinking,* he mused. *One arm wrapped around William. The other clutching onto the rung of a dangling rope ladder. The two of us flying off to safety.*

In the neighboring room, William whimpered sadly in the background.

CHAPTER V

USA

The two-week notice was well written but he reread it once more just to be sure, scanning for grammatical or spelling mistakes and finding none. The content was formal and concise and oozed class.

"So, that's it, I guess. I appreciate the opportunity I had working here. It allowed me to save enough money to get on my feet, more or less. I do appreciate that. But you know, I never really fitted in here."

"So, where are you headed?" Mario asked, not disagreeing. "Do you have something lined up?"

"Well, nothing definitive. But I'm sure something will turn up." A job serving tables in an Italian chain restaurant was in the works, the outcome promising, but he thought that the more distance he kept between the pub and his new life, the better. "I'd say I have another life or two left in this old cat. I have a way of a landing on my feet. Most of the time."

Manager and employee shook hands amiably.

"Take care of yourself. If the head honcho here doesn't fire me out of spite upon reading this letter, then I guess I'll see you Friday night."

An incoming phone call pulled his attention elsewhere and Remy seized the opportunity to exit without much more ado. The heat of the day slammed into him as he swung the side door open wide. He popped his collar out and up to deflect the sun's rays on his neck, stepped out into the scorching Florida sunshine, and strutted back to his car. *That felt right. I don't know exactly what comes next. But that felt right.*

CHAPTER VI

CHINA

"You look like a frog. Like a frog swimming in a pond."

She frowned, dipped and surfaced again, bobbing along the water's surface.

"A sexy frog?" She asked, garbling the question as she submerged. She bobbed up a moment later, spitting water rather unmaidenly.

"Sure, a sexy frog. A young, virile, sexy frog's first-time swimming." Remy chuckled and splashed water at her as she dipped and bobbed seemingly in place, making little progress through the pool. She continued on, focused on the distant edge. At her current speed, she would arrive ten to fifteen minutes later.

"You know freestyle strokes would be a lot faster."

"Too much splash. Not cute." She bobbed again. Underwater her legs splayed and came together again haphazardly.

"Is it cute to watch a frog drown?"

She frowned and continued along. He shrugged a reply and flipped upside-down underwater, standing on his hands, collapsing a few times before giving up and swimming over to the center of the pool where she continued to bob along fruitlessly. He swam circles around her, playfully teasing her progress. They shared a smile when she reached the other side.

"I very good swimmer, no?"

"The best. Maybe you should give up dancing and just focus on the swimming," he kidded, ruining the moment.

Later, as he basked in the meager sunrays that the midday sun had brought, she approached, hair dripping atop the breast of a simple, white bikini equipped with flaps and lacy bits and her shining through it all. No finer medium could he imagine. Hoping to heal fully but slowly coming to grips with the fact that his penis wasn't going to fully recover, lied to, spied upon, and generally immersed in no good. Despite all that, her company brought him joy.

More or less dried, they returned to the apartment, lounging and snuggling. When evening came, they went out for a bite to eat. She longed for an entertaining environment, a nightclub, a pub, but he only knew secretive poker backrooms in which he had tried in vain to track down the culprits responsible for his theft. He wanted to keep that away from her, to keep the pubs where Patrick and his cronies frequented equally distant, while at the same time knowing that she was connected to some of that already. It was an awkward façade to maintain, pretending that what had happened had not. Lovemaking had become an act of vigilance and he took care to remain on top during their coupling. His erection had become sharply curved and slightly painful. He had indeed been maimed. The wound would not heal in the days and years to come.

Late that night, spent and sweating, the couple talked quietly to one another across the sheets, Remy doing most of the talking in a rather one-sided conversation about his job and the people he worked with. He was trying to disclose the minimalist of amounts of the meager information he had accumulated about his theft while prompting her into accidentally divulging more but she spoke so infrequently that such a feat had been proving fruitless. Having failed for the past hour to gain even a single important detail, he abandoned the notion of indirect interrogation and opened up. He was at the part about delving into his own computer system, of having a saved file erased from his memory stick at work, when a flit of peripheral movement caught their attention. Her face flashed a tell of recognition over his shoulder before it settled back to Remy, a tender smile playing about her lips as if to distract and keep his attention fixated on her, while the familiar shadow along the ledge played about along the edge of the bedroom's drawn curtain. It expanded and deepened the shadows emanating from the window, a foreboding presence that was both observed empirically and felt.

He acknowledged the return of the bizarre unknown along the ledge and Monica's dubious newfound interest in his words behind a veil of feigned ignorance, a skill he had become quite adept at throughout his time as a DIY detective and semi-professional poker player. He learned best when those who sought to deceive him thought him deceived. Such a mask had come to serve him well at poker tables and he slipped into the guise naturally, at the same time quelling a very real concern of a being who used building ledges as sidewalks. He continued the one-sided conversation, all the while keeping the darkening shadow affixed in his peripheral until at one point he leapt up, dashed to the window and drew the curtain wide revealing a normal, empty ledge.

"I'd say you were mind-tricking me, but that's a Jedi thing and you're definitely Sith. Not that that's real. But then again, a shadowy figure on a ledge doesn't sound very real either."

She glanced up from energetic texting, though she had been solely intent on his conversation just five seconds prior. "I will go tomorrow."

"I wish you wouldn't. I wish you would take that phone, smash it into pieces, marry me, and live happily ever after in America."

She looked to him with an uneasy smile. "Tomorrow afternoon I go."

She returned to texting, fielding a stream of incoming messages. He made no move to return to bed and instead remained at the window, alternating between staring off into the vastness of the skyline and to the ledge where he was beginning to realize a petite, agile, fearless person could maneuver without too much trouble. Behind him, her thumbs whirled as she texted characters he couldn't read to people he didn't know. He thought of all they had been through, reliving past moments bitter and sweet. Eventually, she slowed to a stop. She clicked the off button and set her phone aside.

"*Sayanora*," he muttered uneasily.

"What you say?"

"*Sayanora*." He put on a brave face, sporting a smile he didn't feel. "Most of the time, the Japanese say 'see you later' or 'until next time' or 'tomorrow, right?' but sometimes that's just not the case. Sometimes you have to say *sayanora* because there won't be a next time."

"Don't be sad. Come." She purred, gently tugging on his elbow. "Come to bed. I make you happy."

"Yeah, that's the problem, Moni." He answered, complying. "That's the whole problem right there."

USA

He landed the new job serving tables at the Italian restaurant and left the pub behind just as soon as professional protocol allowed. There, after six years otherwise, he met a woman that stirred long dormant feelings in the man.

Pretty and clever, confident and kind, Lily and Remy immediately took to one another. They interested one another. She listened, and he listened to her, and perhaps more importantly, they understood one another. When he broached the norm, there she was, right there with him, smiling at the wordplay or sarcasm as if it was her own native tongue. They clicked.

They had been watching training videos for two hours, the subject matter presented as life and death stuff: safety and sanitation, the importance of the proper shoe in the workplace, the dangers of parking lots, how to best wash your hands, and on and on and on. But when an unforeseen influx of customers flooded the front of the house, management forewent the training, thrusting the newly hired into the thick of things, shadowing experienced servers and generally lending aid throughout the restaurant.

The staff rushed about, doing this and that, to and fro. Remy loved these moments, the thrill of it all. Impossible to fulfill all the expectations perfectly but fun to try. He shouldered a tray overflowing with dishes into the kitchen from the floor, tapping into martial stances to navigate through choked doorways while hauling twenty kilos of plates, glasses, and silverware. Stacking plates of various sizes onto according stacks as swiftly as possible, making a game of it, he was interrupted from the flow as he caught the familiar movement of another new hire whose name he could not recall. She was in the midst of rinsing her hands and wore an angry scowl.

"Up to the elbows. Don't forget our training. You need to wash your hands each and every time up to the elbows," Remy stated in a comically bookish voice.

"Are you trying to tell me what to do? Don't even," she hissed, storming out.

Hmmm, Remy thought as he meandered away. *She doesn't quite get it.*

Later, as the rush died down to a trickle, he recounted the story with Lily. "Wait, where are my elbows again?" she quipped. "I always forget that one."

She was something special alright. A rarity indeed.

CHAPTER VII

CHINA

He didn't sleep well that night. Like a sailor on the bow of a ship, uneasily looking to the horizon in apprehension of a storm felt but not seen, Remy lied in bed staring into the shadows of his room. William's unabashed snoring echoed throughout the quiet flat. The hushed heavy breathing of the beauty next to him, whose long hair lay across a generous portion of his torso, coalesced with the hound's, forming a relaxing rhythm. A melody of sleep, and yet, sleep would not come.

His life had become a whirlwind: from conversations layered in double-speak with strangers that somehow recognized him; to the dark truth of Monica's life, past and present; to a compromised internet connection; to the recent maiming; to a presence on the seventeenth-story ledge; to the crime unsolved. Thinking of how best to respond to future occurrences and forming plans to gather more information and evidence constantly filled Remy's mind with vast probabilities most nights. He was constantly fighting a headache in those times, feeling like a boxer in a ring, blows raining down upon him ceaselessly, battered but on his feet, mind racing to find a way out, a way to somehow beat the odds and win. But that night, the night before she left, all of that strangely fell away, leaving a tense calm akin to a lull in battle as soldiers regroup for another attack.

There was a peace to it, but still his mind whirled in contemplation of what may come, running through possible occurrences based on previous experiences, deducing statistical probabilities and the like. More pressure from the school that was also something drastically different was almost certainly upcoming. Perhaps a return of the warring courtyard tribes that he'd observed on day one. He hadn't seen Ezekiel around the office in quite some time. Anyone's guess why but it didn't bode well.

I do know how to get to the airport now, though, he reminded himself as anxiety crept in. *Meeting Monica earlier this week ensured that. If push comes to shove, I can just pack my crucial documents, a change of clothes, toiletries, and my laptop in that black backpack, leash William, and I'm off to the airport to purchase a one-way ticket to America.* Confident in a clear escape path, the panic attack that threatened to creep upon him as he planned an ominous future became manageable. *I love her,* he thought, breathing deeply through widened nostrils, taking in the scent of her, not a perfumed fragrance that he identified with her, but the actual smell of her. *She's not coming with me, though, that's clear. She's not going to fight this wickedness that assails the both of us.* His spirits dipped further. *She resigned a long time ago and I can't convince her otherwise.*

He shifted softly off of the bed careful not to disturb his partner/opponent. He prodded open the cracked bedroom door without a sound and drifted through the hallway and living room silently, ignoring light switches and embracing the darkness. Passing the refrigerator, Remy came to rest at the windowed wall of the kitchen that overlooked the city. Hundreds of windows, perhaps a thousand, lay stretched out before him in perfect horizontal and vertical lines positioned both near and far. From the seventeenth floor, there was much of the city to see. A lone taxi rolled unhurriedly by on the street far below. He held his breath, closed his eyes, and focused on listening. The loudness of the vehicle intensified, the engine clunking along. *Piston misfire,* he reasoned. Nearer, Monica and William slept on, their breathing uninterrupted.

"Come and get it, Guangzhou," he muttered quietly to the city.

He stayed that way for quite some time, leaning against the wall, looking out over the city through a large bay window wide enough to allow a dining room table through if one felt so inclined. No screen across the opening. A bit of iron railing along the bottom of the window and a narrow ledge below that. He anchored himself and swung his midsection out of the window, gazing down a one hundred seventy-foot sheer drop to the street below. He hoisted his torso back in, dizzied. *To access this ledge must have taken more than courage and agility.* He looked down once more, acclimating to the perspective. *Though, it would take quite a bit of both of that. It also means that this adversary, this sneak-thief that creeps along my ledge, must live nearby, or at least be allied with someone that lives nearby.* He opened the window and leaned his body out again, this time looking straight up. Fifty feet or so to the roof. *No, I don't think this thing came and went from the roof. Too far. Too much time exposed. Too much of a strain on the body, too. Yes, I'm reasonably certain this little ninja lives close by.*

He grinned as if he had solved a complicated riddle but as the implications of this discovery set in, good spirits quickly faded. *The enemy is near. Neighbors.* The refrigerator light blinded him as he opened the door and rummaged through its contents for chilled water. William slept on. Monica's breathing had changed, however, and Remy pretended not to notice that she was now awake as he slipped back under the sheets. He kissed her cheek and she continued to pretend to sleep on. Such was their way.

CHAPTER VIII

CHINA

He was certain that the thug from the police station in Nanchang was approaching, though a second look proved otherwise. A reasonable facsimile, however, bearing the same muscular build and thick mustache atop a grim mouth. With squared shoulders and hips, he marched straight toward Remy and William whose mouth opened wide, tongue lolling, oblivious to the concept of a threat.

Remy halted in place near the glass double doors of the lobby, waiting as the man crossed the substantial emptiness of the courtyard, preparing for the imminent altercation. Under a murky sky, William stared off as two children played as toddlers do, kicking a ball, chasing it, kicking it again, sometimes missing and falling down and squealing with delight. William desperately wanted to bound over and frolic but maintained his composure reasonably well. Taking after William, Remy showed no sign of worry or concern, enjoying the simple pleasures of childhood play with his wolfish counterpart. Eventually the man reached his destination, looking even more disgruntled than before.

"Is this your dog?"

"Is that really your question or do you want to try again?"

Fake smile. "Sorry. English not good."

"Brain not good more like it." Remy turned his gaze to the man who stood a respectable distance away, sizing him up, searching for weak points. "Not exactly a language barrier issue, is it? You're uncertain if the dog that I hold here on this leash that I walk around this complex twice a day, every day, is in fact my dog. Pretty sure that toddler over there playing kickball could tell you the answer to that, Tom. Do you mind if I call you Tom? You remind me of a Tom."

"My name is Zhu Hwei." He made no movement to shake hands, or wave, or smile, or nod. Just an announcement of name. His face bore no pleasantry. Nothing warm in the eyes whatsoever.

At hip level, William perspired from an open mouth and tilted his head as a green, plastic ball went flying, kicked off in an unexpected direction. The toddlers shrieked with pleasure and ran off to fetch it. Remy, unappreciative of the tough guy routine and being assailed by a stranger so close to home, such as it was, decided to have a bit of fun with the intruder. He loosened the slack he held on the leash and set his arms whirling about in a swift stretch of sorts. Squaring his own shoulders and hips to mimic the intruder's martial posture he shuffled slightly toward the man, a playful smile on his face. A swift reaction followed. Hwei responded, either not sensing the playful nature of Remy's action or not caring. Like a coiled serpent, he shifted and tensed as if to attack. Remy's smile vanished.

William, still ignorant to the more immediate human interaction happening at the other end of his leash, stood idly between the near combatants transfixed on the children at play. Remy tugged at the leash to bring the hound into a safer position, but the dog didn't budge. He had intentionally kept his family and friends at a distance while he delved into the shadowy underworld, yet his brother's home had been threatened. He had not only failed to protect the woman he loved, she'd rejected and maimed him. Only William remained, the single good thing that he could nurture and protect. The hound stared on, engrossed by the toddlers at play. Since he would not move behind Remy, Remy stepped in front of William which put him within striking range of Hwei.

There was a flash of movement. An attack and a dodge. It was incredibly quick, so quick, that a courtyard populated by some ten or so people were completely oblivious that anything had even happened. The movement, the strike from a muscular semi-clone of the intruder to the police station in Nanchang, and the corresponding dodge by Remy had finally superseded the game of kickball and William turned about reluctantly to face the proceedings, unhurried, cool and calm.

Now that William was positioned behind him, Remy stepped backward, shoving the dog with his shins backward and away from the aggressor's reach. William stared at the newcomer pleasantly as the duo clumsily backstepped. Remy's eyes were all fury.

"You've been waiting for me to come out here. You ambushed me, is what you did. You ambushed me in my own courtyard in the middle of the day among children playing ball. You know the dog is mine, and you asked the question anyway. You understand the English that I speak, but you lie and say you don't. You want me to respect you? Impossible."

He took a half-step forward and was immediately put on the defensive once again. Though Hwei did not strike again, there was a shift of his weight, an almost imperceptible hint of imminent danger. William, while paying attention to the scene, wasn't taking it very seriously. Remy had trained him in the past in playful sparring matches, practicing responses to punches, kicks, and holds but an actual enemy was a different thing. William was a friend, loyal and brave, but he rather floundered his first time encountering an actual conflict. He stood rock-still off to the side, neither a hindrance nor a boon.

Hwei moved forward aggressively and inserted his bulk menacingly. Remy took a step backward and Hwei took another step forward, continuing to exhibit his dominance of the situation. Up close, he was even more muscular than he had appeared from across the courtyard. *A strike to the solar plexus would probably not register, given his muscle mass. Neck, knees, groin, eyes, these are exposed, but his movements portray a man accustomed to swiftly protecting such targets, moreover, such strikes are best delivered as endgame maneuvers, not initial strikes. I don't like these odds*, he concluded. The intruder looked as if he were ready for anything, face grim, muscles tense, body poised. *We've moved on to physical conflict now*, he realized somberly.

Nerves caused an unfunny chuckle out of Remy's throat and he realized he'd been holding his breath. The noise surprised William, who turned quizzically to his partner. Hwei didn't ease his posturing, maintaining spatial dominance as he spoke.

"Your dog stink. Stink in hallway. No dog here."

Remy knew this scrap would not be an easy win, or more realistically, a win at all. He knew that his opponent knew this and was using it as a tool to intimidate. He took a deep breath, his own breath, not a response to anything. Steeling control over self, he inhaled deeply again and let it out with a slow hiss before responding with a voice, cold and true.

"William smells good right down to his paws. I love the smell of dog, and this dog most especially."

"Hallway not good. No dog here."

"There is a dog here. The owner of the apartment approved him and everything. You're concerned about the smell? The fan from his room blows air directly into the hallway. I can't help that. Truth be told, it shouldn't have been positioned to empty into the hallway we all share. That's just bad design. But I'm not going to stop using the fan. And I'm not going to change how I act because you may hurt me." Remy was feeling strengthened the more he spoke. "And you may hurt me. You're a big guy, and honestly, I probably wouldn't win this scrap. You may walk away the winner and I bruised and battered, but I won't change my habits out of fear of pain." Remy smiled, himself once again. "That's just not an option."

He opened his arms wide and splayed his fingers. He took a step closer to Tom II, positioning himself within a meter of the man.

"I will never be intimidated. Do you understand that? It's not that you failed today it's that it's not even possible. I will never obey out of fear. I won't be bribed either, though that would be a welcome change of pace right about now. I'd make a perfect politician but that's beside the point."

"No dog here," he repeated stubbornly.

"Yes, dog here. This dog is here. And as far as I can tell, he belongs here more than you. What apartment number do you live in? Who are you exactly? I've walked my dog twice a day for two months and I've never seen you before. Moreover, you were waiting for me. Lying in wait. It's f^@%ing scary, is what it is. What happened to notes on doors?"

The situation diffused, neither side happy about the result, Remy slid backward in Water form, turned about and walked away, pulling a bewildered William along while they continued their walk.

Fifteen minutes later, they returned inside the apartment on the seventeenth floor. Free from his leash, William bounded over to Monica who was packing her bags in the bedroom. She looked down solemnly and tapped the top of his head twice, still awkward around the dog but liking him nonetheless. Remy opened the kitchen window and leaned out, gauging the ledge yet again and determining the width insubstantial to support his recent adversary.

He's likely working with whoever this ledge traveler is. And an internet banking thief. And a host of 'teachers' at this 'school'. And that first thug in Nanchang, for that matter. And Mike is tied into this, *and that lady-friend Monica teaches with, the old friend from 'dance class'. And, of course, Monica herself. What the f^*# am I involved in? How does one get out of this?*

"Okay, I'm ready go," she sang-sung from the bedroom.

"That makes one of us, Moni." He drank deeply of fermented rice wine, guzzling it directly from the bottle. His stomach churned and warmed and gave the false pretense of a better tomorrow.

She pulled her belongings to the front door. "It's going to get even worse, isn't it?" Remy asked.

"Undoubtedly," the look she gave him said.

CHAPTER IX

CHINA

He tugged the hot pink suitcase over another large crack in the sidewalk, pausing a moment to ensure the thing remained on its wheels as they walked the short distance from his apartment to the Tianhe subway station. Daylight was giving way to shadow, the sky darkening into deepening shades of blue.

"I wish you wouldn't do this. I could do anything with you. You fuel me. Leave it. Leave it all behind. It's poison. Take a chance and stay with me."

She smiled, and while no words passed from her lips, the message was delivered.

"No."

He was a man who had fought men in defense of self or another. Had ended up on the winning end at times, the losing side of others. He had swallowed fear and rising bile to stand toe to toe with taller, more muscular men who were in the wrong. He was no stranger to violence, though he certainly didn't seek it out. He preferred peace. Fought for it, in fact. Refusing to acquiesce to wickedness had brought with it an element of danger over the years. He was no stranger to such things.

But he didn't feel particularly tough or brave as he handed over her pink suitcase. Inhabitants and visitors to Tianhe flowed around the couple, entering and exiting a stairwell connecting the sidewalk to the subway station below. Her smile was forced. The tears began leaking down his rapidly reddening face, a face squinting in the unattractive, pained beginnings of a sob. She said nothing, pivoted and stepped onto a descending escalator step which took her downward unapologetically, pink suitcase in tow, ever-downward until he could see her no more of her. He stayed there for quite some time afterward. Enough time for her to reconsider and charge back up the stairs, joy and determination in her eyes. Enough time for her to travel a few stations first, change her mind, cross tracks, wait for another train and then return to charge up those same stairs. And then he waited a while after that simply because he didn't know what else to do. Abandoned, he descended into the subway station and debated the merits of catching a train to the airport in pursuit, but acceptance of loss won out, bringing with it a new wave of sorrow. With heavy, shuffling footsteps, he climbed back out, half-heartedly waiting on that tiny, waning chance that she would reconsider and return to him.

She did not. The purples of the dusky sky darkened into the black of evening. Street lamps flickered to life around him and still he lingered on. Eventually, all hope was extinguished and he came to, becoming aware of the people around him, of shopkeepers selling their wares, of the traffic and city smells. He shambled through the pedestrians of the busy sidewalk unenthusiastically, reorienting himself toward home.

And just as soon as his journey began, he became aware that he was being followed. In the mass of people, there was one who had locked onto his movements. It was a feeling at first, one hard to describe, but true nonetheless. He turned about and made as if he was identifying high windows above, focusing instead on his peripheral vision. He spotted a man of the same build as Remy and around the same age. A Caucasian, who stood out in the homogenous crowd, though he seemed to be trying to do the opposite of that. Remy pivoted back around and took the first turn available down a slightly less populated area, vaulting up into a comfortable position atop a short wall alongside the sidewalk. The pursuer slowed and stopped to lean against the same brick wall some ten meters away. Remy waited. The pursuer waited. There was no doubt now.

He was torn up and lovelorn and in no mood for spy games. He wrestled with the notion of losing his tail, of taking various subway lines this way and that until he was alone once more but considered his compromised apartment ledge, of the hacked laptop and cellphone. *My exact home address is well known,* he thought. *Protecting its whereabouts is out of the question.*

With this in mind, he vaulted down from the top of the brick wall and approached a vending machine to purchase chilled tea. Roused into continuing the pursuit, his follower shifted nearby. Remy looked about casually for an unwitting assistant and found his mark as a boisterous couple walking hand in hand approached. He ducked behind the couple as they passed, crouching low and timing his steps with their own as best he could. He looked odd indeed from anyone else's vantage but from his pursuer's perspective, he had just vanished. Remy took the lid of his iced tea drink and flicked it into a nice rolling arc that led behind the follower. The man turned around in place toward the sound of the approaching lid as Remy seized every second to detach from the couple and creep up on the follower. As the man turned back around to take note of the crowd, Remy was there, face to face.

Remy scooped up the lid from the tea bottle and straightened himself, taking in all the detail possible: the smell of the man, what the bulges of his pockets might entail, fingernail length and cleanliness, facial characteristics, how worn the clothes were and in what way, and so on. Finished, he looked into the man's eyes and gave a cursory nod, muttering an unfelt apology. The man issued a crocodile-smile in response.

Arriving back at the apartment courtyard ten minutes later, Remy turned around and waved playfully to his tail. He called out, "Be seeing you. Very nice meeting you." In response, his pursuer separated his lips into that unpleasant smile again, crossed the street and walked back the way he had come.

"You know," Remy spoke to himself, "the weird thing is that that isn't so weird anymore."

CHAPTER X

CHINA

Hours later that same night, he lay sprawling, half-hanging from the sofa in the living room. Confined and alone in the relative safety and solitude of his apartment, the worst of emotions had begun spilling out in a great torrent. Loss, sorrow, failure, rejection, confusion, anxiety of dealing with an imminent attack, penile pain, and self-pity melded into something heavy and corrosive to the spirit, leaving him alternating between fierce anger and crushing despair.

He'd hoped to come to Guangzhou, dig around a bit for clues, follow a trail that led to a major leader of the syndicate somehow responsible for simultaneously hiring him and whisking his savings away, gather substantial evidence to prove guilt, present it to authorities, instill justice through a legal system, gain much missed clout and respect, and return home a champion of the people. Nothing like that was happening. It was only after Monica's impromptu confession that he'd even considered a second option -- a return to America with Moni -- and that idea had been instantly dashed.

The pressure was mounting. It was as if a dinner bell had sounded and he was the meal. It felt to him as if a bounty had been posted on his head, and for all he knew, that was exactly the case. *Oh, but I will make that amount soar in value,* he vowed to himself.

Worse things were coming. He didn't know how or where or when, but it was coming and he was finding it difficult to sleep in the face of such an inevitability. He was tossing and turning on the sofa, half-sleeping, half-thinking of what to do next when the sound of an approaching helicopter, just as oddly near-sounding as the first time he heard it, brought him onto his feet and into the kitchen where he searched the sky from behind the wide window, finding nothing out of place and certainly no helicopter, near or far.

Knowing sleep would not come, he donned shoes and escaped into the night. Dressed comfortably in loose fitting clothes, he walked with purpose to the walled fortress of the high school that employed him. The closest gate was closed and locked. It was made of iron: a heavy, solid thing that stood taller than the rest of the walls which encircled the high school, walls laced atop with rusted razor-wire, barbwire, and spikes which curved and jutted outward. *Overkill,* Remy had thought when he first arrived. But standing there in the midnight hour, analyzing the battlements, he came to realize that the fortifications had been installed for a reason, and that he was one of those reasons.

He stood in the shadows undetected by the guard manning the closed gate. He squatted in shadow, observing the distant guard chuckle periodically at a variety show on his mobile device, when a pedestrian approached from around the corner and drew the guard's attention Remy's way. Immediately flanked, discovery unavoidable, Remy straightened as if he had been tying his shoelaces and began walking more or less alongside the pedestrian, as if he too had only then begun approaching. He passed the now vigilant guard, issuing a pleasant nod along the way which was returned in kind, and then he continued on, tracing the campus wall as it snaked around the neighborhood block. The height remained a constant ten feet, no substantial damage to the outer wall, no openings to shimmy through, the top consistently equipped with much sharpness and poky bits. The perimeter wall yielded just two promising points for a discreet entry, both of which between public lamps, dark areas with jutting and/or missing brick to serve as footholds allowing for an easier access to the sharp top. He took mental note of these two entry points, grinning at the prospect of doing more than defending himself day after day, pleased to escape the role of victim.

The second massive gate was designed to accommodate the small fleet of busses and the many cars of parents that dropped off and picked up the student population. Two guards were positioned at that gate, and both were wide awake and well aware of Remy's approach from some distance back. He slowed his walking speed and observed what he could as he strolled by, his attention focused beyond the iron rails of the gate and into the interior of the complex. Lights were on in the foreign studies building where he taught on the third floor. The entire fifth floor, the top floor, was lit up and alive with the noises of people conversing, boisterous and loud. Shadows flitted by well-lit windows representing people in motion.

It looked and sounded and felt like someone's home. Flabbergasted, he stopped and spoke with the two guards who were both intent on his approach. He immediately ran up against a language barrier which suited him fine. The idea was to linger and observe that lit up fifth floor and when the questions he asked in limited Mandarin about when the subway trains stopped and where the nearest hospital was were misunderstood, it allowed for more lingering and more observation. From the fifth floor, he heard conversations compounded. A distant laugh carried across the courtyard to the gate where Remy stood.

A party? Monica maims me, a stranger threatens to attack me -- scratch that -- already attacked me a bit, she leaves and I'm followed from the station back to my apartment just as creepily as you please.

And, oh yeah, invisible helicopters. And now a mysterious late-night party on the top floor of the office where I work.

His mind reeled as he tried to make sense of what he was hearing and seeing. He thanked the guards cheerily, walked away, and once out of sight he drew his fist back and punched the stone wall. A muffled *donk* sounded and pain, cold and real, shot up the knuckle to elbow. Checking the extent of the self-inflicted damage, he gingerly prodded two flaps of skin along his central knuckles that were leaking blood. *They party as I suffer?* Hatred emanated out of the man in crisp waves. He returned home with the gait of a hungry jungle cat, looking to spring upon trouble that did not present itself that night, in the mood for action.

CHAPTER XI

CHINA

The phone chimed pleasantly in the late morning. He was struggling to understand an aspect of how exactly his computer connected to the internet, trying to make heads or tails out of what power certificates held in regards to website connections. As was usually the case, he had no hunger when engaged in such things and no sense of time passing. The sun had seemingly only risen an hour ago. Monica had been gone for days.

His phone's screen flashed the name *Monica Hu* as it chimed again.

"Why hello, Ms. Hu. It is Miss, isn't it? You didn't marry some other bloke already, I hope." An awkward silence ensued. Remy pressed on, good spirits unabated. "Oh, come on now. How are you? It's good to hear from you."

"Alway joking. You alway make joke."

"Well, not always, but it is a very powerful thing, the laugh. Ultimate form of dominion, you know."

Another pause.

"You doing well." She stated, forging a new line of conversation.

"Yes, I'd say so, I mean I miss you and all, but I'd say ---"

"You doing well," she repeated, the tone matter-of-factly.

Remy paused, reflecting on the meaning of this.

"You make new friend?" she asked, a smile practically visible in the singsong nature of the question.

"Friends? No, not at all. You know that. You know what I'm faced with here. Of course, I..." His mind flashed to the stranger at the station. The man with the crocodile smile. *Oh,* he thought. *Him.* All the joy he'd felt reconnecting with her vanished. "What do you want?"

She sounded happier than ever, "You no afraid. No scary."

"I'm sad to be blunt. A lot of sorrow and anger these days. Frustration, too. But fear?" Remy smirked audibly and began to sing, "If you don't know me by now. Then you may never, never, never know me. Ooh-oooh-ooh-ooh."

There was no sound from her end of the phone.

"Afraid of that chap? A man who doesn't know how to square his shoulder and hips? A man seemingly without scars? Perfectly intricate outer ears that showed no sign of cauliflowering. He isn't a challenge. Is he supposed to be scary because he followed me home? Everyone knows where my home is, you ninny, because you know where my home is. Let them come. My little flat on the seventeenth floor will be a cozy tomb if the wrong man enters. Know that, you tiny, petulant thing."

More silence.

"I do miss you, though. Perhaps you've cast a spell on me, I don't know. Shame you've chosen the side that opposes me. I want to rescue you, but I can't."

"Rescue me?" a quirky chuckle followed. "I think you smart man."

"Well, that was your first mistake."

And with that, the tension was severed neatly. They both took a breath, warmed.

"I call tell you, you do good."

"That is a very odd thing to call me about. You're a weirdo, you know that, right?"

"Maybe. You weirdo, too. I call tell you something. Something good."

"That would be a nice change of pace."

"Stop joke. I serious." She paused, dramatically. "I offer you job."

"I have a job. Remember? I teach AP level geography and world history at South China Normal University. Nothing strange about that place, right? The word *normal* is right in the title."

"I hate you joking."

"Alright, alright. What? You want me to teach somewhere else? Back in Nanchang? What's wrong, the new teacher not sharing his banking information with ---"

"Be quiet. I offer you real job. Job you like. Job you good at."

Speechless. Remy had unintentionally held his breath, pondering her words, putting the pieces together. The silence held for ten long seconds while he connected the dots.

"You work with us," she continued. "Do job that make you happy. Important."

"Would I work with you?"

"Sometime. You see me more. Yes."

"And would I be lying to people? Robbing them? Threatening them? Maiming them if they step out of line? Collecting prostitution fees or the like? That sort of job? Or do you mean me gathering data for your side of the fence?" Remy chuckled. "First of all, I seem to be terrible at that and secondly, I would never do that. The weaker you lot are, the better. The more in the dark your team is, the safer good folk remain."

"That bad choice."

"Your mom made a bad choice when she allowed you to go off and join that 'dance school'. This is what a good decision looks like, Moni."

An angry silence swelled. She broke it with all of the warmth of two glaciers colliding.

"Hope you get leak fixed. You call assistant. Maybe she help you."

"What're you talking about? Dear me, you are a strange one, though. Moni? Monica?"

But she had already ended the call, returning to her own life, whatever that entailed. He felt her loss immediately. William rose from a nap, shook himself, nudged his wet muzzle under Remy's knee, and jerked upward. Remy's thigh shot up and fell back to more or less the same resting position. When that failed to bring a response, he set his front paws onto the desk chair, raised himself up, inserted his muzzle under Remy's downcast chin and jerked upward, jolting Remy's head up and back. Remy's face came into view, awash in pain and confusion. William moved in again but this time, Remy swept his hands behind the dog's ears and gave him a gentle headbutt. William danced back, twirled about in joy, and barked a friendly challenge.

"Alright, you dingo of a dog. Alright." he said, slowly rising and brightening a little. "I'll teach you how to get out of a headlock."

And with that, they sparred. Remy threw half-speed blows and issued loose locks that William countered well. The hundred-pound German Shepherd lunged and bit wrist and ankle, gently but firmly, applying pressure but not shredding skin. They drank water greedily afterward and went for a walk, and while Remy's sorrow remained, it was lessened.

CHAPTER XII

CHINA

Drip. The noise registered dimly in the distance just as his conscious mind was drifting into dream. *Drip.* Laying sideways as he attempted to sleep, he repositioned a nearby pillow over his one open ear. He fussed a bit with the sheets, finding a new comfortable position. His breathing slowed and became deeper. He had lost focus of the room altogether, drifting off into complex imagery unconsciously summoned: the beginnings of dream.

Drip. The noise had become noticeably louder for it pierced the pillow barrier he'd erected as if it had sounded previously without the blockage to ear. It was so perfectly timed, that he was beginning to feel cameras must be in place. *How else could that noise appear just as sleep began? And what else explains how the volume increased just enough to be heard through this pillow?*

For the third time that night, he rose from the mattress, spinning about and on firm footing in one deft movement. If he must be kept awake, he would use the opportunity to practice, to prepare for a more physical and less psychological attack. Satisfied with his speed and stance, he flipped on the light switch, exercised a bit, knelt and waited, kneeling as the Japanese do -- heels to buttocks -- waiting in the well-lit bedroom for the dripping sound to reemerge, ears pricked to locate its source. After forty minutes of nothing he turned off the light and returned to bed. His breathing slowed, his muscles relaxed, his form melted into the springs of the mattress.

Drip. He shot out of bed again and dashed into the dining room, returning with a chair that served as a ladder. He probed the ceiling corner to corner, edge to edge, searching for the source of the sound of water dropping and discovering only dryness, nothing out of place. This wasn't too surprising as the noise, while realistic, echoed from too close a position to actually be dropping water; furthermore, it sounded as if it were echoing through an empty cavern, not pooling somewhere above him from a leaking pipe. It was a sound projected through speakers and aimed directly at his sleeping form, of that Remy was fairly certain. It was designed to keep him awake, and keep him awake it did. Dim memories of something called *Chinese water torture* crossed his mind. A single drop -- slow and steady and never-ending -- was said to bring about madness as it landed over and over again on a prisoner, and as the sun began to transform a black sky to darker shades of indigo after two more failed attempts at sleeping, he was beginning to understand the power of such a thing. It infuriated him to be in such a position but his ego kept him from surrendering. *I will not be bullied,* he often thought as he suffered.

After a shower and brushing of teeth, he walked a kilometer to work, still furious, and while the sidewalks were congested no one brushed his shoulders though he made no move to maneuver out of anyone's path. That was the first sleepless night of water torture.

CHAPTER XIII

CHINA

The second night brought more of the same. Remy, exhausted and sleep deprived, could feel his teaching skills leaking away alongside basic cognitive thinking. The monotony of grading papers was especially grueling, each page more or less the same, one after the other, checks and notes and percentages. He nodded off a couple of times at his desk even in the company of those who openly disgraced and mocked and threatened him and his family. Every time, just as chin fell to chest, there would be something that needed being done: a new student evaluation, a meeting about fire safety, an in-office survey that needed to be completed that same-day. The interruptions were irksome and suspiciously frequent but even in the absences he found it difficult to rest, anxious of what was to come.

He returned home around six p.m., walked William with all of the energy of a shambling zombie, took a shower, and began tracking the origins of files that he hadn't downloaded and yet existed on his computer. By ten p.m. he was falling asleep in his chair and so he retired to the bedroom.

Drip. Just loud enough to be heard in the silence of his bedroom. The same sound as the night prior, a droplet of water falling into a pool. Echoey. Distant, yet clear enough to sound as if it was in the same room. Again, he placed a pillow over his head and changed sleeping positions and again the sound intensified to match his attempt at deafening the intrusive noise. It was maddening. At around midnight, a grand idea took root and he crept silently into the living room, dragging a pillow and comforter, taking care to avoid the window line and certainly not turning on any lights. He wasn't certain how it all operated, only that it did, and so took every pain he could to remain stealthy as he lowered himself onto the sofa in the living room, stretching, curling up, smiling at the thought of escaping the waterdrop-torture and doing the impossible: sleep.

His smile widened with each passing minute. That a complicated speaker system was aimed into his bedroom from the floors of the flat above his own was the only way the consistent waterdrop phenomena made any sense. He was betting that such an elaborate auditory system was unwieldly, perhaps even stationary. *I can beat this thing by just sleeping on the couch every night,* he thought after ten minutes of uninterrupted rest. He breathed a deep sigh -- the deep breath one gives after narrowly avoiding an unfortunate fate -- nestled into his pillow and drifted off to sleep.

Drip.

His wailing moan overlapped the diminishing echo of the solitary drop as he burrowed his head into the cushioning of the sofa. As the hours marched onward, the drops fell intermittently until the sun rose and another sleepless night was behind him.

CHAPTER XIV

CHINA

Day four without sleep was beyond anything he had ever experienced or dared to fathom. He had gone through hard times in the past, had known a sleepless night or two through a difficult time, but three consecutive sleepless nights with no hope of sleep in the days to come was quite different. He rose out of bed on the fourth day feeling incredibly out of sorts. Distant. Like a puppeteer living in his own marionette, miles away but vaguely attached.

There was a giddiness that washed over him, a high of sorts akin to an intense caffeine buzz. He was beginning to accept the fact that he wouldn't be able to sleep again in his own home, a concept that not even the homeless can fathom for they know they will fall asleep somewhere, legally or not, comfortably or not. For Remy, sleep, even a nap, was out of the question. It must have taken at least a team to ensure such a transgression continued to plague the man, to make certain that whenever and wherever he laid his head to rest, there would be drips and drops to keep him awake. It wasn't so much the noise that denied sleep, it was the knowledge that he was being targeted.

Two more nights of just that. Dawn broke on the sixth day of no sleep, a Monday, with a full week of work teaching at the school that was something more laying before him and having basically nothing planned. He had returned to poker tables over the weekend a very changed man, statistics and probabilities rolling about in his head automatically, void of care or concern of loss or win, a man set on autopilot. He no longer sought answers to deeper truths of where his money had gone, how and why. Anytime away from the dripping was grand and he accepted it with welcome arms. But dawn came and with it the unspoken rule: no gambling in the daylight hours. And so, Remy had returned home and been immediately and expectedly accosted by periodic dripping sounds that made sleep impossible, all day Sunday -- the fifth day of torture -- and all night until dawn broke the next day, Monday morning, day six.

Such a life was taking its toll on William too, though he slept more easily than Remy, apparently quite accustomed to tuning out intrusive noises. Possessing the hyper-acute hearing of canines this was perhaps second nature to him. While William remained seemingly unaffected, the hound was well aware that something was hurting Remy each and every night. He lied next to him and rested with one eye open, and when Remy sprang up as the sound of a solitary water droplet resounded, so too did William, dutifully trotting alongside the man as he checked the ceiling yet again for the source of such pain. Remy cursed his torturers and their cowardice, cursed the situation itself, cursed himself for remaining in such a despicable predicament, all the while very much grateful for his wolfish counterpart.

"Whatever I've done, or whatever you think I've done, this dog doesn't deserve this. He's good and fair and doesn't deserve this punishment you've set upon me," Remy called out at three-something in the morning to no one in particular, fairly certain that someone was listening. Forty minutes later as he relaxed into a sleeping position, a response of sorts came in the form of the sound of a single droplet splashing into a very familiar pool of water, amplified just loudly enough to snatch him out of sleep. Like a drowning man desperately searching for something buoyant, like a parched man in the desert, so was Remy LeBeau and sleep.

<u>CHINA</u>

That's funny, Remy thought, staring at the milky indentation. *Not funny ha-ha, but funny like, that shouldn't be.* "Funny," he said aloud. "Not like any of this is even a wee bit humorous, though."

He'd returned from poker the night before, twisted the deadlock, turned the knob and like clockwork the folded paper that he had inserted between door and frame as he exited the flat plopped unceremoniously at his feet. Only this time, the paper had fallen pictograph side outward. He had placed the folded card so that the plain white side faced out and toward the opening, and yet, a flash of inky imagery had just tumbled two feet to the floor below. He stooped over and unfolded the business card. Exhausted, he began to doubt if he had simply folded it the other way by mistake before he left but having folded and inserted this card into the doorframe many times since the accosting by the second thug in the courtyard, it seemed doubtful that he would have suddenly reversed his course.

His immediate concern was that of the safety of William, though fleeting for the hound trotted up and met Remy in the entryway within seconds, relieving all fear. *Maybe I just set up the business card backward last night. A week of sleeplessness could have easily provoked such a mistake,* he thought. *One full week of sleeplessness,* he darkly mused.

And so, another night of sleeplessness came and went. He left for work the next day more than exhausted, something else entirely, something that English had gratefully not granted words to. He refolded the business card as always – imagery folded inward -- and prepared to slide it between the door and frame at knee-level but as the door swung shut, he added an additional step, puffing great clouds of baby powder all about the entryway threshold before tossing the container under the sofa in the living room. *Perfect,* he thought, pleased with how the powder and the white flooring matched so evenly.

He left the dreaded office eight hours later, unlocked his apartment door, and the business card fell normally – imagery inward -- unlike the day before. Perfectly normal. Slowly, delicately, he pushed open the door, gently retrieved the folded card and crouched to observe the baby powder he had applied to the linoleum floor. Two and a half sneaker prints were clearly pressed into the drift. The tread and depth appeared to come from a masculine source. *A short, thin man wore these shoes,* he deduced, in detective mode. *The kind of man that could move around a ledge freely.*

"Funny," he repeated, staring at the creamy footprints, not meaning the word at all but falling into a fit of maniacal laughter nonetheless, one that roared into something nasty and uncontrollable. William shook himself free of loose hair and returned to his bedroom.

CHAPTER XV

CHINA

Day eight. *Drip.* Day nine. *Drop.* Day ten. *Drip-drop.*

Thursday. To many, a day signaling the arrival of the weekend and the overcoming of the notorious hump-day but Remy didn't live that sort of life. He fought for hard earned truth about his robbery and current predicament across poker tables with individuals from questionable backgrounds while simultaneously grading assessments and planning lessons and the actual implementation thereof. There were quiet moments that went on for hours while Remy pondered what to do and how to do it as he stared through his kitchen window across the city skyline.

Throughout it all, no sleep. Absolutely no sleep.

Breaching week two of zero sleep, the sound of a *landing* helicopter had been introduced to prevent sleep, supplementing the water drops and the initial auditory mystery of a *passing* helicopter loud enough to buzz by the roof and yet nowhere to be seen. He had heard the helicopter first during Monica's second visit, and a few times thereafter, gradually increasing in intensity until it became a nightly occurrence, an alternative used once or twice each evening in the darkest hours to inspire hope of rescue. An outside presence that knew of his plight and cared enough to send help. A shining ray of light that pierced the gloom.

A false light, however. Once a window was opened, the auditory spell was broken. Still, Remy would often leave the confines of his apartment to ascend to the rooftop where he would be met with a blank night sky. The ability of the sound to carry so well in both the living room, where Remy retreated periodically to attempt fruitless sleep outside of his bed, and also in the bedroom itself, demonstrated that the speaker system engaged was mobile and likely either coming from the apartment above or from below.

Normal people were eagerly anticipating the upcoming weekend but there was no weekend for Remy. It was all just endless torture, sleeplessness the weapon. Friday, Monday, Sunday: it was all the same -- sleepless. Not just torture, but torture in which he needed to attend school punctually, attending meetings and working intricately with others that were likely the same culprits responsible for his unending suffering.

One evening at the end of the second week of such treatment, his mind stretched thin, visual hallucinations common, shadows twisting and turning into unpleasant shapes between the intermittent drops that gonged throughout the home, turning sleep into a faraway concept from a bygone time, the idea of dying shifted from a thing best avoided to a respite from suffering. He chuckled uncomfortably at this cruel shift in perspective, attempting to gain some control over this new outlook on death but the mirth fell flat. Needing sleep, he took a more proactive approach. He exited the apartment, twisting a key into locks out of habit, though the footprints in baby powder had proven locks and keys didn't mean much anymore.

He was beginning to realize that collecting evidence wouldn't mean much as he lacked someone to present it to. He was only proving something he already knew to himself. *I'm preaching to the choir, only I am the choir, and no one else is listening.* He chuckled at his own little joke as he pressed the up button on the elevator panel. Moments later a chime sounded as the elevator arrived. The door slid open invitingly and he stepped inside, muscles moving on their own accord, minimally connected to a brain that had more or less shut down days ago. One level later he exited onto the eighteenth floor in a different mood entirely. A hungry hunter, he walked stiffly through the hallways searching the perimeter for signs of guards, exit/entrance points, tools, obstacles, dangers. Cold, calculated observance. Almost every front door was housed behind a locked metallic gate. Some were elaborate designs of beautiful metalworking. Some forewent aesthetics for a more secure approach. The apartment directly above Remy's displayed the best of both. The bars were the thickest of the floor, and yet, interwoven and twisted into one another as if vines interlaced through branches. Carefully wrought leaves and berries were etched and soldered into the ironwork.

"F*^# you, it's beautiful." He stood directly in front of the gate as a short burst of laughter escaped. *I may be losing my mind a little bit.* "But just a little bit," he said aloud, echoing the thought. He tried opening the gate and found it securely fastened, locked in three places, two centered and one atop. The knob did not even try to budge, the gate itself completely immobile, like trying to open the face of a cliff. *Definitely the right place.*

He took a moment to study his enemy's front door. Newly constructed. Minimal wear and tear. The keyholes of the two central locks showing only the faintest signs of scratching. The top lock covered in a thin layer of dust, pristine and unused. *A careful, sober man, probably not tall enough to reach the top lock comfortably and so it is unused.* The gate itself appeared fresh, untarnished, likely installed at the same time of the locks, within a few months. *Just before I arrived.*

A faint, barely recognizable scratching along the edge of locks came sweeping in from the lower right, identifying the occupant as right-handed and confirming the notion that the occupant was not a tall man. He took several steps back, taking in the scene itself. The floor was kept clean, brushed regularly. No footprints showed for there was neither dust nor debris to make impressions upon. He took a deep breath through widened nostrils. No tobacco residue. No remnants of cologne. Or perfume. *Could this be a woman?* He sniffed the threshold again. There was a faint trace of sandalwood -- a common component of incense – but truly the scent was quite faint, the burning having happened days or even a week prior.

He exhaled and returned to his surroundings. The hallway was still and quiet for a time until a noise trembled from within the flat, beyond the front door that equated to a modern portcullis, within a living room Remy could only guess at. Through gate and door, he heard a helicopter landing, the volume increasing as he stood listening in the hallway, mesmerized. Amongst the familiar audio sharp commands were barked, the voices militant. *Apocalypse Now,* he realized. *This is a clip from the film Apocalypse Now.* As Remy listened intently in the hallway, the sample repeated and on the second go the spoken commands were edited out and the whirling blades of the helicopter looped into a perpetual landing. It was plainly the sound that had been plaguing him, a sound of potential rescue, the sound of crushed hope night after night after night.

He broke the spell by rapping his knuckles against the gate. The sound cut out abruptly. Invigorated, he balled his hand into a fist and pummeled the portcullis. No response came from within. He heard no movement, no hushed voices. Nothing.

"Come on, let's talk like men. Face to face. I'm not going to hurt you. Well, not right now. Not tonight. I'll give you that." No response. "Come on," he repeated impatiently. He waited, listening intently. No footsteps approach the door. No muffled in and out of breathing. He heard nothing, and yet, he was fairly certain that whoever stood behind that Wizard of Oz iron curtain was positioned right next to the door. He felt it in his bones.

"Fine," Remy spat out. "Kinda hard to respect my enemy when he holes himself up and hides behind a locked door. A torturous enemy. I suppose I shouldn't be surprised by your lack of honor. By your cowardice." He felt his words cutting to the quick of someone he could only vaguely sense existed behind a thick wooden door behind a thicker metal gate. "Whatever happens next, just know as I know, that you choose to hide behind locks and I am here. Right here. Here I am!" shouting the finale, "Just begging you to emerge." He stepped away, preparing to depart, but something remained unresolved and drew him back to the doorway.

"On a side note, I'm quite impressed with all of this," he continued. "Quite the coordinated effort. I'm sure that you, whoever you are, work with a team, some members of which I have the misfortune of also working with at that front of a high school. The ledge work shows courage. Not sure if that's you or someone else in your terrorist gang, but that takes supreme agility, balance, and strength. Not much room to maneuver out on that ledge and absolutely no margin for error. Impressive, though I hate you dearly. Want to snatch the throat right out of your gaping neck, actually, but impressive is impressive nonetheless."

He paused, shifting tone and sentiment.

"This sleeplessness, oh, it hurts. You've got me there. As if maiming my penis and leaving my erection warped for the rest of my life was somehow an insufficient punishment. Oh, I can't fix that and believe me, I've tried. Can't bend it back the right way. That's not an option. It's not like taking a dent out of a car frame. The damage there is permanent. I've been maimed."

"And on top of that, there's this sleeplessness," he continued. "I didn't think it could go on like this. Thought the human mind would shut down eventually, that I'd simply pass out regardless of the drips and drops, but nope, your arsenal of noises denies all sleep. At any hour of the day, anywhere in my flat. Truth be told, with a cat burglar on ledges and thug-giants in courtyards and footsteps in baby powder along my threshold behind a locked door, well, falling asleep may very well cost me my life, anyway. I'm one man fighting an army, and I'm losing, oh, how I'm losing, but..." he looked up at an eye hole that showed no sign of life, "here I am, and there you are, cowering. So better me than you, asshole." Pleased with himself, he chuckled a bit and stepped back. "Be seeing you around. Hearing you, really."

Returning home, he bathed and continued delving into the programming and authority chains of his operating system, searching for a clear path to unrestricted internet usage or evidence of who or where the cyber problems originated. Hours later, he surrendered, stretched and lied down to bed. At first it was quiet, as it always was. He waited for a water drop to *plink* and cut the stillness of the night, or for a helicopter to sound as if from far away, approaching rapidly and seeming to hover above the rooftop. For half an hour he waited in silence, until his eyelids grew heavy and a dull feeling was rekindled that he had begun to associate with foolishness: hope to sleep. *Maybe I've have passed some sort of test. It took courage to knock on that door, to speak as I spoke.*

Thoughts of newfound respect swam about his head. And then came a creak. It was not the creak of a door, nor of window. It was the creak of a toilet lid opening and with it followed the sound of a man urinating into a toilet bowl projected directly above his head. Such was the origin of the third audio weapon used to terrorize and torture Remy LeBeau in Guangzhou, China in mid-November of the year 2012. He would hear that same sound many more times as he tried in vain to sleep from his sofa, from bed, from the bathroom floor surrounded by open running taps, from the kitchen floor, cocooned in pillows and sheets, but during the second week of sleeplessness it was new and fresh. He was almost pleased at the diversion and in no condition to realize that Stockholm syndrome was taking root.

CHAPTER XVI

USA

"It's easy to believe in demons. We see them every day. But angels? That takes faith."

Remy sat along a narrow balcony, sipping whiskey, speaking to the sunset. Not the fanciest apartment, but a major step up from the dormitory setting of the homeless shelters nonetheless. Alone on a porch, he could transmute thoughts to a voice in peace and without interruption.

The colors of the darkening sky were turning from bright pastels to darker hues as he swirled ice cubes in a clockwise pattern and sipped.

Road rage is a very real thing, he mused, recounting recent events. *I pulled my car over without any thought. I had zero control of that. I didn't choose to pull over where that moron cut me-off, but I did. A half-second from parking and exiting and approaching the driver. Who knows what would've happen then? Violence, most likely. Driver exits vehicle, enraged, throws a punch or pushes. I respond and pummel or receive a pummeling or get arrested. Probably all of those things.*

It was a far cry from last weekend.

Remy and Lily had met at the cinema after work and watched the second Godzilla movie. It was awful in all of the ways one expects a Godzilla movie to be and great in all of the other. The sequel was a little too sure of itself and, as such, had inadvertently captured some of the original over-the-top Godzilla flare. Lily didn't know this, having little experience with the franchise, but she knew bad cinematic moments when she saw them and wasn't shy about it. He felt an emotional stirring as she quietly heckled poorly designed scenes with cutting commentary hushed into his right ear. He recognized a kindred spirit, a feeling he hadn't experienced in six long, dangerous, lonely years.

"Sorry, Remy," she had said days later. "My boyfriend thinks that going to a play with you would be too much like a date."

"Well, I can't disparage the man for that. Fair enough." And he turned about to a half-constructed salad, gathering olives, distributing tomatoes. He wouldn't show the pain there, not then. But upon returning home a fool who turned right from the left lane without so much as a turn signal, leaving Remy little time to respond to the danger had raised his hackles. He'd turned and followed the car, pulled over, parked and shut off the vehicle when traffic forced the car he followed to stop. Hand on the door handle, something had stopped him and instead of exiting he made a U-turn and drove away.

He sipped and recollected and realized faintly that he'd been shifting sorrow elsewhere. Transference was the proper word for it. America was full of the stuff. Feeling purged, he downed the remainder of bourbon and returned indoors.

CHAPTER XVII

CHINA

Day fourteen? Fifteen? It was becoming increasingly difficult to differentiate the two. Long blinks brought mini-episodes of REM, momentary flashes of dream lasting only seconds. It had become incredibly difficult to tell the difference between eyes lowering in a futile effort to find sleep and normal blinking, between reality and snippet of dream. The line was unimaginably permeable. It took concentration to focus on reality, a concentration that was shortly exhausted and needed several long blinks to reestablish.

Unconsciousness was consistently unimaginably near but somehow the waterdrops and helicopter landings and urinations came all the more frequently. Where once they had only emerged piecemeal to pry him from potential sleep, relative infrequency had turned into regularity.

The weekend was almost over. Remy sat perched over his computer keyboard mining for elusive proof of hacking, laboriously digging into files as he tried to establish control over his operating system. Permissions needed to access his own files, permissions he didn't have and couldn't crack, denied, again, and again, mind firing on all cylinders searching for a path through the digital obstacles, coming up with a clever alternate path and having that shut down, too. All the while, the sounds of a man urinating into a full toilet bowl above him coupled with nonexistent helicopters distracted and reminded him of the futility of sleep later.

He was at times energized and furious and at other times exhausted and complacent as the sleep deprivation continued. He cursed as he was denied permission of a file that granted access to another file that would grant permission to another file that authenticated permission from some outside source. Permission of his own files denied to Remy any which way he could conceive. Out of fresh ideas and having met yet another dead end, he howled and shot out of his seat in frustration. He marched straight over to the kitchen window and flung it open wide to breathe deeply of clean air. A change overcame him and his pulse steadied, muscles relaxed. William trotted into the kitchen to check on the proceedings. Tilting his head, he looked to Remy questioningly.

"Oh, I don't know, Will. I don't know. I'm trying so hard, boy. But I just keep failing."

William bowed deeply, stretching low on his front paws, and shook his wolfish tail back and forth, as if to pounce. Remy smiled, bowed, and shifted to a martial stance. William barked lightly, a friendly challenge.

"You are a fantastic beast, William. But you do know I could mop up the floor with you, even now, right?"

Remy took two steps over, crouched low and kissed his forehead. "Be good, boy. I'll be right back." And with that, he pounced onto the wide window frame of the kitchen, braced his hands on the ceiling, and propelled himself out onto the ledge of the apartment building, a sixty-meter sheer drop on the edge of his toes.

His fingers clutched onto the lip of the outcropping above him that served more as a catch-all than a balcony while his body swayed over a fatal drop. He had stared up from the obscurity of his windows many a night, wondering who was up there, why whoever was up there despised him and how they had come upon the audio torture practices that had been denying him sleep for weeks. Was he the first to be treated this way? A guinea pig? Seemed unlikely given the flawlessness of execution. Sleep-defying noises came at near-perfect intervals and volumes, obtrusive but barely just. It seemed highly unlikely that he was the first to be tortured thusly. *What sort of speakers are being used? Who exactly is manning them and how?* He pulled himself up more easily than he had imagined. *It isn't so difficult if you don't care about that fall,* he thought as his legs hovered over one-hundred eighty feet of nothingness, a sheer drop to an unforgiving sidewalk below.

He braced his torso uncomfortably against the railing of the window above and peered into the flat above his own. No balcony above him, much like his own place, the difference being that this window was equipped with curtains which were drawn shut. He shifted about, inching along the ledge, legs dangling over oblivion, searching for a position that would allow him to see into the lit flat above more readily, finding a break in the curtains that allowed for a clear line of sight within. All the lights were on though the hour was quite late, which made sense as this was undoubtedly where the torturers resided, and yet, he saw only a vacant, fully-furnished residence.

He toyed with the notion of pulling himself up completely to the eighteenth floor and prying open the window. Two things stopped him. The first was an understanding of how two weeks without sleep had been affecting his central nervous system and sense of balance. He had become clumsy and grew clumsier each day. His beat-up mind flashed a warning from a far away place. *Danger.*

The second aspect wasn't a thought at all, but rather a spirit, a presence connected to emotion and not mind. *This is wrong,* it spoke. *You're better than those who hurt you.*

And so, he lowered himself down and into his own kitchen once more. Understanding the ledge even more having traversed it a bit, he was amazed and even more keen to learn how someone could have pulled off the imposition of actually walking along the shallow lip. To maneuver about such a narrow pass required tremendous skill that Remy simply could not fathom. Wicked or not, it was impressive.

Morning came, clear and bright. The sun shone brightly and the sidewalks began teeming with occupants. Out of obligation to the commitment he had made to teach two AP social studies classes simultaneously, he began preparing for the day. He brushed his teeth, testing out several different smiles in the mirror between spits and rinses, dry heaving painfully in the process. He wore a smile to work as he did his tie: uncomfortable and polite. Reflecting back on the school day afterward, he was amazed to realize that his lessons -- though not well-planned – had been taught successfully. Class participation, active engagement in diverse activities, scaffolding, introduction of new material, smooth recap of previously learned material: check, check, check, check and check.

He sat staring off into the darkening sky, contemplating an uncertain future, feeling pinned down and futile. He thrust the window open wide again, halfway intent upon pulling himself completely up and onto the ledge above once again. When his computer crashed, when he was pulled away yet again just as sleep was approaching, when he thought to call or send an email to a loved one and explain the insane predicament he was in -- ultimately refusing to call out for help and thereby bring anyone else into the fray -- during those moments, Remy would open his kitchen window, lean out and look to the ledge above longingly.

He leaned out, locked eyes on a clean, dry stretch of ledge and tensed his leg muscles to pounce but his attention was suddenly pulled elsewhere. "Jump," called the voice. "Jump!"

Startled, Remy looked about, spying no one below or above.

"Jump. Jump. Jump. Jump." Chanted as a chorus, the voices of at least three. Three that, like the helicopter and the waterdrops, were not actually there. "Jump. Jump," they continued. The location of the sound was difficult to pinpoint. From a squatting position along his kitchen window sill, he scanned the street below, searching distant nooks and dark places, unable to find the source. He stumbled back clumsily into his own kitchen and closed the window.

The days fell into and spilled out of one another, amassing into one unrecognizable blob of time. At the end of a day an older workmate, a Canadian, approached him. He had had little contact with the man as his desk was positioned in a corner of the vast open office while Remy's was positioned centrally, surrounded by trouble. The man began chatting with him at the end of the school day, making friendly small talk about nothing in particular, a pleasant change of pace from the normal negativity endured in those days. The electronic chime sounded signaling the end of the school day and he left with the new Canadian in tow, who continued chatting down the staircase, out of the office and out of the school grounds, keeping step with Remy as he returned to an apartment that was also a torture chamber. In the apartment courtyard, the Canadian adopted a more somber tone.

"Do you know about the last teacher that worked here? She lived in your apartment."

"No," Remy answered, becoming aware of what the day's chitchat had been leading to. He intentionally showed vulnerability to encourage the old ne'er-do-well further, chumming the water. "What happened?" he asked through truly tired eyes and a deceptively timid voice.

"She jumped to her death. Killed herself. Guess she couldn't take the pressure."

"Oh, dear. That's terrible."

"Yes," stated the Canadian with finality, newly empowered by the façade of Remy's fear. "Could happen to anyone." And with that, he leaned in and gave a menacing nod. At that point, Remy called his bluff, smirking in the face of intimidation.

"Could even happen to you, old-timer. Your past your due, I'm sure. Care to join me for a spot of tea upstairs? There's a terrific view from my kitchen window." The old man shuffled backward but Remy pressed on, uplifted. "Where're you going? I thought you meant to intimidate me, not flee in terror. Quite opposite things, you know. And this part is really embarrassing. I haven't slept in weeks. Plural. Weeks. And still exponentially your conversational superior. Ouch, right? At your age all you have is words and I better you there, too. That's how much you failed." Remy took in the details of the retreating man. An aging, pudgy homebody. *How on Earth did that guy get mixed up in all of this?*

"How on Earth did you get mixed up in this?! Did I date your daughter once upon a time? Is that it?" No answer came. The older Canadian retreated farther away until he disappeared into the mass of pedestrians. It was much later -- well into the night, when stay-awake noises pierced another fleeting attempt at sleep -- before he was brought low once again. Creeping out of the kitchen window again, he tested the ledge for decent handholds before propelling himself up again. As he pulled himself over the side of the building, initiating a pull-up along the eighteenth story ledge, the older man's words echoed. *Jumped to her death. Killed herself.*

He imagined how little effort it would take to be shoved out of his window from such a compromised position. He envisioned his arms windmilling helplessly as he plummeted five seconds or so before rupturing on the sidewalk far below. *How much simpler it would be to those involved if I died. Dead men tell no tales,* he thought, hanging awkwardly on the eighteenth story ledge. The words clung like poison mist, weakening his resolve until with a heavy heart, he lowered himself back into his own kitchen window, where he lied down on cool linoleum, closed his eyes, breathed deeply, and was met with the sound of a long, loud stream of urination into a toilet bowl directly above.

More than half a month of no sleep with no end in sight.

CHAPTER XVIII

CHINA

Remy's computer was becoming more and more uncooperative, as was his body. Light didn't shine so much as pulsated dully through tired eyes. Shadows twirled and churned into varying degrees of darkness. His mind was doing rather odd things to compensate for the inability to sleep. Combating the consistent interruptions of sleep by purchasing and imbibing methamphetamine to remain vigilant and able-bodied was like putting a band-aid on a gaping wound that needed stitches. His psyche was bleeding out in the process of remaining awake to combat the could-be.

He sat staring at a computer screen, nine windows open, each a more detailed aspect of the window behind it. Nine levels deep, searching for clues as to why certificates had been appointed to such-and-such a program on a date labeled 'October 20, 2035'.

"Pretty sure that hasn't happened yet, William." Below the desk, the hound was half-dozing, using Remy's right foot as a makeshift pillow. He cocked his eyebrows though his eyes did not open. An odd gesture symbolizing two things: A) I care about your concern and B) I don't care enough to actually open my eyes about it.

"Truly, I am envious of your lack of attention, old boy. You actually sleep most nights because of it. I mean, your hearing must be more acute than my own. And yet, when the drips, and sounds of helicopters and urination come in, you just sleep on, unperturbed. Maybe your hearing is so great that you're aware of much, much more than just those three sounds that plague me. Maybe you instinctively tune out twenty piercing noises every time you lay down at night. It wouldn't be the first or only thing you were better at than me but I do have thumbs so suck it."

Remy chuckled at his joke while William raised a tired eyelid and glanced up disapprovingly. He thought to wedge his foot free in the interim, but William was beginning to stir and Remy quite liked the company. He returned to the computer screen, to the layers of nonsensical data, of apps and downloads and software that seemed unnecessary and yet were impossible to remove. Of dates and times and locations that didn't add up.

He thought he had found some ways around the Great Firewall of China, not just by using a virtual private network, but in tinkering with data processing within his own operating system, locating chinks in the armor, as it were. Hours later, he was drowning in data that made no sense, of downloads that had already happened far into the future, or expiration dates in the early eighties, from a time before internet downloads were possible. Google Maps was no exception. The content was quite compromised. By what, or who, and when was impossible to tell, but compromised most certainly.

So, when he checked Google Maps for the location of the Guangzhou International Airport, he wasn't totally surprised to find that no airport appeared in the map of the city. There were no airports in Guangzhou according to Google. To complicate the issue further, his own given location, though in reality unmoving from the flat he shared with William, appeared in random locations throughout the city at different intervals according to the software.

Roadways and landmarks of the city were shown to be in incorrect places: streets labeled incorrectly, Guangzhou Tower to the north appearing in the east, and so on. Remy, having sensed that something like this was on the horizon, had downloaded and stored a file of a correct map of the area into his document folder before the big move.

But nine layers deep into files associated with Google Maps, his computer flashed a warning that it needed to reboot, and reboot it did, and when it returned, some things had changed. One of those things, was the lack of that map of Guangzhou. He set his computer back to a previous time in which that map had existed. Still, the map was gone. He did the most diligent of online searching, using a wide array of web browsers: Chrome, Explorer, Firefox, Opera. He used obscure search engines like Yahoo and Ask Jeeves hoping for truer results but he was unable to find an authentic map of the city available to him on the internet. Most hits led to a website that refused to open, regardless of the most insistent knocking on Remy's part. Some opened to false maps of Guangzhou. This Remy knew in part due to his memory of traveling throughout the city, and also in part because each of these false maps were different from one another. The virus, although such a crude term doesn't take into account how personalized Remy's attack was, denied him access to any real map of the city.

Remy scrolled over to the *shutdown* icon and did exactly that. He unplugged the electrical cord and stared at the dark screen, brooding. A minute later, he folded the laptop closed and removed the battery from the machine. He took up his cell phone and followed the same procedure. Later, as he closed his eyes to rest, the torrent of noises flooded angrily above, strong enough to rouse even William who shuffled off to the farthest corner of the apartment to continue sleeping.

Remy closed his eyes and shut out much of the noise, thinking of how he could work around the massive obstacle before him. He grinned at the decision to leave, at the hope of actually sleeping once again. Above him, a helicopter sounded louder than ever, combining with the sound of a man urinating into a toilet bowl and accented with waterdrops echoing on a watery surface. Someone was unhappy.

He was so pleased that he almost slept that night. Almost.

CHAPTER XIX

CHINA

When the black of night began changing to the blue of day, he felt obligated to stand up and walk around, to drink coffee and change out of pajamas. To dream, to wake up, these things did not happen anymore. Vision constantly blurred. Thoughts trickled in slowly and only with great focus. Sluggish reaction time. His computer not just compromised but completely obedient to a malicious entity beyond Remy's grasp. It was time to go.

He hated the decision but there was nothing else to do other than retreat. Each day brought more suffering. The money was gone and there would be no getting it back. Capitulate to an evil syndicate or leave, there was nothing else to be done. He had little knowledge as to if he actually possessed any evidence of wrongdoing on his computer, though he had effectively frozen all of the malicious software installation data, all of the certificates from times too early or too far, by removing the battery and keeping the computer turned off. He hoped there would be some trace of the multiple maps he had opened, each with a completely different showing of not only his own physical location, but of the general map of Guangzhou. *There must be something registered on a Google server somewhere that proves some of this,* he reasoned. *There might be something to salvage out of all of this.*

In the tumult of cyber-attacking and defending, he had saved data and sent it to what he thought was the official FBI website, a website free from manipulation, though such a thing was impossible to know with any certainty. As the days passed and no response came, it became apparent to him that such an effort to seek help had gone unnoticed or had been blocked or simply disbelieved. It was all quite maddening and he had no energy to persist. He had been wronged and he had resisted, that much was undeniable. He leaned back in his office chair and absorbed that, proud to have fought, though certainly not on the winning side.

I opposed evil, he thought, smiling through the left side of his mouth, a heartfelt smirk. *I resisted. That counts for something. I hate to retreat, but I'm severely outnumbered. Out-teched. Tortured via sleep deprivation. Maimed. Life threatened via a fall from my own window. Strangers entering my home while I'm away. This all has to end.*

He removed a black backpack from a pile of loose clothes in the back of his closet. Inside, a plastic file was tucked away containing his birth certificate, bachelor's degree, passport, and the like. Important papers. Another plastic file contained other personal effects: high school love letters from distant exes, an autograph from a prominent underground rapper, fifty photographs detailing childhood to adulthood on rectangular glossy prints of varying states of wear and tear. Survival necessities: two liters of water, undergarments and socks, eight granola bars, a sealed bag of toiletries. And room remained for the crowning jewels: the laptop and mobile phone, undoubtedly full of nasty programming, override codes, and redirections. While he lacked the ability to track any of it to a specific source, he reasoned that others could in his homeland.

The executive branch will want to know of this. Some of this code could shore up holes in their defenses and they should at least be made aware of what has occurred in this cursed place. This suffering will yield some positivity, I swear it.

Soon I'll be free to sleep. Free from cyber interferences. Free to live a life in which I don't need to constantly focus on protecting my own existence. A first-world nation. I can have that. It's mine, America is partly mine, and it's not that far away. On the other side of Earth, he chuckled inwardly, *but not that far away.*

Despite the inner chortle his heart remained heavy for he sensed what was to come.

CHAPTER XX

CHINA

He attended work punctually and kept to himself, willfully ignoring colleagues that mocked him. He graded papers, prepared lessons, executed classroom activities, led discussions, presented slides on new content, addressed the occasional discipline issue. Normal teaching stuff in an incredibly abnormal environment.

He left the office as soon as school was dismissed, returned straight home and collapsed on the living room sofa. The sound of waterdrops cut through the stillness within minutes.

Roused to his feet, he checked the contents of his bag once more, taking note of the passport which had been recently renewed within the first few weeks of arriving in Guangzhou. The corners were firm and pointed, the pages unstamped. Knowing that someone had entered into his home while he had been away though, he wondered if it had been compromised, if it was some clever forgery that he held in his hands and upon arriving at the airport he would be denied passage.

He ate sparingly, just a bite or two of something leftover, before feeding a far hungrier William and leaving the flat to play poker. His game was falling short, his mind unable to compute statistical probability effectively, resulting in poor decision making. But the losses didn't worry Remy much that night. He strolled down sidewalks, into and out of subway tunnels, all the while focusing on various taxi companies throughout the city. He jotted down four different company phone numbers onto a sheet of paper he kept folded in his wallet, unable to trust his own compromised phone any longer. Lastly, he approached an independent driver not aligned to a company who was parked alongside the roadway outside of a subway exit. Through muddled Mandarin and gesturing, he added this man's number to the list. His mission complete, he returned home in a trance of sleeplessness. He opened a door that he no longer bothered to trap to show signs of intrusion. He was intruded upon: digitally, physically. There was no need to prove it to himself any longer and no one else to prove it to.

William welcomed him home as only a dog can, with unquestionable and unyielding love. In the courtyard later, Remy bounced a tennis ball against a brick wall, enjoying a game of keep away with the hound, who in the heat of the moment could spring over Remy's head. Worn out from the exercise, they abandoned the game and began walking back to the apartment. A familiar mustached aggressor approached from the garden area along an intersecting course, again intent to intercept the duo but this time Remy simply accelerated his gait and entered the lobby quickly, thereby avoiding the man. "Yeah, yeah, yeah," he muttered. "You hate this dog and me. Whatever." He was reminded once more of the man's disposition, his stature, build and movements. He would not be easily laid low, not without a weapon of some sort.

William bounded into the open doorway joyfully. Remy -- still in the hallway -- pulled it closed behind him, a trace of a confused look playing about the hound's eyes as the door shut with finality behind him. With his ally secured indoors, Remy marched back to the courtyard seeking his persecutor but the aggressor was nowhere to be found. In no hurry to return to a flat where rest was impossible, he took the elevator to the top floor and walked about the rooftop. He took a moment to orient himself, located where his own apartment would be several floors below, and approached the edge of the roof. He imagined the view from a lower position, from a familiar kitchen window, and concluded this was indeed the right place.

With enough rope, he felt he could secure a loop around a large air conditioner unit nearby and lower himself down into the kitchen window of the flat of the neighbor above, the audio expert, the stealer of dreams. One hundred feet of rope would suffice. "Of course," Remy thought aloud, "What's to stop anyone from cutting this rope while I'm descending? It's probably safer to climb up from below." He sighed, contemplating the danger. "Safer yet to avoid either one."

Crouched over the edge of a twenty-one-story building, leaning below the roof's edge to get a better view of the ledges, Remy's head suddenly began to swirl. His vision blurred and darkened. Unconsciousness was moment away. In a quick second, he shoved himself off of the lip blindly, crashing onto his shoulder on the hard cement and loose gravel of the rooftop. He groped dizzily for the edge of the roof and when his hands came out over nothingness, he rolled his body the opposite way. There he lay -- a meter away from a nasty fall -- adrenaline coursing throughout his system. His vision came around again, slowly and blurrily. His breathing slowed as he forced his body to comply with relaxation. A plane roared above as it descended, red lights on its wings flashing. A few stars twinkled lazily in the dusk sky, only the brightest of which had a chance of shining in such an urban environment.

And suddenly he realized he was free of the torturous noises. There was nothing above him. No speakers to drive him mad with sleeplessness. No false helicopters. No waterdrops. No sounds of urination into a toilet bowl directly above his resting position. He rolled a little closer to the edge of the roof and howled at the city in triumph, then scurried back from the edge and closed his eyes on the chilly, dirty rooftop. Sleep came almost immediately.

A dream was beginning to take shape. He had just begun to cross the border where empirical senses are replaced by fantasy when distant voices pulled him awake. "No," he moaned groggily, hungry for sleep. Starved, really. But the call repeated itself, growing louder. The voices were directed at him and therefore impossible to ignore. He raised himself onto uncertain legs and shuffled over to the edge.

"Jump!" came the voices. "Just jump! Jump!" It was difficult to see two-hundred feet or so to the sidewalk below, but someone was there. Three or four people took shape as Remy's eyes slowly oriented to the distant source. "Jump!" they called again, mostly unified, their voices playful, jeering. It was all a game to them and nothing more. "Jump!"

He shouted down, "Why don't you just come right up here?! Plenty of room on the roof for all of us. I don't think we'll be bothered much up here." But if they heard him, they didn't acknowledge it and the chanting continued. He retreated back to a more centralized position on the roof and prepared to wait them out but the shouts from below continued on unabated. Thirty-minutes later, the frequency and volume had diminished but was still persistent enough to deny sleep. Preferring this intrusion to the more calculated one inside his own apartment, Remy was comfortable to remain on the rooftop all night. He had even begun dozing a bit while sitting upright and cross-legged on the rooftop when the croak of a door opening awoke him immediately. He sprang up on crouched legs and rolled deeper into the shadow of an air conditioning exhaust fan, on his feet and concealed before the man stepped out of the doorway. He recognized the figure as a security guard from the lobby. He walked slowly about scanning the scene. *He's searching for me,* Remy thought. *And he'll find me, I'm sure. That's the only entrance/exit and there are only a couple of places to hide up here.*

Acting on something he had seen in the movies, his hand groped along the ground as he searched for something to toss. Coming up with only a tiny pebble, he threw it to the far side of the rooftop in order to create a distraction, only it struck the ground with such a whimpered *thwimp* that it went completely unnoticed by the guard. He searched about for something heavier but found nothing suitable: an old plastic straw, tinier pebbles, an empty cigarette pack bleached by the sun.

New approach. He waited until the guard had more or less turned away and then stood up fully and began walking slowly toward the guard, smiling warmly and waving his hand, just as affable as can be. "Wanshang hao," Remy greeted, *good evening,* and continued on his way. The guard looked to say something but Remy was already gone, out of the door, down the four flights of steps and into his apartment. As sleep approached later that night, it was chased away by a fourth addition to the audio torture. "Jump!" came the cheerful voices, this time from the speakers above. "Jump!"

CHAPTER XXI

CHINA

Friday afternoon. Electronic chimes rang throughout the school signaling the end of another week of learning. The weekend had officially begun. Half of the teachers and most of the students instantly swarmed out of the complex in one great mass. Remy remained, note-taking in the margins of short essays and recording grades. An hour later, most of the students were gone and few staff remained. Of the foreign teachers, only Remy and Patrick occupied the office.

Remy sat staring at the man for quite some time, waiting for eye contact that did not come. "I won't miss you at all."

"Pardon?"

"Oh, I was just thinking aloud, I suppose. When you're this tired, thoughts and actions are separated by a very thin, very blurry line. You know what I mean?"

Patrick looked up and their eyes met across desks and computer monitors.

"Well, you do and you don't, Patrick." Remy continued. "Your psyche would likely crumble into dust under even half of the pressure I've endured. You're just a glorified mosquito, Pat. You could've been anything as a child, limitless potential, but here you are: a mosquito. That's what you did with your life. Annoy, hurt, hide, repeat. That's your lot in life. It's pathetic, Patrick. If I actually die, not just the threats which come at me constantly, but actually die, I will die as a man. A whole, human man. Not a mosquito. But a man." He held the gaze of the man who led makeshift thugs that threatened his life, a man who resided in the flat above. His torturer.

"Tortured unto death. That may very well be how I die. But I'd rather die like that than live like you."

Patrick returned his opponent's gaze, showing little sign of dismay.

"No, I won't miss you at all, Pat," Remy continued unabated. "I'm tempted to just take the arrest and leap out of my chair right now and strangle you to death. Do you think you could prevent that? Could you run away fast enough or deflect my blows? I doubt it. I could dislocate your trachea and blind one of your eyes within seconds. Easily. As a man wipes his own runny nose. That easily."

A quick shudder passed through the man.

"There it is," Remy brightened. "There's that fear you've been desperately trying to pull out of me for almost a month."

Patrick flushed angrily, cheeks reddening.

"Oh, relax. It doesn't feel that great to be frightening. I already feel ashamed. You're not missing much." Remy stood, gathering his belongings. "Be seeing you. Or, better yet, never seeing you again."

He was expecting to return to America battered and in need of healing. He expected he may even begin a new life as a protected witness, his true name lost forever. A life inextricably enmeshed with FBI or CIA organizations grateful for the data he had handed over, grateful for the evidence, for the new information gathered. He had visions of fanfare, a makeshift parade along a small downtown square, confetti and streamers littering sidewalks and roadways. Interviews by journalists. The incident he had survived made public on various news networks. Warm handshakes. New policies implemented based on the startling information that he had brought with him. His smirk turned to a wide grin as he thought of crossing that imaginary barrier that separated America proper from the fringe of the airport. *To lie down and close my eyes without an audio attack. To sleep again.*

His smile did not falter the entire walk home, a leisurely stroll, along which he purchased two portions of duck and rice – one for William and one for himself. William gulped down the meal from a tin bowl in the kitchen while Remy slowly chewed the same morsels. He opened his wallet and ensured the existence of his bank card. He checked that his passport was stored securely in his backpack. He sorted through old photos, reminiscing, fingering each one tenderly. He slid his tampered electronics into his backpack and removed the leash from the wall. William trotted outside eagerly into the hallway, joyous. Remy followed more slowly, saving strength for what he predicted would be a difficult passage. He twisted the key into the door lock with finality, preparing to never return.

"Good riddance," he muttered as elevator doors pinched shut behind man and hound.

CHAPTER XXII

CHINA

The corner of the neighborhood block was fairly deserted and the night was thick and warm. Remy lowered himself onto the curb and placed a phone call to the first of the taxi companies on his handwritten list. He was patched through to a dispatcher with some English ability without much waiting. "Okay. We come fifteen minute."

William waited enthusiastically, smiling ear to ear and full of energy. Remy, however, while pleased with the promise of escape and the correlating chance to sleep, was less optimistic. He was uncertain as to the validity of his passport and half-expecting another banking fraud would transpire at the critical moment in which he needed to purchase tickets back to America. He remembered first arriving at Guangzhou, of the gang of taxicab drivers that accosted him at the airport and the driver who intentionally took a winding, nonsensical path after speaking with a school representative. Of the two large groups of men that had filled the courtyard with tense opposition on that first night, the likes of which he had not seen since.

He soberly recalled it all as he stared absently into the distance, sifting through memories, trying to make some sense it of it. Chinese pedestrians passed him on the sidewalk for some time until eventually the taxi arrived. The driver's face was flashed recognition of the German Shepherd as Remy plunged the back door open and ushered them both inside.

"Don't worry. He's a great dog. Peaceful as can be," he told the driver.

He followed this up with a charming smile that failed utterly. The driver retorted with a barrage of Mandarin that was at best half understood. Remy, using Google Translate -- an app that he hoped was working more effectively than Google Maps -- went about the arduous task of communicating. The driver wanted more money because of the dog. Remy thought this unfair: if there were two human passengers the fare wouldn't be increased. The driver typed in a response involving a cleaning fee. Remy replied that the cab wasn't especially clean at the moment, pulling loose papery rubbish from a side door pocket to illustrate. The taxi driver, warming to the negotiations, offered Remy a cigarette which he accepted gratefully. He had more or less ceased consuming tobacco but thought the mutual smoking would better his odds of actually reaching the airport: a faraway, wonderful concept that he hadn't dared entertain long.

Well, at least the translating software is working properly. This negotiation is proof of that, Remy thought after reaching an agreed price. He ensured the driver knew the destination was the international airport and resituated himself in the backseat with William. He had little idea of the correct direction, just a vague sense of where north should be, bluffing his way through the negotiated cab fare with a stern, no funny-business attitude.

Remy chuckled quietly to himself in the backseat, his smile uncontainable. "We're doing it, my furry friend. Just hang in there." He was brimming with joy. Escape had come. And then the phone rang. The screen flashed the name of the one and only Monica Hu.

"Well, hello. Good timing."

"What you doing?"

"I, my dear, am on my fine-feathered way up and out of this hell-hole."

"I no understand."

"Right. I guess that is some strange vocabulary. Forget it. You're calling at a strange time."

"It strange, Remy?"

"Well, not so much strange as coincidental, really. I'm on my way to the airport."

"You go leave China now? You have ticket?" There was a smirk to her voice.

"Yes. And no. Yes, I'm leaving. And no, I don't have a ticket. Everything is so compromised now. I don't trust online purchasing. I get to the form box where I need to input my bank account information and I think, nope. Not going to do that. Not here. Not now. Figure I'll just buy one at the airport."

"I no think you go."

"Oh, but I must, Moni. I don't like running away but a man must sleep."

"Assistant not help you with leaky pipe? Maybe she help you buy ticket." Her audible scoff stiffened his spine. William, nose to the opened window sniffing the passing environ, drew his attention back inside the car. He looked to Remy and returned his massive tongue back into his maw. He closed his mouth and shifted himself to face Remy, aware that something had changed.

"I don't care for your tone, Monica. I know a human heart beats in your chest despite this serpentine façade." He remembered back to the initial bank theft, of how she struggled with herself, and he softened. "I love you, but I cannot stay here. There is only death for me here, either my own or someone else's and then my own after, I'm sure. Terrible things are on the horizon. I just can't do this any longer."

"You good at endure." She paused, shifting gears. "It late. Call me tomorrow morning."

"I'll be on a plane flying east through the sky, but sure, I'll call you when I can. I still must convince you to defect or something once I'm out from under this. Maybe I can pull some strings if any of these devices have something useful remaining on them. I don't know. It's hard to think about anything other than sleeping."

She laughed coyly again. "Okay. Call me tomorrow morning."

He ended the call feeling as though a winter wind had cut through his coat. William was still looking in his direction. "Oh, don't worry about that, boy. We're on our way. Can't be but another half-hour before we arrive at a place too public to be attacked. Too many uncontrollable variables at an airport. We should be safe there. I've thought about it. With vast resources and vast manpower, they can manipulate a defined area to an inhuman degree. Our apartment, our neighbors, a courtyard of people. It's possible. Costly, but possible. But the airport? It's just too public, too many unknowns floating around that could witness this -- whatever this is -- and spread word. They won't risk a thing like that. No, ol' boy. Once we're at the airport, we're as good as gold."

William shook his head back and forth rapidly to remove a buildup of loose fur and stuck his snout back out of the window crack. Remy turned his attention out of his own window, at the blur of the city passing by. Soon after, a Chinese pop tune -- the driver's ringtone -- cut through the stillness. He answered the call, gradually slowing the vehicle the more he interacted with the phone until he eventually parked it on the shoulder of the roadway. He remained on the phone for a few minutes and then the taxi was off again, barreling into the night. Thirty minutes came and went.

Remy called out, "Wumen fujin le?" *Are we close?*

The driver nodded his head, not bothering to look back. Fifteen more minutes passed.

"Wumen fujin le?"

The driver didn't nod his head the second time, focused intently on the road ahead of him. Knowing he had been heard and that the driver was feigning ignorance, Remy smacked the metal bars that separated the backseat from the front. This drew the driver's attention. "Feiji chang?" *Airport?* The driver returned to the road without acknowledgement and Remy's heart lurched.

He forced himself to breathe slowly and deeply despite the newly released adrenaline, and then he placed a call to the taxi company. A new, pleasant-sounding receptionist reassured him that the driver's destination was definitely the airport. She notified him that they should arrive soon and recommended that Remy use his phone to verify his current location. He politely danced around the fact that his phone displayed any number of maps of the area, all of them incorrect, as best he could and, in the end, the dispatcher agreed to call the driver to verify that everything was alright. His rising tension was assuaged a minute later when the driver's ringtone sounded again. The driver didn't slow down as he fielded the second call, however, and ended the conversation abruptly, his mood grim.

They drove on like that for another fifteen minutes or so. Remy watched the urban nightlife give way to ever-darkening, low-income rural sprawl from the backseat of the cab as it cruised along. Homes in need of repair and downright shacks stood along the edge of the roadways. The absence of streetlamps had become noticeable and as the driver turned down yet another unlit road, the asphalt beneath the tires gave way to loosely packed earth, triggering a new rush of adrenaline. William sat upright, perched on tense paws, quickly able to spring into action if need be. Remy moved his hand to pat his head and William veered away. *This is not the time for that,* he communicated just as plainly as words fall on ears.

"Alright, boy. Alright. It's just life or death. You haven't been training for nothing, right?" He chuckled to himself, but it fell flat, empty. "Yeah, this does suck, William. I was hoping to avoid this. Killing. Dying."

He pulled out his phone and called the taxi company again, only instead of the ringing sound signaling a connection, a busy signal flashed in his ears. It was the first time he had heard a busy signal in China. A dull curiosity nipped at him and was quickly pushed aside as the driver made a sharp left on more unpaved roads, axles creaking a warning on worn struts. The next turn brought the cab back onto paved streets though darkness prevailed and residential buildings were nowhere to be found. An industrial area. No one around. Remy mustered his energy for the attack. His worried mind cleared.

He rolled down the back window as far as possible prompting William to pounce over and give the world a good sniffing. Remy pushed him from his lap lovingly, and once the hound was secure, deftly cracked the door open as the driver negotiated another turn. The overhead light sprang on, blinding and surprising the driver who let out a curse in Mandarin. Remy apologized and closed the door shut once again, happily noting that at least he wasn't trapped in the backseat. Even if the door locked, the window was wide enough for both William and himself to exit without too much trouble. He placed a call to the taxi company and was met with another busy signal. There would be no help coming. Remy smiled wide. William, too, had relaxed. He cupped his hand behind the dog's ears and gently drew their heads together in a headbutt. "We won't go easily, ol' boy. You ready?"

Remy began clapping his hands together loudly in a slow rhythm, building momentum for what was to come. His eyes searched the countryside for signs of a waiting vehicle, expecting to be delivered to someone menacing. *I wonder if it'll be that thug from the apartment courtyard,* he questioned himself absently. He leaned forward and took in the dashboard and front seats. No weapons were lying about. He stared a good long time at the driver, analyzing bulges of his pockets for clues of contents, taking in his build, scars and/or marks that individualized the man. Finding the man weaponless and untrained, he turned his attention to the metal railing that separated the backset from the front, rattling the bars a bit searching, testing for vulnerability. Finding none, he relaxed into the backseat and placed another call.

"Strike one," Remy said as he found the taxi company's number in his call log. "Strike two." He pressed the call button, a self-imposed final time. "And strike thr---" but instead of a busy signal, the phone rang. "What's this? A pop fly to center field?!" He negotiated the call to an English-speaker who informed him that the driver had become lost. Remy laughed louder than he should have, still quite close to a breaking point in more than one way.

"Lost getting to the airport? How does a taxi driver not know where the airport is?"

The dispatcher apologized and stated that they would need to return home, back to the pick-up point.

"Well, how will the driver find his way back there if he can't even find the airport?"

"You show him. Okay?"

"Not okay. Not at all. I don't know where I am. Looks like a nice spot to kill a man, though, wherever we are. It's dark and it's dirty and no one is around. We've turned twenty times and were never near a highway. That's a little strange, eh? No highway to get to the airport."

"Okay. Okay. I call him. He take you home. You only pay half fare. Good deal. No pay whole fare, even if he get mad."

"Are you f$&^ing serious? You want me to pay anything for this? My dog and I are about to kill or die and you want me to pay this man?"

"Only half. Sorry. But need to pay gas. Pay something." Her tone had changed, condescending, as if Remy was trying to sneak one by her.

Soon afterward, a pop tune Remy had quickly grown to despise, rang out. The driver fielded the call, pulled the cab over, turned around and sped off. He was relieved to see familiar landmarks whizz by from the open backseat window: an empty field, a familiar trash pile. Eventually, it became clear that they were indeed on the right path back to the apartment in Tianhe, Guangzhou. Thirty minutes later, the vehicle stopped in front of the towering complex.

Remy opened the backseat door before the vehicle had come to a full stop. William leapt out and bounded into the courtyard, leash dragging behind him ineffectively. Remy grasped his full backpack, eyed up the fare and gave the man half. Polite thank you's that neither side felt in the slightest were exchanged. The taxi roared off as he shouldered the bag and slowly followed William as he gave chase to a fleeing rat, ears folded back, smiling as if he was having the greatest of times. His prey found a small crevice in broken pavement to scurry into, leaving William frustrated and without a toy. He bounded back to Remy and the two returned to a flat that was beginning to feel less like a torture chamber and more like a prison cell.

Hours later -- traces of adrenaline still swimming about Remy's bloodstream, William sound asleep -- the sound of partying from the apartment upstairs intermingled with the sound of a helicopter's approach, torture and celebration fusing into one.

CHAPTER XXIII

CHINA

The phone rang around 10 a.m.

"You were call me in morning."

"Had other things on my mind. Killing. Dying. Torture."

"No one kill you."

"I'm not going to argue with you, Monica. What do you want? Speak."

She paused, her sails falling slack, windless. "I not know."

"Great. Nice talking to you. Bye."

He ended the call and returned to a computer he couldn't make sense of. Another sleepless night had brought him no closer to understanding the thing but there was little else to do. Watching films, playing video games, listening to music, idly flipping through webpages, he could enjoy none of those things, his mind whirling around one central question: *How can I escape?*

He tried to gather a better understanding of where the airport was by browsing websites displaying conflicting maps, maps that conveniently neglected to identify the airport. He remembered vaguely that the it was located northwest of his flat and was considering making an attempt via the subway despite the fat that he he had been denied access once before with William. *I could hop on a train without him and arrive at the airport in under an hour. No way my oppressors have the clout to alter trainline schedules.* But the thought was only briefly entertained for leaving William behind was not an option.

Escape will be hard-fought. He opened the wall-to-wall kitchen window and dipped his head out, looking first upward to the tiny, visible sliver streaming from the flat above his own and then down to the sidewalk and street far below. The recent memory of a trio of very real people calling cheerfully, commanding him to "Jump! Jump! Jump!" echoed in his memory. *You could never tell such a terrible thing happened there,* Remy thought, looking down onto a sparsely populated sidewalk. *It would be easy enough to comply, though. Almost fun until the landing, though how bad could that part be? It'd be quick. Not much suffering.* It had been three weeks since Remy had slept. A day or to past the three-week mark, actually.

He cared very little for his own safety. To die then would not have been so bad. As he weighed this new option, a furry presence slid past his outer thigh, drawing his attention back inside the kitchen to the ever-vigilant Shepherd who proceeded to sit underfoot and lock eyes with Remy, tongue lolling out of an open dog smile, reminding him why he must soldier on.

"The things I do for a dingo," he said to his wolfish counterpart who responded by lazily stretching along his front legs. Remy squatted to his level and kissed his furry head. He then delivered a gentle shove which elicited a playful sparring match to play out on the linoleum floor.

They separated as Remy became winded whereupon William retreated to his floor cushion where he curled up for a nap. He had grown to be quite a competent match. As a younger pup, Remy had thrown slow, soft punches his way, and even then, most landed solidly, in time stepping up the speed and solidity of the strikes. He could catch a reasonably swift punch in his massive jaws more times than not. He'd learned to squirm away and out of most generic holds. He'd been trained to defend and his capacity in that regard had become impressive. Remy felt pride knowing he'd raised a hound that could take care of himself. A gentle soul, playful and patient and able to take care of himself if attacked. He was the best of dogs and Remy would see him to safety. Somehow.

He thought back to the earliest of days, a puppy so young it probably shouldn't have been separated from its mother. A furry slug of a pup that could barely walk. A single step of a stairway an insurmountable object, eyes perma-squinted shut. William had come to Remy at a very, very young age. He had casually mentioned to a Chinese acquaintance that he desired a German Shepherd, and low and behold, one week later, a complete stranger delivered baby William free of charge to his front door one evening, refusing payment, not even giving his name.

William had grown into a rambunctious youth, barking at everything that came into his proximity with a ferocity that Remy felt obligated to curb. "Stop!" Remy had commanded. "Other living things have a right to exist, too. We're not sheep in your flock, shepherd." Those were difficult times, William defiant and unruly. Teenage angst. There were time-outs. There were stern talking-tos. There were groundings from pettings and sofa time. Disapproving smacks on the flank.

And then the parvovirus hit. He suddenly lost his appetite one morning and began vomiting constantly, later refusing even water. By the following morning, he was barely able to hold himself upright, focused on each deliberate step. By the afternoon, he lacked the strength to stand. He was fading fast, death all but inevitable.

Veterinarians were few and far between in Chengdu, China in 2010. The idea of caring for an animal beyond its ability to produce eggs, milk, or meat was not a popular sentiment. Remy had only one option, a pet shop that doubled as a veterinarian clinic. Atop an old wooden table, beaten and worn, on a crude patio that shared space with the public sidewalk, William was gently laid down, sleeping a sleep that he could have very easily not awakened from. After a quick onceover, the vet delivered grave news: William had caught the parvovirus. The treatment would be costly and most dogs, especially large breed ones, were killed in the process.

"If you want, I send someone to get shot," the young vet spoke solemnly, knowing the expense of the treatment and the slim odds involved. "It take hour, but then, I not know. He very sick."

And that he was. William had been transformed from a tiresome ingrate to a coma patient on the verge of death in less than forty-eight hours. Death was near. Even a child could see that. "I must try. Please go, ride quickly. Come back soon."

Remy held onto William's paw as the IV was inserted and nutrients were pumped into his bloodstream. He didn't flinch, didn't resist. "Keep bag up. Keep drip. Okay?" the vet prompted him as he exited the shop, mounting his motorbike. Remy nodded solemnly. The vet backed his motorcycle onto the road and roared into traffic, leaving Remy very much alone with his dying pup.

"Don't you die on me. Don't you die, you dingo," he chanted again and again as the night passed on, tears welling and spilling over as he massaged his paws. "You must fight this. Fight it, William! Don't die on me, boy."

True to his word, the vet returned an hour later and administered an antiviral concoction intravenously. Hours passed. The night wore on and was approaching midnight when his puppy eyes opened slowly. Glassy eyes slowly opened and Remy cried tears of joy. William tried to stand but being securely fastened to the makeshift operating table, failed. He immediately began nipping at the IV needle in his leg. "There he is. That's my boy." Soon he fell back asleep, chest rising and falling in quick, deep breaths. Very much alive.

By the following afternoon, William was back on his feet and full of vitality, but nearness to death had changed him. There was no territoriality in him any longer. He stopped trying to control everything and simply let it be, playing as much as possible in the process. He learned tricks because there were treats involved. He eventually stopped eating out of trashcans. Mostly. His love of returning but not releasing fetched balls manifested into playful wrestling which both man and dog enjoyed from time to time. They had grown quite close.

At the kitchen windowsill, Remy stared off into the distant past. "We'll leave this place together, ol' boy. I just don't know how. I don't know how at all." The weight of it all fell upon him then. Defeated. Trapped. Bullied. Exhausted. Sleep deprived. He broke down, eyes flowing as he collapsed onto buckled knees. He placed his forehead to the floor and let it all out. Sometime later, he felt the hot breath of William on the crown of his head, followed by a cold, wet nose nudging and sniffing. William slid his muzzle down, tracing his wet snout down under Remy's jaw and jerked his chin up sharply.

"Oh, you suck," Remy muttered, voice cracking in the process. The hound looked down to the man who remained doubled over on the kitchen floor. "I don't know what to do," he croaked, curling up tightly into a fetal position seeking comfort that would not come for he knew that even in his own kitchen he would be denied the ability to collapse into unconsciousness, that at any minute, a piercing sound would shoot forth and deny him sleep.

"It's not fair, Will," he sobbed.

Remy felt a sharp pain on the top of his right ear, piercing and pulling. He looked up wearily as William braced firmly on his front legs, nipped and tugged on his ear again.

"Ow! What the f%^* are you doing?! Stop it!"

William complied, releasing the ear and taking a couple of calculated steps back. Remy collapsed back to the kitchen floor, hopelessly defeated by his circumstance. A sharp pain cut through his being again as William latched onto the same ear, tugging on braced front paws. Remy shot up, crouching on weak legs.

"Stop it!"

William barked once in response, clear and loud, and made as if to pounce, tail swishing in anticipation.

"I hate you so much," he replied, meaning just the opposite, as he rose on shaky legs. William barked again and spun around.

"Alright, boy. Alright. Let's go for a walk." Upon hearing the word *walk*, William leaped and danced about. They walked several blocks and Remy's mood brightened. He was becoming aware that he had begun drawing a crowd of sorts. Not that he was mobbed, but many eyes looked to him with recognition, curious as to what would be in store next. The neighborhood was very much aware of the plight of this particular foreigner and his dog. They looked as they would to a dangerous wounded beast, which in many ways, they were.

How far and wide does this recognition extend? Five blocks from home, while the effect was diminished, occasional strangers would look upon them with knowing eyes. A new anxiety fell upon Remy then, feeling more out of his element than he ever had: surrounded and outnumbered in unchartered waters. William, however, could not have cared less as he blissfully enjoyed the day and all of the scents it provided.

CHAPTER XXIV

CHINA

William was whimpering disgruntledly, pawing at the kennel door when Remy returned home. He opened the gate expecting him to need to be let out for bio purposes only he didn't gallop to his leash at the front door. Instead, he jogged from room to room, nose to the ground, following a scent trail. He stopped here and there, sniffing the mattress, doorframes and the like as he moved from one room to the next.

Remy followed silently, immediately transfixed as he had never seen him do such a thing before. He thoroughly searched his closet, cabinet and desk drawers, the contents of the emergency backpack. Nothing was missing, though the clothes in his closet felt slightly askew as did the contents of some drawers. Nothing definitive, but with the baby powder footprints at the doorway not too long ago and incessant noises that prevented sleep and William jogging around the apartment purposefully sniffing, he reasoned that his home had been entered into while he was away again.

William would not be deterred from sniffing and resniffing the flat as the minutes wore on. Remy crouched low and murmured kind words praising his diligence that went largely ignored, as did a few tasty treats he tried to give the hound. He shrugged and dropped them into his food bowl, grabbed a small bundle from within his emergency backpack, and left. William barely registered his departure, still hard at work inhaling scents imperceptible to a human nose.

He took the elevator down to the lobby and exited, walking by two security guards who gave him a sleepy look as he passed. *Not much help, those guys,* Remy thought, pushing open a heavy glass door that locked magnetically behind him. *More of a hindrance, actually. I could've fallen asleep on the rooftop if it hadn't been for their interference.*

He marched past a dozen Chinese women in their later years practicing tai-chi while loud folk music played from worn speakers. Their husbands congregated adjacently, watching and chatting amongst themselves. He continued on to the back of the courtyard where he played wall ball and fetch and where a dog's biological needs could be met in relative privacy. He found a clean edge of a low broken wall, leapt up and opened the plastic file he had brought from the apartment, removing the personal effects contained therein.

A hodgepodge of photos of exes from many years ago. A photo of himself at age five lounging draped across a swivel chair playing Atari, big innocent eyes intent on securing points. A photo at age nine -- an acolyte then -- dressed in a long immaculately white robe with worn, dirty sneakers poking out from the hem. Graduation photos. Photos of his sister, twenty years deceased. A photo of his father, almost just as far removed. He reread love letters written in exquisite penmanship from young women who had no idea what they were getting into. Scraps of paper with old rhymes, meant as lyrics or poetry, all but forgotten in those distant days of youth. Reminders of his life printed on paper in varying degrees of wear and tear. Memorabilia.

He took them all in fondly and wondered not for the last time how he'd gotten to be in the position he currently found himself in. He went through each photo one last time before setting them into a porcelain bowl he'd brought from the kitchen and setting them ablaze.

Flames licked over the old papers, coalescing into a bowlful of fire. The gloss covering of the photographs turned to a thick, flaming liquid that pooled and bubbled at the bottom. Black, noxious smoke filled the air. He watched as the photographs of his youth, autographs, poetry, love letters, and ticket stubs melted into a fiery goo. The memorabilia clumped together as the fire fizzled out so Remy licked his fingers and pulled apart charred, fused photos to reignite them, ensuring the faces and especially names of loved ones were destroyed completely. There was little he could do to protect them and removing evidence of their existence from the situation he was currently immersed in seemed best.

As the second fire began to die out, he became aware that the tai-chi participants were distracted. Though the folk music played on, they stood in a rough circle, chatting nervously about something. Slowly realizing that the smell of smoke had caused the disturbance, he poked through the embers and, determining that all the important stuff had been consumed, hopped over the wall, tossing the bowl and its contents into a nearby public trashcan after ensuring it had cooled enough to not pose a fire hazard.

William leapt up and jogged over to the door as it opened, but finding it only to be Remy, marched back disappointedly to his resting pillow. The treats in his bowl remained untouched. Remy opened the hot water tap in the shower with charred, smoky fingers. A second thought came to him then, and as the water heated, he opened the contact list contained in his phone. He recorded his family members' phone numbers by hand on a slip of paper similar to the one that contained the list of Guangzhou taxi providers. He added a few numbers from old friends in Florida before folding it several times and inserting it into his wallet. Scrolling down his contact list, he came to the young man who'd approached him under a tree at the airport while he waited for William's approval at the animal holding office. *I never called him. Not once.* His blackened thumb hovered over the *send* icon. *What exactly would I say to this fellow?* He practiced a few lines in his head, but it all seemed like raving lunacy. *Besides,* he thought, ultimately deleting that and all other contacts from his phone records *That would smack too much like asking for help.*

Personal effects obliterated, he stripped down and washed away the smoke, feeling loss, but pleased with his decision to sacrifice for the ones he loved. He lathered and rinsed and recalled each photo in his mind's eye, committing the details to memory. In another terrible night without sleep, the photos flashed, one after the other.

CHAPTER XXV

USA

"I suppose you'd like the opportunity to scold me sometime tonight. Now is convenient for me if you're available."

The manager, ten years his junior, smiled awkwardly.

"Well, I don't want to scold you. I do want to speak with you though, but I need to use the restroom first," she replied, her mannerisms very maidenly.

"Sure thing. Just let me know when you're ready." He was not swayed but smiled politely. It amounted to the same thing. Speaking. Scolding.

The night had been a disaster: meals constructed incorrectly and late, the parameter of his individualized serving section changed multiple times throughout the evening shift. The back of the house out of plates and ice and lids and to-go cups and to-go containers and clean spoons, and Remy the only one addressing any of those issues by restocking cups, filling ice bins, and hauling heavy plates from the dishwasher to the service line. When the manager, who he felt should have been managing at least some of that, voiced a grievance, well, he found that pretty hard to take seriously. He put on a brave face, nonetheless.

The issue involved a group of guests who had sat down, ordered drinks, had drinks delivered, was not ready to order meals thus requesting more time with the menu. Remy returned, answered a few questions about ingredients and once again the table stated that they needed more time. He greeted and served the table adjacent to their own and returned about seven minutes later. Within that seven-minute window, the first table had suddenly become irate and voiced indignation at inattentive service. The husband/father who was barely able to contain his obesity in a single chair let alone his ire had intentionally shirked placing an order twice and then complained to management as soon as Remy took the order of another table. To the management, the customer's prostrations were well-founded. Customers were obeyed at all cost. Employees were expendable. Right and wrong simply did not exist. Only profit and the loss thereof. America.

He sat down and squirmed as he was expected to squirm, as all American employees are expected to squirm under pressure. Truly, it was the only important element of the dialogue. The manager needed to see that he "cared", and that was only made manifest via squirming. "Oh, what can I do?" "Oh, I tried so hard." Etcetera, etc., etc. He hated it all. Hated what America had become far before he'd moved to Japan in 2003. Hated it all the more in 2019.

The manager had no idea what to do with an older college graduate with experience in Asia she could not in her wildest dreams imagine. She wagged a proverbial finger, taking zero responsibility. She listened and grew uncomfortable at Remy's line of questioning as to how to improve such things in the future. She was unable to give anything akin to decent advice or even make logical statements, her dialogue drowning in contradiction. She was not unkind but it was all so much nonsense.

He returned home and sat on the balcony, the flooring of which sloped and bowled downward. There he immersed himself in self-decorated colorful Christmas lights though summer had just begun -- sulking, brooding, imagining, theorizing. He longed for a bygone time when he lived amongst the Japanese. Their thoughtfulness in word choice. How they didn't flood silence with unneeded words. Their calm calculation. Unimposing, but even when imposition emerged, it was so subtle and intricate that one felt sort of obligated to surrender to it. It was nothing like the blatant forcefulness that had become the very identity of America, if such a thing even existed in a nation so full of variables. So many good. So many wicked. So many afflicted with various psychological issues. Some generous and wise. Some ignorant and demanding. Anxiety attacks and depression had replaced apple pie and baseball as American identifiers. A tumultuous environment that had never felt like home.

Depression so rampant that advertisements littered magazine pages, commercial airtime, billboards, luring the weak and wounded toward such-and-such a pill. "F*(% your doctor," the ads hinted. "Insist on taking these pills until he capitulates to your demands though the side effects are worse than the ailment."

He thought back to Thoreau, of how much he had hated what had become of America, of what Mark Twain would come to call the Gilded Age: a shiny, glittering, beautiful skin concealing a rotten core. "The mass of men leading lives of quiet desperation," wrote Thoreau. *But the desperation isn't quiet anymore,* Remy thought.

Like dogs chasing their tails, so were many Americans. Spinning in place, trying to catch that tip and failing and spinning faster in the process. Trying to pay student loans, trying to pay the mortgage, trying to keep that job, trying, trying and so close to catching that tail. A type of dizziness was to blame for the nation's plentiful and varied psychological problems. Feeling very much like a square peg, he wondered how much longer he could survive in a round hole.

CHAPTER XXVI

CHINA

The sun was setting as Remy left his apartment and returned to the same curbside where he dialed the last taxi number listed that he had jotted down earlier in the week: a private driver he'd spied near a subway station. There was no English-speaking dispatcher to facilitate the call and he muddled his way through a very simple explanation of location and desired destination in limited Mandarin. Some twenty or thirty minutes later, the driver arrived in a dented, blue van. Remy slid the back door open as the van came to a halt and William bounded inside, immediately making himself at home. He verified the destination with the driver in Mandarin -- the international airport -- and one hour later they were nowhere near that place.

"You're an insignificant crumb, you know that? I'm just trying to leave in peace and you won't even allow an exit." Remy was in no mood, concealing real fear with real hate. "You're a tiny thing," he continued. "You've a smaller build than my last girlfriend. You've been in a scrap or two, though, I bet. I can see that in your beady little eyes. But so tiny. I have twice your reach." Remy laughed maniacally at himself, the driver, the situation.

But the driver didn't share in Remy's mirth. They were, yet again, in some backwater area outside of Guangzhou. Few streetlights shown. Fewer houses than normal. The same sort of environment as he had been taken to the prior evening, only he felt no fear this second time for a violent and unhealthy desire for action had taken root. William's head rested on his lap, his eyes closed, mostly napping. Remy shifted the hound's head gently aside and bounded into the passenger seat, surprising both dog and driver.

"I'm tempted to just commandeer your vehicle and drive to the airport myself. Just shove you right out of your own door. Wouldn't that be something? What could you really do about that?" Remy smirked, and for the first time, began honestly contemplating force in order to escape. *Definitely possible,* he thought. *Minimal, if any, injury to self.* Remy played it out in his head, smiling wide and not liking the feeling that came along with it. Feeling reduced to the same evil that plagued him, his mood soured. When he spoke again it was without the fervor, without the mad joy.

"Just take me back to the apartment," he muttered, returning to the backseat.

He looked up the sentence in Mandarin on his phone and spoke again in the driver's native tongue. The driver chuckled -- an annoyance barely tolerated – turned and began the journey back. The familiar urban sprawl reformed, pedestrian and vehicular traffic condensing to define the city he had come to know as torture incarnate. Within half an hour he had arrived back home, such as it was.

"Sixty dollars," the driver barked in Mandarin. Remy slid open the back door, pushed a suitcase out, shouldered the emergency bag, and ushered William out. He faced the driver.

"You're scum. You just denied me the ability to leave this place. I am imprisoned in Guangzhou. Denied escape. You lied to me about taking me to the airport. You know where it is, you told me you would take me there, and then you didn't. I shouldn't pay you anything."

"Sixty dollars." The driver repeated, looking antsy, tight. Dangerous.

"Ooh, is it go-time? Are we going to do this? You know what I think? I think you owe me sixty-dollars. How do you feel about that?" A maniacal smile had returned to Remy's face, brightening his mood in all of the wrong ways. He shifted back to the front seat and with that simple action, the driver flashed a pocket knife: extended, locked in place and ready to go. Remy paused.

"Well, you have a decent chance now, I suppose."

"Sixty dollars," the driver repeated in Mandarin.

"Do you know what happens next? I take that knife away from you. You may very well cut me first, but only once if at all. After that, I disarm you and repeatedly stab you until you flee or die in the process of me defending my own life. Then, I drive your van to the airport, wash up along the way, bandage or stitch up a wound that you may or may not have been able to inflict, change my clothes, purchase a ticket back to the U.S. and fly far, far away from this place. Oh, how I hate this place, this hell on Earth." He pondered the idea a little longer while keeping an eye fixed on the blade. He was uncertain as to if his passport had been compromised, but all signs pointed to his mobile phone being so hacked that it was likely used as a GPS tracking device for others, as well as a microphone and video recorder. *Could very well be in use right now, which means I would never get to the airport.*

"Alright, scummy. You win. This is a dead end."

"Sixty dollars," he repeated. Feeling strengthened by Remy's clear surrender, he brandished the blade closer.

"Yes, you've made that clear." Remy shifted forward until the point of the knife poked into his chest. "Is that what you're after?

You're going to carve out my heart or pierce my lung? Unlikely given that dinky thing. But here it is." Remy stared into once cold eyes that were melting nervously. The driver pulled the knife away.

"Didn't think so."

Remy relaxed into the backing of the front seat, no longer focused on the blade. He looked out of the window and found William uncharacteristically sitting patiently next to the suitcase on the sidewalk. "That's the weirdest thing about this whole night," he mumbled to himself.

He slid his hand into his back pocket and brought out his wallet. "I'm going to give you twenty dollars. That should cover the gasoline used, and a little for your time. Paying you to do this to me does not sit well but this amount feels right, so here it is." Remy handed over the yuan. The driver counted it quickly, thumbing through it while awkwardly continuing to hold the knife.

"Not enough. Sixty dollars. Forty dollars more," he demanded in Mandarin, Remy's comprehension skills barely sufficient to understand the gist.

"Nope. Be seeing you, cowboy."

Remy exited the vehicle, gathered William's leash and his own suitcase, and returned to his flat where hours later torturous sounds repeated throughout the night as he tossed and turned, yearning for sleep that would not come.

CHAPTER XXVII

CHINA

Remy stood leaning against the kitchen window watching the sun set below the skyline when his phone chimed.

"Why you no call me?" she ordered.

"Yes. I'm fine, thank you for asking," Remy replied pretending to hear something more pleasant. "Actually, not fine at all but you know that which sort of answers your original question the more I think about it."

"I no understand."

"I will leave this place," he said unperturbed by her misunderstanding. "I don't know how. I don't know how long it will take. I'm sure -- I mean, I'm absolutely certain -- that it's not going to be easy, but I will leave. I'll find a way to the airport and I'll fly back to America. Or I'll die in the process. One of those things is going to happen. Surely, you and I both agree on this."

A long pause and then, "I know."

"It's a shame you didn't marry me when you had the chance. I'm quite the catch, you see."

She laughed prettily and he was reminded why he loved her. "You want marry me still?"

"I don't want to marry all of the baggage you carry, that's for sure. But you and me, on a deserted island making babies and farming for sustenance, yeah, that sounds pretty good."

"That not happen."

"Yeah, I know. I know. Listen. Don't hurt William. He's a good dog and he doesn't deserve this. Well, no one deserves this, but definitely not William. Promise me that if something happens, he'll be taken care of. The resources are there. All of this must be so costly. I've been crunching the numbers. From this new job that is more than teaching to the taxi interruptus, to the labor of cancerous neighbors above, to the hardware costs of an audio system I can only speculate on, to the personalized consistent hacking. There must be living human beings on the other end of these actions countering my efforts to secure possession of my own phone and computer twenty-four hours each and every day of the week. All of that can't be cheap. Wish I could make some sense of it, though. The cost must outweigh the $8,000 stolen from me. If I remain employed at this weird school another month or so, I will have earned more than the amount in salary alone, the same school that had something to do with the theft to begin with. It doesn't make much sense to me, Moni. Why spend all of this money to hurt me? Is your gang paying to cover their trail, to make a madman out of me so that no one believes the truth I've plucked out of all of this? Or is there some underground bounty on my suffering?"

He waited a long time for an answer that did not come.

"I miss you very much, Monica Hu. I hate what you've done but I love who you are. I am a man torn. I know to kiss you is to be home but I also know you're quite aware of my circumstance and feign otherwise. Loving you is very painful."

"Loving you very painful."

"Alright, my little parrot. I'm going to go now. To my own computer that I cannot control. To my own home that is entered into by whomever, whenever. To a sofa, or bed, or chair, or bathroom floor, in a perpetually failing effort to sleep. It's coming up on one month now. One month of not sleeping. That has to break some record."

They spoke for some time afterward of things that didn't matter. The fact that he was in no hurry to end the call and return to his plight balanced with the knowledge that he knew it was no coincidence that she had called him as he tried leaving the first time, just before the taxi driver had fielded a mysterious call and began taking an alternate path to nowhere. He engaged in playful dialogue and took the call to the rooftop, enjoying the fresh air and chance to escape the apartment. There he paced and chatted for a couple of hours, well after the sky darkened from dark blue to black. Distant Chinese folk music floated up from twenty stories below as the women gathered and began practicing tai-chi. They came and went and the lovers chatted on.

Afterward, he perched along the lip of the roof's edge, at first scanning the horizon for signs of the airport before settling into a blank stare over the city, lost in thought. Having exhausted his tired mind, he tumbled backward along his lower back and across his shoulder, popping upright a meter away from the cusp. There he teetered before falling down comically, splaying his arms and legs across the roof, as in the first step of making snow angels. There was perhaps a moon in the sky somewhere but he didn't care to find it. He heard a plane roaring in the sky outside his field of vision. It was like sleeping within enemy territory during a lull in battle. He was uncertain in what state he would awake, of what would happen to William in the process, of the security of his passport and personal effects. But after four long weeks, sleep finally found him that night. He snored and twitched for the better part of five hours, awakening to the sound of songbirds eagerly chirping about the impending sunrise. Amazed to have slept, he marched downstairs to freshen up and prepare for work.

CHAPTER XXVIII

CHINA

Sleep. Remy's head had cleared and while not quite firing on all cylinders, he felt well-lubricated, both mentally and physically. It was only after achieving sleep that he became aware that there had been something off about his thought process. Not that memory had failed to serve him during the month of sleep deprivation. Nor had some alter ego taken over and acted on his behest. There were no hallucinations. But as the weeks of sleeplessness dug in, it was as if his mind was slipping into deep waters far from shore. Pressure building as the miasma coalesced. Clarity dimming. Hope waning.

A decent night's sleep had eased the burden life had become. He felt sharper, more agile. He brushed his teeth with gusto and drew a comb through thick hair in need of a shearing. On his way to the elevator he juxtaposed past occurrences, analyzing his enemy's actions, remembering past acts in cool detachment, a fly on the wall to memories, calculating. By the time he was on the sidewalk merging with the pedestrian rush hour, a plan of sorts was taking shape. He nestled himself into his office desk chair, having replayed the plan several times along the sidewalk, making small adjustments with each imagining, honing the edge into something sharp and useful.

None of the office thugs spoke to him any longer. After he realized that they wouldn't actually strike him on school grounds, their ability to upset him was vastly diminished. He took a bit of comfort in how far they had slipped from their initial positioning: from dread-bringer to nuisance to a whisper in the wind. At least in the office. His apartment was another thing entirely.

Returning to work after the dramatic exit on Friday was a huge loss of face, though. There was no way around it. When Patrick strolled in a minute or two before the first bell rang, Remy put on a wide smile and forced eye contact until it was held. "You got me. You won that round. I tried and I failed and you won."

"I don't know what you're talking about."

"Right. Okay. Well, that's fine. But I will get to that airport. I will leave this place. One man and a dog. Little more than the clothes on my back, I imagine. Maybe a few thousand in the bank, maybe not. Not the safest entities, Chinese banks. But I will get to the airport and I will fly away and it will be a sweet, sweet thing."

"Where is the airport, Remy?"

This gave him pause. He was unclear on that matter. He'd witnessed low-flying planes from the rooftop and had developed a vague understanding that it lied somewhere north. He vaguely remembered looking at a map of Guangzhou several months ago from his laptop in Nanchang, but given all of the cyber problems he'd encountered, he couldn't be certain as to its validity or even remember the details clearly. The certificates and files on his computer showed that he had lost control of his operating system long before he arrived in Guangzhou, if any of those dates and times were remotely accurate. Such was the downward spiral. His head began to swirl with a stream of possibilities that he cut short abruptly.

"Pretty sure it's near your mom's house." He replied, amusing himself. "Isn't your mom from China?" Remy began cracking up. It was obvious that Patrick came from Anglo-Saxon stock. Anglo-Anglo-Saxon. "You haven't told me much about your mother. How is she? Is she even alive? Does she love you?" Remy grinned wickedly. "Oh wait, does she know what you do because if she knew that, I'm pretty sure she---."

In response to the stream of questioning, Patrick stood and exited the office.

"Has it always been that easy? Amazing what a little sleep can do. I feel good. I feel right."

A teacher two seats down turned to Remy, the older Canadian who'd walked him back to his apartment, the one who spoke of a former teacher killing herself by jumping out of the window of the flat Remy occupied.

"How was your weekend, Rem?"

"Go f%*^ yourself, Buck," Remy chuckled, spirits high. "Or if you keep talking, I'll walk over there and do it for you."

Buck was not his name but Remy couldn't remember hearing another for the man. Buck smiled awkwardly, took a breath, opened his mouth, and Remy lunged out of his seat, on his feet and headed Buck's way. The middle-aged man closed his mouth, exhaling audibly through his nose.

"You get it now, right, Buck? You see where I'm at. Just nod your geriatric head." He didn't nod nor did he open his mouth again. "I needed a friend, and you came and threatened me with a tale of a suicidal teacher preceding my arrival. We were basically strangers and that's how you initiated a relationship with me."

"I don't know what you're say---" he began as a childish smile of a man who knows he's lying played about his lips. The pen Remy flicked bounced off of the crown of his head, interrupting his sentence.

"I told you to shut your rancid, decaying mouth, Buck. Zip it. No more words now. It's quiet time. Let's get to work teaching. Because that's what we are here. Teachers. Just a normal bunch of teachers teaching students. Nothing to see here, folks. Nothing abnormal at all."

And with that, Remy opened up files and documents and went about tending to the tasks that normal teachers have: recording grades, printing worksheets, and the like. To be fired would mean a swift exit out of the nation and he welcomed that idea. The Chinese government wouldn't allow an unemployed foreigner to remain in the country. To be fired would trigger consistent sleep, a home not broken into habitually, an escape from the role of bullied detective. But he had made a one-year commitment to instruct AP Geography and World History to the utmost of his abilities and he would do exactly that.

He was not fired that day, though technically he assaulted a man with a disposable pen. As the week wore on, sleep-deprivation was reestablished and the section of seating around him became vacant. At first this seemed like a victory but it was actually the worse of two evils. Loneliness turned out to be more bitter than conflict.

Another day of teaching at the strange school came to a close and thousands of students began filing out of the schoolgrounds. The director of the English teachers offered to accompany Remy along his walk home, in much the same way that Buck had done earlier. Sheldon Smith -- a beanpole of an Englishman -- kept pace with Remy as he marched toward home, all the while hinting and insinuating terrible things that could happen to Remy if he didn't start playing ball.

"Look, Sheldon," Remy said, stopping abruptly on the busy sidewalk. "If you're trying to threaten me right now, be clear. Are you saying that my job is in peril? Fantastic. I've thought about that and please feel free to imperil the thing. Are you hinting that I may not be able to rest at night? That would be terrible, to not sleep every night. Sleepless, night after night after night. Whatever you may be trying to threaten me with, it's not as bad as what I already endure. Each day, I don't know what I'll come home to: my dog missing or murdered, my passport gone, my clothes thrown out of the window. My home is entered into when I'm not there so any of that could very well be possible. I live with that every single sleepless day. Oh, and I'm threatened by a large man in my apartment's courtyard bimonthly. What's left, Sheldon? What more can you take from me? You see, that's the problem with torturing a man to this degree. There's nothing left to take. You don't have a bargaining chip." He turned away and continued the walk home, fading into the crowd. Sheldon remained rooted in place.

"I think I should call your family."

Remy halted and slowly pivoted to look back at the man. Sheldon continued, "That's what I should do. I have their contact information on your application. Your mother, your sister. I should call them, tell them to come here. To join you."

Remy's face flushed, as the fight rather than flight aspect of adrenaline took its course. His enraged mind flashed to his simple family: an elderly mother who couldn't struggle to escape like he had, like a rat on one of those sticky mats, she would not be able to break free. Of a sister and her husband that weren't ideal human beings but were family nonetheless. *They would die of fright and stress if they were exposed to even half of this.* His mind drifted to tar pits, of how one primitive beast would become caught in the goo, and in dying call out for help from the pack, which would in turn lure a well-meaning helper to the same demise. He had intentionally not done this, not called out for help, taking the nobler path and suffering alone. He thought, too, of how his credibility would drain away into nothingness if his family came and scooped him out easily. Or if there would be no audible torture when his family arrived, his enemy too smart for any of that, leaving Remy to rant and rave about something that didn't appear to exist. A lose-lose situation, either way.

Remy walked back until he was uncomfortably close to Sheldon. "I would kill you in the process. I wouldn't box you. I wouldn't call you nasty names. I wouldn't shove you menacingly. I would murder you in broad daylight if you brought my family here." Remy's attention was pulled outward as a familiar, muscular, mustached Chinese man appeared in the crowd, distant, but certainly focused on the scene. He slid back a bit to keep both men in his line of sight, forming a triangle of sorts.

"You have a wife. A toddler. How would you like them to come visit me? How would you like it if your family came and lived in my apartment, my sleepless torture chamber for even one single night, Sheldon?! How would you feel about that?!"

Remy pivoted and sidestepped, putting Sheldon directly in the way of the rapidly approaching guard, body weight shifted and poised to strike the Englishman's exposed neck. He reared back to hit a man that had not thrown the first blow, a man that likely had no idea how to fight, a man that was only now coming to understand where Remy had shifted to. Shame swept over Remy and he returned to a relaxed position.

"You have heart, kid, and heart goes a long way."

He slid backward gracefully as he exited the scene, keeping Sheldon directly in an intercepting path of the upcoming guard. He sensed a clustering of teenagers walking in the general direction he needed to go and faded behind them, crouch-walking awkwardly away in the throng. He didn't disappear so much as was obscured for ten seconds or so, reappearing quite far away, far enough. Technically a smooth escape and yet all he could do was return to his apartment which was anything but.

He didn't sleep all that night, but such things were terribly normal.

"Do you mind I sit down, Mr. LeBeau?" asked a mediocre student with lazily untapped potential.

"Sure, if you can find a seat," Remy replied, smiling at his own joke amongst a sea of empty chairs.

"I am applying university this year."

"Good. You should be applying to at least four. They want to see good grades, high SAT scores, volunteer experience, and a well-written letter explaining just how awesome you are and why you would make their campus a better place." Remy paused. "Do you have any volunteer experience?"

"That's why I come. I need help."

"Well, that's my job. What can I do for you?"

What the student wanted, after much hemming and hawing, was for Remy to compose his personal statement to universities. As if this wasn't enough, he was to add details of volunteering that came from imagination alone.

"I know what you want me to do but there's no way that I'm going to do that. If you write a letter, I'd be happy to edit it, give you some pointers, but I---"

"No, I rather not to write it."

"Yeah, well, what you'd rather not do isn't the issue. You have to write this. That's a major part of how a university gets a feel for who you are." Remy stiffened in his chair. "You're asking me to write something *as* you. That's not an option."

"You should. That your job. Teacher do this."

"That does reinforce something I've been thinking about for a while."

"Why you make everything too hard? Everything too hard with you!" His voice hadn't raised in volume but the inflection was wholly unpleasant. He stood up, realizing a dead end when he came against one, and stormed out of the office.

Remy returned home later that afternoon thinking of that conversation, of the thousands of foreign high school students sending letters to universities that were actually composed by English teachers. He thought of this spread throughout the fifty states, throughout the Canadian provinces, Australia, England, South Africa. Anywhere a foreign student applied to an English-speaking university, there very well could be that deception at play. Principals of foreign schools endorsing -- enforcing perhaps -- fraudulence. Of how deeply entwined the Chinese government had been with the past two schools that had employed him: Nanchang, once home of the philandering Principal Tan, appointed into a position he used to manipulate underlings into sex abuse and Guangzhou, a school that had threatened his family, kept him sleep-deprived and ensnared within city limits. Of the billions of dollars in foreign student tuitions. Of the many millions of dollars in foreign teacher salaries paid abroad.

He thought this knowledge would prove useful when he escaped, that some governmental agency back in the U.S. would appreciate this tidbit gleaned in the gloom, along with the data on his computer that showed huge irregularities of software certificate ownerships, false download dates and the like. Cyber evidence he had; proof that students weren't composing their own personal statements, not so much.

More sleepless nights led to the end of the work week. A meeting was held in which the head director -- the equivalent of a principal -- informed the staff that the winter holidays would begin earlier than expected. Effective immediately, the first Friday of the month of December in the year 2012, winter vacation officially began at South China Normal University and would continue well into January 2013. Remy thought of another month without sleep piggybacking on an already grievous month. *Surely, I will be dead before the new year arrives.*

Remy raised his hand and politely waited to be recognized. "You're actually going to pay me, I mean us, during this time? An extended paid vacation out of the blue? I mean, wouldn't this be a good time to let someone go? You would save money that way, you know." He glanced over pleadingly to the bookkeeper seated in the back of the crowd of forty or so and found her intently focused on her own shoes.

"No one is going anywhere," said the director, a finality in his tone. Something like a smile emerged from underneath a thin, tight mustache. The meeting concluded soon thereafter.

As the teachers gathered their things and exited, Buck turned to face Remy from across the meeting room. "You going home for the holidays?" he asked snidely, knowing the difficulty, the pain.

"That's the plan, Buck. That's the plan."

CHAPTER XXIX

CHINA

Remy journeyed back to the familiar poker haunts, drank excessively, lost a ton of money, and couldn't have cared less. All motorized services denied him passage to the airport. He'd been flagged somehow, someway, and most definitively. He'd begun to lose certainty northward was even the proper direction.

It had become apparent that stating his destination was the *airport* amounted to him being delivered anywhere but, and so north had become the new command to drivers that he flagged down in streets many blocks away from his own address hoping to not be recognized. Within a quarter hour or so, he needed to state that he was actually going to the airport and then came a phone call, derisive tones and sideways glances into the rearview mirror, mocking chortles, turns down side streets that led to nowhere. One of the most strenuous failures involved him riding the Tianhe subway line for a few stations, transferring to another train, exiting a few stations later, then hopping in a taxi waiting curbside. Things seemed to be going well until halfway into the trip when the driver received a call and bad turns were made once more. Twelve out of twelve taxi drivers in Guangzhou just couldn't figure out how to get to the airport.

With the vice-principal's thinly veiled threats and endless failed taxi rides and Monica's phone calls, Remy was drowning in hopelessness. As he finished off one full liter of whisky and smoked all throughout the night, he escaped in the only way he could -- inwardly. For some hours, he played cards and chatted about the banal as if he wasn't the focal point of some insidious plot. It wasn't sleep, but it was the next best thing.

He returned home as the sky began to lighten, taxis having no problem taking him to and from other Guangzhou locations. Through a foggy mind, he filed that information away as meandering drunken steps took him across the apartment courtyard. *Maybe I can hail a cab to a location near the airport and walk the rest of the way? If I only knew where the airport was.*

He sang some of the lyrics to *Free Bird* in tuneless hope of escape as he staggered into the lobby and up the elevator to the seventeenth floor to an apartment flat that soon cascaded noises far louder and more regularly than normal so as to pierce through any possibility of him passing out drunk. Dawn turned to morning in this manner. Soon after the torrents fell about him, he entered into the intricate cyber web, trying and failing as he did to procure solid proof of what was occurring, or better yet, to free himself from whatever had rewritten its way into his life and access the real, uncensored internet. To access emails in knowledge that nothing had been deleted or altered from his inbox. To access an actual map.

He spent the entire day fruitlessly following digital paths that led to nonsense into the night until the following afternoon when his computer crashed. When he rebooted, which he'd done in the past under similar circumstances, not only were most files and software missing – the exception being ones that he had no control over, faux files with download dates that couldn't be, which rebooted just fine

-- he could no longer connect to the internet. Turning to his phone, he found the same problem. No connection, impure or otherwise.

He felt the walls closing in and struggled to secure a connection in a variety of creative ways, one failed attempt after the other. By nightfall, he surrendered. Knowing that he would again be denied sleep, he slipped his phone and wallet into his pocket and boarded a late-night train headed for the airport. The train rolled on, accelerating and decelerating every three miles or so as stations came and went. He read the map displayed atop the subway doors which showed the airport as a final destination along his current path.

Then three stations away, for no apparent reason, the subway doors failed to shut as they normally do after letting in passengers at a station. A minute later, an announcement in softly spoken Mandarin played through the cars and everyone began filing out. Remy exited lastly and only under some protest, the doors sliding shut behind him as the train skittered off in the same direction it had been going all along. He looked at its passing longingly. He watched two more trains arrive and go through the same process before he resigned himself to his fate and boarded a train headed back to Tianhe.

I can't do four or five weeks of this. I just can't, he thought as the sound of a helicopter landing looped for the umpteenth time above his bedroom ceiling. If he hadn't been an atheist, he would've prayed, long and hard. As it was, he fumed. The sound of water dropping into deeper water echoed throughout the apartment as he schemed in darkness later that night.

The next day he fed William and ventured into Guangzhou once more using the same subway tunnels and trains that had denied him access to the airport twelve hours prior. He changed trains and veered away from the airport, heading east to the computer district. Exiting the darkness of the subway, he ascended into the full light of day to find himself surrounded by signs in colorful Chinese symbols that promised discount prices and grand service.

CHINA

"Come, come. Look. Cheap DVD."

He harkened to the call, more for something to do while he took in the massive indoor mall than for any desire to make a purchase. He had amassed over a hundred bootleg DVDs and video games throughout his four years in China. Having no access to online streaming television services from his homeland, he'd made use of the many bootleg shops scattered throughout the Chinese cities he had inhabited. A true, original import was easily twice the cost of the American equivalent which far exceeded his budget and oftentimes was simply nonexistent. With television viewing completely in Mandarin, he had swiftly turned to this form of piracy as a way to stave off homesickness and to relieve the tensions that work instilled. Living on a teacher's salary, he saw no way around this practice, and while he took no pride in piracy, he had used these one-dollar disks a fair bit.

"Good quality. Very good. For you, only three dollar."

Remy chuckled, "Oh, come now. That's far too much and you know it. I'm not some tourist. The price is one dollar. That's the normal price."

"Two dollar."

"The price is one dollar a disk. Everyone knows that. It's the only consistent price for a good in this entire nation."

"For you, good price. Three disks, five dollar."

"I feel you're not really listening to me," Remy continued, becoming absorbed into negotiations. "The going rate is one dollar.

A flood of muttering of unpleasant Mandarin, and then, "Okay. One dollar." More disgruntled Mandarin followed.

"Yeah, but I don't really want to buy any of these. Do you know where cellphones are sold?"

"Aye-yah!"

With no directions forthcoming, Remy left the exasperated lady and entered into the mall. Two floors above, he stepped off the swiftly moving escalator and found himself in a realm of mobile phones. The entire third floor was designated to these devices: phones ranging from new to various degrees of used, iPhones and Androids, accessories, batteries, screens, motherboards. One shop seemed to sell various parts gouged from a wide array of mobile phones, undoubtedly very used, some components bordering on obsolete. An adjacent shop also sold mobile parts, only each of these were new and shining, top-end stuff: new screens of various dimensions, tiny chips and batteries meant to be soldered onto motherboards, and the like. It was the first time that Remy began to suspect that his software alone wasn't the issue. With the proof of break-ins illustrated in powdery footprints on the threshold of his front door coupled with a worried hound's frantic sniffing about the apartment yet nothing missing, he'd been asking himself a very simple question for a month: *Why break in?* It was only then that a potential answer had emerged. *Perhaps, to alter or substitute the hardware of my electronics.*

"It's sort of like James Bond meets the Jawas from *Star Wars*," he joked to himself.

He walked through the vastness of it all, wall to wall to wall to wall, north to south, east to west. Many small shops were partitioned only by thin sheets of cheap cloth or plastic that hung like shower curtains separating one store from the other. Some shops utilized folding signs near the entryway to advertise their wares, others banners, and many shops operated without any sort of marker indicating a business. Having perused every shop on the floor, he made his way to the fifth floor and snacked on fried octopus tentacles, drank cold tea, recuperated a bit, and returned to the third floor, to the realm of all things mobile phones had to offer. He found a SIM card dealer and negotiated a lower price for one month of service reasoning that a change of SIM and service might throw cyber hounds off of his scent and allow him to move more freely about the city. Perhaps even access the internet again, tainted or otherwise.

"Okay. Where your passport?"

"What? Why do you need to see that?"

"I need passport. I need see visa. Show you work here."

"Well, I was hoping to forego all that, my man. You see, it would sort of defeat the purpose of all of this. My name precedes me in all the wrong ways."

"I can no turn on SIM card without visa."

"Well, if you associate my name to this new SIM card than I'm sure I'll just run into the same trouble that I came here to escape. I'm trying to lose my pursuers. Give 'em the ol' slip. Know what I mean?"

"I no know what you mean."

"Yeah, yeah, I know." Remy stepped back, unsure of how to proceed. The man behind the counter kept his attention on this strange foreigner, not wanting to lose a sale, but unsure how to proceed.

"Look, I hate to even ask this, but could I pay you more money? What if I paid for the SIM and service and then added this on top?" he asked, fanning out Chinese bills equaling twenty dollars.

"Why you give me this?"

Remy didn't answer, hoping that the silence would explain it all. Embarrassed that it didn't, he continued, "Look, I'm bribing you. I'm trying to bribe you. I'm in a real bind. People enter my home. People threaten me with violence, many people, like a surprising amount of people. And sleep, they've taken away sleep. You can't know what that's like. You shouldn't know. No one should. It's awful. It's a terrible thing to do to someone. I slept last week on a rooftop but now I'm right back on fumes again. Sleep fumes. My body relaxes each night -- well, more or less -- but never my mind. Never that. I suffer from massive cramps daily, though the muscles still bend and pull and contract enough to get me around. I'm barely surviving this. I must escape." He stopped, realizing that this merchant understood only bits and pieces, his English vocabulary likely limited to business transactions. He exhaled everything in his lungs, closed his eyes, inhaled deeply, opened his eyes, and put on a fake smile that inadvertently caused the merchant to take a step back. This had the ironic effect of bringing about a true, warm smile across Remy's face. *Oh, how I must appear these days,* he thought.

"I give you this money. You don't register my name. Just activate the SIM without my name. What do you say?"

"Impossible."

"First of all, nice English. I wasn't expecting that. Secondly, damn. Damn!" he slammed his fist into his open palm and stepped back, cursing. He squatted low on his heels and moaned miserably. The merchant, no longer interested in the sale, was far more concerned with ensuring that his merchandise wouldn't be damaged by the angry foreigner. Remy's ire faded upon noticing the shopkeeper's concern.

"I'm sorry. Truly. I don't mean to worry you. You're not the one keeping me awake every night. You didn't basically empty my bank account six months ago. You didn't forge a path into my heart and then rip it out of my chest. It's not your fault," he said with a sad smile.

They spoke a bit more and Remy told him that he may return later with his passport, though inwardly doubting such an event would bring about the change he needed. He turned about and began exiting the vicinity, descending an escalator, staring out at nothing as he contemplated the possibility of establishing a phone number that connected service to a newly purchased SIM without connecting it with his name via a merchant, and therefore with the government. *The government must be a part of my treatment. Or at least be aware of it. I must find a way out of this net.*

Yet another escape plan in the works. His peripheral was all but shot, deep in thought as he was and lacking sleep. He almost missed him. The same foreigner at the subway station the evening Monica had left his apartment, rising up the adjacent escalator. The same one that had followed him home. That guy. He was rising up to the third floor, to the floor Remy had just descended from. They both took each other in through peripheral alone, subtly intent on nothing else other than each other.

Arriving at the second floor, he began jogging to the nearest emergency exit stairwell, through the doorway and down stairs leading to a loading area that opened out onto a secluded alleyway connecting two main streets. He continued jogging toward the farther street, putting the face of a building down the road between himself and the would-be pursuer, failing to flag down a passing taxi in the process. A vacant taxi sitting curbside sped away as he lifted the back-door handle. Two other taxis nearby zoomed away without passengers before he was close enough to hop in. He took out his phone, cursing loudly at no one in particular. His arm tensed, ready to toss it down and dash it into pieces but thought of the data it potentially stored -- possible proof of hijacked privacy, perhaps the only proof procured. Grumbling to himself, he jogged on until he found another indoor electronic market, this one more rundown and smaller, and ducked inside.

He walked briskly towards the back of the building, catching his breath. The stores he passed targeted medium-sized businesses, not individuals. Much of the merchandise on display were samples, the idea being to order in sets of tens or hundreds which would be delivered to a business later. Acclimating to the environment and no longer winded, he took on the personification of a semi-wealthy foreign business owner perusing goods as he made his way to the second floor and positioned himself within eyesight of the escalators and doors, commanding a clear view down to the first floor. He kept his eyes open and shopped without shopping for some twenty minutes, until something striking caught his eye.

He negotiated a quick discount before making the purchase, mind whirling with yet another plan of escape in the midst of losing his current tail. He trotted down a nearby stairwell and stopped at the foot of the stairs. There he removed the backing from his phone, the battery, and then the SIM card, depositing the tiny golden chip into his front shirt pocket. Task completed, he crouched low and tucked himself behind the stairwell.

His legs were beginning to cramp and he was doubting the wisdom of lingering when he heard a solitary person descending the staircase. Soon, a familiar form came into view. If it had been the same foreigner that had followed Remy home after Monica left, the one he had just fled from, that would've been unsettling on its own. To see Monica trot down those stairs would've been a surprise, sure, but fathomable. Instead, an older man Remy had played poker with back in Nanchang came down the stairwell. A city one thousand miles away where his bank account had been emptied. Home to the bizarre incident at the police station. That city.

He recognized the man clearly, a man he had dealt cards to, a man he had bluffed, a man he had lost and won money from over cards. He was going on sixty-years old, perhaps older, light grey hair, thinning to the point of baldness atop his crown, nobody's fool, a man with a gruff disposition, not a close friend, a casual acquaintance, but a clearly recognizable man nonetheless. Richard. A man who had no conceivable reason whatsoever to be standing where he was.

Remy emerged from underneath the stairwell, stunned. Richard turned to face him and muttered one simple word.

"F*%^."

Perhaps he suspected Remy of attacking him, and indeed, such a thought was not so out of place there and then. Instead he walked around the man, giving him a wide birth and taking care not to turn his back to the anomaly, even more at a loss for words than Richard. At the exit he jogged away, crossing several streets in an effort to lose a proven tail or two. He found a taxi and hopped right in without a problem as most people do who seek taxis.

He gave the address of his apartment back in Tianhe, ensured that the fare machine began at zero out of habit, kicked back and enjoyed the ride. A couple of minutes later, having assured himself that the taxi was actually headed in the correct direction, Remy reinserted the SIM and battery into his phone. Immediately, the phone signaled a call coming through.

"Well, hello, Monica."

"Where you going?"

"Nowhere. I can't go anywhere. I can't leave. Oh wait, actually, I'm going home. Get it?" he laughed mirthlessly. "Home!" He had little idea what the following conversation entailed, his mind racing, feeling very much hunted and trapped, in need of procuring escape more than ever. The first numbing tendrils of fear had begun to take root, a feeling that would rise in caliber as the sleepless nights continued.

He was near maniacal the entire day. Psychologically overwhelmed. He returned to his flat and walked William, who was less animated than normal. Such a barrage was obviously taking its toll on the hound, too. When night came, Remy journeyed to the rooftop, leaving the mobile phone behind and did something he was simultaneously proud and ashamed of. Removing his purchase -- a green, military-grade laser pointer, capable of shining outward for many, many miles -- he aimed high and flashed it in three sets of three: three short, three long, three short. SOS. He did that intermittently for the better part of an hour, aiming in the direction of an occasional plane overhead if one happened to fly near enough to be noticed. Exhausted and overwhelmed with what had become his normal everyday life, he took his que when a security guard opened the rooftop door, returned to the flat, plopped down on his bed, and was immediately accosted by wicked sounds played at torturous volumes and intervals that denied him the ability to fall asleep all throughout the night and into the next day.

CHAPTER XXXI

USA

Another dull day. He had taken a late nap after a mind-draining conversation with his roommate over proper thermostat etiquette in the two-bedroom apartment they shared. Chuck took it upon himself to change the temperature of the AC unit fairly regularly. Hot during the day and cold at night, the idea being to save a few dollars by living in misery. Remy had tried but could reach no compromise with the man.

Chuck was the sort of fellow who always knew better. If you liked to eat sandwiches, Chuck would tell you why pasta was better. If you wore a necktie, Chuck would sing praises of bowties. No matter what beer brand you drank, Chuck would be swift to inform you of a better one that you weren't imbibing. Every six weeks or so, Chuck was fired from whatever job he had gotten himself into. A man who had not once made his bed in six months and still slept on an inflatable mattress. Not exactly a go-getter.

The fact that he was reduced to sharing a life with this fellow was proof of just how far he had fallen. Chuck was a desperate, lonely man reaching out the only way he knew and Remy wanted to find compassion in his heart for him. He just couldn't.

Not that Remy's depression was all Chuck's fault. A huge disconnect existed between himself and America, a divide that only grew wider the longer he remained within her borders. He found the culture manipulative, condescending, crass and deceptive, her people waiting for chances to speak in conversation rather than listen. Rainy weather reminded him of bygone times, the sound of waterdrops preventing sleep, memories that refused to be shook loose.

As did the rainchecks and postponements of the recently elusive Liz. He had for the first time since Monica felt that romance was not completely out of the question but over the past month, such thoughts and feelings had come crashing down around him. Liz operated on his wavelength but she danced about, coyly feinting and dodging his advances while flirting a bit to keep the attention coming. He was growing tired of the pursuit, rare though a meaningful connection was and rarer still a romantic one. The inevitability of continued isolation was becoming apparent and in its wake came a deep, dark sorrow.

He left the apartment around ten p.m., the plan being to drive to Lake Eola in downtown Orlando and brood, to reflect on what had been, to make sense of it somehow, or perhaps to tip over the cusp into something more desolate. He had never felt more alone and out of place than in his homeland.

He blasted electronic music from assembly line speakers through open windows as he exited the interstate and onto downtown roads. The drive had raised his spirits and so he ducked into a basement bar, ordered a double shot of bourbon and danced. Early in his teenage years, he had snuck out and raved and danced, danced, danced, returning closer to dawn than midnight, creeping back into his bedroom window to prepare for a full day of high school.

A chubby gal in her early-twenties smiled and approached, swaying rhythmically. He returned the smile politely and shuffled elsewhere. On the other side of the club, a thinner gal in her thirties approached, sweaty and shiny-eyed from drug use -- probably ecstasy -- the characteristics of such all too prevalent in her mannerisms. She danced close and moved closer still but ultimately Remy fell back and another took his place. He had lost his taste for such things.

Still, in the midst of such immaturity, depravity some would say, his spirits had lifted. Sipping on a pint of beer later at a quieter pub, he reminisced. *How soft and squishy it is here.* He held out his hand and stared at the wrinkles and scars that had accumulated over the decades. *At one point I suffered the unimaginable. Now there is nothing. I own a reliable car and rent a two-bedroom apartment, certainly a step up from the homeless shelters and lightyears from the horrors of Guangzhou but it doesn't feel like much. Life has become bland. Flavorless.*

He moved from a table to the bar, ignoring a soccer game on the many televisions mounted on the walls. He found a bartender he was familiar with, a young twenty-something who seemed to legitimately appreciate his quips. She wasn't overweight -- a rarity in America -- and as such was well sought after by a variety of suitors.

"Do you ever feel appreciative -- grateful even -- but at the same time, completely the opposite, hungry for more, knowing you can do more and angry that you can't?"

"Yeah. That's not strange. Most people feel that way."

He left the pub in a better mood knowing he wasn't completely alone, social interactions and alcohol having lifted his spirits temporarily, pleasant distractions from the miasma of depression. He was a man who was burdened by loss, happiness welcomed but never sustained. There was no light at the end of the tunnel, no escape from what his life had become.

CHAPTER XXXII

CHINA

The days and nights continued bleeding into one other. Without work, there wasn't much to separate the two.

Remy's mind was collapsing. He sat staring at his laptop, at lines of code, at a dozen open windows, each a deeper aspect of the inner workings of his computer's operating system. He had forgotten why he'd opened the first box, of what in particular he had set out to understand, what the original plan had been. He moaned and rubbed his face, abandoning another attempt at connecting to the internet. He sat back and closed his eyes and was immediately inundated with unkind sound. He howled curses and returned to the fruitless endeavor.

He'd exhausted every taxi number. Each driver had done the same thing: driven far out to nowhere, feigned ignorance of where the airport was and turned about, returning Remy to his apartment and demanding payment of the full fare. He'd traveled alone, not wanting to subject William to such depravity, testing the waters for any sign of a respectful taxi company that would do the right thing and finding none. During the most recent encounter, he had sat in the passenger seat with the driver, flashing translated Chinese along the way, both written and spoken, leaving no room for misunderstanding. That night, the driver had crept his right hand into the lining of Remy's backpack which lay on the floorboards during a wait at a red light. He caught the movement, smacking the driver's hand in the manner teachers once employed to misbehaving students. Afterward, he had found it difficult to discontinue assaulting the man, and as such, promptly exited the vehicle. The driver immediately circled about and demanded payment. With a hungry and unhealthy gleam in his eye, Remy marched up to the cab driver who promptly sped away. He had no clue where he was. Multi-storied buildings surrounded him on all sides, none of which looked familiar. He chose a direction that seemed more urbanized and set to the task of trying find his home. He walked for hours, stopping people along the sidewalks to ask for directions. Few seemed to know the name of his apartment building or of the street or even the district where he lived, well known though it was, and those that did grinned wryly and pointed in a direction that often conflicted with another's.

There were some who recognized him, some whose eyes lit up, a condescending smile emerging as they became aware of his presence. Hours into the long walk, he had accrued a handful of followers who seemed content to trail him distantly and enjoy the spectacle. *My tale must have spread far and wide throughout this city. They know I want to leave and they won't allow it and they derive pleasure from it all.* The word was out. There was no doubt about that. Remy had become the laughing stock of a fair amount of the city's inhabitants, a mascot of foolishness.

Fierce anger was giving way to real fear as he followed directions and walked down sidewalks filled with pedestrians that at times glanced knowingly as he passed. Yet again, he approached a stranger for guidance and was pointed back the way he had come. When that new heading began feeling incorrect, he approached another stranger and was given drastically different instruction of where to go. Misdirection repeated for about an hour as Remy began to realize just how outnumbered he was. Sensing he had been recognized yet again, he put on a wide, no-nothing smile and approached a twenty-something couple waiting to cross the road to ask for directions. The man stepped forward, keeping his date behind him, a young lady whose pleasant features were melting into discomfort. *To see my suffering isn't as funny as the story of it all,* he realized as he doled out basic Mandarin requesting help. He pointed Remy off in a direction, smiling wickedly in the process while his date studied her shoes. After insincerely thanking the man, he began walking in exactly the opposite direction. Within seconds, the man jogged back to Remy. "No, no," he stammered in English. "That way," pointing vigorously in the opposite direction, the direction he sought to lead him down. He ignored the man and simply continued along the opposite way.

The man and his date joined the small cluster of followers that trailed far behind, exposed only in rare moments when Remy doubled back unexpectedly. He had done this a few times in the beginning to test if he was indeed pulling a crowd and again to test their response to his approach. *Is there a phone app of sorts to track my movements throughout this city?* he wondered dully from a far away place.

He plodded onward in the opposite direction for more than one hour but not quite two, doggedly trusting his assumption about the last guide's true intentions and was eventually rewarded with familiar buildings signifying that he'd returned to his own neighborhood. The night had grown quite late, the streets mostly emptied of pedestrians and vehicles. His fan club had dissipated behind him the further he marched into his own neighborhood, strengthening the notion that he was traveling along the correct course. By the time the towering apartment complex came into view, he was alone once again. His legs ached and his back was sore from hauling his back-pack for hours as he zigzagged throughout the city. His emergency backpack stayed with him at all times in those days -- while bathing, sleeping, toileting, cooking, walking William, always -- out of concern for theft or tampering of his passport. He collapsed into his bed sweaty and stinking, utterly spent but of course denied sleep.

A sleepless night came and went. The next morning, he threw a tennis ball into the distance, encouraging William to exercise and play. The hound slowly trotted over to the tennis ball, bit down on it and returned to Remy. He stood by Remy's legs, eyes downcast, head and tail drooped. Passionless. "I'm sorry, William. I'm so sorry." In the courtyard, along the backwall of an unused utility building, he sank to his knees overcome with despair and cried. William, having no encouragement to offer, released the ball and walked away.

CHAPTER XXXIII

CHINA

It wasn't sleep but he occasionally found fleeting peace on the rooftop for a few minutes prior to a security guard breaching the serenity and ushering Remy back to the sleep deprivation he called home. A fairly standard routine had developed. Inundated with foul noises as he tossed and turned and failed to sleep each night, he would rise and quietly slip away, out of the front door, and onto the rooftop. It was blessedly silent, cool, and open. Free. Then just as he would begin dozing, the rooftop door would swing open and an apartment security guard would march out, ruining everything.

Before the inevitable disruption, he tended to stretch and practice his katas, maneuvering reasonably deftly in simulated disengaging, blocking, and take-down techniques. He was most certain he would be needing to rely on such things soon and kept himself sharp in the interim. He thought back to his high school and college days, of practicing swordplay and hand-to-hand combat in backyards with peers that shared similar interests. Hours each day, most days each week for a couple of years. Maybe one thousand hours of drills, sparring, and thrown weapon practice. Hundreds of matches, armed and unarmed. He moved about the rooftop in good form despite his condition.

On this particular night, he perched along the roof's edge as might a gargoyle, toying with the sensation of falling, testing his balance. He tumbled backward and sprawled out comfortably on the cement and gravel that made up the flooring of the barren rooftop. From his pocket he procured the military-caliber green laser pen he'd purchased during the tailing incident a week ago and shone it into the night sky, flashing three short, three long, three short bursts. He heard a plane crossing above and flashed the same signal in that general direction, a green flashing line cutting through the darkness, the action more or less a habit. Throughout the week, he had noticed a trend in that the occasional aircrafts seemed to be roaring by at lower altitudes, the outline of the plane becoming clearly visible even at night, no longer just blinking lights on wings in a far-away part of the night sky. *Progress,* he thought warmly, *a delicate and rare thing in need of nurturing.*

No work. No sleep. No cyber progress. No clear way to get to the airport. Phone calls from Monica limping in from time to time, little more than heckling on her part. Hopelessness and anxiety dully blurred as the sixth week of sleep deprivation continued.

He was sipping coffee in the late morning on a day of the week impossible to tell, working on restoring his internet connection when a soft *click* reverberated throughout the living room. So soft in fact, that neither Remy nor William recognized the intrusion. A moment later it returned. *Click.* Remy paused and closed his eyes, waiting for its return. Time passed, and then, a *clack* sounded from the kitchen window. He paused his futile attempt at connecting to the internet and focused solely on the window. The noise had undoubtedly come from something small bouncing off the pane. Like a pebble, though that made little sense on the seventeenth floor. Angered, he stormed over and slid open the window.

"I'm right here, you insignificant f*^#s. I'm here. Just knock on my door, and I'll open it." In response, there was but one word, "Jump!"

Looking straight down fifty meters, he spied a familiar trio of people grouped and lurking. They seemed to be looking right back up at him though it was hard for him to tell given the distance to the ground, just tiny blobs far, far, below. "Jump," the distant group repeated. "Jump!"

He had no idea how a pebble could have clattered off of his kitchen window several times. In hindsight, he would come to think that perhaps it had swung down from the definitively troublesome flat above his own. A simple, string tied around a pebble-sized object and swung at an arc downward would have done the trick. At that time though, he had no idea how any of that could have been possible. More importantly, he had no idea who the people were that triggered his approach and then beckoned him to jump to his death. What he did know was that he was ready to meet those individuals head-on. Hungry for it, in fact. All three of them at once. He leapt out of the front door, habitually twisting the deadbolt home as he spun about and bounded down the hallway to the elevator. A minute later he was on the ground level and clearing the lobby door, jogging off toward where he had last spied the trio.

He rushed to the scene as a cat does to an area it thinks it spotted a mouse with much the same attitude: murderous curiosity. But as he jogged alongside the perimeter of the building, he spotted nothing out of the ordinary. He scoured the area where he'd spotted the trio from his window in great detail and found nothing. No discernable footprints. No recent cigarette butts. Not even litter in the area to analyze.

Content that they had fled from him, he crossed the street and ordered a couple of duck and rice lunch meals from the only ma-and-pa restaurant he could rely on in those troubled times. While the other food stalls had all turned away from him in time, treating Remy with ever-increasing disrespect each time he ordered food and increasing meal costs, the duck restaurant -- luckily his favorite -- had remained true. Their prices had not risen. Their portions remained constant. Customer service just as it had always been, nothing magnificent, but fair and in its fairness special. He brought the food home to William and they ate with the stoic acceptance of their situation. Nine hours later, the sun fell and Remy returned to the roof to flash mile-long laser beams in the general vicinity of descending aircrafts, unsure how or if such a course of action could help. He descended the familiar stairwell, returned to his torture chamber and settled in for the night, a night like the one before and the one before that, a night of being accosted by insidious sounds aimed at him from above until the dawn broke and a day of much the same began anew.

CHAPTER XXXIV

CHINA

Almost daily Remy shouldered his emergency backpack -- a bag kept within arm's grasp at all times -- and ventured into the city searching for a way to the international airport. Taxis failed him time and time again. Each and every company in Guangzhou. He had tried the subway system again, and again the train stopped short prior to reaching the airport. He had exited the subway station, ascending stairs that brought him so close to the airport that he could see and hear planes descend, feel the tremble in the air. He marched up and down foreign city blocks but was unable to find roads that led to its source. Guangzhou trains simply would not complete their journey to the airport if Remy was aboard.

I'm marked, he thought, analyzing the situation during another sleepless night. *The only proof of wrongdoing lies in this phone and in this computer system both of which keep me pinned down, easily located. Even with the battery and SIM removed, somehow my movements are monitored.*

He was drawing progressively larger crowds with each failed outing to the airport. Each long walk to nowhere entailed an audience of sorts. Where once they had been content to give misleading directions and follow from a distance, they'd soon graduated to following just a step or two behind, almost shoulder-to-shoulder, at times ridiculing Remy openly along the way. They had become brazen and only by Remy physically checking some of them by walking up and inserting himself into their ranks, nose-to-nose in some cases, would they back away enough to allow him a bit of space to think clearly about which way was north, and once north, where the airport might be located.

Such were the long walks in those terrible days and nights. The majority of the city he interacted with recognized him on sight by mid-December, some following him about to enjoy the spectacle of the foreigner who wanted to leave but couldn't, but most simply turning away from the scene compassionately. A thirty-something pair of men, well-dressed, clean-cut, suddenly appeared from around a corner during such an excursion, approaching rapidly while a sizeable crowd followed nearby. "Come with me," one said, speaking in fairly clear English, beckoning Remy toward him. The two men quickly crossed the street and Remy, desperate for guidance and allies, quickly followed. The two men jogged in earnest with Remy in tow and soon the crowd was left behind.

The jogging was not so easy on Remy. Always in those days he had that backpack resting heavily on his shoulders and in short time he was quite winded. Sensing this, the two clean-cut newcomers shared a smile and made a turn at the corner. Remy followed, panting. Two more blocks they ran as Remy called out questions as to where they were going, who they were, what the plan was. No response. He slowed to a quick walk as hope began leaking away. He took a deep breath, arms at the ready, and came around a corner to find the two men and the crowd that had initially been left behind altogether laughing heartily at a winded Remy.

Most of the time the jeering mob followed from a respectable distance. Remy would pass street merchants from time to time selling their wares along the sidewalks throughout the labyrinthine city during the long walks. He'd purchased physical maps of the city, which, much like the conflicting reports his computer had been showing him, showed distinct differences when compared to maps purchased in other parts of the city, the airport either entirely absent or displayed in differing locations. He'd purchased bootleg Windows installation disks so as to make his tattered operating system usable once more, though these Windows bootleg discs automatically installed unnecessary files with suspicious certificates from dates that made no sense and were impossible to override or delete. They did allow him access to a tattered and highly-altered internet once again but reinforced the same problems he was trying to free himself from.

The weapons the street merchants sold were a temptation. He had browsed an assortment of folding knives, pepper spray canisters, cane swords, traditional swords, tasers, and even more exotic fare such as *sais*, *shurikens*, and hatchets over the course of many failed excursions. He took his time working out the balance, testing the tipping point longingly as he flipped promising instruments over in his hand. They were all poorly crafted -- mass produced, weak alloy rubbish -- but most did have a sharp enough edge and that did bring a small smile to his very tired face. The mob would evaporate into thin air during those moments, leaving only non-adversarial Chinese milling about the vicinity. Two or three blocks afterward, the flash mob would return, forcing him to quicken his pace in order to maintain a comfortable distance.

With these fresh memories swirling about an exhausted and tormented mind, Remy found himself once again hiking along hostile streets. He shook his head back and forth as a dog might when dislodging water, dislodging miserable sentiment instead. With a clearer mind, his thoughts turned to how best implement the new addition he'd brought with him as he marched down another long stretch of sidewalk. He continued heading toward what he thought was north based on sunrises and sunsets and what he hoped was the north star, fairly certain of the direction, the problem being that the northern part of the city seemed to be off limits to pedestrians once he traveled ten kilometers or so northward. He had reached a similar point, this time turning left, heading west on aching, cramping legs as he searched for a way to turn right and head north again.

Perseverance paid off. Sometime later, he spied familiar Chinese symbols on a road sign marking an upcoming airport along a nearby interstate. After weeks of long walks with cruel crowds, he'd found definitive proof of the general vicinity of the airport. It was a hard-fought gain, albeit one that left him quite far from his goal.

No sidewalk veered upward alongside the onramp leading to the interstate and Chinese characters warned that pedestrians were forbidden entry. Putting the interstate and the airport that followed on the backburner, he crossed the street at an opportune time so as to forge some distance between himself and his entourage and headed toward a line of mid-sized apartment buildings. He slowed his pace, searching the scene. Up ahead, a pudgy woman threw open glass doors and exited. He jogged up, grabbing the handle before it closed and let himself inside. The door clicked shut behind him with a sound Remy hoped meant that the outside world had been locked out. Not knowing this for certain and already seeing familiar faces in the throng crossing the street toward him, he turned from the glass door, gave a knowing nod and quick smile to the lobby security guard before hurrying up the stairwell.

Up the stairs he raced: passed the second, third, and fourth floors, to the fifth where he ducked through a doorway that opened into a very modest hallway covered in faded and frayed carpeting. Dark stains of unidentifiable origins dotted beige colored walls and floor. He spied an exit sign on the opposite end of the hall, dashed over and raced up a different flight of stairs to the sixth and seventh floor. There the stairs ended and Remy made his move.

Following an old ploy that seemed to have granted him a temporary reprieve from tracking, he removed the SIM from his phone along with the battery. He hastily tossed the mildly disassembled parts into a plastic bag and removed fully-charged hair clippers from his emergency backpack. In the stairwell, he stripped off his hoodie and sheared all of the hair from his head. From far below, the faint sound of pursuit rose up the stairwell. He stripped down to underwear and socks in a very open environment, quickly changed into slacks and a suit jacket, and shoved the original outfit into his backpack. He looked down at the hair clippers lying in a pile of hair. *This only works once,* he smiled. *Besides, no more hair left to cut.* He kicked the recently cut hair and clippers to the edge of the wall then repositioned his backpack to carry it in a duffle bag sort of way. Trotting downstairs, he began practicing an unconcerned pleasant smile while listening intently to the sounds below, ascertaining that his pursuers were moving up the same stairwell he was on. On the sixth floor he ducked out of the stairwell and onto a dingy hallway that looked remarkably like the fifth floor where he dashed back to the original stairwell that he had first ascended from. He approached the ground floor swiftly and on quiet feet, taking note to not let his shadow pass where it should not. Listening. Watching. Smelling. Feeling. The senses coming together as one as adrenaline flooded his system. He leapt down the steps three at a time, all six flights, but slowed at the end to take a deep breath as a diver does before plunging into deep water. Centered, he rounded the doorframe armed with a Hollywood smile. The security guard was surprised to see him. No recognition played about on his face. *So far, so good.*

As he opened the lobby door and exited the building, a young Chinese couple in their twenties entered. Remy couldn't determine their intent, but began the process of illusion anyway. *"Bonsoir,"* he said as he passed the couple, doubling back to look meaningfully and obviously at the stairwell adjacent to the elevator doors. "Idiot," he stated in the best French accent he could muster, half-gesturing with a nod of his head, as if someone quite troubling was back there. The couple gave each other a knowing grin and took the bait, quickening their steps and heading toward the stairwell. Satisfied with the guise, he turned from the retreating couple and swung the exit door open wide. All business, cool and calm. A businessman late for a meeting. He immediately flicked his jacket sleeve back to check the time on a fine wristwatch that did not exist. "*Merde*," he cursed. He spoke sharply to himself in a hodgepodge of French and English. The overall effect allowed him to pass through and away from his pursuers. One block away and the air smelled sweeter, the pressure lighter, population density much thinner. Escape. He turned, crossed the street, and entered a taxi.

Success and freedom washed over him as he climbed into the backseat of an aging cab where he kept the driver's focus on his shaved head and fine suit. The driver, unlike what Remy had grown accustomed to, appeared to speak a little English and asked where he needed to go. Remy answered in a French/Mandarin/English medley, "North, along the interstate." Adding, "I am late for a meeting." The driver eyed him dubiously in the rearview mirror and made no move to comply.

Remy shrugged, "Fine. *Mercy beaucoup, monsieur.*" In a brave bluff, he opened the car door and took a step outside, already feeling the unsettling presence of the mob resituating itself.

"No, no. Sit. Sit. We go." And away they went.

He found it difficult to not grin as the taxi entered the same on-ramp he had spied earlier and merged into the flow of high-speed traffic along the interstate. Airport bound.

Ten minutes later, the driver queried, "Where you go?"

"North. You're going the right way. Keep going north," he replied, scanning the passing signs for indicators of the upcoming airport. He searched the dark horizon hungrily for landing lights, for an opening in the city sprawl of a suitable size to host landing strips. He cracked the backseat window open in the hopes of hearing a landing plane.

"You going airport?" the driver asked. There was something in the tone of voice that gave Remy pause, something accusatory.

"No, no, no, my good man." Accidentally delving into an English accent but recovering swiftly back into French. "Passed the airport."

This satisfied the driver and they drove on. Ten minutes after that, the unbelievable occurred. There it was in all its glory. It started off as a flicker of lights that flashed in the spaces between homes in the distance. A long set of parallel lights. As the taxi barreled onward, a stretch of wooded area to the side of the interstate opened up and for a moment, the strip and the terminal appeared in the distant, dark horizon. Overwhelmed, Remy had forgotten to keep his smile checked, and so the driver asked again, only it wasn't really a question that third time:

"You going to airport," he stated angrily.

"Get that through your thick skull, driver. That's exactly what I will do. I will get to that airport. I know where it is now." Remy shrugged away the driver's contempt. "Unless, of course, you want to save some time and drop me off there now." The driver said nothing. Within minutes the airport was fading away behind them.

"I say," Remy continued, "To the airport, driver."

He repeated the request in passable Mandarin. The driver glanced back in the rearview mirror and turned off of the interstate. Soon, they were on backroads -- racing down them really -- driving much too quickly through deserted streets. Within fifteen minutes, he had raced down many a road, turning randomly, U-turning and immediately turning left or right, only to U-turn again. Remy was rapidly becoming disoriented, as was the driver's intent. Knowing this, he closed his eyes, rolled down the window, and smelled deeply of the world around him, of the oils and metallic scents in the air, of old, wet earth. He ignored the racing and turning and thought back to the interstate, to first entering the taxi, of the way the taxi had progressed down the interstate until the airport flashed through, stopping, rewinding, replaying while the driver raced angrily through deserted streets. Remy took a last, long whiff of freedom, smiling, as he cranked up the window back to a closed position.

He shifted in his seat, leaning forward until he could make eye contact with the driver in the rearview mirror. He stared until the driver was forced to stare back 'less he lose face -- a Chinese term for being disrespected -- fury in his eyes, a child's mirth in Remy's own.

"I fooled you, you vile little man. I duped you good and plenty." Remy kicked back and laughed. "*Parlez-vous francias?*" Remy laughed again heartily. "Because I don't."

"Where are we going?" Remy continued. The driver said nothing. "Oh, come on. You spoke English twenty minutes ago. Cat got your tongue?" The driver continued racing no one, turning nonsensically. "Fine, driver. Fine."

Remy looked over at the backseat door. Locked. He pulled up on the knob along the backseat door to disengage the lock. The knob immediately shot back down, locking.

"Oooh, aren't we displeased. Last chance. Airport."

Repeating the command in Mandarin though it elicited no response. The driver continued along the erratic path, silent as stone. Remy cranked the backseat window open and reached his arm out of the backseat until his hand found the exterior handle. With his other hand, he pried up the locking knob, forcing the automatic lock up at the same instant that he opened the backseat door from the outside. The overhead light shot on and the driver began to curse loudly in Mandarin. The lock shot back down ineffectively on a door that remained cracked open.

"Yeah, yeah. Your dead mother. All that stuff. Whatever."

Still the taxi raced on. The opportunity for escape came four or five minutes later, a long time when in such a situation. Remy waited patiently, keeping the door cracked open until the taxi was forced to slow at a congested intersection. He immediately leapt out of the moving vehicle, stumbled, found his feet and was on his way. He knew that he wasn't to be murdered outright or he would've been dead already and so he took his chances that the driver wouldn't turn around and run him down. The driver did spin the taxi back around and seemed to consider the notion, ultimately zooming off into the night instead leaving Remy absolutely clueless as to where he was in the predawn night.

He picked the direction most traffic seemed to be moving away from while he thought of what to do next. When the sun rose an hour later straight ahead, Remy realized he'd been traveling east, not south. Orienting himself to the rising sun, he turned right and headed south toward a torturous flat he called home.

CHAPTER XXXV

CHINA

Overall, the experience had heartened him. He'd seen the airport, knew roughly of its location, and although the hike to the interstate onramp where he entered the taxi had not been a linear one and he was uncertain as to the path he had hiked back home, he was closer to escaping than he'd ever been. He had discovered the location of the airport, a massive step toward actually leaving.

Exhausted though he was, he did not sleep when he returned for such a thing simply didn't happen in those days. He lied down and stretched tired limbs after inserting a random DVD and raising the volume to counteract the audio assault from above. He grimaced as his leg muscles contracted violently throughout the day. Severe cramps on the bottoms of his feet distorted his soles in excruciating arcs. Knotted calf muscles clenching into agony barely tolerated without screaming. He spent the day periodically writhing in pain with teeth clenched, gasping, and then panting with pleasure as the cramp subsided.

Famished, he limped to the duck restaurant in the early evening and placed an order. The owners smiled as he approached but the expression was strained. They didn't ask why he was more or less dragging his right leg behind him, his left leg barely any better. They didn't ask why his hair had been sheared to the barest of peach fuzz. They didn't ask why he still shouldered a backpack, the weight threatening to tip him over. They didn't broach the subject whatsoever. He found this to be the only pleasantly false thing in his life. He ordered food and pretended as the older couple and grandson of the propriety pretended, that everything was fine, and in that mindset, there was hope, false or not.

The cramping had subsided by the following night. Remy shouldered a familiar backpack filled with the essentials: toiletries, a change of clothes, important documents, a liter of water, his mobile phone and laptop separated from their batteries. This time, unlike the rest, he brought William with him. The hound leapt about, twirling, in celebration as Remy removed the leash from the wall and clipped it onto his collar. One hundred pounds of dog streamed out of the door with Remy pulled along in tow. He pulled back on the reins at the threshold and searched his pocket for a key to lock a front door proven susceptible to intrusion even while locked. William pulled on the leash, eager to get going.

"Probably right, old chum. Why lock it when they enter in anyway?" More out of a refusal to give up a good habit, he forced the hound to wait while he clicked the locking mechanism home. And then they were off. William was ecstatic, pulling so hard that if Remy had been donning roller skates, he wouldn't have needed to walk at all.

The physical aspect of walking long distances was much easier as William muscled forward, towing his human cargo. The problem was the mob. William was a loving, trusting beast, the mob a malignant force that he needed to be sheltered from. They would coax him into taking wrong turns, tempting him this way and that with "aaawwww's" and "oooohhhh's" and pettings. William didn't see through any of that and was very much enamored by the attention. Remy steered him northward away from distractions for hours. Squatting alongside a sidewalk to take a break, he waved away an approaching ne'er-do-well, exhausted and baring teeth as if to snap in a way that William simply never did.

"Look, you lovely, stupid beast, we must travel north."

William looked him in the eye then looked away, panting heavily. Remy slowly poured water in his cupped hand and Will lapped it up thirstily. Remy took a few swigs from the plastic bottle before returning it to the emergency backpack. Three young men approaching the duo altered their course upon making eye contact with Remy's glare, giving the man and hound a wide berth as they passed.

"Look, some of these guys are innocent and just want to say hi. But some of them very much mean us harm. They flatter you. They pet you. They coo loving things in your ear. Some of them are fine, I know, but I don't have the energy to sift through it all and sort out who is who. We must flee this place as soon as possible." Remy lovingly grasped the Shepherd's head in his hands, a head approximately his own size, and pulled their skulls together in a tender headbutt. "You must focus and follow my lead."

Later, exhausted and parched, they arrived at the northern outskirts of city where Remy tried and failed several times to hail a cab. They would slow down, recognize the man and dog, and then speed off again. Realizing his inability to hail a cab directly he instead crept up on an unsuspecting taxi and just leapt in, taking the driver by surprise as he awoke from a nap. He asked to be taken to the airport and away they went, until the driver received a phone call and turned off the interstate well before the airport exit. Remy and William exited the vehicle immediately after the driver began the detour hopeful that since they had crossed the northern barrier, they could walk the rest of the way to the airport, but hours of urban hiking proved that to be misguided. With dawn threatening to break, they began the long walk south, returning well after the sun shone brightly in the morning sky.

This procedure was repeated again and met with the same result. The only good coming from those failed attempts was an increase in William's ability to tune out the crowds. Remy gave public transportation a try with William and found that fruitless, as well. Subway station officers physically prevented them from entering open doors, which would have upset Remy more if he had any faith that the train would have actually taken them to the airport. Bus drivers around his neighborhood and even miles away, refused them entry, physically inserting themselves in their path when they tried to board or simply refusing to drive the bus once they entered and took a seat.

"Go," the driver commanded, an older man, pointing firmly toward the bus doors that Remy and William had just entered in from, doors Remy had pried open with his elbow and forearm while the driver failed to seal them shut in time. He thought of tossing the driver from the bus and driving himself and the passengers north to the interstate and beyond to an airport he could recall in perfect clarity but couldn't actually get to, but he doubted he would arrive before being intercepted by authorities.

Certainly wouldn't be able to board a plane like that though. Not without hostages. Hmmm, hostages, he began to ponder before shaking his head vigorously side to side to dislodge such evil thoughts. *I cannot let this change me.*

Muscles knotted, body bruised, mind tattered by hopelessness and a need to sleep, they exited the bus and began yet another walk back home.

<u>CHINA</u>

Remy nudged his way past the subway officer, navigating a leashed William to the back of the train. He sat down heavily on a subway bench and William curled up at his feet. The train sat motionless on the tracks, the doors open wide. On the other side of the window, Remy watched the first officer engaged in conversation with another. Spying a third transit officer coming down the steps, he abandoned his latest futile effort to escape the city of Guangzhou. He walked toward the opposite end of the tracks, found an exit up and out, and was gone.

Another failed attempt. He seethed with the impossibility of it all, fear of an unwinnable situation shifting into a cold fury that he mostly kept quelled, a resource to be tapped into if need be. Almost a full week had passed since he'd finally broken through and located the airport from the passing taxicab. He'd traversed several different paths since then, each more fruitless than the last. William was not allowed on busses or trains and taxis were no longer an option with or without the German Shepherd. They would slow down, recognize, and drive away.

Several evenings were spent recuperating from the long walks to nowhere, nights full of wincing through crippling muscle spasms of the lower body and more failed attempts of asserting dominance over his phone and computer software. He was delving into the nuts and bolts of his computer during such a recovery period, the physical components -- albeit shallowly out of fear of ruining the only proof of what he was enduring -- when a fresh idea came to him. A new hope.

He limped down the apartment hallway, down an elevator, and into the open air of the metropolis. He turned down a few streets along his neighborhood trying to not focus on the inhabitants' attention to him before arriving at an electronic store that sold cellphones and accessories. *Bingo*, he thought. Stepping gingerly on agonizing leg muscles, he entered the store.

"I am plagued in so many ways -- hardware, spyware, threats and that damned speaker system -- so I'm sure a single change won't solve all of my problems, but hey, if I can fix something, why not? A private phone with a clean connection to the internet would be really nice these days. Maybe the problem is in the phone battery. Physical spyware would need to be powered somehow so attaching such a device directly to the battery makes sense. I've definitely found limited success escaping my torturers after removing the thing. It's as good a place as any to begin."

"I no understand," she said.

"Not sure how anyone would understand that. It sounds insane," he replied, removing his phone to input English phrases into Google Translate, translations far more accurate than the mapping system. She gestured for the phone to read the contents more clearly and then proceeded to take it with her into the privacy of the back of the store against Remy's delayed protests. *Perhaps she just erased any record of wrongdoing. Perhaps she's made matters worse and just installed some new protocol that will amplify the preventive sleep noises. Though, truth be told, that couldn't be any worse than it already is. It's perfectly evil as is.*

She returned and they sifted through more talk about the purchase before eventually arriving at a price for a compatible phone battery: 300 yuan, $43. Not a great price but the alternative would have been to keep searching for another store. His tale had spread so far and wide that the odds of finding a retailer that would treat him properly was quite remote. He could have walked another five miles on his battered legs and still found the same or worse pricing on a single mobile phone battery.

"I'll take it, you impudent wretch," Remy agreed smiling sarcastically. "Wow! What a deal."

She exited into the backroom and returned several minutes later with a small, white cardboard box that contained a fresh, new battery. She motioned for Remy to hand her the phone but he had had enough of that.

"Never mind. Here's the money, harpy." Remy propped up three, one-hundred RMB bills on the glass counter. "I'll insert it later."

She took the money. And then she procured a calculator from behind the counter. She clacked away and spun the device around, showing a totaled sum of 480 yuan, $68. Remy's blood turned cold in his veins as fury began to bubble forth.

"Three hundred was an awful price but we agreed on that sum. We had an agreement."

She smiled and pointed to the increased amount, very pleased with her cunning. Remy's upper lip involuntarily snarled back into a growl and his right arm moved without his consent toward the calculator. Overriding instinct, he forced his right arm back and spoke through gritted teeth.

"Look. I'm sure you feel pretty good about your decision to cheat me right now, but it would be best if you just give me that battery, keep my money, and let me go about my night."

Her smile waned and she became mouthier, letting off a stream of unkind Mandarin and pointing more and more to the calculated sum of 480.

"Ma'am, and I use the term loosely here. Ma'am, I implore you not to do this. You already have the three hundred yuan. I'm going to take this," Remy's hand shot out and snatched the battery and box from atop the glass counter that separated them. "And then I'm going to go home."

She cursed in Mandarin. A lot. He felt ashamed and guilty after snatching the battery, though she did still have the 300 yuan they had agreed on. He remained in the shop while she berated him with Mandarin curses, unsure of the proper course of action, torn between feeling like a thief and not wanting to be robbed. She turned to her own phone, quickly looking up a translation before placing a call.

"I call police," she said.

"Fan-fu*^$ng-tastic. You do that. I was thinking of doing it myself, but if you feel that would be best, I'll wait right here."

He found a decent place to lean on the other end of the store while he waited. Given his experience in Nanchang half a year prior, he had mixed feelings about what may happen next. Ten, long minutes passed. Not the ten minutes of watching an enjoyable film, or even a terrible one, but the ten minutes of a boxer in the ring. Ten long, slow, awkward minutes passed while they waited for an authority of justice to arrive. He would've been content to have his three-hundred yuan returned. He would've been content to walk away with the battery. He had faith that one of those two events would occur after a police officer arrived.

A short, thick, stocky fellow walked into the establishment with all of the bravado of a gunslinger stepping into a saloon. He noticed Remy off to the side and approached the owner of the shop. They conversed back and forth for about a minute, all the while, the officer of the law stealing increasingly judgmental looks back in Remy's direction. The conversation ended sharply and he began marching toward Remy menacingly.

Remy leapt gracefully down from the countertop he had perched himself on and raised his arms in the surrender pose, also the initial stance of Air in the martial art style of Ninjutsu. "Look, ruffian. I don't know what she said to you, but hear me out. We agreed on a price of three hundred yuan. It was crystal clear. She even typed it up on her calculator. I gave her that amount. She returned with the battery and then demanded more money." Remy held up three digits, arms still raised by his side. "Three hundred yuan. She has that right now. And I have this battery, so what I'm going to do is walk away with the agreed upon product."

Before he'd taken his second step toward the exit, the man wrapped his fist firmly around Remy's belt buckle, gripping and twisting the waistline of his trouser until it pinched his sides tightly. He locked eyes with Remy with all of the compassion of a hungry shark.

"Really? It's like this?" he pleaded not wanting violence. "Do you even understand the words that I'm saying?"

He didn't answer with words. The officer shoved him backward against the glass counter. He didn't use his free hand to call for back-up and that more than anything concerned Remy the most. He had waited for him to arrive, surrendered, and offered no resistance. The stocky brute had a hand free for a back-up call, and he just stood there, dominant and pushy. That was enough for Remy. Uncertain if the man was even a police officer or something akin to the fellow who had taken over his case in Nanchang, he acted.

He began by sliding his weight through his hips and pivoting them from side to side while moving backward, shifting from Wind into Water. The brute clamped his second hand onto Remy's waistline, overlapping his original grasp in a professional manner before twisting mercilessly making a weapon out of a trouser waistline. *Finally*, Remy thought, smirking a half-grin, feeling no guilt about what would come next.

His attacker was half a foot shorter than Remy, a few years older, muscular and lean. Remy's grinned wider as he redirected all his troubles with China onto this one man. He looked down at hands that were folded over themselves, clenched tightly in order to secure the tightest grasp to a man he hadn't bothered speaking with.

"You feel pretty secure in that grip?" he asked, looking straight into those shark eyes, feeling the man's resolve waver a smidge before he made his first move.

He removed the topmost hand from his beltline by grasping onto his attacker's thumb muscle where it branched from the palm and rotating it obscenely, with purpose, on his way to wrenching the entire arm outward if possible so he could land a blow in the newly opened area. Instead, the man released his other hand from Remy's belt, bringing it up defensively as he took a step away.

"There you go! Nice job. I was worried I was just going to just dominate this encounter but you know what you're doing, right?"

He took a quick glance behind to orient himself and inserted himself between Remy and the exit.

"Bravo, good sir. Bravo. I can't fault you for that. Loyalty is a fine thing. It's a shame that you're such a moron, though. A blunt tool. Obedient to women, regardless of their guilt. F^*#ing idiot."

He accented his verbal assault with a swift jab toward the face designed not to land but to show his opponent's reaction time, his style which turned out to be basic hand-to-hand training. Normal stuff, stiff and uncreative, nothing special.

Remy relished the moment, finally able to physically resist what had been plaguing him month after relentless month. "You know you should leave now. You must know it. You have to feel it."

There was true concern in his opponent's eyes but certainly not fear. He wasn't enjoying the situation as much as Remy was, though. As Remy approached grinning, his opponent released a haymaker with is right fist, all too predictably. Remy rotated around to the man's left as it whizzed nearby. He countered by lightly smacking his opponent's left cheek as one applies cologne, enjoying the confrontation all too much. His attacker responded by removing a retractable beating baton.

"Well, then. We should probably step outside, don't you think?" Remy asked rhetorically, knowing there would be no response. He purposefully turned his back to his assailant and moved toward the exit, keeping the man in his peripheral. He rushed up and swung the baton so as to deliver a blow to the back of Remy's head but Remy dodged by pivoting and ducking a bit to the outside, having expected the man to seize the dishonorable opportunity. The attack whizzed by and Remy struck him with both open palms, one to the shoulder to interrupt an arm rearing back for some nefarious purpose, the other dead center in the chest. His attacker stumbled back, tripping on his feet, remaining upright but barely just.

"Come, little one. Outside."

His attacker performed better on the open street and sidewalk. As soon as they exited the building, a crowd took shape around the confrontation. The man knew how to wield his beating stick, lashing downward and upward and side-to-side in combination with well-timed punches. His opponent turned out to have quite some skill with the baton and for all of Remy's strong beginning, he was quickly caught up in something far more challenging than he had first imagined.

It was a beautiful dance if you are into that sort of thing. They feinted and turned this way and that, delivering meaningful strikes that mostly missed their mark. Remy thought he was possibly fighting a protector of the law -- thought there was no badge and no backup called -- someone he would've preferred to fight alongside rather than against. Two minutes later, a very long time in such an environment, he had thought of no decent endpoint to the confrontation. He wouldn't flee, but he didn't want to land solid blows and actually hurt this man, aggressor or not. The crowd had grown thick, numbering more than two dozen situated in a rough perimeter around the action. Phones were up and recording video that the government would swiftly remove from social media just as soon as it was posted. He pivoted away from a baton strike to chest that turned out to be a feint, the actual blow landing squarely across his left knee. Sharp pain cut through his senses.

"You're doing so well!" Remy replied in the midst of combat, a bit winded. "But check this out."

Taking a deep breath, he unloaded a flurry, keeping himself on the man's left, his weakest side. From this point he delivered a rich series of face slaps and shoves unwilling to punch or kick the man lest he was in fact a police officer, pulling back on strikes as one would when sparring, not meant to harm but rather prove that he was swifter and better positioned. They were warnings unheeded, however. His attacker's response to the flurry was swift and brutal, the baton a wicked blur of strikes that Remy struggled to remain on the other side of. Ducking under and away from one strike, he back-stepped too slowly and the baton landed squarely on his left bicep.

Remy pivoted to avoid another savage blow, this time leaving a trap of sorts. He kept his left leg too close to his opponent and the man gratefully swung at the easy target. Remy quickly returned his leg resulting in the officer smashing his baton into the pavement. The weapon came up curved a bit into a saber, crescent-moon shape. Pleased with his successful ruse, he did not predict the swift follow-up strike that followed. Unlike Remy who was intentionally pulling back from full-powered blows, the officer buried his deformed baton into Remy's right shin, the blow further warping the baton and splitting open skin to the very bone itself.

"Holy shit! My bones are stronger than your beating stick. Did not see that com---"

And then his attacker was on him again, charging forward while swinging the damaged baton wildly. Remy pivoted as bullfighters do and brought Crane's Claw down onto his opponent's left eyeball, fully able to scoop it out of socket. Instead, he clumsily tapped the man's face in passing before dancing back a few steps, clearly more winded than his opponent.

"I'm not going to do this. You're not my enemy. You're an idiot, but you're not my enemy."

Remy caught a glancing blow as he pivoted away and slid to the side. "You're duped, just like I was, by a woman who dripped poison in your ear. I don't blame you for that." His opponent struck out with his damaged baton and planted it firmly into the same wound, widening the opening.

"Okay." Remy raised his hands in surrender. "No more." He stopped moving.

His assailant continued the attack, however. Remy brought his leg up and out as the man struck at his bleeding shin a third time, pivoted his opposite foot and delivered a stomp kick to the baton, ejecting the weapon from his opponent's grasp. Remy followed the bouncing weapon, catching it before it had a chance to come to a rest. He barely had time to test the feel of it before the officer was charging at him again. Remy hurled it over the thickening crowd before sidestepping to avoid a punch, catching a glancing blow along the way.

"Well, what the f^%$ am I supposed to do now? You just keep coming! All this over a phone battery that I paid the agreed price for?!"

He lunged forward. Remy pivoted clumsily and backstepped, maintaining as much distance as possible with the man. Being disarmed had made his opponent cautious, allowing Remy time to catch his breath and think.

"Why are you still attacking me? You saw my hands up. Twice. And still you attacked."

Speaking the words aloud, Remy realized he needed to change things up. He dissolved a martial stance, squared his hips and shoulders to his assailant and bowed deeply, head out and low. In response, the man approached again fists at the ready. Remy backstepped and turned to narrowly avoid a heavy punch. Time was running out. Either he was going to curl up and take a serious beating or he would need to seriously damage his opponent. Neither option was very appealing and he was inwardly debating the choice when he sensed someone approaching. He spun about and maneuvered into a position so as to keep both his attacker and the newly arrived person within his line of sight. A pudgy young officer in his mid-twenties emerged from the crowd and began demanding in broken English for Remy to stop.

"I've been trying to stop but…" Remy gestured toward his opponent as he prepared to strike yet again. "He's stuck on rampage mode."

Remy held out his hands again, raising them up. The young officer ran to the older one and they began speaking to one another. Remy took the opportunity to kneel down on both knees and catch his breath. Surrendering to the moment, he closed his eyes and waited. He was manacled with great pomp by his opponent and openly mocked to show his dominance to the crowd that had gathered. He was ushered into a cage for humans that had been incorporated into the back of a pickup truck. While there appeared to be official emblems painted decorating the sides of the truck, Remy was still uncertain to what people he had surrendered to. His mind turned to the thug in Nanchang posing as an officer and he considered the possibility that he may very well be driven somewhere secluded and murdered. A calm had overcome Remy and even thoughts such as this did not panic the man. *To die here and now wouldn't be all that bad. At least I would sleep finally.*

A quarter of an hour later, the truck stopped and the cage was unlocked. He clambered out and was led inside a dimly lit building to an interrogation room ripe with the stench of mold and mildew. On filthy white walls were dark smears made by hands and shoeprints from top to bottom. One handprint started off perfectly clear and then smeared away into a faded streak, as if someone had been dragged out of the room. The young, chubby officer secured Remy to a strip of piping that rose from an interrogation table bolted securely into the floor and left the room.

Remy seized the opportunity and fell asleep almost immediately, the room having the opposite of intended effects. His breathing slowed and deepened as his mind wavered from reality to dream before the door slammed open.

"Son of a bitch! I was almost there," Remy yelled at no one in particular. The pudgy officer and a new, older officer who seemed to run the place entered.

"You are here," said the pudgy officer.

The two officers conversed for a time before the older man left, leaving the pudgy man alone with Remy. He took a seat on the other side of the room and leered.

Remy rattled his manacle with a mirthful smile. "Care to unshackle this? I'm not a violent man. I wouldn't strike you. I never strike first. Pretty proud of that fact, actually. That thug you probably look up to initiated combat with me and then got his arse whooped good and plenty."

"You bleeding," the officer replied coldly.

"Touché. The dog does have a few teeth after all. It's actually mostly scabbed over now. He wielded a weapon while I held none. Did you ever find that baton, by the way? Or did I throw it too far after I kicked it out of his hands?"

Remy leaned forward and lowered his voice.

"I was all over that cat. That's why he's not in this room. He's shook up. I was attacked and I chose not to injure a man who reached out and manhandled me for no good reason. A man who obeyed a woman who lied to me about a final cost, and likely lied to him, too. He attacked a man who waited patiently for ten minutes for an officer of the law to arrive, a man who was immediately restrained without provocation. He's heavier than I am and it's all muscle but I don't think I lost that one, cowboy."

Remy leaned back in his chair as comfortably as he could while cuffed to a pipe. "Let me tell you, I feel pretty good right now. Despite this Halloween Horror Nights thing you have going on in here." He nodded outward with his head. "Look at that one. Do you mean to tell me that someone smacked their hand against the wall at near ceiling-level and then was dragged back down to the middle of the wall where the smear ends? Did you arrest Harry Potter in here? Was there a quidditch match that went horribly awry right here in this room? That would explain the prints at awkward heights. Doesn't explain why they're all the same handprint though. That's the exact same handprint all over the walls. Doesn't explain why they were all applied at that same time, either. The paint, or mud or whatever that is, is faded exactly the same all throughout. Doesn't explain why you haven't bothered to repaint the walls white again after this wayward quidditch match ended either. Oh wait, I'm supposed to do this." Remy began shaking, trembling in his seat. His face took on terror, his eyes desperate. "This is so scary."

Remy relaxed and laughed heartily and to his surprise, the young officer laughed with him.

"Quidditch," the pudgy officer repeated through a chuckle.

"Right? I mean, I guess it was team Slytherin because Gryffindor wouldn't be in here, am I right?"

They shared a laugh after that one, too. The young man looked meaningfully to Remy, no longer leering, shook his head and exited. At the door, he turned back to Remy still shackled to the table. "You wait here."

"Everyone's a comedian," Remy muttered as the door closed, shaking his manacled wrist.

He desperately wanted to sleep but his mind raced with what had happened and what may occur next. He glanced down at torn and bloodied trousers that would need to be thrown away. Through a shredded pantleg, he gingerly probed the wide split along the shin bone. Blood had congealed into a dark, fat clump. "That's going to leave a mark," he said to himself, and it did, for the rest of his life.

He listened attentively to his surroundings, hearing voices in the distance but not understanding the language enough to translate what was being said. The general tone was softening, however. Laughter pierced through once which Remy attributed to the relating of the quidditch match joke, or the wait-right-here joke. Within an hour, a calm had spread over the vicinity and he was having a very difficult time understanding that. *I was involved in a violent struggle with one of their numbers and a few jokes have cleared the air?* It made no sense to Remy. *Does this mean I can return home and actually sleep at night?*

In time a detective arrived, announcing he'd been summoned from Shanghai to help deal with the matter. He spoke English extremely well and sported an immaculate trench coat, looking every bit the role of detective.

"Nice coat. They didn't check it at the door for you?" No response. "Shanghai, you say? I've been shackled to this table in an interrogation room decorated for Halloween at most two hours." Remy leaned forward and smiled falsely. "So, you're from Shanghai. Tell me, how far away is that exactly? Because unless you were helicoptered in at the exact moment that treacherous sales clerk called the police, and you weren't, you gorgeous-haired bastard, I don't see how you could've arrived from Shanghai so swiftly."

The man maintained a somber demeanor.

"Because, you know, the only way to travel that distance so quickly would be by helicopter but that would have ruined that magnificent hairstyling you have going on, but whatever, I've grown accustomed to being lied to. Do you think I should be expelled back to America? That would make sense, right? I committed a crime in your eyes undoubtedly. Defending myself from attack. That's probably illegal these days. Shouldn't I be expelled?" A tinge of hopefulness creeping in.

"No. You just need apologize and they let you leave."

"Oh, really? They'll let me return to my apartment where sleep is impossible? How nice. Fine. How do I apologize and leave this place?"

An official form was presented to Remy, the header printed in Mandarin and mostly incomprehensible. He wrote the following with his left hand, his right still manacled to the table:

I am sorry that you suck so much. Sincerely, Donald Duck.

He added a date he'd seen attached to a certificated file he had been unable to remove from his computer: October, 12, 1912.

"So, is that it? Are we good now?" Remy asked, rustling his handcuff.

"Don't do this again," the detective warned as he unlocked the cuff.

"If I'm not grappled again, this won't happen again. Say, do I get that 300 yuan back or what? I should have either the battery or the money."

"Goodbye, Mr. LeBeau."

CHAPTER XXXVI

CHINA

More failed attempts at securing his internet connection. More nights on the rooftop lasering SOS into the night sky. One plane, a small aircraft capable of seating only a handful of passengers, had flown directly overhead so closely that he could see the faces of the pilot and copilot. He waved his arms about as those seeking rescue do but the plane simply continued on its way, trekking across the night sky at an extremely low elevation until it disappeared into the horizon.

More long walks, legs cramping from toes to heels, up calves to thighs, twisting and churning, transforming Remy into a tangled ball of muscle and agony. Always he could reach the northern boundary, some nights easier than other nights, but there he was held in check, unable to proceed. Only vehicles were allowed on the interstate and no other roads led to the airport. There was simply no way to walk to the airport.

His phone hadn't rung in a week, Monica having left him alone to struggle and fight like a hooked fish. She was the only one aware of Remy's plight that had displayed an ounce of concern. He opened the call with a smile.

"Remy! It's so good to hear you, son. How are you?"

"Mom? Mother is that you?"

"Yes. How are you? How's my son?"

He paused, trying to wrap his mind around the situation. He didn't want to drag her into the tar pit he was sinking into, but hated dishonesty. *How am I? I'm flashing lasers at low-flying aircraft to seek escape, long walks to nowhere, altercations with police or whoever those people were, scaling the ledges of my apartment, torturous denial of sleep, week after week after week. Not great. That's how I am.*

"Why are you calling me?"

"I love you very much, son." The sound of welling tears came through clearly in her voice.

"I know that, mom. I know. Why're you calling me? You've never called me before. I mean, the occasional email, but never a call. Not in the ten years I've been living abroad. Why now?"

"I worry about you. Aren't I allowed to worry about my son?"

"Yes, and this would be a perfect time to do exactly that, but stop avoiding my question and start telling me why, out of all this time I've been away, why you're reaching out to that son you love so much now?"

An awkward pause.

"Sheldon called. Do you know him?"

He thought back to the walk home after work when the vice-principal had threatened to bring his family crashing down into the midst of his assault. Of the bodyguard that had appeared. Of the thug-teacher who had brought up his brother's home address on Google Maps. Of Patrick. Of the lone good one in that whole mess, Ezekiel, whom he hadn't seen in weeks. Of the apparent norm of foreign teachers composing university introduction letters on behalf of high school students.

"Son, are you there?"

"Sort of."

"I don't know what that means."

"Yeah, that's a trend these days. No one understands what I'm saying anymore. It's not easy to explain any of this." A pause. "Things are bad here, mom. Real bad."

"Hello? Can you hear me?"

Remy cursed and rushed to the kitchen window in order to receive a better signal though his phone's screen displayed a full bar reception. He changed the subject and began speaking of other things: how distant cousins were faring, of his niece's grades, of his aging mother's own health and retirement. In response to the shift in discussion, his voice began coming through clearly.

"Well mother, it's getting late over here. Nice chatting and all. Don't feel obligated to wait until a complete stranger that leads a school that's torturing me contacts you before you decide to call your own flesh and blood and check in on him."

"What? I can't understand you. Your voice is breaking up."

Though he had apparently been censored, his spirits brightened as he gave voice to his concerns. Happiness quickly evaporated as he was forced to repeat himself, an echo of his own voice wavered and chopped in and out. He glanced down again at his phone as he leaned out of the kitchen window. Full bars.

"This place sucks so much," he muttered to himself.

He took a deep breath and returned to the call. "Here's the deal, mom. I fell in love, but she robbed me blind. I resisted the theft every which way I could and ended up deeper and deeper into unfathomable muck of which there are no words to describe properly." As he spoke, an echo of his voice wavered and faded in the tiny speaker of his mobile phone, making his words indiscernible.

He pressed on anyway though. "This city opposes me. I know that sounds crazy but the subways won't take me to the airport, nor the buses, and don't get me started on the taxis. The internet won't show me where the airport is. False maps have been made and sold to me by sidewalk merchants. I kid you not. My laptop, my phone, this very phone you cannot hear me on, has had its physical hardware altered, I imagine. At the very least the software overwritten which is why you can't hear me speaking right now."

As if to prove the point, she called out to him questioningly, "Hello? Son? I can't..."

"Exactly. Exactly that."

He sighed and walked away from the kitchen window where he'd been called upon to jump, jump, jump. Where he'd pulled himself halfway up to the apartment above on the eighteenth floor.

"I've walked and walked. At least a hundred miles these past few weeks. Maybe two. Maybe more. I don't know. I'm so sleepy and I'm denied sleep. The effects of that I can't begin to explain to you." He paused and gathered his thoughts. "I'm very tired, mother. Very tired. I think you will live your entire life and never know what this feels like." Static began clicking in. "Nor should you."

"There you are. I couldn't hear you. I was about to hang up and call you back," she said, thinking that would actually solve the problem. "Sheldon thinks I should come visit you. Bring your sister and Apr---"

"No! No! Do not bring my niece here. She's only ten. Just don't come here, mom. Don't do that." His voice became murkier as he pressed on. "Look, I love you. You made massive, massive mistakes in your upbringing of me, but I love you. You love me." The echo was clearing. "Maybe. Anyway, do not -- I repeat do not -- come to China. Not now, not ever. The end."

He contemplated a future in which his family would arrive and somehow the taxis would all respond normally. They'd all leave the apartment and assemble into a crowded cab and sail off to the airport to be delivered safe and sound to the good ol' US of A.

And then he thought of all that he'd suffered recently. Guangzhou continuing its trend and ensnaring his family just as had been threatened in the teacher's office via demonstrating that thugs knew exactly where his brother lived. Possibly worse, they arrive and all of the troubles would disappear, transforming his own family into proof that Remy's ordeal had never even happened. *I may die trying to leave this place but I will not allow all of this to be erased. This happened and the world will know one day.*

"Just stay away. Stay far away." Static popped and Remy altered his approach, hating that he was responding to threats of censoring his speech as prompts. He spoke again in the most sarcastic voice he could summon, "Everything is perfectly fine." The line cleared immediately. "Don't worry about me."

"I worry about you."

Fine time to start. "Well, stop. I'm all grown up and fully capable of taking down an aircraft carrier all by myself if need be. You needn't worry."

They shared a chuckle.

"I have to go." Remy kept his voice light. "Do you remember when I was a boy and would go swimming in the pool in the backyard? You'd put a towel in the dryer so I I had this warm, soft towel to dry off with when I came out. Do you remember that?"

"Not really, Remy."

"Well, it was lovely. I can't speak much to your parenting after age nine, but some of that younger stuff was phenomenal. It's almost like you're one of those people that love puppies and ignore the dog when it gets older. Yeah, that's it exactly. That's how it's always felt with you. But those puppy days were pretty good."

No static now.

"Goodbye, mother. If I don't see you by New Year's, be sure I'm dead."

"I couldn't hear what you said just now. Can you move to a window or something?"

"Oh, it's far more complicated than that. Just know I appreciate those warm towels. And don't come here. Not now, not ever."

They shared an uncomfortable farewell before he shut off his phone, knowing there was a high probability that she wouldn't come, feeling she was safer for it. He reclined on the sofa, closed his eyes, and was met with the loud sound of a man urinating above him via a speaker aimed downward that prevented him from sleeping each and every night and day.

CHAPTER XXXVII

CHINA

Remy hiked east after breakfast in search of a new approach to the airport. By late afternoon it had become apparent that there was no way to head east and then swing north or northwest to the airport. Northeast was an option but it wouldn't have brought him any closer to escape and after a full day of hiking he was too exhausted to continue. On his last reserves, he staggered into a westward train in a subway on the eastern outskirts of Guangzhou. No seats were available so he squatted on aching legs and then promptly collapsed into severe spasms of both calves and both soles of the feet. A young foursome motioned toward Remy and began chortling. The alpha of the group broke away from his gang and walked by him as the worst of the pain subsided, intentionally passing gas as he walked by. The stench filled the train car and set the foursome to fresh tittering as the leader returned to his group.

Remy began muttering to himself, his voice rising in strength until it cut through the entire car. "Can't you just leave me be? Just leave me in peace. Is that so impossible?!" There were no answers from the passengers that Remy eyed wildly, especially not the foursome. "I don't even know who you are. I've never seen any of you before this moment. You know I'm wounded. Even if you don't know my backstory, you see me here collapsed on the ground, obviously suffering. This is how you treat a man too injured to stand?!"

Surprisingly, he found a sympathetic eye here and there looking back at him, strangers careful not to stare and draw attention to themselves. Mostly he was met with cold indifference. The mood of the once brave foursome had shifted significantly as a realization sunk in that treading on this man a second time may be costly.

He kept a firm eye on the pacified gang until they exited at the next stop. Later he changed trainlines and began heading northwest, bound for the airport. Again, the train stopped stations away from its destination and the passengers filed out dutifully. *I haven't the foggiest clue how this is happening. It's barely past five p.m. Surely, some of these passengers will miss their flights due to the rerouting. These train delays must be upsetting international airport schedules. The cost and long-reaching effects are staggering. So much time and manpower and money on me? I wouldn't believe it if I wasn't living it.*

It made little sense to him no matter how much he thought it over that evening during yet another long walk home. A long shuffle home, really. One foot, then the other, the strides short and jerky. Minute changes of the pathway he treaded were enough to cause him to stumble, occasionally culminating into a painful landing. He had failed to find an alternate path to the airport. *The only way is along the interstate,* he realized.

He spied an alley cat munching on bones in the shadows and crouched low, more for an excuse to rest his leg muscles than an interest in the cat itself. He cooed and tutted his tongue, beckoning it closer, but the scraggly grey cat bounded off, leaving behind a partially devoured rat carcass.

"Oh, so you got the memo, too?" he asked, chuckling at his own joke.

Hours later, deep into the night, he returned home equipped with a new plan. William leapt up to make level eye contact with him as he entered. "Relax, my friend. Relax. I wouldn't leave you here." As if in answer, William stopped bouncing and began intensely sniffing his trousers, groin to cuff. His final verdict was a sneezing-snort.

"What? Is it the cat? Come on, man! I was bored." William turned about and mouthed the leash that hung from the wall, tugging it free. "Really? It's like that, is it?"

William barked once, loudly, one sharp bark, and then nothing.

"Is that a *yes*? Your English really is quite good. You are a weirdo, dingo, but you know I love you." He crouched low and brought their heads together lovingly. William licked Remy's nose in appreciation.

"Come now. Let's take a stroll. I believe we may actually get out this mess soon, old boy."

CHAPTER XXXVIII

CHINA

In perfect response to the burgeoning idea of hope, the tenants upstairs doubled down on the audio affliction. Remy found the sounds to be less troublesome near the kitchen window as the noises of the city seemed to counteract the barrage and so he spent most of his time there, staring off, his vision limited to a peripheral haze while he analyzed the past and predicted possible futures. He had decided to rest and wait and heal before implementing the new plan. He had been leaning against the windowsill most of the morning, ironing out the upcoming details, stretching his mind outward as he imagined possible challenges along the way. William had long since grown bored of his human counterpart and was taking a nap.

Immersed in thought and probability, his mind didn't immediately recognize the disturbance below. Something wavered in his thinking and his vision sharpened, snapping his mind back to the reality that surrounded him. On the street far below, an elderly couple was lowering themselves with some difficulty into the backseat of a sedan, the make and model too distant to be seen clearly. He wasn't sure why he'd been snapped back to the then and there until he glimpsed a bit of the face of the older woman, a face that had maintained kindness to Remy while he struggled to order food in Mandarin at the local restaurant across the road from the apartment complex. The duck restaurant. His go-to sidewalk restaurant. She was not quite resisting but clearly uncomfortably rushed into the backseat. Nearby, her grandson was arguing with two muscular men in button-up Polo shirts, pressed slacks, and sunglasses. A familiar look he had learned to associate with strife.

The grandson was furiously waving his arms about, causing a scene. One of the men put his hand on the twenty-something's elbow and the grandson shrugged it off and took a step back, a step that was followed by the other man moving forward, flanking the grandson. The grandson showed concern then, realizing he had little choice as they wrapped him up gently, one on each elbow. Remy's face dropped into sorrow and his heart cried out: *Do something!* He dashed to the bedroom to change into outdoor clothes, pulling trousers over pajama bottoms, sticking bare feet into shoes. He muttered a quick prayer and took a last look out of the kitchen window to the scene below, unsure of what to do but accustomed to feeling that way.

The grandson was already secured into the backseat with his grandparents. Judging by the manner in which the two well-groomed thugs kept him in their line of sight while they discussed something among themselves, his ire had not been much assuaged. Having concluded their conversation, the muscular men began moving to the passenger and driver's seat. *I will not make it in time*, he realized, feeling relieved and disappointed. He threw open the kitchen window and shouted across the block, yelling and waving his arms about as would a man trying to catch the attention of a rescue helicopter.

"It's okay!" he shouted through a forced smile that couldn't even be seen from so great a distance. "It's all okay. Don't get hurt because of this. Don't do that." *I don't think I could bear that weight right now.* The grandson turned back and gazed up in Remy's direction, drawing the attention of the thugs, as well. Remy waved with a warmth he didn't feel. "It's okay! You're a good man and not forgotten. Be well and good. Thank you for treating me with respect during all of this." A pause. "Thank you."

Perhaps, the altercation had nothing to do with the restaurant being the only one he ate from, the only one to treat him with compassion. It would remain yet another unsolved mystery. The dark sedan drove off and he never saw them again. For dinner, he walked straight over to the ma and pa sidewalk restaurant expecting to find it closed. Instead, he found a completely different older woman there, a completely different older man, and no grandson figure. The new caretaker and Remy smiled knowing fake smiles to one another as Remy expressed his desire to eat in simple, heavily-accented Mandarin. After ordering, he asked about the whereabouts of the previous managers and was misunderstood several times until it became apparent that the subject was off limits. The meal was terrible and expensive. Just rice and meat and vegetables slopped together, everything overcooked. Few people visited the restaurant after the original family left. It went from being one of the most popular sidewalk eateries to nearly permanently deserted.

Remy's diet began taking a turn for the worse. He ate crummy food from the old woman who ran the shop for three more days while he stretched and endured cramps and recovered. And then, as the sun disappeared beneath the horizon, he took up his backpack and attached a leash to William's collar. The hound was eagerly anticipating the opening of the front door, already pulling on the leash, chomping at the bit, so to speak.

"Ease up, boy. It'll be a long trip."

CHAPTER XXXIX

USA

"It's not that I'm your enemy because I'm not. What I am is hugely disappointed in what you've become," Remy said to no one in particular from his bedroom window on the second floor of a cheap apartment that overlooked nothing special in Orlando, Florida.

"I hate it here. Cracked and potholed roadways. The people in the supermarkets, the people on the roads. Most of my fellow employees, employers -- not just this job but the last and the next -- have so little in common with me. David Bowie sang a song about being afraid of Americans and I get that. I don't fear you, but I could see how someone would. How entire cultures do. You're abrasive and often fail to peacefully disagree. Everyone so polarized. So consumed with placing themselves in comfortable labels."

He took a deep breath, collecting his thoughts. "Your students' international scholastic scorings continue to decline. The percentage of educated Americans that migrate abroad, leaving behind their homeland indefinitely, increases each year. Crime rate perpetually on the rise despite your bloated employment of police officers.

You're a violently ignorant lot that live in vast income inequality. An inflated police force won't solve that. You're going to have crime in an environment like that no matter how many coppers you employ but instead of providing a society in which crime has no place -- a nation with a decent minimum wage and social safeguards, a place where medicine and healthcare is available to all -- you focus on instilling fear in criminals. Your laws safeguard fat cats, dishonest employers that mistreat their employees regularly. Suicide and murder and violent outbursts commonplace. A population thoroughly medicated. You are no role model of mine." He pivoted, crisscrossing a well-worn trail across the living room, feeling the flooring dip down and rise up as he paced.

"You've been given the entire world. No one disagrees with who rules this planet. It's undoubtedly you. And what have you done over the past seventy years of world dominance? The economy: minimum wage so low in each state that it can't support an individual's life expenses. The wealthy regularly negligent in paying taxes through the use of shell companies and offshore banking. The infrastructure: roads so poorly maintained that tire and alignment damage is an unavoidable daily occurrence. Public transportation: walking a kilometer or more to and from bus stops in the summer heat and chilly winter mornings. Bus stops often without benches, neither paved nor protected from the elements. Public transit in all forms all throughout America rarely punctual. Trains and buses swimming in litter, the seats damaged. The environment: from the depths of the ocean to the tip of the atmosphere, poisoned. The working class: employee rights practically nonexistent in an environment flooded with immigrants – legal or otherwise -- that accept unlivable wages and unjust treatment because it's a slight improvement to their own native lands. Low-skilled immigrants dominate blue-collar jobs with a surplus on standby, effectively denying workers the only power they have ever wielded: the ability to strike. Most of us are unable to provide for ourselves and our families. We live paycheck to paycheck. Home ownership, college tuition for our children, insurance and medical expenses impossible to fund on the wages we receive. Little room for savings. Yearly vacations a thing of the past. All the while we must take great care to show no signs of displeasure in being treated inhumanely for fear of immediate termination. Personal safety: most Americans lock themselves in their homes both day and night and still have panic attacks, night terrors, depression. You know what all that stuff is, though? Awareness. Awareness of what you've become. A monster. A thing more oppressive than England ever was. And while I'm wise enough to know that the enemy of my enemy is not at all my friend, I am severely disappointed in what you became. You had everything in front of you, everything, the Earth's resources, and this is what you did with it. I'm more often ashamed to identify myself American as proud."

He pivoted, pacing back. "And I'm not alone. If the massive numbers of university graduates migrating elsewhere aren't proof enough than how about your ever-decreasing voter turnouts? How about jurors that hate to be called in even though it's an escape from their own miserable jobs? How about just breathing the air, opening your eyes, feeling this country, and knowing without a doubt that we the people have absolutely no connection with the decisions made by our government for you serve the wealthy and consume the majority."

He halted, straining his sharp ears, listening to the parking lot below where a handful of Haitians began laughing heartily. Neighbors or friends thereof. The night before they were screaming in anger, a lover's tiff of some sort.

"I belong here about as much as a potato belongs in a tiger's mouth."

He inhaled deeply, pivoted and retraced his steps, pondering an exit strategy. He had come to America to forge a comfortable existence for himself among his own people. He had suffered and endured the indecency of homelessness, toiled through indignities of working for people who lacked common respect. He saved and saved and there was always so little to show for it. Hard work, dedication, and honesty had not brought him out of poverty. Years of discomfort. Years of disgrace. He was trapped. Lost at sea, barely able to bring his head above the waterline and breathe before the waves came crashing down again. America. Depression.

CHAPTER XL

CHINA

He had exhausted the northern perimeter. All roads may lead to Rome but no sidewalks led to the Guangzhou International Airport. Trainlines deterred. Taxicabs noncompliant. Rejected at bus stops. A private pilot or two had been made aware of his dire situation via the emergency flashing of SOS from the rooftop, of that Remy had no doubt for small aircraft had buzzed right over him. Extraction, however, was apparently not going to happen. Just what exactly could a pilot do anyway? Land and then drive to where he thought the signal had come from, knocking on every door of each apartment complex in the area to ensure the residents were not in need of rescue? *At least the flight path pointed me in the correct direction of the airport.*

The elevator doors pinched shut and the chamber descended. William looked up, eyes as wide as his gaping maw. "Oh, sure. You're happy now. Just wait a few hours, my furry friend." He stooped low and mock-jabbed William's side. They sparred good-naturedly as puppies do until the elevator doors opened. William bounded out of the doors at a swift pace, pulling Remy in tow. *If I were only wear-*

ing roller skates this trip would be a breeze. This is more like steering a horse than walking a dog.

Northward, choosing unexplored roads along the way to combat boredom having lost hope of encountering any kind of a boon a long, long time ago. His mind wandered as each footstep overtook the next. A hazy image of a concerned Southerner watering plants in her yard alongside the sidewalk appeared, her expression faltering as she took Remy in, exhausted and marching onward, determined and grim. "Can I help you, son?" she asked, real concern playing about her face. "You don't look so good."

He smiled, staring off into the horizon, his chin dipping down to his chest, blinks slowing as he was pulled forward step by step by a tireless hound.

"Howdy, ma'am. I have seen better days, that's for sure. Could I trouble you for a glass of water? I've a long way to go."

"Honey, you just wait right there."

And she bounded off, returning with a glass of iced tea that Remy gratefully accepted, gulping down a good portion, leaving William the bottom third to lap up from the tilted receptacle. They began chatting about the weather, about William, what it was like living in China. She asked about where he was headed and why he looked so worn. He hinted about some of what had occurred, focusing on his need to get to the airport, of the taxis and the buses and the trains that had prevented such things.

"You poor dear. Don't you worry no more. I'll drive us there right this minute."

She dashed off into her home and returned with jingling keys and off they went, Guangzhou in the rearview mirror where it belonged. His thoughts turned to memories of Monica: good times and bad. Of sneaking about, immersed in shadow as he watched that damned black sportscar arrive to pick her up. Of holding hands on the sofa while a movie played, the two of them chatting about something else entirely. Of the way her neck smelled. Of the robbery, her frantically snapping away at the ATM keyboard as she funneled his savings else-where. *Probably in someone's pocket around here. Wait, where is here?* He jerked his head up, eyes peeling open under protest. Nothing looked familiar. *Did we turn during any of that?*

William maintained a steady quick pace, tugging at the reins.

"To the airport, William. Take us to the airport, okay? You know how to get there, right? Maybe you can smell jet fuel in the air. Does freedom have a smell? Follow that. Go there. Get us to the airport."

William thundered on unmindful of the chatty human in tow.

"I feel fairly confident where it is. I've watched the blinking lights of aircraft ascend and descend from roughly the same distant point in the horizon from our rooftop. The few times that small airplane descended to check out the SOS flashes, it passed overhead and con-tinued on northward. Dead ahead. That night in the taxi I saw it, William. I saw the airport. I know it exists. We will get there tonight. Good times, old pup. Good---Hey! Stop!"

He snapped to and yanked William back from marching straight into the oncoming traffic of a busy four-lane road. Remy crouched and the hound pivoted back to his face a consoling lick. "I appreciate your energy but be safe, my friend. Be mindful of your surround-ings. More mindful than me, at least." William turned back around, taking absolutely no heed to the words whatsoever, waiting impa-tiently for the opportunity to continue marching onward.

An hour later the pull along the leash had lessened, not tremen-dously, but some. An hour after that, William's pace had slowed sig-nificantly. Needing a rest, he brought them to halt on a dry spot of cement where sidewalk met a wall that separated private residence from public streets. William panted, perspiring heavily from his mouth in the form of drool. Remy drank from a two-liter water bot-tle and then poured some of its contents slowly into his opposing, cupped hand. William took the hint and began lapping up the water as it cascaded, the majority of which was not wasted. When they set off again much of William's pep had returned.

The high-rises of Guangzhou proper lay behind them, presumably to the south. The roads around them were pockmarked with cracks and potholes. The exterior of shops and homes, the edges of which laid flush against the sidewalk itself, were in need of repainting. Walls that separated homes from sidewalks were often affixed with broken glass glued to the top in order to deter trespassers. It was not the type of place one generally felt safe being in, and yet, Remy was heartened.

"This is good. I recognize this area. I mean, I think I do. One graffitied wall adorned with rusted barbwire sort of blends into another around here, but this part of town strikes me as familiar."

William marched on, uncaring.

Shortly thereafter the path ended at a T-intersection and Remy brightened again.

"See? It's harder to go north now. I remember this place. There were wild dogs roaming about last time I was here and enough broken glass that I worried about your paws." He studied the pavement and found it sparkling with tiny pulverized shards. "Yep. This is the place. Be careful where you step."

They crossed the street to a wall surrounding a section of homes that prevented northward progress: east or west being the only option of travel. He studied the details of the jutting broken glass zigzagging atop a stretch of wall alongside the sidewalk, dropped William's leash, leapt up and shoved his fingers into an open pattern, slightly lacerating only a single digit in the process. Pulling himself upward just as he had pulled himself up from the kitchen window to the eighteenth-story ledge above his flat. He peeked over the top of the wall and across a shabby garden thick with foliage where a family of four sat around a dining table chatting amiably. The father poked a pair of chopsticks into a steaming pot and coerced a morsel of something onto his plate. A teenage daughter and son laughed together, sharing an unknown joke while the mother spooned rice onto each family member's plate. Remy hung there observing the quaint scene, lost in the moment, forgetful that the reason he'd leapt up was to find a bearing north. The mother's attention soon shifted through the glass door and across the garden, spying something odd on the edge of the wall. And so Remy fell back, lowering himself onto the sidewalk unceremoniously.

"I do believe it's time to go." He looked up and down the street but William was not there. "Oh, don't you do this, you dingo." He closed his eyes and listened with purpose. The family eating returned to the fore. Someone -- a couple? -- approaching from behind, across the street. Distant engines approaching and fading away, one new and purring, another old and clunking. A soft jingle sounded from the left. His eyes shot open and he followed the sound, moving as swiftly as one can without running. He rounded a corner and found William relieving himself in a clearing of trash, cement, and a few dead shrubs. He muttered a quick prayer of thanks and folded his arms menacingly across his chest, all bluff, his heart singing with joy to find the hound.

"William, you come here right this instant!"

In answer to this commandment, William kicked dirt over his puddle and trotted back to Remy with a wolfish grin. He returned within arm's reach but when Remy bent low to scoop up the leash, he leapt back and ran off, much faster than he needed to. A good distance away in the midst of an abandoned lot in south China, the Shepherd turned back and issued one solid, playful bark. *Come get me!*

"I don't have time for this, dingo. Well, time I have. Energy I do not." William barked once again, repeating the challenge, and then sprinted a figure-eight, showing off before returning to his original spot.

Remy smiled sardonically and shot both his thumbs up into the air. "See these?" He wriggled the digits about. "Don't you wish you had these? You can barely remove eye snot with your stupid dew-claws." He opened his hands and wriggled all his digits. "I can control the world with these things. Ha! What do you say about that?" William barked once in response and crouched low, tail wagging.

Remy began walking away, keeping the hound in his peripheral but appearing to abandon him, a trick he had learned from Japanese mothers when dealing with unruly children. William followed along as Remy marched forward, half searching for an opening to cut northward and half focused on the hound.

"Well, this is definitely the place, old chum."

He stopped walking and looked down. William mirrored his movements and looked up at the man. "You're a great dog and a good friend. But, oh my god, what's that over there?!" Remy suddenly glanced up, staring off a distant point. William's snout shot up and he began sniffing the air, ears perked. Remy slowly stooped over and easily retrieved the leash.

"Oldest trick in the book," he said, gently rubbing William's scruff. The hound detached and shook his head, rejecting the petting, displeased at being duped. Remy trailed along bringing forth memories of the night of the haircutting a couple of weeks prior in order to determine the direction of the interstate, feeling that it likely existed westward. He inferred that it snaked from north to south throughout the bulk of the city and that they would stumble across the highway that led to the airport eventually even if it wasn't at the same on-ramp he had previously discovered. He searched the dark and crumbling neighborhoods for the apartment that he'd ducked into earlier to change clothes and shave his head to no avail. They continued on, resting and drinking periodically -- Remy growing more uncertain of the interstate's location; William's powerful pull weakening as they went.

"Just wait," Remy panted, "until your third trip like this."

He heard the interstate before it came into view: a dull mass of buzzing engines in the distance, a welcome addition to the quiet streets of the city outskirts. He had learned he could no longer trust his hearing but hope still brought a bounce to his step as he rounded a corner to discover the exact same on-ramp the taxi had taken earlier.

"The proverbial golden brick road."

William turned back to Remy tiredly, as hesitant to enter the interstate as Remy was eager. "Don't give me that sourpuss. Come on! Follow the golden brick road! Follow the golden brick road!" Remy sang, half-maniacal that the first part of the plan was finished.

William, unimpressed, crossed the street and headed toward the onramp, Remy in tow. A solitary taxi waited in the distance but he knew better than to try. He squatted at the intersection adjacent to the onramp and forced eye contact with the Shepherd.

"Listen to me. This next part isn't safe. I mean, nothing has been safe for a long time now which is why we have to do this, but I digress." William looked away, sniffing a breeze. "Hey. Back here. Pay attention. If you run away, play your come-chase-me game up there, you will die. Splattered and smashed and very dead." An image of that incident flashed: screeching brakes, blaring horn, a silenced yelp. His eyes watered and his throat tightened. William closed his maw and began paying better attention.

"It's got to be around ten o'clock. There'll be plenty of traffic, lots of speeding traffic." Remy tuned in to the sounds from above. A cacophony of vehicles rushing by, the flow of traffic swift and incessant. "If you don't take this seriously, you could die. Do you understand? I don't know what I'm expecting from you right now. It's not like you can answer me but you're a bright boy. I hope some of this is sinking in. Follow me now. Okay? Understand that? You," Remy poked his finger into William's forehead, "follow me." Remy brought the same finger back to his chest. William looked on politely.

"What the f#^% am I doing?" Remy asked himself. William shook his head back and forth to clear away loose fur or perhaps to say *I don't know.* "You're my ward and I will see you to a better place. If it costs me my very life, so be it."

Remy straightened up, stood, and shot back to the ground, trying in vain to straighten a limb that was contracting horribly. Before the pain really settled in, Remy snatched the leash and clutched it tightly as the spasm rocked his being. Eventually, the calf muscle relaxed and Remy's vision returned. Two rows of large pointed teeth loomed above. A spot of drool landed in his eye. "Gross." William, undeterred by such a petty insult, bent lower and sniffed Remy's breath intently. It was an odd gesture, and after a few long seconds, it was over. "Okay, weirdo. Everything okay with you? Did I pass your physical, Dr. Dingo?"

William stood nearby, waited for Remy to find his feet, no longer tugging at the leash. They walked side by side, the leash only a formality, all but unnecessary. Abandoning the comfort of the sidewalk, they were intercepted by a waist-high metal barrier designed to prevent pedestrian access. Remy leapt over this with surprising dexterity, turned, bent over and scooped up one-hundred pounds of William, depositing him on the other side. He maintained a position closest to the passing vehicles, sandwiching William against a guardrail marking the edge of the interstate. They ascended the onramp and began traversing along the highway, marching north. The other side of the guardrails quickly and frequently became choked with vegetation, forcing the duo to occupy a goodly portion of the rightmost lane of an interstate lacking a sufficient shoulder. It was also very dark. Powerful streetlights illuminated patches of the roadway every half kilometer or so but everything betwixt lay in near perfect darkness until a speeding vehicle whizzed up and by, headlights elongating and rotating their silhouettes in the process. Often motorists would blare their horns and veer into the alternate lane. More often, they did nothing, failing to notice either the man hauling a full backpack or the large German Shepherd until they were in the midst of passing, if they noticed at all as they whizzed by at one-hundred kilometers an hour, easily within arm's reach.

It was an incredibly dangerous thing to do. Each minute was full of close calls. Semis hurtled passed, the air pressure pulling Remy toward the onrushing big rigs and then shoving him aside as they roared by -- a feeling akin to standing in one place on the beach as the tide comes in -- disorienting and dizzying. Each minute was like this. Each long minute. There were stretches of highway that opened up and allowed them to cross back over the guardrail and into relative safety while they continued marching north. They accepted such treats gratefully, having marched kilometers with no margin for error acceptable.

They pressed on for more than an hour in this way, soldiering on until Remy spied a decent place to rest along an opening in a thicket of woods some seventy feet away. The ruckus of the interstate dimmed into a manageable hum as they marched into underbrush. He found a smooth chunk of stone to rest on along the edge of a short ridge that descended thirty feet straight down to another patch of flora that ran along a small road running parallel to the interstate. He thought to abandon the interstate and follow the far safer path below but was uncertain how long the road would continue north and if they both possessed the ability to climb back up the sheer face should it not.

He looked over to William who was casually grazing grass. "We're going to the airport tonight. I know this is hard now but it'll be smooth sailing after this. I remember looking out of the backseat passenger window and spying landing strip lights to the right. It's over here somewhere. We're not so far away now."

The hound walked over to Remy and plopped down, resting his wolfish head upon his lap. Remy twisted the leash around his wrist twice and then sank his chin to his chest, not quite passing out though he was asleep within moments. He collapsed forward onto the back of William and they rested this way until he awoke to a familiar sound. A voice he'd heard before.

"Jump!"

Below him, alongside the parallel road below, a car was parked, its headlights shining onto the base of the ridge where man and hound rested. Both doors of a sporty car were open wide and around the car, three people stood in darkness behind the shine of headlights, their collective body language showing ease with one another and defensive posturing toward Remy's location. Remy and William were blanketed in darkness, the headlights unable to cast upward and the interstate lights too far behind them to be a factor in displaying their position. And yet, there they were. Whoever they were.

"Jump! Jump! Jump!" they chanted, giggling. Remy looked down upon their dark forms concealed behind high beams. *One is a woman, or at least short and thin and small-boned. The other two are certainly men.*

"Safer for me to jump from this height than enter that highway again," Remy called down. They stopped chanting upon hearing him, focusing their attention to his specific location. *Well, they needed my voice for that. There's some limit to their capabilities, at least.* They spoke in hushed whispers amongst themselves before breaking into soft laughter, apparently enjoying a private joke. They chanted for him to jump again, but it lacked unity and there wasn't much heart in it.

"That's strange," Remy shouted below. "It almost appears that you're human from up here. But you're right, I should come down." And with that he searched the ridge for a winding way down to street level, hungry to destroy the evil below. Having spied a promising path, he rose on shaky legs and shuffled downward intent on attributing a face to the torturous gang, planning on provoking the gang into violence so that he could respond without hating himself the next day for what he wanted to do. *It couldn't be Monica, right?* he argued with himself. *I'd recognize her voice anywhere. But what other women do I know that live here and would be involved in this? Or are they just strangers from a flash mob?*

It was reckless to approach people who obviously meant him harm but there was still a mystery to solve and something burned in him seeking vengeance. He was hungry to put his hands on some trouble and throttle it, smiling unhealthily as he made his way down the embankment. Beginning his descent, he glanced down to find the trio dispersing. Car doors slammed shut and the vehicle reversed onto the road and sped off. Remy couldn't read the license plate from his position nor could he properly identify the car. *It wasn't that black sports car that picked up Monica back in Nanchang, was it? That doesn't seem probable. But then again, what's been probable in any of this?*

He turned about as the car fled, needing both of his hands to aid in the climb back up the bluff. *Both hands. No leash. Shit.* Realizing his mistake, he rushed back up the bluff. *Don't be gone. Don't wander off. Please be there.* Pleading with a very distant god as he clambered back up the ridge. He listened for the jingle of tags on collar and heard nothing but engine after engine roaring by. He crept low as he half-ran up the peak of the slope searching the darkness for any hint of William's whereabouts. He retraced his footsteps and found William waiting exactly where he had been, laying down in high grass, head on his paws, exhausted. Remy crouched low and kissed him on the crown of his head.

"Not exactly top-notch parenting skills. I'm sorry." He looped his hand into the leash handle and William rose slowly, reluctant and tired. It hurt his heart to see him like that. "I was hoping to save you from all of this, you know. Come now. Once more into the fire, old friend."

They marched back toward the interstate where soon it became necessary to travel on the dangerous side of the guardrail again. They both came to a stop, hesitant to put themselves into such close proximity to death again. It was insanely dangerous but it was also the only way Remy knew that led to the airport.

"Come on. No one lives forever," Remy joked. William was not amused. Tractor trailers and pickup trucks and sedans barreled by honking, frequently coming close to careening into the duo at high speeds. Almost another hour passed by like that until through the bland landscape below and to the right a very special thing emerged: a long strip of lights at first so distant that Remy couldn't distinguish it from a stretch of neighborhood streetlamps. Landing strip lights. They had found it. He shouted in joy and howled wildly, raising his arms in celebration. William remained unamused. At the next opening, they crossed the guardrail and found their way down to the quiet streets below, Remy half-pulling William along to their destination.

Close and growing closer with each step. His vision became dazzling clear. The air smelled sweet and fresh. Hope rushed in unannounced.

"We're in the money!" he sang, "We're in the money! We've got a lot of what it takes to get along!" He glanced down to William who was tired but enjoying the mad human at his side. "Lighten up, furry one. We're here. I can sleep soon. In a faraway land where none of this routine bullshit is routine at all." They walked on. "I still have no idea what to do when we get there, though. I guess report the incident to a customs agent. Then they'll send us off to federal agents, I suppose. Or maybe we make our way to the United Nations where we make a formal statement and present proof. Or we just land in California and sleep on the side of the road without strange cars and stranger people pulling up and telling me to jump to my death. Any way this goes, it'll be better, my friend."

The good times were not to last, however. Remy's pace slowed as a painful realization crept up and began permeating his well-being. The roads were all but vacant. Only one van had passed them since they'd exited the interstate. The landscape consisted of vacant fields in preparation of rice season. A whole lot of nothing lay sprawled out before them. The airport, though distant, was in clear view and much smaller than expected. One long strip of parallel lights led to that building and the more Remy took it in, the more he realized just how short that strip was. He studied the airport as they approached. Though quite dark, he could not make out a single aircraft on the ground. He turned his attention to the sky and found no aircraft above either.

Reality sank its nasty claws into his chest. *This is not the international airport. This is a local airport. I won't find any passenger flights there, only pilots and their personal aircrafts which are unable to cross the Pacific Ocean.* He'd fought hard to reach a dead end at best.

His knees buckled and he collapsed hard onto the pavement, curling into a fetal position alongside the road as the realization solidified. He wept in the dirt, but not liking the feel of that much, he soon rose to his knees and wept knelt. In time he regained a bit of composure and crawled toward William.

"I'm sorry. I'm so sorry. But we have to turn around now. I don't know what else to do. I don't know..." He collapsed again, overwhelmed and straining to breathe. In response, William bit the nape of his neck sharply. Remy shot up and shoved William before he had much of a chance to brace himself. The hound fell to one side, surprised. "And what would you have us do? What do we do now?!"

William rose and shook himself from tail to nose in order to shed fur or perhaps to say, *I reject this.* He then began marching in the opposite direction they had come, southbound on vacant dark roads, leash trailing behind him regally. A need to keep him safe cut through the gloom. Unconsciously, Remy rose and soon caught up to William.

"I don't know much but I know I'd vote you in as president if I could. Are you old enough in dog-years to be president?" Remy did the math while he stood on legs that barely held his weight. "Nope. Need another year or two." A minute of silence as they marched on. "And you weren't born in America."

They didn't take the interstate back and as luck or something else would have it, a lone taxi came hurtling down the road within a half hour. Spying headlights, Remy walked into the middle of the road without thought or concern for his own safety. If the taxi had plowed him over, that would've been just fine. But the cab stopped and even offered a reasonable fare to return them back to Tianhe. It was almost as if the city had exhibited compassion, though the driver dropped them off a good half-mile from home while demanding full fare.

The hour was late, the streets deserted. He unclipped William from the leash and the hound trotted about happily, reinvigorated, jogging this way and that, sniffing rubbish piles and chasing the occasional rat, obviously pleased to leave such hardship behind. Remy shuffled forward, one foot and then the other, limping and too tired to think about much.

A sharp squeal of brakes cut through the stillness of the night. Remy pivoted in place to find William, maw open, panting, staring directly at a public bus that had stopped just a foot or so from plowing into him and ending his life in the middle of a once vacant road. He rushed over and clicked the leash onto his collar, dragging him to the safety of the sidewalk while the bus driver cursed loudly out of the window. Back home, they both guzzled water thirstily and would have fallen asleep immediately afterward if not for the dripping sounds and whirling helicopter noises. Remy rested his battered mind and body as best he could in the tumult, breathing deeply, slowly, relaxing and stretching worn muscles, contemplating alternative methods of escape.

CHAPTER XLI

CHINA

Dawn broke hours later and the city awoke, its citizens filling the sidewalks and streets. Just another perfectly ordinary day. Remy embraced the façade, spending most of the day recovering, nursing leg spasms and the like. William napped most of the day and was not eager to take a walk in the morning, rising only after much encouragement. Remy passed right by the same man who had ambushed him in the courtyard a month ago, brushing shoulders with the man in the lobby, wholly uncaring.

Where the courtyard met the apartment's parking lot, he spied a vehicle with its engine running parked, both front doors open wide, no owner in sight. An odd spectacle anywhere in the world. Odder still because just earlier that morning Remy had spoken aloud to William: "You know, I may have to just steal a car in order to leave this place. Hotwire a car and drive it to the airport as fast as possible, buy a ticket there and hope to depart before my actions catch up with me."

He approached cautiously, keeping a healthy distance of the vehicle while observing the perimeter. No sign of the owner. No one around at all, actually. *Why isn't anyone around? Guangzhou is teeming with pedestrians. This is definitely a trap. Why else would such an oddity materialize just after I mentioned it? The flat is bugged, or the microphone component to my cellphone's software has been overridden to allow outsiders to listen in. Or both. Probably both at this point.*

He declined the invitation and turned his attention back to escape, wondering absently if the international airport had ever existed to the north. Even if it did, he had no clue where specifically that might be. Engaging in another series of long walks to find its location filled him with dread. He began considering another type of long walk, this time southward until he reached the shoreline, then turning right, heading west and hugging the coast until he reached Macao, the closest foreign nation, although it wasn't all that foreign, having recently been officially returned to the Chinese government. So too with Hong Kong which was positioned not much farther away than Macao. *No,* he thought, *I would need to walk past Macao to Vietnam to ensure an escape. Six hundred miles or so hiking west along the coastline. Thirty miles a day, each day. One long walk after the other and twenty days later, Vietnam.* He turned his gaze to the napping hound across the room and wondered if William could hack it. Wondered if he could hack it. Wondered how much longer either of them could endure their current hardship if they stayed put.

I know where Vietnam is, far though it may be, but I just don't know about this airport anymore. I could spend a year and never stumble across it. Vietnam makes more sense. It's too large to remain hidden. It's the next step. But first let's give them a show to remember.

Beaten and worn and smiling, he was beginning to feel that he was walking on solid ground again as ideas of striking back solidified into working concepts. His mind raced mischievously and a cruel grin creased his mouth as he returned alone to the parking lot only to find normality where the bizarre had once been. He strolled about the spot where the vehicle had been parked searching for some sort of a clue -- a discernible footprint that might match what he had witnessed in the baby powder trap he had laid at his own front door, or a newly discarded cigarette butt, a familiar black sports car in the parking lot perhaps --- but ultimately finding nothing of interest, he returned to his flat. He was crossing the courtyard toward the lobby when two men approached suddenly from opposite sides, flanking him. They wore identical jackets, each holding something undisclosed and bulky in their right pockets. The courtyard almost entirely vacant as they approached rapidly, pressing in on their target. Remy pretended to not notice and opened the door for the arrivals, politely insisting they enter first. In response, they stood erect and unmoving, right hand firmly pocketed in large coats, waiting. Remy reluctantly entered the lobby and they fell about him, one on each shoulder. He made eye contact with the lobby guard in passing, a middle-aged man who was staring absently out of the window.

"Really, guard? This is totally okay with you?"

No response.

"Fantastic. Fine," Remy muttered to himself as he entered the lobby elevator, "Which floor? Oh wait, let me guess. Could it be the eighteenth? The flat above my own. I'm just going to press eighteen here." The elevator doors pinched shut, securing Remy and the two men as the chamber rose. "So, what's in the pocket?"

The men smiled arrogantly, silent and looming far too close for comfort.

"I said, what's in your pocket? Pistols? Or beating batons? I hope they're pistols. I could use a pair of those." He shifted and pivoted and faced the two men whose confident smiles were transforming into something else. Emboldened by the concept of his very life being threatened, Remy prodded one man's elbow, tugging sharply at the forearm and thus removing the hand from its pocket. Fully expecting a pistol to emerge, he kept himself behind the first man's line of fire using one of the two as a shield from the other and staying out of any direction that a barrel may be pointing from within a pocket. As the arm moved out of the coat pocket, something bright and spherical flashed into view. An orange. The other man mimicked the first, procuring another orange whereupon they fell to laughing.

"It's just a huge game to you all. My shin wound that has scarred. The debilitative cramps. The sleeplessness. Dear god, my penis, forever marred. I'm sexually disfigured now and it's all just a joke to you. You enjoy the suffering of others. You're evil. This is the very definition of evil." The elevator chimed and the doors opened. The men kept chuckling, loving the show. Remy exited, seething, wanting to murder both men with his bare hands but knowing he would never get away with it. He marched over to the door of the flat above his and banged long and hard on the finely wrought iron gate that protected a more tender front door. He paced furiously up and down the hallway and then returned to the gate, banging again, yanking violently, rocking the doorframe as a gorilla trying to escape its confinement, trying to loosen something vital in the foundation. Nothing shook loose. The gate remained impenetrable.

"Fine. I'll just wait here then. You have to come out sometime."

He sat in the hallway and waited, fury cooling only slightly as one hour passed into the second. A couple returning to their flat walked down the corridor to their own flat further own the hall, trying not to stare at the foreigner as they passed. A middle-aged gentleman exited another flat sometime later, walking as far around Remy as possible in the process. He showed obvious concern for his own safety.

"Yeah, that's not good. I'm not the bad guy in this scenario, but they don't know the difference, do they?" He rose on stiff legs. "Alright. I'll return to an apartment that is bugged and denies me sleep. Coming up on two months now. I slept once in all of that. One time. And I'm sure I won't sleep tonight. I don't strike first but I've never wanted to break that rule more than I do right now. I took an oath to never throw the first blow and it shall be kept. I took an oath to only speak truth, to never lie, and I mean to keep that, too. This story shall be told, you little shit hiding behind a gate. The world will know what happened here. Someday."

Later at the wide, sliding kitchen window overlooking Guangzhou, he schemed resistance.

CHAPTER XLII

CHINA

Remy began searching the inner workings of the machinery of the devices in his flat, looking for anything out of the ordinary, some technical component that looked newer than the others. Anything suspicious would do. A component newer than the rest. A piece of hardware with a flashing light or an antenna.

Using a variety of screwdrivers purchased earlier, he disassembled everything in his flat. The rice cooker, television, Xbox system and accompanying joysticks, lamps, the DVD player, remote controls. He removed the plates covering each electrical outlet and shone a flashlight inside the walls before taking apart the flashlight itself. The blender, speakers, toaster, modem. He scrutinized the dimensions of each piece of furniture intently, establishing no room for false compartments, removing drawers and shelves as he searched. He carefully felt every inch of fabric from curtains to linens to the clothes he wore. He wrapped his knuckles against each wall, listening for unusual hollow places.

The refrigerator proved a tremendous challenge. There seemed plenty of room to place a bug in the bundle of parts underneath and along the back of fridge. He poked around a bit, returned the grate to the frame and contented himself with simply unplugging the machine, hoping this would trigger some response, or more hopefully, somehow end the ability of sound to pour down on him wherever and whenever he tried to sleep.

All day and night and into the next morning he toiled, finally resting on the sofa, a massive pile of equipment to the side, most of it reassembled into a functional state though one of the speakers was destroyed in the process and the toaster lever needed to be shoved down with quite some force in order for the locking mechanism to hold. The home had been scoured and nothing resembling a microphone had been found.

When the sound of a landing helicopter swam overhead, he growled and moved to the kitchen floor near the window where the noises dimmed, his mind whirling with possibility. *Nothing much left,* he pondered, *there's the sofa, I suppose, but I don't feel right gutting that thing. It's not mine and I wouldn't be able to put it back together as I have the rest of this stuff.* His breathing slowed as he relaxed into the notion that he had done all he could. The listening and tracking device either came from the phone and/or laptop with or without a battery and/or SIM chip or there was a distant microphone pointed his way. Either option was beyond his ability to alter, just as he was powerless to prevent the audio torture from depriving him of sleep. He smiled softly, laid down on the kitchen floor and curled up into a ball, the linoleum feeling just as soft as silk. Within moments, his breathing turned to snoring, triggering the sound of loud drops of water echoing directly overhead, rousing him just before sleep manifested.

He rose and plugged the fridge back into the wall triggering the machine to hum back to life. William jogged up to examine what the commotion was, snorted derisively, and left the room to return to his floor pillow, leaving Remy where he had found him, staring directly at the ceiling above. *Just beyond that ceiling, that's where all the evil emanates. It's a thin divide, really. Sound waves pass right through. Just that floor and my ceiling. Unless,* Remy sprung to his feet, *it's not coming from the flat above at all but rather from within my own ceiling.* He leapt up, nudging the rectangle boards that intersected the ceiling ajar, revealing a hollow space above.

He jogged over to the next room, pulled the dining room table over into the kitchen and climbed atop. He removed several boards from the kitchen ceiling, found a handhold and pulled his head into the half-meter space above the ceiling panels. Various cords came in from the walls and from the flooring above, snaking a path across the hollow space between kitchen ceiling and floor above. Wires of various colors and widths and groupings crisscrossed their way through the dark space. The area was equally dust encrusted, dark and powdery. No clean spots existed to mark that something had been introduced recently.

There were many more wires up there than Remy thought necessary. Some led to an overhead lamp, some to outlets in the kitchen. One bulky set led to the AC unit. And some wires he just couldn't place at all which was unsettling but a far cry from proof a listening device or a malevolent speaker system. He had done all he could do. All signs pointed to the microphone function of his laptop and/or mobile phone coupled with some sort of an override of the GPS function that he'd turned off within the first week of sleeplessness and a speaker system aimed at him from above. *Who will believe such a thing? This is the stuff of madness.*

He rested and then set about returning things to their basic order throughout the home. By the time the sun began dipping into the horizon, the apartment had been returned to its original state. He inserted a disc labeled *Casablanca* into the DVD player and relaxed with the masterpiece. When it was over, he pressed play on the remote control to restart the film and swiftly changed into dark, loose-fitting athletic clothing. He left his phone, laptop, and emergency backpack behind and tiptoed out of the house so quietly that not even William heard him leave.

Project Mischief was underway.

CHAPTER XLIII

USA

I tell myself a hundred different things.

King of the jungle. The star of the show. Cleverest of foxes.

Low and depressed, beat down, worn thin.

A wolf without a pack, alone and unrelatable. Keeping Guangzhou a secret. Bury it deep. Never share that part of your past. Hide, little turtle. Hide.

I'm not still in love with her. It's been seven years but I'll be okay. I'll find a woman with similar interests and settle down, a family of my own, a child to love and raise strong. Spirit as light as any songbird.

*But if it hasn't happened in seven years it probably won't happen at all. Not this year. Not the next. It won't ever f^%*ing happen. Get that through your thick head.*

Poisoned twice. All signs point to intentional poisoning. Doesn't happen to most people. Once in China and again years later on a bus trip from Thailand to Laos for a visa renewal. Not malaria. Not food poisoning. Not dengue fever. No one I have ever spoken with who dealt with those afflictions were unable to drink water. No one was so parched, so deliriously thirsty -- wanting nothing more than water, crazy for the stuff -- but upon taking a tiny sip, violently expelling it. Throat almost swollen shut due to the strain. Bloody vomit. A fountain of mucus and saliva. Hours of that. Drowning in the stuff while dehydrating to death. Ironic. But through a kindly soul who nursed me back to health in a small town along a bus route in Thailand, I survived. Some herbal cocktail poured down my semi-conscious throat from a pharmacist awakened in the middle of the night and here I am, alive. Intentionally poisoned but this badger lives to tell the tale.

I'll eventually pull myself up by my bootstraps and get out of this quagmire. I'll sell the book and buy a home of my own, provide for a retirement. Planning ahead. A wise, old owl.

What if I'd remained in the states the entire time? Never left to teach abroad. Would I fit in now? Would I belong? Just another sheep in the flock.

There's a place for me here in America. One day things will be better. Somehow. Someway.

Yes, I tell myself a hundred lies and I believe them all for they come from an honest man.

CHAPTER XLIV

CHINA

He wasn't carrying much: his front door key, the keycard to reenter the lobby, superglue, and a lighter. After weeks of hauling a backpack filled with necessities around the city, he felt like he was springing off of clouds as he walked down the hallway following a trail of wiring that led from the wireless router bolted near his apartment door along the upper edge of the hallway to a plain metal door adjacent to the elevators upon which a sign was posted in Mandarin that warned of electrical danger. There he emptied half of the superglue into both the deadlock and the doorknob keyholes. He then bounded up the stairs and squeezed most of the remaining superglue into a similar looking door directly above that one.

He had changed the properties of his online connection many times as the sleep-deprivation continued and his situation deteriorated and each time whatever he altered returned to its original form within an hour. He was halfway certain that a human in charge of the network was manually overriding his changes, preventing any lasting effect, and that denying said person access to the control room where the router wires led may help him access unfiltered, unredirected internet. The other half of him simply enjoyed lashing out against the place that had tortured him for nine weeks. He toyed with the idea of gumming up the locks of the flat directly above his own, but that would have been only raw vengeance and Remy was above such things, beaten and torn though he was.

He took the stairs downward, light of heart and quiet of step. As the stairwell door shut behind him, he began applying a thin coat of super glue to each of his fingertips and thumb, careful to spread his finger wide as the glue dried. Six flights later, the glue bottle empty, he removed a lighter and set fire to the bottle, so as to remove any fingerprints. Once thoroughly ablaze, he dropped it and stood by while the fire consumed the bottle and extinguished itself before exiting the stairwell and taking the elevator the rest of the way down. There would be no evidence to link him to what would come. He was in business mode and not to be trifled with and he loved it.

The elevator doors slid open, revealing the same lackadaisical guard who had failed to intervene during the incident with the two flanking strangers. "Hey, there f^#*face. How's it going? Busy staring at the wall like a moron, I see. Cool. See you around." And Remy was out of the door, hungry for action.

The city could not have been any more deserted. It was as if the citizens of Guangzhou had mysteriously vanished in the night due to an alien abduction. He took a deep breath and for the first time in quite a while, he didn't feel like a victim. Quite the opposite, in fact. He was so energized that he began to run, not jog, but fully run to his destination. Street corners and intersections came into view and faded behind him. A quiet night. Even the late-night snack food shops had closed down, shutters drawn and fastened shut.

As the blocks rolled by, he felt renewed, reenergized. The pressure of mounting failures and unachievable escapes, threats to self and family, pain in all its forms, simply did not exist then. It was as if he had already died and was haunting those streets as a specter, so light was the burden of life at that point. To hurt, to live, to die, to run, to breathe, to blink all melded into one. Somehow the city knew this for there was no one on those sidewalks, nor cars on the roads.

There was a guard at the gate though, the only person Remy had seen since exiting his own complex which was in and of itself particularly strange. There were always stragglers walking the sidewalks at any hour. But not that hour. The guard rose, a grim demeanor on his face. Remy slowed to a trot, in full beast mode. No smile.

"You," he pointed sternly at the rising guard, "Back. Sit down. Back!"

The grim demeanor turned to something more yielding, confused and semi-compliant. The man halted his approach and Remy took the opportunity to leap upon the massive locked gate, scaling the long vertical bars up an over the perimeter. He searched the surroundings for any trouble and finding none sprinted off to his target: the foreign teachers office.

It didn't shock him to find the school grounds completely uninhabited, though he had been somewhat expecting the foreign teacher's office's top floor to be awash in light and revelry again. He assumed the director of the school lived up there as he had jogged by while exercising from time to time and had found the normal signs of human occupation: people chatting, the smell of dinner cooking, shadows that moved behind curtained windows. But like the streets, all was silent there, too.

He tried every door along the outskirts of the building, violently yanking the handles in an effort to dislodge a locking mechanism. Failing that, he inserted the lobby keycard between door and frame in order to work free a deadbolt. That too failed. He gave thought to smashing through glass in order to enter but did not like the idea of destroying property. No entryway presented itself. Resigned to the fact that an in-person declaration would not be possible that night, he took several steps back and hollered to the top floor.

"Hear me now and know this: I'm not taking it anymore! I'm striking back now, get it?! This city, this cold, dead city, this poison that you are. You cower in the shadows now. A thousand against one. Here I am and there you all are, cowering in the shadows. No more games. No more threats. No more words. You hear me?! No more words!"

He ran to the far gate and scaled over it, landing in the midst of two expectant guards. They immediately began closing in, speaking sharply in Mandarin. Remy moved forward toward the weaker of the pair menacingly, feinted and cut around them both and then onward, running down streets and alleyways, turning and doubling back, making a trail that would prove hard for any bloodhound to follow let alone a human, much as the first taxi driver that had taken him from airport to apartment had done. Eventually he threaded his way through Tianhe to return to his miserable apartment. He took the elevator up, changed clothes, and adopted a calm persona. Project Mischief was complete.

He lied down to sleep and as soon as the sound of a helicopter landing overhead began looping, he shot up and ran upstairs to the apartment directly above his own, shoved a screwdriver into the iron gate's keyhole, jabbing and stabbing repeatedly, gouging and twisting and ruining the mechanics therein. He walked away slowly, all swagger, daring anyone to intervene. No one did. Back home, the looped helicopter audio assault was swapped out for constant water drips, and Remy immediately shot up from this, too, this time climbing out of the window, perched solely on a thin ledge barely wide enough for toes to find purchase. He shuffled along the ledge, two hundred feet of plummeting below, removed a large kitchen knife from his waistline, and thoroughly sliced through the freon tubing of the AC unit to his apartment, a tubing system that connected to each AC unit in the complex. By the time Remy climb had returned to his kitchen window, the entire side of the skyscraper was immersed in a cloud of freon that soon grew in size until it encapsulated the entire building in a dense fog.

He left the kitchen window open wide. Thinking back to the initial presence along the ledge in the final days of Monica's visit, he poured a little milk into a saucer. "Here you are, you pussies. Here, you pussycats. Here's some milk for you." He slammed the plate of milk down on the kitchen counter, splashing the contents. "All you have to do is take it."

There were no challengers. Hours after dawn, he strolled down to purchase an overpriced breakfast from the recently transitioned ma-pa shop: hard-boiled eggs soaked in soy sauce atop steamed rice. As he turned to leave his attention wavered to a television in the back of the shop. The local news station was on, broadcasters speaking formally. A familiar image flashed of the school where Remy worked, and then another shot, a short video clip of Remy's hooded form disappearing over the top of the main gate of the school.

"Oh, shit. That's me. I mean, he. That's the guy who did it," Remy rambled, though there were few people around to hear him and no one who spoke English. Feeling guilty, he whistled the most suspicious of tunes as he exited the shop and hurriedly returned to his flat.

CHAPTER XLV

CHINA

He was thoroughly and constantly exhausted, unable to think clearly and consistently enough to plan. *South. Walk south until the ocean, turn right, and walk until Vietnam.* He repeated this mantra internally throughout the day and night, careful not to say it aloud thereby alerting his torturers to his plan. It was all he could do to remember those simple words. Dreams stole upon him in the blink of an eye and were washed away just as swiftly by another wave of audio assault. Simple chores around the house required the utmost of concentration.

He had broken down what would come to be into two camps: A) he would be arrested and sent back through legal channels to the United States, or B) he would begin the long walk to Vietnam. Because William had the potential to get lost in the shuffle of A, Remy focused on B. But before leaving, there was one last thing to do. He donned his finest suit and tie and replaced the emergency backpack with a nice over-the shoulder laptop bag. He grabbed the leash from the wall and after the normal relieving of doggy biological needs, man and hound continued on to the school that was more than a school. The gate that he had scaled two nights prior was open wide. Remy smiled to the doorman, gave a nod, and passed through.

It was a brisk mid-December morning. The majority of students had long since returned to their respective homes leaving the school-grounds almost entirely vacant. Remy unleashed William as they crossed the threshold of the gate and the hound took the opportunity to dash about, sniffing everything he could get his nose into. He reveled in the freedom, catching scents and following trails that led to nothing and then dashing off again to sniff something else. It was William at his happiest.

A few students of various ages walked about the campus chatting pleasantly with themselves, children of teachers who had come to school in order to prepare upcoming lessons. He bounded right over wearing a wolfish grin, tongue lolling. The students immediately took to him and began cooing over who would pet him next. Nearby, apprehension showed plainly on the faces of a few adults overseeing the activities.

Remy's heart was full of pain. Hatred and fear and suffering had coalesced into something quite unpleasant. Guangzhou as a whole had done him wrong. Very wrong. But something softened in the man as he took in the scene. The kids knew Will to be safe and friendly. It caught Remy off guard, the students love of the hound, their purity and fearlessness.

"Truth be told, I kinda hate and love the fact that you aren't afraid of him. I wasn't expecting to leave this place with any positive memories. Sort of gives me hope for the future, not that you have any idea what I am talking about right now."

"He is big dog. Very big. What do he eat? Do he eat people?" one of the students asked, laughing at his own joke and running off before Remy could come up with an answer. William took off in playful pursuit easily catching up with him, running circles around him, yipping happily: *I am the fastest, not you.*

"Oh, for crying out loud. I didn't want you to like him. I didn't bring him here untethered thinking we would be warmly received. He was supposed to be unfairly attacked so I could defend him." Remy said, half to himself, half to the small group of merry teenagers playing tag with William. "Seriously, though. Do you not know what goes on in this place? They've threatened me and my family. Tortured me with sleep."

"I no understand. What is torture?"

"Oh, kid. I'm not going to teach you that one. I hope you never learn it."

Remy whistled a long, whirling tune and William came bounding up whereupon he was fastened to a leash again. "Sorry, my friend. We have somewhere else to be."

William's attention remained focused on the congregation of youths who waved to William and Remy as they walked away, though more to the hound than the man. Remy waved back politely.

"A more humanizing event could not have transpired and it's all your fault, dingo."

He smiled and gave William a playful shove, caught off guard when he responded by charging right through Remy, bowling him over as he ran past. The Shepherd dashed back to his teenage fan club running around them, in and out, chasing and being chased, his leash streaming behind. Remy sat up on the ground and simply absorbed the spectacle.

"How can your children be this, and you be that?" Remy asked aloud, knowing no answer would come. "I would kill or die to protect what I'm seeing right now." He stood and brushed himself off. "It doesn't make much sense, China." He whistled again but William refused to tear himself away from the action, in no hurry to be tethered again. Remy raised his voice, shouting through the din, "William! Now!" The children slowed to a stop. William gave a last juke and then sprinted pell-mell into Remy's grasp where he was leashed again.

As the elevator doors slid shut in the foreign teacher office, Remy unleashed the hound. They stood side by side while the chamber ascended -- William overjoyed with the day so far, Remy more cheerful than he had been since the torture began. The elevator doors slid open and the duo walked together in unison to his desk where William curled up at his feet as if they were home.

He worked in silence on the second semester's lesson plans. Quizzes and projects, worksheets and charts, brainstorming new ideas and flushing out details of prior ones. Normal teacher prep work though he knew undoubtedly that whatever happened next, he wouldn't be implementing any of it. He typed up instructions for implementation, printed them, and placed them atop his desk adorned with a sticky note that read *Use Me*, hoping that the next teacher, whoever and whenever that may be, would follow through. He thought of his brother's address displayed on a screen, shown to him as a threat from one of Patrick's teacher/thugs. Of the student that expected him to single-handedly compose his university introduction letter and lie in the process. How the files he'd worked hard to isolate and save as proof of hacking from his home had been erased right from the very same desk. *This is an evil place*, he thought. *It should be burned down to ash. Why am I leaving behind solid lesson plans and teaching notes?*

"None of this makes any sense," Remy spoke aloud to the empty office. "But these lesson plans are gold and should be used." He tilted back in his chair and interlaced his fingers behind his head. William was a hot ball of fur on his feet. He closed his eyes. His breathing slowed and grew deeper. The beginnings of dream whirled about and began congealing, and then he was jolted awake to the sound of the glass door shutting. In walked a Chinese teacher, doing a terrible job of pretending to not be solely focused on Remy.

"You just won't let me sleep."

"Excuse me?"

"If I must, and it would seem I must."

He closed his eyes again hoping the intruder would leave but he remained, clacking away on his keyboard for no reason whatsoever and staring, making sleep impossible yet again. He sighed in stoic acceptance, stood, and walked toward the exit. William rose, shook himself, and followed. The man blanched.

"You need rope for dog."

"I need rope for you. He's not the one that should be contained. He's fine."

With that, Remy exited and returned to his apartment to suffer.

CHAPTER XLVI

CHINA

The air-conditioner -- used more to heat the home in early winter than to cool it -- wheezed tepid air through its open vents. It rattled and moaned and accomplished little, reminding him of his own limited progress since the banking theft in Nanchang had set him on his present course.

He shut off the machine and returned to the kitchen window to look out over the city. His mind drifted away from the skyline as his mind turned inward, anticipating how far he would be trailed during the journey to Vietnam, what his pursuers may do to prevent sleep as he bedded down on streets and pockets of undeveloped land each night. Each day hiking roughly twenty miles westward. He gave consideration to the idea of needing to defend himself from an organized combined attack by a mob. Of the many varied possibilities of how that could go down. Like a cat grown tired of a wounded rat, perhaps his torturers were growing weary of the game and would move to end his life. The thought of dying did not bother him for death offered an escape to sleep-deprivation. Surpassing his own selfish desire to rest one way or another, his thoughts turned to protecting the hound. He analyzed many possible scenarios, each with layers of potential responses, divergences and statistical probabilities echoing and spreading like webbing throughout an overworked mind.

She called later that night.

"Well, well. Look what the cat dragged in," he began.

"Me? A cat?" she replied. "You leave gift for cat, yes?"

Remy thought back to the plate of milk, of furiously shoving the window open wide on a crisp, cool night, hungry for action that never came. Somehow, she had known that. He had scoured the place for cameras and microphones and found nothing. Yet, there it was, all the proof you needed in one short, broken, rhetorical, pompous English question. Not exactly court-worthy evidence, however. And she knew it. She pressed on with an audible smile.

"Cat. You cat? I cat," stating the last part with finality. "You feel mouse?"

"Yeah, I was just thinking about that." He didn't like where the conversation was headed and changed the subject, shaking off cold tendrils that had begun wrapping about his heart. "I'm leaving soon."

"You always leaving."

"Oh, one of these days, Alice. Biff. Bam! To the moon!"

"Who Alice? You have other girlfriend? Maybe she help you."

She was honestly confused about the Alice reference, her tone shifting from gleeful confidence to quelled anger. Emboldened, he responded swiftly, using the opening to shift the conversation into a more positive light.

"There is only you, love. Only you. A cat, you say. But that isn't exactly it. You're a tiny piece of a cat. A whisker or two. Half a twitchy tail. One person couldn't do this to me. It's taken scores, if not a hundred." He thought back to the trains, to the pursuers on the long walks, the taxi companies, the cellphone shopkeeper, the sleep-deprivers. "Hundreds, maybe." Remy smiled wide. "You're just a fraction of a cat. And I am one whole mouse. Not so bad when you think about it."

They shared a silence, as they had many times before, feeling each other through the silence.

"I wish I wasn't so connected to you, Monica Hu. I wish I didn't love you like I do. It would be nice if I had a say in who I love."

More silence.

"I really am leaving soon. I can't not sleep anymore. My mind is so starved of dream that it begins finding it in any darkness. Even a long enough blink brings immediate dream: hallucinations manifesting, whirling about, dissipating in the flash of an eye. Sleep has been made impossible, but honestly, these days lowering my guard and falling asleep would be reckless. It's terrifying to live this way, which makes you lot terrorists, don't you think? Creators of terror. Terrorists."

"I don't think," she responded in double-speak, meaning *I don't agree*, and also, *I choose not to think about it.*

"I know, snugglebunny. I know. That's your problem. I'm not even sure you know how to think."

"You think too much. Alway have."

"No such thing."

The silence that followed hung like thick fog, separating them in a way silence never had before. His eyes misted.

"I hate that I love you."

He could hear her voice weaken, catch on words and break softly like waves on a sandy beach. "You should have better. You find someone. Someone make you happy."

"Sounds pretty easy. I'll just go and do that then. Fall in love with a nice girl who likes balloon animals, long walks on the beach, and is super into yoga. Do you honestly think I'll love again? I've tasted the forbidden fruit and my happiness is forfeit. How could any woman

I will ever meet understand this? I am screwed right and proper even if I survive this mess, which I may very well not. I'm prepared to die. Literally prepared for death. Looking forward to the rest it would bring, actually. That should f^%*ing scare you and yours. I'm sort of hoping for it at this point, actually."

She spoke again but her voice cut out and became choppy as voices had been distorted when he mentioned uncomfortable realities of living in Guangzhou with his mother.

"You have to say it again, Moni. I couldn't hear you."

"I say, forget.... Go and be....I not... just....." There was nothing more. He growled angrily into a phone line that showed the call continuing, the seconds ticking by. He held the line open for three long minutes hoping for her return until he finally surrendered and ended the call. He sank to the linoleum of the kitchen floor and wept quietly. "It would be so much easier," he gasped, needing to voice the thought, "if she didn't have a soul tucked away in there."

It was some time before he was able to compose himself. He wiped tired eyes with the back of his hand with the finality of one who hates that he continues to cry. He stood on shaky legs and returned to the window, a makeshift stage, a soapbox of sorts. Throwing the window open wide, he took in all of the city. From distant landmarks barely visible to the pedestrians and motorists near and far. To the microphones and cameras that must exist somewhere and yet remained undiscovered.

"I am leaving! And woe, woe, to you who gets in my way. I walk south, and then west, and if anyone interrupts my sleep along the way, I will kill you or die in the process. If you try something cute, to distract me and lead me away from my path, oranges in pockets for example, I will murder you. Savagely." He wasn't boasting or proud. He wasn't pumping himself up for what may occur later. The words didn't empower him nor was he ashamed. He didn't wonder if he was being taken seriously. He didn't care about any of that. He simply wanted to issue a fair warning.

He could feel a shift through the floor, the walls, through the open window, and even through the ceiling.

"Two things," he commanded to a city that loathed him. "One, if I fall, take care of this dog. You know him to be pure and good. Tend to him if I cannot."

"And two, and this one is because I hate you, I mean like down to my bones hate you. You see, the woman I love, the woman you've used as a weapon against me, a woman I cannot rescue from the evil that is you. She called me just now to gloat that she was in charge and to verify that I was a fearful victim. That was the purpose of her phone call. She compared me to a mouse. To a rat. Now a rat in twenties slang was anyone who snitched, or in proper terms, reported the truth about a crime that had occurred. Oh, and I will do exactly that. This story will be told as long as I have breath in my body. Maybe I'll die before I get to my destination. But I think my death would arouse unwanted foreign attention to this scene. A dead American would bring serious foreign professionals in with clearance to investigate. That's probably why you haven't tried already. I registered the incident with Interpol and if I end up murdered, well, that would sort of solidify my claim now, wouldn't it?"

"Of course," he continued, "It wouldn't be too complicated to stage a suicide. Not so farfetched at this point." He paused midspeech, absorbing this revelation. "I do want to die now anyway. It would be so nice to not be awake. Sort of a win-win situation though when one's own death is part of a win-win, it's tough to call that a real win. I suppose you could just attack me. Beat me with batons again. And maybe you will. I care very little. Come, if you will come. Here I am. I'm as prepared as I can be, but I digress." He took a breath and steadied himself. "You called me a rat, China, and that might be true. It reminds me of one of the finer American poets. A man who survived horrors, as well. Poe. Edgar Allen Poe. He wrote once, '*If a rat to madness tease, why even a rat will plague you.*'"

"I am that rat," he spoke to neither William nor himself, knowing he was heard nonetheless.

CHAPTER XLVII

CHINA

He hiked south, shouldering a bag he couldn't trust to remain unmolested without constant supervision. He had become so accustomed to the heft slung over his shoulders that he felt as if he was missing an article of clothing without it, even during minor tasks such as checking the mailbox or grabbing a meal. Southward for hours before cutting right. Then westward for hours. Congested urban sprawl transformed into Chinese suburbia: live chickens strutting about on littered sidewalks, wild dogs patrolling deserted lots, rundown sidewalk shops filled with the working class. Broken glass regularly speckling the sidewalks and streets reflected light through variously sized shards. *Odds are good William will injure his paws within the first week. Maybe the first day. Not good.* Wild mutts barked ferociously as Remy passed, quickly losing their bravado and fleeing when he turned his attention to them. He wasn't sure how William would respond to such rude challenges and didn't look forward to assisting him with every aggressive mongrel that crossed their path. Having come across two small packs in the four-hour venture southwest and extrapolating that over a month-long journey, he was dismayed by the expected upcoming frequency.

Plodding down miles of sidewalks, thinking. *So, it may take two months, not one. Not ideal, but doable. If my Chinese bank account actually holds the amount shown via online banking and no one robs me again, I will be able to provide food and water for the both of us during the next two months, though this is the same internet that displays vastly differing maps of Guangzhou each time I search for a clear path out of here. If my bank account holds up, I should be able to afford the journey to Vietnam and be able to purchase a ticket for William and I to return to the states from within her borders afterward. Nothing left after that but what does that matter?*

His mind drifted to a potential future in which his story was broadcasted over the airways during primetime television. There was a United Nations briefing in which he gave testimony of what had transpired. *How could this not be international news? How could this incident not reshape international relations? Surely, the world will want to know what has happened here these past months. The story is far more intriguing than anything I've ever read in the papers or watched on television.*

There was a time that William had broken toes of his front paw as a rambunctious teenage pup in Nanchang and needed to be carried, slung over Remy's shoulder like a wounded soldier, up and down four flights of stairs in order for the hound to release his bowels and bladder each day. That had happened for weeks, almost a full month. It had been incredibly burdensome but he had endured the weight, and William the indecency, twice each day. In time the hound had healed and life had returned to normal.

So too with this. This suffering will end. The journey will be arduous and long but we will cross the Vietnamese-Chinese border, legally or not, and we will find a way back to America. Beyond exhausted, almost certainly injured, but this thing will happen. Focus on that fi-

nality each day until you reach America. Know that you may be denied access to your own bank account as soon as this begins. We might need to walk in hunger, eating from trash bins, drinking water from unclean sources. Stealing to survive. Fending off attacks. Infected by something along the way, medicine unavailable. Many possibilities stretched out before him, all of them gruesome.

A deep stoicism had taken root by the time he returned to the flat. William, vigorous as always upon Remy's return, faltered in his step as he bounded to the front door to greet him, perplexed by the change. This man was distant. Detached. He trudged passed the quizzical hound, bathed, and plopped down on the bed utterly exhausted whereupon he was immediately assailed by blaring noises from above. No growls of anger. No cursing the neighbor above. No moaning in despair. For the first time, he accepted the sleeplessness from a far-away place deep within.

CHAPTER XLVIII

CHINA

He came to the next morning in no rush for what was to come. It was to be the last night spent sleeping on a mattress so when dawn cut through the darkness, he delayed acknowledging its arrival and savored the cushiony goodness. Around noon he rose with a heavy heart and began preparing. The plan was to walk the dog, eat lunch, and begin the long trek south, hopefully reaching the coastline before dawn.

They exited the lobby, entered the courtyard and were immediately accosted by a mighty thundering from above. It was as if construction work was being done in the clouds. A deep drone emanated from amid the white clouds above. Focusing his attention upward to the source, he was shocked to witness five helicopters in a V formation, like geese migrating, navigating through the sky slightly above the skyscrapers that defined Tianhe district. A slow, unnerving realization that this was a military operation washed over him. William couldn't have cared less, plodding on toward his usual bathroom spot wholly uninterested in the activity above. The roving helicopters continued a wide loop centered on Remy's towering apartment building. Beyond the steady chopping of the powerful helicopter rotors, the roar of fighter jets pierced the scene. It felt like war, like vast bloodshed soon to come.

He had attended airshows both in America and in Japan. Proud pilots showing off their capabilities. A celebration of aircraft skills. Maneuvers done in designated areas with spectators cheering them on. What he was witnessing was no airshow. There was real tension in the air, a pressure more pronounced than any upcoming thunderstorm.

The SOS flashings into the night sky and the failed ventures toward the airport, while seemingly hopeless endeavors, have actually triggered a rescue? Such a thought was too optimistic to consider, and yet, the choppers above were definitely making a tight circle around Remy, close enough that he could see pilots in cockpits as William evacuated his bowels in an unused corner of the courtyard. Chinese pilots and Chinese aircraft. No doubt about that. The situation surreal.

The roaring of nearby jets in the distance was unignorable. A culmination of multiple jet engines piggy-bagging atop one another as they appeared to approach and veer away accented the continual chopping of air by the helicopters above. There was a feeling in the air, an energy difficult to put into words, that signified that the helicopters and jets were opposed to one another.

The new ingredient of military-grade aircraft on opposing sides of an imminent aerial conflict filled Remy with dread. He hated how he had been tortured mercilessly over the past two months -- sleeplessness, flash mobs, home invasions, internet manipulation, violence, maiming -- and hungered for a permanent ending to such things but when it came right down to it that cloudy day, he was mostly filled with concern for the families of soldiers on both sides, the potential of lives lost.

A plethora of emotions churned within him. He longed for freedom from his tormentors and sought assurance that the actions he had endured would never occur again to anyone else. A need for justice prevailing and the wicked laid low. To sleep unmolested. He needed these things to happen. Vowed it would be so. Yet there he stood, staring into the busy sky, uneasy with the concept of human lives paying the cost. The world weighed heavily on his shoulders as the helicopters rounded about again in formation, the sound of diving jets in the distance.

The sound of jets rushed downward from behind the cloud-filled sky as helicopters marched about the perimeter, all seemingly centered on Remy and William. The streets and sidewalks were deserted, however, many worried faces peered out at the sky from darkened windows. Across the road, a huge white sheet waved in the wind from an open window on the top floor. The parking lot of the apartment complex was strangely void of cars save for one. The principal of the school, Daniel Zhou, and vice-principal Sheldon Smith, stood alongside the vehicle. *Just like that day with the car running and the doors open wide*, Remy mused. *No one around for a hundred meters. Maybe even the same car, actually.* He turned and faced them, locking eyes.

"What do you think of the airshow?!" the principal called out.

"F*^$ you. That's not an airshow. I've seen airshows. This ain't that."

"They've been preparing for months. You must've heard it. Quite the show, don't you think?"

"First of all, I'm not going to discuss what I've heard or not heard with you at all. Secondly, no. I've never heard fighter jets come screaming in, plunging down and flying up and off only to hear the same dreadful noise again a minute later. Never witnessed a formation of helicopters patrol around me. Never seen someone fly a white sheet out of their window, either. It feels like war out here. Like the edge of battle. Like a wave, cresting and falling upon itself as it approaches the shore. That sky is hostile. You know it and you won't say it but there's something serious going on up there above our heads."

Zhou said nothing, smiling foolishly.

"You're vile and wicked men but not fools. Stop smiling like an idiot and engage in the truth, alien though such a concept that must be for you. Put your pride aside and think about people dying."

The principal's smile held fast. "I don't know what you mean. I'm here to inform you that your services are no longer needed. We've terminated the teaching contract. This van will take you to the airport." He motioned with an outstretched hand to a minivan parked curbside in the distance. "We wish you the best, but you've been acting strange and ---"

"Spare me. I'd prefer that we both die in a fiery explosion than listen to your lying mouth." Remy smiled then, free with his words. "You act in cowardice as you've always acted. It was cowardly to gang up on one man and it is likely only in cowardice that you allow me access to the airport. Cowardly to lie about an air show, too, while we're at it. You're trying to tell me that a helicopter was attempting to land atop my apartment for the past two months and that's why I couldn't sleep. Practicing for an air show? Doesn't explain the waterdrops or the sound of a man urinating into a toilet bowl amplified at all hours each night and day. Doesn't explain the intervals, just as I'm about to sleep. Doesn't explain why I never witnessed that helicopter of yours even though I've spent quite a lot of time on that roof examining the sky. Doesn't explain public transportation denying me access to the airport."

Spent, he disengaged and began returning to the apartment.

"If that van is still there when I come back down, I'll enter and just see where it takes me. I have a feeling that today it won't drive around in circles and pretend to misunderstand me and go anywhere but the airport. You have no idea how lowly I think of you. You can't fathom such a depth. Or much of a height, the more that I think about the lot of you."

The principal of the school that was more than a school said nothing, his smile cold and unwavering. Sheldon, too, had nothing to add to the proceedings. It didn't take Remy very long to pack a suitcase as all of the vitals were already in his backpack, ready to go. The rumbling of helicopters and jets pressed through the closed windows of the apartment, leaving him with the distinct feeling that the cavalry had actually arrived. *I'm still not exactly sure what's going on out there but that air show explanation is about as bogus as it gets,* he thought, gazing across the city skyline for the last time. He didn't engage in an elaborate goodbye to the apartment that had proved itself to be listening. Instead, he found a sheet of paper and a pen and wrote a single sentence which he placed atop the coffee table. It read: *If a rat to madness tease, why even a rat will plague you.* When reaching the lobby downstairs, the security guards stopped him, requiring he return the key to his apartment and the plastic card that demagnetized the locks of the lobby door. "Sure," Remy mumbled. "Whatever. Just get me out of this place."

He opened the minivan door and ushered in a fully-packed suitcase along with William and his kennel, his backpack within arm's reach at all times. The sound of helicopter blades spinning in earnest and the distant roar of jets was all but muted as the back door slid shut. Without a word, the driver sped off and for the first time Remy felt he was actually airport bound. Within ten minutes the vehicle had entered an interstate heading north, a simple act just as surreal as the aerial conflict above.

CHAPTER XLIX

CHINA

He seems to be in a good mood. Strange given the circumstances. Remy returned his attention to the backseat window. The highway was all but vacant. Only a smattering of vehicles along the way. A handful at most. A stiff stillness of spirit blanketed the circumstances. A tense tranquility that threatened to turn to something much worse very soon. Something akin to when gunfire on both sides of a battleline diminishes into silence. Something completely unrelatable to most people. The passengers of the van barreled down the interstate wordlessly. Ten minutes ticked by with only three vehicles in either direction along the interstate. *Definitely not an air show.*

"Oh, it will be good to be gone," Remy mumbled. William, mistaking this for a call to action, rattled the kennel door with his paw. "Be still, old boy. Everything is fine."

The driver took an off-ramp, following a familiar sign for the airport written entirely in Chinese characters. Remy had been down this path twice before, the last time by foot when he realized the airport was only local one. Adrenal glands activated. His fingers unconsciously stretched and flexed into fists. He had prepared to begin a long hike to Vietnam and was instead met with air forces focused on his apartment. A monumental day to say the least. Quelling the adrenaline rush, he consciously took a deep, slow breath, rolled down the window, and stuck his head out, analyzing the sky for signs of aircraft. There were no longer helicopters visible in the sky nor rhythmic chopping of wind that had echoed in the courtyard a half hour earlier. No roar of fighter jets either. No evidence of what had been was found above.

He dipped his head back inside, rolled up the window, and took another deep breath. In the very back of the van, William whimpered and rattled the kennel gate again with his paw, accurately predicting what was to come. Remy shifted in his seat, tensed up and pounced into the passenger seat in two quick steps, landing gracefully, focused and poised.

"No games this time," just as cold as ice. "I'm not going to threaten you. I don't even know if you speak English. It doesn't matter. This is the warning. Maybe you understand it. Maybe you don't. I don't care. If you jerk me around this time and fail to deliver me to the airport, there will be consequences. Swift and severe consequences. The cavalry is here and I'm leaving and that's all there is to it."

"Wait," the driver replied, relaxed and unperturbed.

He returned to driving and Remy returned to the backseat. Soon the familiar local airport appeared from behind a wooded region. Fighting to suppress a snarl, a fresh wave of adrenaline coursed through dilated blood vessels. He made eye contact with the driver through the reflection of the rearview mirror and pondered when it would be best to make his move, not wanting to cause a high-speed collision during a struggle for control of the vehicle. *Best to wait for him to stop, wherever/whenever that is. Be quick and end it immedi-*

ately. William battered the kennel gate again with renewed ferocity. "I love you, boy. But just stay where you are for this next part."

He cleared his surroundings of any obstacles and extended muscular, perpetually cramped legs. Yawning, he stretched his arms outward to test his reach, studying the surroundings of the minivan for advantageous tools and potential hazards while the van rushed onward. A security booth to the private airport came into view, the driver barely slowing as a guard waved them through, their arrival expected. Within the compound, the driver brought the van to a stop alongside a perimeter fence that separated hangars from the parking lot. Remy began considering a new concept: being ushered away in a private plane to parts unknown.

Private aircraft can't hold enough fuel to cross the Pacific Ocean. More likely I'd be flown to some other place. Deeper into Chinese territory? Is this the beginning of a hostage situation? he wondered absently, dazed at this new thought. *I suppose I've been held captive for almost two months now. Cavalry or not, wherever they are now -- somewhere not too distant I hope -- they could only intervene by firing upon the general vicinity thus forfeiting my life. Aerial strikes are not known for pinpoint accuracy, though at this point, that wouldn't be so bad. It would make for a great epitaph, if I had the money for such a thing. Which does bring up a fair point. Why is any of this happening? Not just the fighters or the helicopters, not just the empty interstate today, but why bother torturing me with sleeplessness and holding me hostage in Guangzhou for months? Because I poked around and searched for my stolen money? I suppose I did ruffle some feathers along the way, though. A whole lot of feathers, actually, the more that I think about it. Man, there is just a trail of feathers leading to me.* He chuckled at the imagery. The driver turned back to face Remy, interrupting the levity.

"We wait. Here. Wait here. Look."

"What are you saying? I don't know what you mean. You want me to wait and look?"

"Look." The driver pointed across the private landing strip to a series of hangars in the distance.

"I don't know if you're about to kidnap me or what, but sure, let's look at something together. Whatever."

He followed the driver's gaze along his pointing finger, passed the docking bays, to...

Remy let out a breath he didn't know he'd been holding, feeling like he'd been socked in the stomach by a prizefighter. "Son of a whore," he cursed. "That's it, isn't it."

The driver at first stifled his desire to laugh, though upon turning around in the driver's seat and seeing Remy's astonished face, he abandoned the attempt.

"Alright, alright. That's enough out of you, toady. You look like a toad, you know. Squat and short and sort of hunched up. Prominent lower jaw. Definitely a toad."

The driver realized he was being insulted which had the effect of softening the intensity of the derision. He stepped out of the van, turned back again, looked at Remy, and laughed anew.

"Yeah, laugh it up, toad man. Very funny."

"Close. Too close," the driver said, shutting the door. "You wait here. We leave soon."

Remy sat staring into the distance where on the other side of the private airport, two kilometers away at most, the bulk of the international airport clearly stood in the distance. A commercial passenger jet descended, creating a distant rumble of engine, albeit a distinctly different rumble than what the unseen fighter jets had produced just an hour ago. He listened attentively as the plane landed, comparing the recent audio memory to the current observation and finding no connection. *There were definitely fighters up there an hour ago. All quiet now, though. Guess it's up to me.*

CHINA

He waited for a while after the commercial jet touched down, staring absently through an empty sky while he thought of what to do next. A few minutes later, he slid the side door open and exited. In the distance, the driver smoked and laughed with a peer. The skies were quiet, all traces of an aerial conflict gone. The tension in the air had thinned significantly. *I need to press forward while the incident remains fresh in everyone's minds. Strike while the metal is hot. This is a solid opportunity to escape.*

"Hey!" Remy called over. "Oy! Are you going to drive me to the airport or not?"

The driver and his buddy casually glanced over. "You wait. We go soon," the driver said around a self-serving smile before returning to a smoky conversation. Remy felt his rage quickly mounting into something intolerable. An involuntary snarl contorted his face and a growl rumbled within him. A presence pushed on him to approach the driver and his buddy, a flood of horrific events playing about in his mind's eye. He took a step out of the vehicle and promptly halted in place, snapping back, coming down, regaining control of self, calming. William was slapping away fervently on the kennel gate with both paws, the hinges threatening to tear loose. Remy's snarl faded into a twitching of the upper lip and soon subsided completely.

"Hey now. It's okay, boy. I'm back." The Shepherd remained unconvinced but ceased pounding on the gate. "Let's get out of here."

He tossed his suitcase out of the vehicle, shouldered his backpack, freed and leashed William in one fell swoop, and pulled the kennel out of the back of the van. He tried unsuccessfully to balance the kennel atop the luggage a few times before giving up and looping the leash around the same arm that pulled the heavy suitcase along behind him. The other arm was tasked with dragging the bulky dog kennel. William kept an awkwardly slow gait with the cumbersome mound of possessions as they clumsily shuffled toward the distant international airport. A scraping sound cut through the smoker's conversation, turning the driver's attention to the spectacle. He threw down half a lit cigarette and jogged over.

"Okay. We go now."

"F%^* you, toad. Go jump in a pond."

Instead, the toad jumped into the driver's seat, started the van and easily caught up to the duo lumbering awkwardly down a stretch of vacant roadway. He spoke from the driver's seat as the van idled along beside Remy and William, the idea being that they should return to the van. Unresponsive, they continued slogging onward to the point along the horizon where the terminal had appeared, the rise of nearby buildings having soon obstructed Remy's view. The driver gave up after five minutes or so and sped off, cursing profusely in his native tongue.

"I wonder what he called me, Will."

The hound glanced up as the corner of the kennel swayed back and into their legs again. The suitcase posed the same problem, often jamming into the back of Remy's heel, calf, and thigh at random intervals and locations, bonking into William's flank as well, while periodically getting stuck in cracks and debris. It was slow going, laborious, frustrating, and painful. They stopped shortly after the van sped away and drank deeply from a water bottle stored in the emergency backpack. William licked his bruised legs and side. Remy awkwardly rubbed strained and newly bruised leg muscles with fingers that were contorting into hooks as cramping took effect there, too. He furiously shook his wrists to relax the binding muscles to minimal success. Minutes later, they marched on with fingers slightly less locked into crescents.

Warehouses, storage facilities, and open lots filled with industrial machinery came and went. Remy looked straight through it all, feeling with certainty they were headed in the right direction though the terminal remained uncomfortably unseen. In the midst of this he spied a familiar sight.

"Hey, look over there. That's the quarantine building I picked you up from when we first arrived. When was that? Back in early-August? Four months ago. Wow, just four months ago. Feels like four years has gone by."

They rested again at the new site, exhausted though having only traveled a short distance. Fastening the leash to the outer edge of the kennel rather than to himself gave William freedom to walk less impeded on the outskirts of the shambling mound of suitcase and kennel. It was still burdensome and awkward but only Remy's legs were in harm's way as they continued along to the terminal. Close to an hour they travelled like this until they arrived at the fringe of the international airport's parking lot. Renewed at the sight, they pressed on, a clumsy mess creeping ever closer to the terminal, a massively odd thing shuffling its way across the parking lot, blobbing along in a beeline for the first visible entrance. Crossing the threshold of the closest automatic sliding glass door entryway, Remy found a bit of wall off to the side, and collapsed into the heap, panting and grinning from ear to ear. After catching his breath, he rolled over and kissed the floor.

With a paper-light heart, he rose to his feet but a wave of dizziness and a severe calf cramp brought him crashing back down into his battered possessions. Embarrassed, he came back up on the other leg, clenching his teeth in pain and trying in vain to not cause a scene. He had shouldered his backpack and was beginning to pull his suitcase upright when he noticed an airport employee approaching. He waved and forced a strained smile through the pain of the muscle contracting. The employee did not smile back. She showed only concern. Deep concern.

"Sir, are you alright?" An innocent question.

"Am I alright?" Remy tried to laugh but it came out in a coughing hiss. "No. No, I'm definitely not alright. I need help."

"Certainly, sir. I will find a cart." And she briskly walked away.

"Well, I guess that's a start."

She returned later with a cart and a man dressed in managerial fashion along with a grumpy, muscular security guard who loomed in the background.

"Sir, dogs not allowed in airport, sir."

"That's a lot of *sirs*. But don't worry. This is William. He's not just any dog. He's very well mannered. Calmer than most people, actually. And he's on this leash here there shouldn't be a problem." The trio of employees remained stern and unyielding. "Okay. Fine. I'll put him in the kennel." He opened the gate and William bounded right in, happy to lie down and relax while being moved about.

The conversation shifted to destination and to Remy's lack of an airline ticket, which brought more concern and mistrust. Four months' salary minus frugal living expenses and the cost of substances designed to keep one awake in a war zone tallied up to more than enough to purchase a one-way ticket to the United States, even a same-day one.

"Why didn't I purchase the ticket ahead of time? Good question. That is a fine and normal question to ask," he replied, stalling for time to think of how to best proceed. "You really don't know what's been happening to me here? I don't know where to start. Thought everyone here knew the deal. Well, I've been experiencing computer issues, the depths of which are staggering. Far beyond the realm of viruses and hacked identity. Honestly, I wouldn't be shocked if my bank account is totally wiped out but I do have around six or seven thousand dollars in cash with me." Expressions shifted almost imperceptibly toward skepticism. A subtle change in body positioning and a softening of the eyes were clear signals to Remy, though.

"Here, I'll show you. You obviously don't believe me." He poked around the contents of his bag and came up with a bundle of cash in a worn envelope. "This is all the money I possess. Can't trust bank accounts. I'm a little shocked you don't know who I am, actually. You honestly have no clue what's been happening to me?" The faces before him showed no sign of recognition. *After all this, there are Guangzhouans that don't know?*

In time he was able to purchase a one-way ticket for himself and William to depart Guangzhou, China and arrive at Los Angeles, California on December 20, 2012. To say that he did not trust the inhabitants of Guangzhou would be an understatement unto folly. The shortest, most direct path to America left the least amount of room for trickery and interference and had the benefit of shielding the location of his family from a place that had tortured him. The counter clerk was obviously uncomfortable with the cash transaction and Remy's starry-eyed expression when the ticket was handed over. To hold the thing in his hand was truly special. He brushed it across his cheek, savoring the way it felt against his skin, sniffing it lovingly. His eyes watered with joy.

He checked his suitcase and was told he needed to speak with the quarantine specialist about William before passing through the security gate. There he was told that since William lacked a health check identification form -- a document only veterinarians could provide -- he would not be allowed to board the plane. Remy assumed the next step was to take William to an onsite vet but no such person worked at the airport.

"Well, what am I supposed to do?! What can I do now?! I just spent over two thousand dollars on a rushed ticket out of here. Now what?" The more he breathed, the less air he seemed to take in. The blood rushing to his head almost caused him to pass out. He leaned heavily on the counter, recovering. "Can't I just give you money and you bring a vet here? Why isn't there a vet here if such a thing is necessary? Can't the quarantine department issue the document? Just take my money. Take this money and let us go." He held out the remainder of cash from the envelope.

The quarantine officer stepped back. "I am sorry. I no take that."

There was no getting around it. The only vet Remy knew had an office three blocks down the road from his apartment/torture chamber. The hour was approaching six p.m. It would be the next day before he could even start the process.

"You have no idea how hard it was to get here. You just don't have a clue. I thought everyone in this city was to blame but I see now that some of you don't have the faintest idea what's been happening to me. None of this makes sense to you, I'm sure. I have to go back there?" Remy wiped his runny nose and teary eyes with the back of his hand. "I don't have a choice. You won't transport William without this document and I won't leave without him. I must do this somehow." He struggled but found some composure. "And I will. I have to so I will."

"Yes," the official replied through a strained smile. "Goodbye."

Remy left, explained the situation to an airline clerk who refunded 75% of his ticket cost and returned his suitcase. Five hundred dollars spent on nothing. He dragged the shambling mound into an elevator, across the airport subway station and onto a southbound train. Forty minutes later, he clambered out of the subway station and trudged through familiar sidewalks. Outside of the apartment lobby, two security guards refused to open the door for him. After much banging on the glass, one of them cracked open the door to shoo and point him away. The guards refused to listen to Remy's Mandarin. Refused to read writing on an app on his phone. As the shooing turned to physical touch, Remy cursed their families loudly and left. Untrusting of taxis, he dragged the material components of his life three blocks east to the sidewalk of the vet's office. Well into late evening at that point, he tucked himself off to the side and for the first time in his life slept out on the streets. The night brought freezing temperatures, the wind cutting through layers of clothing he'd donned from his suitcase. Shivering, he opened the kennel door and laid down against William's warm fur. Within minutes, he was unconscious. Blessedly asleep.

He awoke in the middle of the night feeling something was amiss. Ducking his head out of the kennel, he spied a bent figure rummaging through the contents of his suitcase. "Hey! Get out of here!" he cried out as he crawled out of the kennel. The man ran off, surprisingly light-footed. Remy began to give chase but stopped himself halfway down the block, thinking of the foolishness it would be to leave William behind with his backpack containing evidence, money, and passport. He spun about and returned to the kennel.

"Not exactly a guard dog, are you."

William yawned and returned to sleeping. Remy, on the other hand, spent most of the evening worried about his suitcase. From the perspective of those few individuals that passed by the strange mound of possessions that cold December night, the only sign of life was an outstretched arm emerging from the depths of a large dog kennel that came to rest atop a grey suitcase. With a numb hand he dozed lightly, vigilant and unconvinced he would ever sleep again.

CHAPTER L

CHINA

Dawn lit the sky, rousing the well-rested German Shepherd and warming the air. Remy clambered to his feet and began the long process of loitering about the vicinity waiting for the veterinarian's clinic to open. A few boring hours later, an employee arrived. Taking note of the strange heap of possessions of man and dog, she smiled awkwardly and ushered the pair inside. The vet arrived soon afterward and the situation was presented to her whereupon Remy was told it would take most of the day for the necessary bloodwork to be drawn and analyzed, perhaps even two. On his last reserve of strength, he nodded dully, accepted a gracious invitation for his luggage to be stored in the backroom, and left William in capable hands. He strolled down blocks he had hoped to never see again, passing the ma-pa restaurant that had transformed under new management, eliciting memories of the elderly couple and young man's forced removal. He had no reason to purchase anything save for a frugal lunch and having zero desire to shop, neither wanting to further burden his luggage nor possess a souvenir of his suffering, he walked about without purpose for as long as he could stand before returning to the veterinarian's office where he proceeded to wait and hope for test results to arrive.

Hours later as the office began going about the closing process, Remy's mind turned to the reality of an additional night sleeping on the streets and all that would entail: another day and night without bathing, clothing rumpled and stinking, another winter's night exposed to the elements. He sat surrounded by magazine covers sporting jubilant faces in the waiting room brooding as Chinese pop music played softly through hidden speakers, contemplating another grim night, wondering absently if a taxi would even take them both to the airport. Another long walk, a dangerous portion of which rested alongside the interstate, back to the local airport and beyond, to the international, all the while hauling backpack, suitcase, kennel, and William. The short distance from local airport to the international had proven exhausting. He would need to allot himself a few days to travel the twenty miles or so to the international airport. A sour prospect indeed.

He was wondering if he would see the sky filled with military aircraft again or if that ship had sailed when a middle-aged lady entered carrying a rectangular block, a casserole dish wrapped in tinfoil. She looked about the room as she greeted the receptionist, searching for something or someone. Remy. Their eyes locked and she offered a curious smile, equal parts warmth and sorrow, quite unlike the crocodile smiles and mocking jeers that he'd grown accustomed to.

She walked up slowly, tentatively, as one would approach a wounded animal which wasn't so far off the mark.

"This is for you. It's lasagna."

"I'm sorry. Did you say 'lasagna'?"

"Yes. Do you like it?" she asked, legitimately concerned that the dish would be unacceptable.

Remy was flabbergasted. "Sure. I mean, yes. Ma'am, I would love some lasagna. Thank you."

She held out the glass casserole tray, filled from edge to edge with freshly baked lasagna.

"Oh, no. I forgot a fork. How are you going to eat this without a spoon or fork?"

"Or chopsticks. Those would work, too." He met her gaze and smiled while he attempted to make sense of the situation. "Ma'am, it's really no bother. I'll find something to eat it with. Disposable chopsticks should be easy enough to find."

She brightened, backed away and spoke with the vet's receptionist, soon returning with exactly that: one pair of wooden chopsticks. Remy received these gratefully, clueless as to what was happening.

"There you go. That's better." She paused, taking in Remy and the casserole dish, mental gears clicking. "Only you don't have a plate either, do you? I didn't plan for this well at all." She mumbled to herself in Mandarin, chiding her lack of foresight.

"Ma'am. This is fine. More than fine. It is a wonderful thing, this lasagna." He bowed deeply in appreciation, a gesture he'd picked up from the Japanese many years ago. "Thank you very much for this feast. Shall I leave the container here? I don't know how else to get it back to you."

"No," she smiled warmly, "No, just take it. Or throw it away. It's nothing."

"Well, it's certainly something to me." They shared a pleasant silence. "So, do you often bake lasagna and enter into veterinarian clinics to gift your dishes to strangers?"

"No," she laughed. "You're the first. The first time I've made lasagna, actually. I hope you like it."

"I do. It smells lovely."

They smiled at one another, bigger questions looming.

"So, why are you here?" Remy continued. "I mean, I hate to pry, and don't want to seem unappreciative of the gesture, but it is a little odd."

She smiled coyly and began heading for the door. "You just looked like you could use some lasagna."

"A dish you've never baked before."

She paused in the doorway. "God bless you. I'm sorry." And she was gone.

He stood transfixed, staring at the closed door, the twinkling of the bell atop the doorframe dimming into silence. He looked down at the full pan of lasagna, unsure what to make of what had just transpired but trusting the woman implicitly. She felt wholesome whoever she was and he set about to filling his stomach with the homecooked meal. As the hour approached five, he set aside the tray and began preparing for another cold night outside. He was in the process of requesting his belongings when the door flew open. A courier rushed inside, dropped off a Manila envelope and dashed off. Several minutes later, the chief vet approached the front desk and waved Remy over, beaming.

"These are your papers. Show to the quarantine counter at airport."

"Really? This is all I need? Just show them this?"

"Just show them papers." She reached out a thin, strong hand which he shook. "Good luck, Mr. LeBeau."

"I'll take all the luck I can get. Thanks again." He turned to the receptionist in order to gather his possessions and a thought came to him. "Actually, if you don't mind, would you call for a taxi? I feel you may be better at that sort of thing than I am."

She smiled awkwardly, discomfort playing about at the corners of her mouth. "Are you ready to leave now?"

"Oh, yes. You could say that." Remy situated back into the lobby seats comfortably. "Now would be better than later."

CHINA

"I'm sorry, sir. But you must remain in seat during take-off."

Remy looked to the flight attendant: young, petite, pretty. He flashed a toothy grin, feeling moxie rejuvenating, energized. "*Habla no ingles,*" he stammered, followed by, "*Gomenasai, anatano koto-baga zenzen shiranai.*" The culmination of Spanish and Japanese spoken by a Caucasian was enough to confuse her into complacency. She had seemed on the verge of unbuckling herself from the folding chair she perched upon but resituated herself in her seat instead and accepted the noncompliance. He turned from her and gazed out of the emergency exit window, insistent on watching China disappear from view beneath and behind him.

It's over now, he thought absently, reflecting back on the past several months of Guangzhou and laughing uncontrollably. Catching the eye of a few worried passengers, he reeled the laughter back to an enthusiastic chuckle and returned to his seat.

He set his sights to the various windows lining the walls of economy class, watching the ground dip and twist as the plane arced upward, climbing to higher elevations. Soon the only indication of the horizon was a stretch of lights that grew smaller and dimmer in the distance. He leaned nearly over the lap of a passenger in the window seat next to him working hard to ignore the intrusive presence. Remy flashed a middle finger and thumped it vigorously against the plastic window of the passenger window seat and howled in joyous rapture as the last of Guangzhou disappeared from view. He continued staring absently into the distance for the better part of an hour adjusting to the new reality of successful escape before settling into his seat to watch a film that he cared nothing about.

The usual line was, "Chicken or beef?" or, "Chicken or fish?" Chicken always one of the options for some reason. Which is what Remy overheard in the dull dialogues behind him as the cart clunked its way up the aisle, but when the flight attendant approached Remy, the question shifted.

"Mr LeBeau? Are you, Mr. LeBeau?" The stewardess asked, flashing a toothy smile.

"Most people call me Remy, but technically, yes, I am Mr. LeBeau."

"Here is your meal."

"Shouldn't you ask me if I want fish or..." But she was already gone, tending to a new line of passengers ahead.

Between William and himself, half of the lasagna had been devoured before passing the security gate of the airport. That had been about four hours ago, and while not especially hungry, he was in the mood to celebrate. Whiskey over ice and a tray of food that resembled a meal sufficed. His thoughts were a churning mass focused on landing in America, of what to do next, how to best move forward.

Immediately approach the nearest custom's officer, ask for a supervisor and report the long and complicated tale, or check on family first? Those with the means to do what has been done to me must have the means to strike outside of their nation, as well, he pondered, sipping whiskey, nibbling on chicken, rice, and a vegetable medley that was somehow both overcooked and undercooked. Weighing out what exactly to say to an authority figure in his homeland. Something to think about besides escaping was a massive shift and he was finding it difficult to adjust to the fact that he was actually free. He mulled over a few introductory lines, but it all sounded like so much nonsense, the ravings of a lunatic. He glanced down at his crumpled and stained clothing. *Soon to be three days of not bathing, too. I don't appear credible. What to say? Where to begin? It just sounds like madness if I start halfway into it.*

He was trying to string together a concise, formal statement when a sharp stomach pang doubled him over. It started in his lower abdomen and spread quickly throughout the intestinal tract. Searing pain. His face winced in discomfort as the pangs came and went, increasing in severity and frequency. He excused himself and waited in line for the restroom at the back of the plane, grimacing through waves of intense pain. Feeling control of his bowels and esophagus slipping away, knowing that had just been ingested would soon be expelled one way or another, Remy fell to the floor and curled up into the fetal position, clutching his agonizing stomach in a last ditch attempt to keep everything within.

Hearing the click of the restroom latch unlocking, he pushed through a slowly exiting passenger and locked the door behind him. There he remained for the next five hours, expelling food and drink every which way imaginable. He vomited, almost asphyxiating in the process, gasping for needed air between interims of heaving, minute after minute, hour after hour. The world spun wildly in erratic spirals, fluctuating in and out. Closing his eyes only magnified the effect. He hoped to remain half-unconscious on the bathroom floor for the rest of his life but was ushered out by an attendant as the plane began its final descent. From the nearest open seat, Remy promptly slid onto the floor, panting, digestive tract a mess, respiratory system stressed and weakened. He didn't sleep nor was he entirely conscious. Wheezing. Coughing. Moaning.

Poisoned, he thought as he failed again to sufficiently fill his lungs with a deep breath. *Why else insist on clarification of my name before handing me the meal? I don't have dietary restrictions. Except for poison. Maybe I should've mentioned an allergy to poison when I checked in.* He wheezed a little chuckle though his head was ringing like church bells. He flexed legs that felt incapable of supporting his own bodyweight. Checked hands that twitched about and could not be held still. He chuckle-choked again at his sorry state, in pain and very much looking forward to arriving in his homeland.

CHAPTER LII

USA

"I don't know."

"What is that supposed to mean?" questioned the officer. A gruff, no-nonsense sort of man, all posture and positioning. Absolutely nothing in the charisma category.

This man's mind would have ruptured within the first week of what I went through. Remy smiled at the thought, a gesture his counterpart found visibly frustrating.

"Do you not know what 'I don't know' means? I'm not sure how to explain the concept to you."

"I'm familiar with the phrase, sir." The *sir* was drawn out and sharp, truly meaning *asshole*. "I need to know where you are going."

"Well, being a citizen of the United States, I'd say anywhere is fair game. Isn't really any of your business, is it?" The officer stiffened. *This isn't going well at all.* "But you do have a fair point, I suppose. Sir." Remy returned the same *sir*, tit for tat, grinning wickedly. "Most people have a destination. A specific address they're going to."

They stood, separated by a chest-high counter facing one another and not liking what they saw.

Prince Charming was expecting Remy to continue. The silence hung for a bit first.

"So, I guess just stamp that passport there and I'll be---"

"Sir, I'm going to have to detain you if you can't provide me with an address." He turned his attention away and began searching the area for a colleague to take over his counter. *He's not bluffing.* Still woozy from the flight, Remy took a deep breath and leaned against the counter.

"Look, I understand your plight. Officer..." Remy searched the man's uniform and badge for a name. Nothing. "Officer, I get it. You're charged with keeping the border safe and I seem like a problem to you. Hair all over the place. Clothes wrinkled and stained. I don't smell like roses right now, either. Probably the most haggard person you've seen come through these lines today. And here I am apparently refusing to tell you where I'm going."

The guard softened, not much, but some. Remy pressed the advantage. "Only I'm not refusing. I just don't know. I really don't. I've been fighting so hard just to get here, anywhere out of China, as weird as that sounds. It's been so hard to get to this point. I'm spent. Pretty sure I was just poisoned. Every---"

"Poisoned?"

Sensing an abrupt shift away from compassion in the officer, Remy weighed his options before replying. *I'm not speaking to a sympathetic man. This man sees me as a threat. He's listening only to spot a reason to detain me.* "Metaphorically speaking. I've had a little whiskey on the ride over, you see." Walking a fine line along the edge of truth. "Listen. Everything I had in me has been poured into getting to this point. I haven't given much thought at all to what happens next." He paused, the past flooding in. "What to do now, I mean," he added dully, forcing himself away from the memories, vision clearing.

"Tell me your home address, then," he commanded, opening up the passport page, preparing to stamp an acceptance symbol.

"Yeah, I don't exactly have one of those."

The officer looked up with cold, dead eyes, set the stamper aside, and flipped the passport closed.

Based on the recent, likely intentional poisoning and the antagonistic reception at the airport, Remy decided right then and there to check on his family first which would allow him time to find a way to say what needed to be said and to determine who exactly it needed to be said to. To rest and heal. He could feel three days of grime sticking to his skin. Being detained wouldn't have been awful, but it would've put him off to a bad start, a position from which he would undoubtedly be disbelieved. He thought of William waiting patiently somewhere in his kennel somewhere near a luggage carousel. He straightened, resolute to end this back and forth favorably.

"Well, not in the traditional sense. It's been a while. I've been away from the ol' U S of A for a good many years now. You know how it is," Remy smiled warmly, looking for agreement and finding none. "Or maybe you don't. Anywho, thirteen twenty-two, Shady Glen, Winter Port, Florida. That's my address." And it was, or rather, had been thirty years ago when Remy was a lad, the address having long been cemented into his memory long ago by a protective mother insistent that memorizing it would be critical for his own survival one day. *Maybe she meant now.*

The officer was warming but nowhere near sold.

"Look, man. I don't know what else to tell you. Some crazy stuff happened to me in China. I haven't lived in America in over ten years. I feel like a refugee seeking asylum, but as you can see, I'm an

American citizen, so that doesn't exactly apply. I'm tired. I'm so very tired. Please just let me rest."

The officer seemed to enjoy Remy's breakdown. He stamped the passport and handed it over.

"Welcome back to America, sir." A normal, respectful *sir*.

"Yeah, I was hoping for a hero's welcome. A parade or some balloons. This isn't a great start."

"Beats detainment. Next!"

Still unable to stomach water without initiating a wave of vomiting, Remy shuffled through the airport on weak legs, leaning heavily on his baggage cart for support. He had dreamed of returning to the United States for two long, torturous months. Home. He had made it. He was soon reunited with William at the animal quarantine department of LAX where he received a thorough face-licking before exiting the building in search of a suitable place to meet the dog's long overdue biological needs. Afterward, the duo relaxed on a distant bench where Remy quickly realized he had no idea what to do next.

CHAPTER LIII

USA

His first thought was to fly out to Orlando, Florida: the closest port to home. *From there, I could rent a car, drive to mother's and hopefully she'll be unmurdered and happy to see me. After that, I check on the siblings, ensure their well-being, and then practice telling my tale while I sleep for a week. If everyone's fine. Pretty big if, the more that I think about it, but first things first. I need to get to Florida.*

"Okay," the middle-aged lady snapped, chewing gum and punching away on her keyboard. "I can get you on a flight in two days, December 23rd. It'll be a redeye." She looked up smiling as if she had just solved the problem of world hunger.

"Two more nights here? How much are hotel rooms this time of the year? A hundred bucks?"

"You won't find one at that price this time of year." She smacked her gum to emphasize the point.

"Well, how much is the ticket?"

"Twenty-four hundred dollars."

"American dollars? That sounds like the right price in pesos. Do you mean twenty-four hundred pesos?"

"American dollars," she chortled, appreciating the joke.

"Look, you seem nice so I don't know how to say this, but that's an absurd price." He paused, doing the math. "I spent less than half of that to bring myself and my pooch across the Pacific Ocean. Does that price include my dog?"

She just laughed.

"Okay. Glad you find it funny."

"It's because of Christmas," she related, matter-of-factly.

"Doesn't feel much like Christmas on this side of the counter."

She chortled again, "You're pretty funny."

"Do you offer discounts for comedians?"

"I wish."

"Twenty-four hundred dollars, two nights later." Remy mulled over the number, a sizeable portion of all of his savings. "Plus an additional fee to ship the dog."

"Can he fit as a carry-on?"

Remy's turn to laugh an answer. "So, closer to four thousand with William?"

"More."

"This is a far cry from a hero's welcome, you know. I was hoping for a: 'Way to survive that harrowing ordeal. Thank you for the evidence. You fought well.' Something like that. I mean, there was military aircraft filling the sky at the end of it all. How did things shift from that to this?"

"Are you a soldier or something?"

"Something like that. Merry Christmas."

"Merry Christmas!"

He wheeled the cart away, nowhere in mind, just pushing and walking and thinking. *I don't want to sit around and wait two nights, just to pay way too much to fly to Orlando. Trains? Amtrak is still a thing, right? I think they still transport people by train in America. I should check on that. Of course, I would need a car just to get to the train station. Taxis are too expensive. I could just rent a car and do it myself. To Orlando? Drive to Orlando?* It was as if a lightbulb lit up above his head. *Drive to Florida. Five thousand kilometers east. Across the highways and interstates, taking any road I please, stopping wherever I want to stop. Freedom.* He thought back to being repeatedly jerked around by taxi drivers, trains that had stopped just short of the airport. Of the many long walks. *I could drive wherever I want, as fast or slow as I want. See America in the process.*

There was a peace that came with the finality of his decision. Shaking off the last of the poisonous effects, he wheeled William and his suitcase to the parking garage where he searched for the best deals among the various rental car companies of LAX. Doing some mathematics in his head, he concluded that he would spend around eight hundred dollars to get to Florida all things considered: gasoline, a night or two in a cheap hotel room, the rental car cost. Another couple hundred for living expenses in Florida during the holidays. Conservatively, another five hundred to return the vehicle back to L.A.

And then what? Visit the United Nations? Report the incident to local authorities? Send Interpol an email again? Contact Homeland Security? All that aside, is my family safe right now? After what I went through, anything is possible. I may return to a missing mother or worse. Those responsible for my torture certainly knew the exact address of my brother's home. Breathe, Remy. That's it. In and out. Deep, slow breaths. I'll have time to plan while I drive. This is good. This is what should happen.

He twisted the key and ignited the engine of the newish Dodge Dart. William leapt into the passenger seat confidently, maw open wide, tongue lolling. He hadn't turned the mobile phone back on after landing for fear of erasing some important bit of data when the system acclimated to the new environment, potentially updating and erasing important evidence in the process. Thoughts of using the phone filled him with dread akin to utilizing a Ouija board, and so it remained tucked away in the worn backpack.

Baggage stored, he turned his attention to driving the Dart, a thing he hadn't done in years. *Just drive slowly until it feels comfortable again,* he advised himself. *We may even reach ma's house by Christmas morning.* He checked the time on the dashboard display as he set the radio stations. Midnight was fast approaching, bringing an end to the date of the end of the world according to the Mayans: December 21st, 2012. The American media had twisted this concept into meaning the end of all life on Earth, facts once again taking a backseat to ratings. Truthfully, the Mayans held many calendars, some as short as lunar months, menstrual cycles, and harvesting seasons, and some as grand as the end of the old way and the beginning of the new. *Beginning of the new.* Remy echoed, smiling wide, thinking of the long drive ahead. *I like the sound of that.*

The employees of the rental company were grouped together engaged in a lively conversation as Remy returned.

"Excuse me. Could you just point me towards east?"

"Point you toward east? I don't think I can. I just Google it and zing, I'm there, you know?"

Remy smiled awkwardly, uncertain how to broach the fact that his phone was many things but definitely not a helpful device for navigating. The lead employee just continued on unabated.

"Do you one better. Here." And he slid over a map of the Californian roadways, folded like an accordion, if accordions were delicate jigsaw puzzles that could never be put together again.

His mind flashed back to false maps sold to him by sidewalk merchants in Guangzhou while he pushed himself onward through streets, a ridiculing flash mob in tow, pouring himself into finding an escape, failing again and again, exhausted, injured, sleep-deprived. *This is not that. I am home now.* He quelled the darkness and smiled. "This is good, my friend. Thank you. Merry Christmas."

He returned to find William in the driver's seat, peering out over the top of the steering wheel. "Look, you're not going to drive this thing. Just kick back and enjoy the ride. You've earned it." He lowered himself into the driver's seat and William hopped over. As he studied the map of southern California, the imagery began fading as memories flooded in. Fighting to shake it off. Fighting to escape what was. Eventually his focus returned to the outstretched map in his hands. The airport itself wasn't marked so he took an educated guess and plunged into the chilly night, eastward bound. He drove slowly, reading each sign he passed, looking for directions to an east-west interstate, later enjoying the rush of speeding down it. By three a.m. most of California was behind him. He took an exit ramp that connected to a narrow two-lane highway, a detour just for the sake of detouring, just because he could. Freedom.

The speed limit was significantly slower but it had the desirable quality of being vacant. Finding a comfortable shoulder, he pulled the Dart over onto the hard-packed sand of the southern Mojave Desert. Interstate traffic growled in the distance, a stream of glowing headlights. Above, something Remy hadn't seen in a very long time. Stars, hundreds if not a thousand, clearly shining at differing intensities lightyears away. They formed constellations he couldn't remember, peppering the darkness of night.

"It's gorgeous. I had forgotten about the night sky. William, you really should see this." He tore himself away from the jeweled sky, glancing over at the general direction where William had run off to release his bladder only to find the area empty. "Come on, you dingo. Don't be lost in the desert."

He called out his name in the sing-song style that meant *come* and waited. Nothing.

He closed his eyes and listened, picking up a dull jingle of collar well behind the parked car. He stormed off, closing in on a William-sized shadow in the distant darkness.

"There are rattlesnakes out here. Scorpions, too. If I get bit by a snake, I'll be pi---"

He halted midstride, suddenly aware of what had captured Will's attention. Ten feet ahead, Will was devouring the rotting carcass of an armadillo. His muzzle shoved into the shell, ripping decaying flesh from bone. He threw back his head to whoof down the prize and then dug in for more.

"Foul. That's disgusting." He stooped over and hooked his fingers around the hound's collar, tugging him away from his prize. Grudgingly, the hound obeyed. "Come. I'll buy you a hamburger soon. Or a burrito. A burrito sounds nice. Haven't had one of those in ages." He marched on, fingers hooked around the collar, William glancing back over his shoulder intermittently at the rapidly retreating corpse with obvious regret. "You are so gross. If you get intestinal worms right now, I don't know what I'll do. I really don't want to stop in Oklahoma for a few days while you pass worms."

He flung open the passenger's seat and William jumped in happily, all concerns of leaving an uneaten feast behind replaced with the joy of travel.

"The stars are lost on you, carrion-eater."

The hound smiled on, unperturbed, tongue lolling, breath remarkably nauseating. Remy sighed, twisted the ignition, rolled down both windows, and off they went, eastward until the sun broke the darkness of night dead ahead. He had planned to pull over and rest during the day, to drive at night when traffic would be less congested, but as night became day, he just kept driving, all day and into the next night.

CHAPTER LIV

USA

Eighteen hours on the road, taking only the most Spartan of breaks along the way to tend to biological needs. California, Arizona, New Mexico, and into Texas. Several hours had passed since the offramp indicator for El Paso and judging by the more definitive road atlas purchased at a truck stop along the way, he had quite a way to go before reaching the midway point of both the Lone Star state and the entire cross-country journey. The idea was to press on until San Antonio and bed down there for the night but his eyelids were uncompliant. Blinking was becoming soothingly rhythmic and despite loud music and open windows and a sharp smack to the face, he was fading fast.

He took the next exit off of Highway 10 to a township in west Texas which consisted of little more than one motel and one gas station. Tumbleweed blew by in the distance. Two roads divided a landscape peppered with scrub brush and little else into four equally vacant quarters.

"We have four rooms," the Indian clerk announced. "Two of them are small and the A.C. does not work in one of them." He waited for her to go on, but she was finished.

"Do you have a room with a bathtub? And hot water?"

"All the rooms have hot water. Where is it that you are coming from?" Inflection rising throughout the sentence in the bubbling way of the Indian accent.

"It's a long story, ma'am. But I'll take a room with a bathtub, wherever that is. I don't much care about the air conditioning. It's winter and I'm pretty sure I'll just pass out until check-out time even if you have a scorpion infestation."

"We do not have anything like that here, sir."

"Fantastic. I'll take it. I do have a dog with me, though. More of a wolf, actually. How do you feel about that?"

"There will be an additional cleaning fee if he makes a mess."

"Oh, he doesn't do that. He's a good ol' boy. No worries. Do you want my money now or later?"

"Later will be fine, sir. Come with me and I will show you your room."

It was nothing fantastic. Tile floors that had seen better days. Rugs that could use a vacuuming. Musty air. The entry door was set two feet above the floor of the motel, an architectural anomaly that made little sense to Remy. Three steep steps down to the room's floor. Window panes sat loosely in a frame that had seen better days. Queen bed and a bathtub large enough to recline in.

"It's wonderful," he said, meaning it.

She brightened. "The sir is very kind. We will be seeing you at checkout."

He smiled and they exchanged pleasantries and the key. William bounded into the room shortly thereafter and gave the place a thorough sniffing that ended in approval. After dinner, he was forced into a bath that he would have preferred to do without. Remy was quite literally losing consciousness as he lightly brushed the hound's teeth, staying awake only long enough to collapse onto the soft mattress. He awoke twelve hour later, groggy and blissful at having slept undisturbed for the first time in almost two months. It was almost too good to be true. He half-expected the hotel room slowly coming into focus was a dream of some sort, that he would soon be jolted awake from an elongated blink in his flat in Guangzhou, trapped and aching. He accepted the reality of his new situation gratefully. *You made it,* he reminded himself. *You're safe now.* William slept on, curled up, tail covering his snout atop Remy's clothes, having made a nest of the open suitcase.

Within an hour, they had checked out, eaten a fast-food breakfast, and were back on the open road. San Antonio dead ahead, Louisiana far in the distance. Florida farther still. He mostly kept to the speed limit, predominately occupying the middle lane of interstate traffic, driving with the determination of a marathon runner, focused on arriving at his mother's home by Christmas morning. Highway 10 carried him into Houston around sunset on December 23rd.

CHAPTER LV

USA

Pasadena, then the Louisiana border. It was well past midnight when he began toying with idea of foregoing checking up on the family and settling into New Orleans for the holidays instead. The city had been devastated fairly recently when Hurricane Katrina tore through, destroying a nearby dam in the process thereby flooding the downtown area for weeks. The property damage had been vast. Mildew and mold and water damage had destroyed the foundations of homes and apartments, hotels and businesses, from the French Quarter to the distant outskirts. *In the aftermath of such destruction,* Remy reasoned, *rent prices will be quite low.* New Orleans, one of the finest places to take in jazz, dating all the way back to Dixieland jazz in those early days of the first world war, arguably the very birthplace of jazz itself. It was a tempting notion he mulled over while filling the gas tank thirty miles west of the city in the late hours of December 23rd.

"What'd you say, cracka?!"

A tall, dark-skinned man with a shiny, metallic mouth loomed from the other side of the gas pump Remy was using. He was halfway into filling the tank, staring absently into a wooded section of trees, entertaining the notion of a Cajun Christmas. To relax with some jazz and think of what to say and who to say it to.

"Am I the cracker you're talking about?"

Remy looked around, finding only himself and the thug nearby. On the opposite end of the parking lot, a middle-aged man rushed into his car, reversed and exited the parking lot in record time.

"Cracka, you know you a cracka."

"Okay," Remy replied, not really sure how to handle the situation. Outsmarting the man was not an option, or rather, not outsmarting the man wasn't an option. He was large, slightly more muscular and a good half-foot taller. They were alone. Not such an unfair fight.

Remy continued to fill his tank, deleting all ideas of enjoying New Orleans for the holidays. "So, you hate crackers, then. That's cool."

"Damn straight, cracka." He just loved that word. Shiny plated teeth reflected dim light cast from gas station lamps filled with an accumulation of dead insects. A pause, and then, "Cracka."

"Yeah, you mentioned that."

William had been roused from slumber and was sniffing at the crack of the window toward the transgression. Indeed, there was cause for alarm. If he moved with hostility towards this man, an attack would ensue. No doubt about it. It was in the air, like the feel of rain before it falls. To be within arm's reach of those who had definitively been responsible for his sleep-deprivation would have been lovely. But this random, ignorant fool just wasn't on Remy's radar. He was vile but Remy had no burning hatred of him.

"Merry Christmas," Remy said, hanging up the gasoline nozzle. "It's a tough time for me, too."

That stung the man, who mumbled a long series of nothings accented with the word *cracka* here and there. There was a feeling of a near-miss which dissipated as the gas station faded away in the rearview mirror.

"Don't pretend that you're a guard dog, all of a sudden. Just because you sniffed around when an ogre threatened to attack me doesn't mean that you're some benevolent protector. Where were you in Guangzhou?" Remy thought about that as he adjusted to a new speed limit.

Stopping at a red light, he turned to the hound in the backseat. "That wasn't fair or even an accurate thing to say. You maintained your cool really well back there. You are a fine, fine beast, William, and I love you very much, carrion-eater."

William opened his mouth to pant and smile.

"Go back to sleep, now. We have a long way to go." And he complied not so long after the command, curling up in the backseat in the wee hours of Christmas Eve as Remy sped the Dart eastward towards the Mississippi border.

CHAPTER LVI

USA

Mississippi. Alabama. Then a sign issuing a warm welcome to Florida just as dawn broke. He pulled into a highway rest stop to stretch and toss a tennis ball around with Will as he pondered the immediate future, playing a series of events over in his mind's eye. Arriving home to find the family pleasantly shocked at his arrival, jumping up to deliver hugs and cheek kisses. Surprising the family as they sat huddled around a colorfully decorated tree, in the midst of a discussion that Remy could just slip right into.

Darker possibilities. His brother's home vacant, signs of forced entry and an ensuing struggle. A memory flashed of the thug teacher smugly displaying his brother's address on Google Maps, of that open threat and a more subtle one issued by the vice-principal to bring his family into the torture, of his mother's voice on the other end of a phone call that cut out at all the right moments. He stood staring off in the distance, lost in thought, coming to when he felt something drop on his foot. A tennis ball covered in dog drool rolled off to one side. William looked up happily.

"Did you actually return the ball? What is wrong with you?"

Remy dove to retrieve it but William was faster and snatched it away, engaged in a game of his own design involving sprinting about and pretending to fetch. Remy gave chase for the hound's sake, wholly unable to shake thoughts of his family imperiled. Once the hound had tired, they returned to the car. Remy grabbed some loose change and placed a long-distance call to his mother's house from a payphone. *Surprised these still exist,* he thought absently as the phone rang. An answering machine clicked in, his mother's voice identifying herself and politely reminding callers what they should do when they hear a beep. He dragged out the message, allowing her time to identify him and pick up the phone. Two minutes later he hung up, frustrated and even more concerned. He called again and left another long message thinking to wake her, but again there was no response.

Not good. Remy began struggling to breathe deeply. *She's always been an early riser.*

The air soon felt as if it lacked oxygen. Forced, deep breaths yielded no better result. He squatted as a wave of lightheadedness turned the world black. Hyperventilating. He was dimly aware that he was drawing attention to himself. Exhaustion from driving from L.A. to Florida in fifty-five hours came upon him all at once. He focused on controlling his breathing, inhaling and exhaling consciously. When he was able to stand, he placed a call to his brother. The phone rang and rang, ten, fifteen, twenty times. He hung up and called back twice. Nothing. Neither his mother nor his brother was home on Christmas Eve morning. Remy didn't like it. Despised it. Was frightened by it. The coins that he shoved into the payphone to make a third call became lodged in the slot and so he squared his shoulders and hips and struck the machine with his open palm. A wave of cold snapped through his right arm from wrist to elbow.

"F^$*!......F%*#!!!"

He looked around and spied children playing in the distance. "F$#*," he repeated more quietly. His top of his right radial bone lumped menacingly around the center of his palm, severely dislocated. He poked the endpoint of the newly situated bone in the center of his hand triggering another wave of cold that weakened his legs to the point of collapse. Unable to prevent collapse, he could negotiate how he landed a bit and took care to fall on his left side.

"Yep, that's the problem. Fantastic, Remy. Just what you need right now," he chided himself, as he dragged himself upright, clumsily using only his left arm.

The change return slot had burst open. Silver coins lay scattered about the vicinity. Opening the lid released the contents of the coin bank, around twenty dollars in coinage. He filled his pockets with one good arm and returned to the Dart. William sensed something was amiss and calmly moved to the backseat without prompting as Remy sank into the passenger seat. He took a deep breath and reevaluated the arm he'd been cradling across his chest to prevent from swinging about painfully. *My arm is broken. That must be what this is. You know that bone shouldn't be where it is. You know where it should go. All you have to do is put it there.* He rolled down each window a crack and took a diver's breath. Mustering courage, he bit down hard against his own teeth and used his left thumb to shove the bone protruding into his right palm, sliding the radius back into the depth of his right forearm, straight down the wrist. There was no terrific popping noise, no tearing sensation, just a wave of cold emptiness that pulled him into unconsciousness.

He awoke an hour later, drool covering the top of his shirt. The arm was throbbing and unresponsive and an icy chill pulsated from its core. The unnatural lump had been replaced by an angry, dark bruise. His whole body ached but the arm felt aligned properly again. After freshening up in the restroom and filling his stomach with tap water, he unfastened several buttons of his shirt, tucked the injured arm into the opening á la Napoleon Bonaparte, and set about exiting the rest stop. Reliant solely on his left hand, he awkwardly merged into the flow of highway traffic, grim and determined to reach his destination.

CHAPTER LVII

USA

He drove on, five, six hours barreling down the highway with one arm resting in his shirt and the other navigating the roads. Onward. No lunch. No break. Just onward. The sun was setting when he pulled into her driveway. He parked the car and absorbed the scene. Everything looked in order, though his mind raced with the possibilities of what he may find inside. He removed his arm from the makeshift sling and refastened the buttons of his shirt. *I may need this arm, broken or not. This may be very bad indeed*, he thought as he approached the front door. Inside a small dog began yipping, negating the need for a doorbell. Almost immediately the sound of thumping footsteps approached the nearby window. An older woman, mid-sixties, short and chubby, peered out from behind an upturned flap of curtain. A rattling of chains and locks and then:

"Remy!" she exclaimed, as if he was a rock star. "Come in!" He was greeted with a kiss on the cheek and wrapped up in a firm embrace. In short time, he was ushered into a spare bedroom, where he unloaded his belongings along with Christmas gifts for family members he hadn't seen in years, trinkets picked up along the cross-country drive. After introducing William, he led the hound into the backyard, where he ran about joyfully chasing an unfortunate squirrel.

"How are you, son?" she asked, cozying into a plush chair in the living room. Remy reclined along the sofa and stretched his legs.

"I've been better." He searched for a deeper description but didn't know where to begin. "I'm glad you didn't come to China. And it's good to see you alive and well. I wasn't sure what I'd find." Trailing off at the last sentence, realizing how odd that had just sounded.

She picked up on it, face scrunching up uncomfortably. "Sheldon worked with you at that school, right? He called me."

Remy's face flushed an angry shade of red remembering Sheldon accompanying him during the walk from work to home, the thinly-veiled threat of bringing his family into the mess, the strange bodyguard that had materialized from the crowd, intent on the imminent scuffle.

She pressed on, "Said you had a culture shock."

"Culture shock? Well, that culture was certainly shocking but we really are using the word *culture* pretty loosely here. Culture shock. Nope, though that does cover up their tracks nicely." He paused, thinking of the defensive position the school had taken. It was a pretty strong argument. Difficult to refute though Remy's mind immediately began doing just that. "Doesn't explain why I was afflicted by this cultural shock three full years after I'd settled into China, though. Culture shock occurs within the first week. Maybe a month. What about the first couple of years? Nothing shocking then." That about summed it up. Refuted. End of story.

His mother went on, unaccepting and unconvinced. "He said you were having delusions. Hallucinating. Believing things that weren't true."

He sat up, relaxation woefully leaking away. His mother had chosen a side before he had even arrived. The other side. The side he had painstakingly tried to escape over and over again. The cause of his concern over her safety. Irony. "I'm telling you the truth, mother. What happened to me was not culture shock." *No solace to be found here either,* he silently realized. "I'm your son, you know. How are you siding with strangers on this?"

"I know that," she said good-naturedly, changing the tone. "It's so good to have you back for the holidays, Remy."

Enthusiasm and discomfort warred within her as she took in her son for the first time in years. She kept up the cheery façade as she moved to the kitchen, preparing to shift the conversation to food, of which she'd been consuming way too much having gained at least twenty kilos since he'd seen her last. As she rummaged through cabinets in search of cooking utensils and ingredients, Remy evaluated the situation. *She's safe. Always was safe, I guess. So's the rest of the family or she would have mentioned it. Wouldn't be thinking me as delusional right now. Now what?*

"I don't know if you're proud of me or ashamed or what." He waved his hand dismissively as she began to reply. "No, no. I know you'll say proud. I know. Forget that." He searched for words to describe some of what had occurred during the dark times. "It wasn't easy. This past half year has been so hard." His mind flashed back to the previous winter, of creeping through shadows to follow his live-in lover as she sped away in a black sportscar. The lies that followed. "This whole year has been...taxing."

"Because you lost your money."

"I didn't lose it. It was stolen from me." He chuckled coldly. "I didn't set it down somewhere and forget where I put it. I was robbed. I was robbed and so much more. Events you cannot begin to fathom, things I hope you never understand. Unsupportive though you may be -- and let me tell you, your disbelief right now is downright corrosive -- you are my mother and I love you and I don't want to see you troubled."

"Trouble me. Tell me what happened."

"Alright," he began, "I was tortured. That's the worst of it, for sure. The sleep deprivation. I wasn't allowed to sleep for close to two full months. I was intentionally kept awake by malevolent forces in Guangzhou, China." He looked to her, analyzing her mannerisms for an understanding of her true thoughts.

She did not believe him.

"And there it is, mother. You don't believe me. You think I'm making this all up."

"I didn't say anything!"

"I've transcended the need for verbal confirmations from those I interact with, but okay, fine, I'll play along. Do you believe what I just told you?" he asked, knowing the answer but needing her to catch up.

"I believe that you believe it."

"Wow. That's just great. Thanks for that. So, I'm delusional. Me, your son, the guy who came out of your womb, and some stranger you've never met before, a guy named Sheldon who you only know as a disembodied voice on the other end of a phone, is the honest one. He's the one who has earned your trust." He stood up and eyed the front door.

"I'm sorry. Sit down. You must be tired." Love and concern in her voice.

"Yes. You have no idea. You have absolutely no clue just how tired I am." He processed that, softening. "You just don't know any better, mom. It's just who you are. It'd be great if you supported me, believed in me, but you just can't. It's just not in you. I'm trying to draw water from a stone. I should go."

"I'm sorry you feel that way," she replied matter-of-factly. "Why don't you rest in the spare bedroom?"

"Sleep would be nice." Simply saying the word brought with it a yawn. "Okay. Thank you. I appreciate the offer. I think I'll take you up on that, actually." He sat back down and stretched his legs. "I wish we had a better relationship, you and me."

"I want that, too."

"Well, I'm here now. Let's make the most of it." He smiled genuinely. "So, what happens on Christmas Eve? Don't we open one present tonight and the rest on Christmas morning? It's been a while." He looked about the living room, taking in the details for the first time. "Wait. There's no tree here."

"I'll be at your sister's this year, but not 'til tomorrow. My little granddaughter is growing up so fast. She can speak three languages, you know." She was beaming, full of grandmotherly pride. Everything Remy had hoped for poured into his niece.

"You're the sort of person who loves a new puppy and hates the older dog, aren't you?" He asked, in the habit of vocalizing his thoughts. She shrank back, hurt.

"Why would you say that?"

He changed the subject, not wanting to argue. "Thank you for the hospitality, mom. If we're not doing anything tonight, I'll sleep until the morning. I could probably sleep for days, actually. But wake me up in the morning. I have gifts that I want to give the family. My lovely, loving, encouraging, nurturing, trusting family of mine."

The bed was tiny. A child's bed set up for his niece to use during trips to grandma's house. He needed to curl up in order to fit on the mattress, mimicking William who slept tail on snout on the floor below. It was uncomfortable and did little to alleviate the muscle cramps that had become a normal part of his life. Spasms shook his body, prying him from sleep throughout the night but only temporarily. The pain subsided and sleep returned. There was no sound of water dripping. No helicopter. No man urinating directly above him. No chanting commands to "Jump!"

A child's smile played about his face as he slept throughout the night and into the next day.

CHAPTER LVIII

USA

He almost slept through Christmas morning. The sound of pots and lids and water faucets mixed with boisterous, muffled voices engaged in a lively discussion. *That's the family out there. If they had experienced anything akin to what I went through, they would not sound like that. They're unaffected and I escaped. We escaped,* he corrected himself, glancing down to the Shepherd underfoot. *Now what?*

He delivered unwrapped and unreciprocated presents to a family he hadn't seen in years, doling out gifts among awkward smiles and the massive elephant in the room. No one asked if he had experienced culture shock. They just assumed it to be true based on the cryptic answers he gave. They followed his mother's lead, rejecting the tale of sleep-deprivation and entrapment, not even entertaining the notion really. *He's either crazy or a moron that confused reality.* Their inner thoughts were almost audible to Remy so plain to read were their faces. A strained, uncomfortable Christmas. *With family like this, who needs enemies?* Remy thought, chuckling to himself at the private joke. *Needed enemies,* he corrected. *That all seems to be far away now.*

As December turned to January, Remy and his mother tried in vain to stoke a fire of love and mutual respect that had never burned brightly. His sister and her family eventually came to openly condemn Remy's tale and made it a point to reject his presence. No matter how gently he broached the subject of what had happened, his mother simply would not believe the difficult parts. She thought him delusional and clutched tightly to a normality that just hadn't existed then and there. Faced with such doubt, he reanalyzed the past year in China, revisiting memories as a skeptic, critical and objective. His mind raced with very real memories of actual occurrences that were impossible to erase or disregard. Only with great purpose was he able to dull them into submission in the quiet moments.

He found little support from her beyond food and shelter. Emotionally, she offered little support. Her disbelief intensified into a real concern that her last born son was no longer sane. He soon stopped trying to convince his mother of what had happened and focused instead on acclimating to America. He began seeking work in early January, first applying to jobs that he truly desired and felt capable of performing well: administrating charter schools, teaching the Inuit of Alaska, assisting private detectives. Finding no success there, he broadened his search to jobs that relied less upon education and experience until eventually he found himself applying for work at fast food restaurants and grocery stores. But no one would hire Remy LeBeau. Overqualified one way and lacking experience another. By the end of January, he remained unemployed and was almost completely out of money. He signed up for government food assistance and used the funds to purchase groceries for a home that he was feeling increasingly more unwelcome in. Because he had been working abroad, he did not qualify for unemployment benefits. Food assistance became the sole form of income coming in each month.

By mid-February, his mother had gotten into the habit of ridiculing him daily for not working. He had sent over one hundred resumes to employers, oftentimes filling out online applications that repeated his resume word for word, a fine indicator of just how little American employers were concerned for a would-be employee's time. Pressure at home was mounting. Mother and son argued more than they conversed. Words turned to daggers.

He took a long drive and purchased a .45 semi-automatic handgun, thinking that it may be time to end the suffering rather than endure it. He researched the most complete method of committing suicide via gunshot online, feeling secure of exactly what part of the brain should be targeted to ensure a quick death. He slid the full magazine into the handle until it clicked in place, switched the safety off, and took a long pull from a whiskey bottle. Finding putting a gun barrel into his mouth undignified, he repositioned the barrel behind his ear, aligning it just above the brain stem. He inhaled deeply and exhaled slowly. There was a kindly written note for his mother, apologizing for the ensuing mess and ensuring that she was not to blame. *It is as it should be, as it must.* He breathed again, slowly, deeply. All was calm. There was no inner voice screaming: *Don't do this!* Acceptance. Empty acceptance.

He flexed his right index finger, a soft smile barely turning up at his lips. Only nothing happened. He remained locked into position, barrel behind ear, rigid grasp on the handgun. He took another deep breath and focused on squeezing the trigger of the device. Again, there was no response from his digits. He set down the .45 and drank deeply from the whisky bottle.

"Alright," he muttered, eyes pooling with tears, vision distorted. He did not cry, though. He was far too detached for that. "So, I have to live than, I guess."

A week or two later, his mother -- feelings especially hurt by wording during an argument -- called the police, unbeknownst to Remy. He was reading a novel on the sofa, shifting gears into something more productive and peaceful. A knock on the door caught

Remy off-guard and brought a chubby officer inside. Once inside, his mother set about telling a tale that Remy had attacked her, had thrown her against a wall, had held her down against her will, a fabricated lie that rolled off of her tongue with ease. He was surprised by the arrival of the officer; he was stunned by the remorseless lie. His mother looked truly distraught though he hadn't touched the woman. There had been no struggle. Neither of their voices had even risen above a normal speaking volume. No one had even cut the other off in conversation. Mean things were said, words that cut to the bone in the way that only those who know each other well were spoken, but a physical altercation had simply never occurred.

It was clear that she wanted him gone and instead of clearly declaring that to her son, she had called the police and lied to an officer of the law. He packed his belongings into his suitcase and left later that day, calling an old friend from high school who then offered him a sofa to sleep on. Remy was a mix of gratitude and sorrow. Hating the burden he had become, the lack of options available, he drove on in no hurry, wallowing in the juxtaposition of rushing across the country to ensure his family's well-being, a family that had wholeheartedly rejected him. Dusk was approaching as he arrived in east Florida. There was drinking and catching up on old times. Shots and beer. A bonfire. Reminiscing. Honest laughter bubbling through the mire.

Spring was emerging, made manifest in blooming flora and warming weather. A season of renewal and growth to many and quite the opposite to Remy.

CHAPTER LIX

USA

As Remy's life spiraled downward, Monica remained in touch with him via Skype. An ever-worsening winter with his mother. She was there. Sleeping on a sofa at an old friend's place in the spring. She was there, too. Remy didn't know why, but she was there through it all.

By April, he had lost hope of explaining the unimaginable to officials. He was introduced to an available sexual encounter with another woman at the new place but it just felt wrong. He was bound together with Monica Hu, connected through a shared experience that proved impossible to put into believable words. There was a love he could not shake, despite it all. He was tied, alright. Knotted firmly.

He missed her a great deal. Happiness only returned during those periodic video chats in which he could look upon her and give voice to the drivel that had become the makings of his new life in the states. She denied and deflected and refused to discuss the Guangzhou torture. She didn't much enjoy discussing the bank theft in Nanchang nor the well-dressed thug who entered into a police station and ushered out a legitimate police officer. If Remy could have forgotten such things, he would have found true happiness then. Erotic pics and videos helped satiate carnal desire.

He wore the scar on his right shin with pride, though he had come to realize that explaining its origins immersed the listener into a story that was quickly dismissed as the ravings of a lunatic. He read the faces of the few he began explaining the details to, saw friendly demeanors shift from concern to worry to mistrust and disbelief. Would-be friends kept their distance thereafter and he soon learned to just keep the story to himself. It was unbelievable and he was losing potential acquaintances in the process of relating it.

The mobile phone and the portable storage device that potentially held some evidence of the cyber-torture that had plagued him, once of utmost importance, fell into the void that welled within. He had practiced relating the tale for months and still people thought him mad, dismissing the conversation before much of the story had even begun. He had lost all hope that authority figures would be sympathetic to hearing him out and analyze the electronics. No one cared about the torture he had endured. No one had believed it even occurred.

He had very little money remaining and the old friend that he'd reconnected with had grown tired of him sleeping on the sofa after a month. Remy dutifully continued to search for work but found none, as unemployable as he was unbelievable. Poverty, real poverty, was becoming the new norm. Unable to pay an upcoming car insurance premium, he photographed his newly purchased, very used vehicle and prepared to sell it online. His thoughts turned to the handgun, of using it to steal and rob in order to put some cash in hand but after a long night of soul searching, he reasoned that such an act would only delay the inevitable, and more to the point, was wrong. He gave away his handgun to the newly-reconnected, newly-disappointed old friend in an effort to compensate rent for occupying the man's home, an act that meant very little to him. He just wanted him gone, all the novelty of rekindling the past long gone. He accepted the gun and an old engagement ring that had never found its true mark as payment for rent and continued being a rude and hostile presence.

It was all collapsing around him. There was nothing left. No friends, old or new. No family. No job. No home. Only William remained. Ever-joyful William, just as happy as always.

<u>USA</u>

"You have to get rid of the dog, Remy."

"I can't do that. That dog's been with me through thick and thin. You don't know, don't believe, what I went through to get him here. He kept my spirits above water in drowning times. He's my anchor. Don't do this. Think about what you're asking of me."

The pleading went on for some time but Josh didn't care much. He had lost his fire long ago, a realization that had come within the first week of catching up with the man, a realization that Remy had tried his best to disguise.

"The dog has to go," he repeated, clearly annoyed at not being immediately obeyed. Remy tried to find a halfway point that would satiate the man to no avail. No clear reason was given. No compromise was acceptable. William had become a backyard dog from day one, enduring the Florida heat against Remy's wishes. The pistol, the groceries he kept supplied, the engagement ring, constantly cleaning the house, all insufficient. Begging a cold, hollow man did no good.

With the heaviest of hearts, Remy set about to finding William a new home. He placed an ad on Craigslist which praised the many merits of that champion hound. He wrote of his pedigree, being pure German Shepherd, fairly young, in good health, sweet and playful and basically obedient and then he submitted an ad online to give away the only friend he had left. A friend and a son of sorts that he had pledged to deliver into safety, far from the torture that had gripped them in Guangzhou.

There were a few replies that were quickly dismissed. Remy was prepared to suffer the consequences of expulsion from the volatile home before putting William into the wrong hands, and more than a few of those types responded, and this was put to the test as the hollow homeowner tried to speed up the process, threatening to evict him from the house if he didn't surrender the Shepherd to the first available responder. Remy swallowed a desire to beat the man senseless and smiled placatingly. He loathed him but continued to endure the cruelty. It was another week before a proper reply came in, an email from a man and his wife, owners of an aging female German Shepherd who wanted a playmate around to keep her company. They owned a nice house. Not a mansion, but it was well-kept and cozy.

William was sitting in the passenger seat alternating between sticking his snout outside of the open window and peering over the dashboard, thrilled to be on the road again. Remy held onto his paw as much as William would allow during the long drive, teary eyed and sniffling. At red lights he would bend down and stick his face into his fur and inhale deeply, filing the scent away in a special place in the memory bank.

They arrived at a park filled with high grass and old, gnarled oaks that cast the field into shade regardless of what the sun intended. He shut the engine off and turned to the Shepherd.

"You have no idea how much I don't want to do this. But I'm just being selfish. It'd be best for me if we didn't part ways. Whatever happens next, you'll make it better." Tears fell and his voice broke. "But that's selfish. I may get arrested soon for beating the sh!t out of Josh or robbing a grocery store in order to pay for a hotel room. Either way, I'll probably end up homeless or imprisoned soon. That would mean you wouldn't have shelter, old boy. Or steady food."

He smiled weakly. "This is the right path for you. It just hurts so much." He broke down then, choking on words that became loud sobbing. William moved over to the driver's seat and sat on Remy's lap. All one hundred pounds of him. "Now, you're getting it, dingo." More sobbing. "This is the end for you and me."

He held him in a tight embrace and spoke into his fur. "Don't forget what I taught you. Howl at the thunder, don't hide from it, you baby. You escape from holds pretty well and dodge blows with the best of them. You probably won't need any of that stuff where you're going, but you never know. Don't jump on people, no matter how excited you are to see them. Poop outside. Keep out of the trash. All that stuff." He relinquished his hold on the Shepherd. "I love you very much, William. I'm sorry I couldn't provide for you. I tried. I just couldn't do it."

An unforgivable imposition had been imposed upon him that day and he would never be the same. Humanity had irrevocably failed him. The cheap phone in his pocket rang and five minutes later Remy, red-faced and weepy-eyed, was standing across from the man who would take William as his own. He smiled wide in an attempt to mask deep sorrow, failing utterly.

"I don't know how to do this," he said, choking on the words. "I don't know if I can do this."

"Do you want to keep him?"

"Of course, I want to keep him. This is William. He's a marvelous dog. I raised him. We shared a life together. You're separating a son from his father is what you're doing."

"Well, then…"

"No, please, take him with you. Take William. And love him as I do. He'll be in a good place with you. There's no way around this. It just hurts, is all." He took a deep breath and collected himself. "So how do we do this?"

"You give me the leash."

"Just like that?"

"That's the only way to do it," he replied patiently, compassion somewhere on the fringes.

He tried to say something uplifting, something clever, but his mind was blank and hurting. Instead, he slid the leash over into the man's hand. William accepted the transfer pretty well, enjoying the newness of it all.

"And then, I'm going to go for a walk. It would be best if you weren't here when we get back."

"Ouch. But that sounds right. Okay." He crouched and held the hound's forehead against his own. "Be good, William. I'm sorry. I love you. Be good." Tears flowing. "Goodbye."

The man marched off into a thicket. William was happy to trail along. Within seconds, they disappeared into the brush. Remy straightened up, returned to his car, and parked in a similar spot in the semi-abandoned lot. Within a few minutes, William and the caregiver emerged. William paused as he returned to the clearing, coming full stop and looking about, sniffing the air to the right and left, searching while the man tugged him toward his car. Remy turned the ignition thinking to swoop in and undo what he had done but his hand froze at the gear shift. Inner turmoil welled and burned before he turned off the engine and watched as William was pulled into a nice, modern sedan. His muzzle jutted from a cracked window, ears pricked, searching the surroundings for Remy as the sedan sped off, merging into traffic and then gone.

It was quite some time before he felt in control enough to drive but just two blocks later, he began sobbing so intensely that he couldn't breathe. Blinded with tears, he pulled over to the side of the road and wept, crying out, "I'm sorry" over and over until his throat was raw and noncompliant. He did not speak after that for a few days. Something had shifted within him. Something irreversible.

CHAPTER LX

USA

"I'm sorry."

"Yeah, me too. He's in a better place than me, though, so there's that." He forced a smile at the camera to the only one in his life to have said *I'm sorry*.

"You were a good daddy. A dog daddy," she giggled, a step beyond anything Remy could muster.

"Yeah. Look, I'm going to go, okay. Take care."

"Wait. I want show you my new outfit. It very cute."

There was no desire in him. Not for her, not for food, not for waking up.

"Some other time, Moni. I should go."

With the connection severed, he returned to going about the process of selling his car. The sale brought in some cash but his funds wouldn't last much longer even if he continued to avoid paying rent. It certainly wouldn't last more than a month if a motel was needed. He checked his email before lunch, not looking forward to the disappointing stream of rejection letters to job applications. Many more applications were met with no response whatsoever. Melancholy everywhere he turned.

"I was going to save the world once upon a time," he spoke to an empty house while the computer started up. "All that hurt had a purpose. I had a reason to press through then but there's nothing now." His lips turned upward, somehow failing to become a smile. "At least I brought William to a better place. He's probably napping after having had a swim in the pool. Going to chase some squirrels later."

Rejection, spam, spam, rejection, car insurance cancellation confirmation, spam, spam, spam, employment offer, sp--.

An employment offer? Buried among potential car buyers and leftover interested parties to take care of William and a heap of less interesting material was indeed a job offer to begin teaching a summer program in July. He was fairly certain he could survive until then. *Just need to purchase that airline ticket and the rest should take care of itself. It'll be tight, but this is possible. Thank God. Now, where am I going?*

Guangzhou, China. The only position offered to Remy in the past four months was an offer to teach English and Social Studies at Huamei International School in Guangzhou, China.

Can't be a coincidence.

He pondered a return to Guangzhou -- the only alternative to homelessness -- for a long time, weighing out the pros and cons, the statistical probabilities such and such would happen and how to best respond. Days passed in which he made a last push for employment in America, utterly failing again. At the end of the week, he woke up on a couch with purpose for the first time in months. He sent an email thanking the school for the opportunity and finalized the details of something he never imagined doing: return to Guangzhou.

<u>CHINA</u>

The money didn't last.

Shortly after an awkward birthday that he was neither in the mood to celebrate nor financially able to, the old friend turned enemy became intolerable: belittling Remy daily and demanding more out of household chores that were already completed thoroughly. By the end of May, he'd taken to locking Remy out of the home during the day as he left for work. Unable to ignore the writing on the wall, he began searching for a short-term roommate situation near Guangzhou for a couple of months until the summer position kicked in. Somehow through a listing on Craigslist, he found exactly that. The flat was tiny and lacked air conditioning. The bed was stiff, narrow, and short. There was no washing machine. No refrigerator. No stove.

The Chinese government seemed to provide small, two-bedroom barebone apartments such as the one he stayed at in the spring of 2013 to most of the impoverished citizens of her nation, fairly free of charge. The lady who posted the ad was seeking to increase the minimal income she generated working fulltime at a cellphone shop. For the price of $200 a month, Remy enjoyed a room of his own in an apartment in the far western outskirts of Guangzhou where he read two Hemmingway novels he'd brought with him, jogged the neighborhood in the evenings, and basked in his new freedom, miniscule though it was. The interior of the apartment was hot, dank, and musty and the air stunk of mold but he was happy for the improvement in living conditions.

It was strangely nice to be back in China. Walking through crowded streets, dining on low-cost dishes cooked to order, ingredients hailing from local farms. He ate sparingly of dumplings, fried rice, and noodles of all shapes and sizes, constrained to a budget so tight that there was no need for a bank. All the money he owned fit easily into his wallet.

Depression, panic attacks, corpulence, violent outbursts, anxiety, fear, while prevalent in America, were all rarities in China. His torment half a year ago warred with respect for a populace so lacking in psychological disorders. From the alpha-male wickedness of Josh to the pathological lying of his mother in a ploy designed to imprison her son, America had proven herself to be thorny ground. He was apprehensive, expecting Guangzhou to strike as soon as he lowered his guard, but a twinge of hope bloomed uninvited.

The sun shone fiercely on his neck and shoulders as he returned from the local market carrying, among other odds and ends, a large bag of powdered laundry detergent to mix with lukewarm water in a bucket, forming a soapy mixture in which he'd scrub his clothes clean. Halfway into the procedure, hands pruned from soaking, he began contemplating the purchase of a washboard. The balcony lacked even a wire to string across the dilapidated balcony. *Need to buy the whole set, I guess. That's odd. How has this woman done laundry here in the past without such things?* He quelled rising suspicion as he plunged and scrubbed jeans. *How much longer will this China hold? No one has turned against me. I can sleep each night. No damnable noises piercing in at the perfect time.*

It was the normalcy that got to him. He had expected to return to Guangzhou and be immediately accosted in all the familiar ways. Instead, he took a perfectly normal train to a station, ate a nice dinner, and fell straight to sleep in a musty room. The woman he shared the room with seemed nice enough. She was a tad older than Remy and seemingly attracted to him. Nothing happened, however, as any other woman just felt wrong. There was only Monica who journeyed over to visit a greyer-haired, more worn Remy LeBeau. She was untouched by their time apart, poised, dignified, as graceful as she was beautiful. He felt alive again. Alive, but barely just.

He had been certain he would never walk and talk with her again, yet, she had returned in the flesh. She hadn't left his side through all the hardships of America and Guangzhou and he hadn't the faintest idea why. It was a joy to meet with her again, though. That he knew.

She brought all the energy and hope that spring had failed to deliver though unanswered questions still remained: her premature exiting of the police station; the muscular thugs, one in Nanchang and two in Guangzhou; the theft itself; the warning of an imminent leaky pipe, a precursor to sleep deprivation. She refused to discuss anything from those dark times, comfortably deflecting even his most measured and carefully crafted questions woven eloquently into perfectly normal conversations.

She stayed in a cheap motel on her own dime for a week which came complete with an old AC unit that periodically wheezed out dismal wisps of slightly cooled air. They dined on dishes purchased at local markets on carefully budgeted allowances. It wasn't much fun for her but only someone who knew her very well would've noticed. To hold her in his arms was undoubtedly a joy but most other pleasures had become muted, darkened. He had grown less interested in the highs and lows that life offered. A dark cloud had formed and twisted itself around Remy's spirit and while there were moments in which the man that she cared for shined through, there was a looming gloom that proved difficult to penetrate.

She left a couple of days earlier than expected and while he wished her to stay, he couldn't blame her for leaving. He'd expected to be immediately assaulted, a rat batted about by a thousand-person cat; instead, he slept soundly, undisturbed each night. He was confused by the normalcy of it all, though some things would never be normal again. There was the scar on his shin where he had been beaten by a baton. There was the curve of his erect penis, a consistent killjoy.

He was saddened as she disengaged her hand from his and entered a train headed for the airport, but even those feelings -- the only feelings anymore -- were dim. June turned to July. He moved from the far western outskirts into a mediocre apartment across from Huamei International School to begin teaching middle-school students English in a playful weekday environment over the summer. He planned and implemented lighthearted activities and learning games in a vigorous classroom full of game-oriented students.

July turned to August and the academic year began in earnest. His charges shifted to high-school students and expectations became more serious. Assessments and lesson plans began to fill his days. New staff members were introduced. Meetings were held. After work drinks and movie-watching meetups took place. Evenings in downtown. Karaoke.

The simple pleasures of life wouldn't hold, however. When it began to fall apart, he was as pleased in its coming as he was sickened. Finally, the expected emerged. A relief of the worst kind.

CHAPTER LXI

CHINA

It began with an attractive teacher newly arrived who taught middle school students in a different wing of the school. She was quick with a quip, light on her feet, confident, easy to talk to, attractive. Curiously, there was something in her mannerisms that portrayed familiarity toward Remy though he had never seen her before.

She was an American, as was the entirety of the foreign teaching staff. No British or South Africans or Australians. Only Americans, which was in and of itself, an oddity at an international school. Such were his expectations of Guangzhou and he found comfort in the shift into unsettling occurrences, to be back on familiar footing, suspicion fitting like an old glove. Monica had seemed capable of shirking answers indefinitely so Remy saw a quasi-suspicious, semi-romantic relationship with the new colleague Mary as an opportunity to find answers.

They got along well, chatting amiably at meetups at colleagues' homes for dinners and whatnot, occasionally venturing into the now perfectly normal downtown environs to attend Latin dance classes or trivia nights at pubs. Normal dates that usually ended with her joining him back at his apartment where she would sleep on his sofa. The next morning, they would split ways after breakfast. Rinse and repeat. Such was the routine they shared for a month or so.

During this month, Remy tried unsuccessfully to pull answers from Monica. No one had proven as challenging as her. He had never been pushed so far or stretched so thin, and yet, she'd been the only one to care for Remy during the bad times. The only constant in his life in a period of so much loss. She was everything to him, but she would not budge on the big issues, questions that burned in Remy's psyche. *Why did she abandon me at the police station? Why remain a presence after the theft? Why offer me a position to work with her? What exactly would that have entailed? And how had the opening to teach at Huamei -- literally the only job offer in the world -- come about? And in Guangzhou, no less? Again?* None of it made any sense and that absence of understanding was maddening.

He loved her but knew she would never relate the truth in its entirety to him. At best he was fed morsels shrouded in hints and subtlety, and so, failing to find answers through Monica he turned to Mary, the mystery of her, how she had seemed prepared for him in some way, had recognized him before he had even met her. With English being her mother tongue, it required less patience and concentration to engage in conversation with her. They had long discussions on topics ranging from Hollywood to politics. Remy took a shine to her as he sniffed about for clues as to why he had looked familiar to her, or better yet, of what had transpired in round one of Guangzhou.

Meanwhile, he had been thrust into the role of teaching not just the subjects of social studies and English, of which he had agreed prior via a signed contract, but also science and mathematics, subjects he was far less experienced and comfortable teaching. He taught every core subject to each and every one of the students in the international high school program, doing twice the work agreed upon for the same rate of pay. Trouble was brewing.

CHAPTER LXII

CHINA

"I'm sorry," Remy chuckled. "Did you just call it your snail?"

Mary looked up coyly and slid an empty shot glass over to the side.

"That's what it is. It's my little snail. And what're you doin' looking at it?" she asked, trying to sound accusatory through a drunken haze, though the grin portrayed a different meaning altogether.

"What am I doing looking at it? I'm being a red-blooded man is what I'm doing. What are you doing wearing a skirt without panties? How about that?"

"I don't like to wear them when I sleep. Is that okay with you?" Softly snide.

"It most certainly is. Your panties are your own. Do what you like. Just know that if we're sitting on the floor playing cards, shooting whiskey and you're wearing a high skirt, well, my eyes may wander a bit, deviants that they are."

She shrugged and eyed the bottle again. He took the hint and poured another round. They cheered and clinked shot glasses and downed another shot. A third of a bottle remained, most of its contents split evenly between their two stomachs. She discarded a seven of diamonds which he eagerly drew into his hand, completing a mini straight.

"It's more of a slug than a snail," Remy said, considering his discard. He decided on the ten of diamonds and tossed it down it smugly. She immediately scooped it up. "I mean, you don't have a shell or anything for it. Looks more like a soft, fuzzy slug from here," he continued, leaning over to get a better view.

She refolded her legs, pouting cutely. "The shell is on the inside, get it? You can't see it. The part that you can see is the little body that slides along through the garden."

"That's a long way to go for a snail analogy."

"You just don't understand the female anatomy."

Not liking the discard pile, he turned to the deck and pulled a card he needed to complete his gin hand. He kept a straight face concealing the fact that he had already won, looking deeply at his cards as if he struggled to decide which one to discard. "Do they like being petted, I wonder? Some snails are poisonous, right? Some snails you should touch, and some snails you shouldn't. I wonder what's going on with your snail."

She looked up from behind her hand. "My snail is *not* poisonous."

"Good answer. Gin, by the way," he said, fanning out his hand as he lay them down, eliciting a groan of displeasure as she threw her hand off to the side. "Can we go to bed now? It's late and I'm drunk and sleepy."

She moved to the couch, her normal sleeping spot.

"I was thinking you should sleep in my bed tonight. All this talk of poisonous snails has me a little frightened. I'm not sure if I can sleep alone. I'll be thinking of snails coming down the walls, through the windows, under the door." He outstretched his open hand. She peered at the it, considering. "Come on, Mary. This isn't such a crazy idea. You've been crashing on my sofa for a month. We've smooched a couple times, you know, just to keep our skills sharp and all."

She grinned a bit.

"You want this. I want this. So why don't we do it?" he asked her. "Every weekend you end up here. You must kind of want this, too, right? So, let's just do it."

After a little more cajoling, she placed her hand into his and off they went to the bedroom, where they caressed and kissed and loved and more. Later, he awoke and slipped into pajama bottoms before quietly slipping through the sliding glass door that led to the balcony, stargazing from the third floor of his apartment some fifteen kilometers west of downtown.

Maybe twenty or so up there tonight. And that one might be the ISS. Nothing compared to that night in the Mojave. The night I finally touched down and escaped, William munching on a rotting carcass under hundreds of sparkling dots of varying sizes and intensities. Around the world and back again, right here at ground zero. How did I end up in Guangzhou again? Nothing makes much sense anymore.

He stretched and contemplated things that were and may be. The door slid open behind him bringing Mary equally half naked. She was short and buxom, wide at chest and hip, with a pretty face that seemed to be holding something back most of the time. She laced her fingers around his chest and embraced him from behind, her ample bosom pressing against his back pleasantly in the warm night air.

"From no panties, to only panties. I may never figure you out."

"Good. I wouldn't want to bore you."

He turned and kissed her before taking a seat. She perched on his lap. They sat together and talked of constellations and horoscopes, of the distant future and potential for life outside of Earth, challenging each other's perspective as often as agreeing. *Sometimes up is down and foes are friends. I still don't understand why on day one, minute one, she looked to me like she already knew who I was, but this is nice. This is good.* And it was. For a time.

CHAPTER LXIII

CHINA

It didn't last a month, although in all fairness, one month in Guangzhou could last a very long time indeed. As September began, Remy was finding it difficult to maintain a relationship with Mary. He had tried explaining some of what had happened to him six months earlier. Tried to drum up an answer as to why she seemed to take a shine to him right away. Tried explaining the bank theft and what had followed, how it had changed him. Of the trauma he re-lived in the still, sober moments. With each revealing she grew more distant and mistrusting.

In the midst of this growing divide, a teacher he had never seen before began making appearances throughout school hallways and weekly meetings. A tall, thick, chubby man, bearlike in stature and stride. He moved into the apartment directly across from Remy's and from that day on, the audio assault began again. In the begin-ning, someone would knock sharply on his front door and then dash off, sometimes up, sometimes down the nearby stairwell before van-ishing into a flat. The sound of a door quickly shutting was Remy's only clue. Catching glimpses in pursuit, he began realizing he was chasing a Chinese boy and so he soon gave up the notion of catching him. *Restraining him would likely ruffle feathers and my limited Mandarin wouldn't be enough to interrogate the kid,* he thought, feeling much like the fox from the sour grapes fable as he returned to his flat after one of these chases.

Door poundings began occurring more frequently and at later hours as time wore on. After a week, Remy was once more thrust into a state of sleep deprivation. The loop of a helicopter landing above had been replaced by a physical banging on the front door but the effect was the same. Sleep-deprivation. Within a week, it took another form. Above his bed, or sofa, or bathroom floor, wherever he lay down in his flat exhausted and hoping to sleep, directly above him a familiar audio track of a man urinating into a toilet bowl sounded out, denying him slumber.

When Mary came to visit, the torture wouldn't manifest itself. No knockings. No audio assault from above. Everything was fine until she left, and then it would begin again in earnest. It came to the point where he was tempted to invite her to live with him just to allow him access to sleep, but such a thing reeked of desperation. He tried explaining the audio assault to her but it just came out as nonsense. She was growing increasingly uneasy with him and needed more coaxing to visit each time until they drifted so far apart that communication was reduced to sporadic texts that she only obligingly responded to after days had passed.

In time, Remy decided to inform higher-ups at his work about what was happening to him at home. The vice-principal of Huamei International School listened politely to Remy as he explained the noises from above and the knock-and-runs, a fake smile dutifully stretched across her face. Her advice was to wait it out, which of course, did nothing to alleviate the problem. He was on his own.

Days later, he walked by the bear-man in the hallway before classes began and doubled back to catch up with him.

"Hey," Remy called out, jogging up to the grim man. "We were introduced once at a meeting, I'm Remy." The bear shook his hand without energy, eager to move on. "Look, I just couldn't help but notice that ever since you've moved in, I don't sleep well. Many strange noises, day and night, triggered exactly when I want to sleep and wherever I lay down. Which should be stranger than it is but I digress. Do you know anything about that?"

"I don't know what you're talking about," he replied behind a smug smile that displayed the opposite was true.

"Right," Remy smiled back, "of course, you don't. No one knocks on your door and runs off at night? Daytime, as well."

The eye contact was not friendly. The thug smiled on, a knowing smile, not a confused, uncomfortable smile, but an *I-know-exactly-what-is-going-on* smile. Remy hated it. Wanted to stomp it off his face.

"Alright, we'll talk more about this later. I wouldn't want that trouble to spread your way. We'll figure this out together, I'm sure. What's your name again? I fear I've forgotten it."

"John."

"John? Well, I'm Remy LeBeau," He held out his hand. "It's nice to meet you," he lied. "John what, if I may ask?"

"Smith."

"John Smith," Remy sighed, finding it difficult to take the conversation seriously. "Your name is John Smith?"

No response.

"Okay, sure. Whatever."

They broke off and Remy returned to teaching all four core subjects to the same students for the entirety of the school day. It wasn't a fun predicament for either the students or the teacher. It was proving a challenge to keep things fresh and hold their attention throughout each day while the nights were filled with piercing noises that turned sleep into an impossibility. He began spending more and more time on the building's rooftop above the fifth floor in order to find solace and catch something akin to a nap. Once again in imperiled, he returned to the stretch of sidewalk along the interstate where he had made certain purchases during the first Guangzhou incident. There he navigated through pimps' offers of prostitution and secured something to keep him vigilant throughout the night attacks, uncertain as to what the city might throw at him next but wanting to be quick and alert when it did.

CHAPTER LXIV

CHINA

Mary left in the autumn, leaving Remy shunned and isolated. The last to hear of outings with colleagues. Received with an up-turned nose when he attended social events. He had mixed feelings about being excluded for as the audio bombardment continued, he just didn't feel up for jolly good times with workmates, of which one or two were likely connected to the return of torment. *At least the bear and one or two others,* Remy thought, thinking back to the first round of Guangzhou last year. *Such a feat requires multiple people working shifts in order to cover me twenty-four-hours a day. A single tormentor would suffer from the same lack of sleep being inflicted. And nobody can endure what I endure here. Yes, more than one person is involved indeed. The giant across the hall and who else?* For a time, he enjoyed the mystery of it, attempting to deduce who took part in his sleep deprivation and who didn't. He needed to think of something, after all, since he was forced awake all day and all night as the weeks ticked by.

On a cool Sunday morning, Remy hauled one large box packed with Mary's clothes, toiletries, and whatnot from his flat, through the apartment parking lot, across the street, and into her flat located in the school dormitory. Feeling abandoned and knowing the audio assault would come in more forcefully afterward, he did not wish her well. There was no warmth in their parting.

The situation did worsen significantly in her absence. The sleeplessness was more sternly regimented and websites, once normal in nature, were showing signs of tampering. Addresses that had once operated normally began showing signs of tampering in the form of odd coding in the address bar and new digital content overlaid atop the original. His computer warned him of certificate inauthenticity and the like -- issues Remy wasn't able to mend -- and soon thereafter, stopped warning him altogether. A familiar attack had begun again, and while this was the Guangzhou he had been expecting, he took no joy in his prediction coming to fruition.

He continued to teach, hating the burden of teaching the additional unpaid classes but preferring to be employed and housed than not. He made it clear that he found teaching all four subjects indefinitely with no increase in salary or benefits unfair, but when the school officially stated that there would be no change, he had little recourse.

To pass the time and fight encroaching fear, he annoyed his attackers as often as possible. He had narrowed it down to the bear, John Smith, and a short, thin, athletic man in his mid-twenties who palled around with him. Looking out over the vast courtyard from just outside his classroom on the third floor, he spied the duo chumming it up. They quieted their personal conversation as he approached, looking him up and down disapprovingly as he strolled into their midst. Remy pretended not to notice.

"Howdy. What's shaking? What are the two of you up to? Whatcha talking about?"

Cold stares served as replies. Glares that Remy savored. His only means of fighting back, as it were. They muttered something and walked away. Remy enjoyed that part the most, that he could just walk up and they would hush up and scatter. That more than anything proved cowardice and he grew to develop a taste for it. He had never been truly certain who was responsible for the audio torture during round one of Guangzhou. Probably Patrick living above his flat and at least a couple of others.

Round two of Guangzhou was a bit different in that only the big man and little guy were the obvious culprits, though the director of the school showed such callousness as to Remy's plight that she could not be discredited altogether. Remy would walk alongside John Smith in the hallways when we could. The bear hated it and Remy continued to pretend not to notice, blissfully chatting away amiably at the dismal man. To annoy and deceive the man simultaneously was one of his greatest joys. It didn't make up for the lack of sleep, but it bolstered his endurance thereof.

But as October rolled around, Remy was losing his moxie. He could feel his energies ebbing away with each loud fist-banging on the front door in the middle of the night, never rushing out swiftly enough to catch the perpetrator in the act. Responding more slowly as time wore him down. Undoubtedly, once again, his neighbors were to blame. Not one to curl up and accept abuse, Remy engaged his tormentor one day, jogging up to the lumbering brute as he lumbered down a school hallway one morning. No longer in a playful mood.

"So, you rattle my cage. A lot. The sick part -- and I mean sick like you suffer from a psychotic problem sort of sick -- is that you it. Yet, every time I rush up and growl at the bars that confine me, you're nowhere to be found. That sort of pumps me up, you know. I doubt that's the effect you're looking for, but there it is nonetheless. You're a coward. A giant, bear of a man, but you don't stand toe-to-toe with me at all."

The bear slowed, not the quickest wit but realizing that he was on the wrong end of the conversation.

Remy pressed on, enjoying himself immensely, "Anyway, just thought you should know all of that. I've always wondered why this is happening, though. You must be connected to someone who means me harm, though truth be told, there must be more than a few of those types. I don't accept injustice wherever I am to whoever is around me, so I know I've accrued enemies." Recognition played out on the giant's mannerisms.

"You see, I do suffer, that much is undeniable," Remy continued. "You're certainly doing your job. Food has lost its flavor. Constant headache. Physically weak. Off-balance. Clumsy. Tired. Sore. Sleepy, but no sleep for me! All of this hurts. Don't you think whoever is doing this wants me to know that I'm being hurt by, blank. Fill in the blank here, bear man. By....blank."

Remy was way too chipper, virtually chirping the sentences out as they walked side by side down a rapidly congesting hallway filling with rambunctious youths.

"He drove a black truck. In Florida. That's your hometown, isn't it?" John asked, knowing the answer. "You remember a black truck, LeBeau?"

Bells were ringing. Only Floridians way back when called him by his last name alone. Remy, surprised by the success of this ploy, broke eye contact and turned his gaze off to the side, searching his memory. "I need more than a black truck. You mean a black car? A black sports car? I know one of those."

"It was a truck, a new truck. New then. This was twenty years ago."

"I really have no idea what you're talking about. A black truck from Florida twenty years ago?"

His opponent had grown tired of the game. "Jimmy." Ominous, meaningful, serious. The bear smiled through clenched teeth.

Remy stored the name away for later ponderance, deflecting the pressure.

"Oh, great. Well, tell Jimmy I said hello. Give him a big hug for me."

The bear brightened. "You don't remember him, do you?" he chortled. "You don't even remember."

That wasn't quite right. Remy's mind was harkening back a score of years, to a black truck and a man named Jimmy. A man he'd purchased pick-me-ups from once upon a time, though he didn't owe that man anything. The only incident had been insisting that he not follow through and attack another man Remy had called a friend, back in those times when he had such things. Hadn't seemed so important at the time, just a request to give an old friend more time to pay a debt. A teenage squabble.

"Jimmy doesn't make sense at all." But that had to be the guy. Twenty years ago. Black pickup truck. Florida. Jimmy. No denying those connections. Only one man fit that description.

The bear ambled through a classroom door, pausing and turning about to face Remy, grinning terribly. "Give it some thought tonight. Maybe you'll dream about him." Something akin to a laugh came out of his mouth as he pulled the door closed behind him.

Jimmy. I can't even recall his last name. That guy? Why would he want me tortured? He had compiled a list of potential individuals that he had offended to the point that they would literally torture him and actually had the means to do so. The list was filled mostly of ex-girlfriend's fathers, though he had bested some wealthy poker players out of their funds with much bravado and had thrown a couple of those names into the list, as well. Triad members associated with Monica Hu. Any of those would have made sense. Jimmy did not. *Unless he moved up in the world.*

"I finally protract a name and I'm even farther from solving this thing," he muttered to himself as he returned to his classroom on the second floor, passing Mary's class along the way. The students were on their feet, dashing from one side of the classroom to the other in response to something she was reading aloud. It looked to be great fun. He slowed and stopped, sliding into an unobtrusive place while the class carried on. Mary looked great, smiling ear to ear, leading well. The students were laughing, enjoying whatever it was they were doing. He continued watching, glad to bear witness to something wholesome and good. Eventually he caught Mary's eye and her smile abruptly lost its luster. He raised his thumbs up, signaling approval, proud of her. She turned away, saddened.

It was one of the most obtrusive nights of Remy's life, the noises piercing through the ceiling regularly throughout the entire night. True sleep had been an impossibility for quite some time but that night, his apartment was flooded with water drops and door poundings and looped urination noises. A new addition was added to the barrage which Remy attributed to an actual hammer pounding on the floor of the apartment above him, hammering that went on all night and into the next morning.

CHAPTER LXV

CHINA

Another week without sleep came and went.

"Hey, those look like comfortable shoes. Going for a long walk tonight?"

"I hear you like hiking, right?"

"Hey Rem, how do I get to the airport from here?"

Etcetera, etcetera. The open jeering, lack of sleep, and isolation were consuming him. He couldn't objectively take much pride in his lessons any longer. Too sleepy to plan properly and victim to an employer's mistreatment, he was just winging day to day teaching. Due to his considerable experience teaching abroad, this still amounted to a fairly decent performance, albeit much less than what he was capable of.

He had brought up Jimmy to the bear and the little man a few times afterward and had been met with poorly veiled ignorance. The well had run dry. Not that he took part in much detecting having lost hope in a better future, of justice coming along and saving the day. He was just trying to survive which had really been the only thing leading him back to Guangzhou in the first place. He'd lost faith that those guilty of the crimes against him would be punished. Even if he'd procured evidence that proved the identity of those responsible, the executive branches of both China and America had proven uncooperative. He had come to grips with the fact that he wasn't going to be able to prevent this from happening again, either to himself or another, if such a thing even happened to anyone else. Through hopeless depression, the attacks continued and not being the kind of man to just curl up and die, Remy resisted. Like punching wind, he resisted.

Another week of sleep deprivation and ridicule had sucked most of the moxie out of him. His feet dragged and his eyelids drooped. Slow to think. Slower to respond. He found himself knocking on the door across from his flat, uncertain how he had gotten there or what he would say if someone answered. He waited at the doorstop, hearing dim voices inside. He knocked again. Waited. Knocked again. A hushed conversation came to a hissing end as the door creaked open.

"What?" croaked the towering bear.

"Look, I'm sure you don't want me here. I'm not trying to cause any trouble. I guess that's why I'm here at your flat right now. I just want to teach and save some money and enjoy a home of my own one day. I'm not trying to solve the case anymore. There's nothing I can do about that theft. No one believes me anyway."

"Yeah, I heard about that." Smiling a knowing smile. Remy swallowed the desire to climb up the man and remove the derisive gesture.

"I'm sure you did," Remy replied flatly. "It's gone. It's gone and it's not coming back. Those that robbed me got away with it scot-free. I don't like it. I hate it, actually. But I can't change it." He took a step forward and spoke more softly. "I'm not hunting you and yours. I'm not trying to find out the how and the why and the who. You mentioned Jimmy, and honestly, I don't even know his last name. Haven't seen him in twenty years. Can't you just leave me alone?"

"He knows your last name."

"Well, f*%$ing fantastic! He wins the f^*%ing gold medal for last names then."

Both men stiffened. Remy took a step back.

"Sorry. It's hard to live without sleep. Just let me sleep, man. Please." No response. "I'll lose this job if I can't sleep. I'll lose my mind if I can't sleep." No response. "What's the point in continuing all of this? There's nothing to deter me from. There's nothing left. There's nowhere to go. No one to tell the tale to. My friends and family are gone. Just let me sleep. Please."

"No one's stopping you from anything. Do whatever you want." A stupid, crocodile smile followed.

"I want to sleep. Are you telling me I can go do that right now?"

"No one's stopping you."

"I hope so. That sounds real nice. Man to man, please let this go."

Remy returned to his apartment, cuddled up in bed and was immediately assaulted with the sound of a man urinating into a toilet bowl projected downward via speakers from the floor above at a volume much louder than would naturally occur if for some reason a functioning toilet had been positioned directly over his bed.

CHAPTER LXVI

USA

He voiced concern to his employer again about the noises keeping him awake at all hours, of the banging on his door, of the ridicule and bullying he faced from the duo of fellow employees at the school. The director of the foreign language department showed zero concern. Remy called a private meeting with the vice-principal of the school in which he voiced the same concerns. He cared even less.

A week later, Remy was cut loose, fired although he hadn't missed a single day of work despite a rather serious injury to his Achilles tendon while jogging. While not exactly firing on all cylinders, he had led classes adequately. He hadn't missed a deadline. Had arrived punctually every day. His contract was terminated nonetheless and within a week he was shipped off to the airport. He slept most of the way there, groggily checked in his bags, semi-dozed while standing in line, and promptly fell unconscious upon taking his seat on the plane, only waking as the landing gear skidded along the LAX runway. He navigated through customs pretty easily, telling them everything they wanted to hear with a bright smile, retrieved his luggage from the carousel and waited for William's kennel to appear before he remembered the loss. Round two was over. He found a seat on a bench and pondered what to do next.

There was nothing to do in L.A. He knew no one, had no chance of finding work or housing with the paltry savings he had accrued during his most recent stint in Guangzhou. His financial worth amounted to less than two thousand dollars. For hours he searched his mind for any way out, any opportunity, any promising lead. His friends and family had proven treacherous. He had no job offers to fall back on. Almost half a year of searching for work in Florida had only yielded one opportunity for work. The concept first whirled about in the distant background of his mind's eye, a peripheral thought as he contemplated a more promising focal point. But as the hours progressed and possibilities vanished, there was only that one thing left to do.

He clicked the Skype icon of his phone.

"It early, Remy. Why you calling me?"

He smirked at the grammatical mistakes. Her accent, her voice, the only comfort remaining.

"Look, I just wanted to say I'm sorry to put you through so much. I still don't know how you factor into everything. It sucks that you left me high and dry at that police station in Nanchang. The theft itself. That damn, black sportscar. Your lies. Why am I apologizing to you? What am I doing?"

She looked on quietly. Her calm was infectious and soon stilled his rising ire.

"I love you, Monica Hu. I know that doesn't make any sense. But I do. And that's it. That's the only thing that hasn't gone anywhere these past years. These hated years." He felt something he'd been holding onto for quite some time break off and drift away. "I hope you do good things and improve this world. I hope you find comfort and love, even if it's not me. Be good, kid."

From sleepy to calming to alert and nervous. Quite a range of emotion played across her pretty face. "Why you tell me this? What you tell me now?"

He shrugged noncommittally. "I just want you to know how I feel, Moni. I love you. I always will." He turned his face to keep watery eyes from showing. "Get some sleep, okay. I should go."

She pressed him again for an answer he wouldn't give, wanting to know why he called and what was going on. He smiled sadly and disconnected, then sat staring off for some time, gathering courage, collecting himself. An hour later at a branch of his bank in downtown L.A., he closed his account, easily inserting the balance directly into his wallet. He then took a train right back to LAX, where he rested uncomfortably in the lobby all night while he waited for an economy one-way flight back to Guangzhou departing the following day.

CHAPTER LXVII

CHINA

Round three was brief.

"Yes," he answered, opening the passport to the page containing his previous work visa, "I'm here for business. It certainly isn't a vacation." He shared a charismatic smile with the immigration officer, feeling good about what was to come, light, unburdened. The officer stamped Remy's passport and he was on his way. He patiently waited for his baggage to arrive, in no hurry. Calm. Distant. Detached. Floating overhead looking down on the proceedings from the vantage point of a helium-filled balloon butting against the ceiling. He was all smiles and smoothness as he exited the Guangzhou airport in the early morning, marching right through a familiar grouping of taxi drivers, ignoring hands extended for handshaking and passenger-pulling. He returned to the very same pillar he had spied on the taxi drivers from back during round one, reminiscing as he puffed on a cigarette, an indulgence he had recently rekindled.

The early morning shone hues of yellow and orange across a blue sky full of fluffy white clouds. Remy was down to a backpack and a single suitcase, half-filled with clothing, half-filled with odds and ends: a fairly decent coin collection; an unopened 12-year-old bottle of fine scotch; a few paperback novels; a harmonica; electronics with batteries detached, and furthermore, the battery charges themselves worn down to near empty levels, just in case, though he had no need for these things any longer. There was no one to call. No one to touch base with.

He whistled a peppy tune as he schlepped his belongings back into the airport and down an escalator to the subway below. Aboard a southbound train, he recalled painful memories of round one. Trying again and again to get to the airport. Prevented by taxi drivers, by trains that had stopped prior to arrival at the airport station, by buses that denied William entry, of William himself, and then, for quite some time, he paused, frozen, muscles locked and mind distant, feeling very, very heavy. Subway tunnels and open air stretches alongside the trainline blurred by while he recalled raising the hound from a pup. A grin emerged among watery eyes as he reminded himself that William was in a safe place, a good place, with a peer, and resources, and healthy food. *The best thing I could have done for him.* He took some comfort in that and in so doing felt the heaviness subside. He tossed the remaining bit aside, returning to blissful detachment as he hailed a taxi at Huamei Station.

He arrived at the very same intersection he'd departed from earlier that same week. On one side of the road, the vast campus stretched out behind a long wall topped with looping rolls of barbed wire; on the other, the apartment complex where he had been kept sleepless for the second time in Guangzhou. He exited slowly, paid the driver and stretched, soaking it all in. He rolled his suitcase down a cracked sidewalk, distancing himself from the devil and the deep, blue sea. Two blocks later, he spotted a cheap motel of sorts and secured a room for three nights. It smelled old and contained only a single hard bed, an aging dresser, and a makeshift shower/toilet area in the back corner, resembling the flat he'd shared in the summer during the roommate situation. It wasn't pretty, but it was cheap and nearby. That's all that really concerned him.

He bathed in tepid water that posed as hot, grateful for the cleansing. Light as a feather, he strolled down to a local market and purchased a few dragon fruits to munch on later along with the highest quality kitchen knife he could find. A long blade ended into a stainless-steel handle of substantial heft. He wiped it clean of dust and tested the edge gingerly against his index finger, before firmly tucking into his beltline atop the small of his back, edge facing outward, lined up for a menacing draw. He then tossed the tail of his untucked button-up shirt over his beltline at the small of his back, completing the concealment. Comfy snug in its new home. *Step one, complete.*

He walked down a block to the entry of Huamei International School, smiling wide to the security guard barely manning his post as he entered, expecting no confrontation and therefore finding none. Assuming the role of a potential new-hire -- well-dressed and donning the slightest of nervous appearances, just enough to be believable, not enough to be suspicious -- the guard cheerily pointed him toward the director's office on the upper floor where interviews for a newly available position teaching every main subject to the same high school students everyday would be commencing. One out of sight, he deterred from the given path and approached his actual destination.

Mary sat at a desk situated at the head of her classroom. Her students were running rampant this time as she had made the mistake of finishing her lesson before the period was over. *Rookie timing issues,* he thought, as he knocked on the door while simultaneously opening it.

"Hello, everyone."

A chorus of student voices, droning as one, "Good morning, teacher."

"And a very good morning to you, too." Remy smiled and made the rounds like a celebrity at a press conference, high-fiving and shaking hands and asking simple questions in English that were happily answered while he gradually made his way up to the teacher's desk across from a very concerned Mary.

"You look like you've seen a ghost."

She nodded dully.

"Well, I'm not dead yet," he chortled, "Not for a lack of trying, though."

"Why are you here, Remy?"

"You always were a deep thinker, Mary. Why are any of us here? To strengthen the good and weaken the evil, I suppose. That's the best way I can describe a meaningful life. Can't strengthen much good these days, so here I am."

She smiled warmly, stirring something within the man that he hadn't prepared for. Something heavy and disorienting. He winced, quickly smiling in response to mask his discomfort. He pivoted and took in the room. Thirty-five middle schoolers milled about, some leaning in close to spy on the conversation, others using the opportunity to infringe on classroom rules. "And you really need to get a firmer grip on time management. They'll rush your lessons if they know you'll just surrender at the end and let them do whatever they want. They're the enemy, you know," nodding his head to a trio of girls literally leaning in, eavesdropping on the conversation. They giggled and fell back as Remy made eye contact. "Case in point."

"They're not enemies. They're just girls."

"I know, I know. But they do have an agenda of their own and it isn't to learn as much as they can from you. Food for thought. Take it or leave it. I mean, it's rare wisdom from a master educator, but you do what you want with it."

She relaxed visibly and a little of that old flame kindled in her eyes. "I'm sorry," she began, "about what ha---"

"Yeah, that's enough of that. How about lunch? Do you have plans for lunch?"

She nodded.

"Yes? You have plans for lunch?"

"No, I was nodding that I would go to lunch with you."

"Well, okay then. A little confusing but let's do it. Lunch."

He faded back into the crowd and mingled with the students, weaving through simple conversations, listening patiently to replies and questions riddled with grammatical mistakes until a bell sounded signaling the end of class and the start of the lunch break. Mary gathered her belongings and they left, navigating through hallways teeming with teenage life, strolling shoulder to shoulder. They spoke of trivial things until they exited the school gate, whereupon she shifted into action.

"You have to talk. Now. Why're you here, Remy?"

He glanced at her sideways as they continued on, crossing the street toward the local ma-and-pa restaurants of the open market across from the school. "You spent a month sleeping over at my place coy and flirtatious the whole time and you just rush right into this? Demanding what you fail to deliver. Ain't that a dame."

"Yep. I'm a dame. Whatever. Talk to me."

"I am talking to you. You'd just prefer a different topic."

"I could go right back to the school again," she said, stopping in midstride.

He didn't take the bait. "But you won't," he replied, speaking over his shoulder. "You're far too curious. Come along, little cat. I'll buy you some fish. I know a good place up here. It's a little spicy, but you like that sort of thing." He slowed his gait, allowing her ample time to catch up.

"You're crazy, you know that?"

He held his hand out and she relaxed into it, their fingers interlocking. They walked hand in hand to a nearby restaurant where they sat on old, plastic chairs and ordered their respective meals.

"First of all, let me say that it's good to see you. So pretty and full of life. I liked you from the moment I first saw you, you know. I've always had a good feeling about you." She flushed and looked away. "But I also felt like you were keeping things from me from the very beginning. Important things." She looked back crisply. "And I'm not expecting answers to my woes from you right now. I'm not expecting you to come clean but you need to know that there are repercussions to all of that. Any decent girlfriend would be very concerned about the issues I had with banging on doors and late-night noises keeping me awake, but you, you dismissed it like it was nothing." She flushed again, looking away guiltily. "You've felt like a plant from the get-go regardless of any of the secondary stuff. Stuff you won't talk about."

"I can't talk about nothing. There's nothing to talk about."

"Oh, but there is. There definitely is. Must be very comforting for you, believing that it's nothing. Well, it's something to me, Mary. I was forced awake for months in Guangzhou. I didn't make that up. I was tortured and I suffered sleep depravity to an extent you cannot fathom. The least you can do is acknowledge that it actually happened. But you don't and here I am, upset over nothing, right? Nothing. You're half right, though." He took a breath, entering into a dialogue he'd semi-prepared for. "I have nothing now. Nothing at all, Mary. No friends. No family. No one believed my story. No one believed that the truth was the truth. I tried rephrasing the tale, each time twisting and folding it into something more palatable, something more easily digestible to the listener, but in the end its always just too much to believe." He looked away and smiled to mask the pain. "Everyone thinks I'm insane. I don't have a job and don't see one coming in the near or even distant future. Certainly not a decent one. No money left. No light at the end of this tunnel. No future."

He forked eggplant into his mouth, chewing slowly, allowing her time to respond. She said nothing but held his gaze firmly.

"Nothing," Remy reiterated. "Well, I shouldn't say nothing. I could beg for money to survive but I won't. I could kill myself I guess, but that's easier said than done. Death or begging. I know which one I prefer."

"Remy, you'll be alright. You're being dramatic, if you ju---"

"Dramatic!!!" he bellowed, flinging the fork in his hand in a wide arc across the road and over the school wall. He didn't follow the trajectory, didn't care. "Dramatic," he repeated, cooling some. "Could you be more demeaning, I wonder? Is that even possible? But I guess I am being dramatic. This," he said, locking eyes with her, "is definitely drama. You're not wrong about that."

He relaxed, opened up a chopstick container at the table, and returned to his light meal. They dined together in silence for some time.

"Are you going to tell me why you're here?"

"I will. I am. Here it is. The best thing that I can do with this life of mine is to end the life of those who do evil. It beats begging, that's for sure. I wish my existence had more merit. I wish the good that I could do throughout the rest of my life outweighed the evil that I will remove soon, but it doesn't add up that way. My life just sort of fizzles out from here. Doesn't take a prophet to see that. But I can end some wickedness before I go and that doesn't sound too bad to me at all. Makes for a pretty decent tombstone." He chuckled, "As if there will be a tombstone."

She fumbled with her wallet, searching for money to pay the tab.

"No, no, my dear. I'll take care of the bill. Allow me that. I want to pay."

She politely declined and they went back and forth out insisting the other, but in the end, Remy was able to pay for both meals. The goodbye was swift and decisive. She walked away quickly and didn't look back. *Step two, complete,* he thought, checking off a box in a mental list as he watched her cross the street and return inside the school compound.

Miyamoto Musashi wrote of a technique called startling the snake from the brush in his memoir *The Book of Five Rings.* He spent an entire chapter on it, in fact. The idea was to bray and shout and feint in order to scare a beast out from a safe place where it lay hidden and/or well protected, in order to line up a clear shot. So too with a swordsman who momentarily drops his guard in the face of a sudden rush and barbaric yell. As Mary left his line of sight completely, Remy felt fairly certain her upcoming gossip would indeed startle some serpents into action. *It won't be much longer now,* he thought to himself, sliding a half-eaten meal away.

CHAPTER LXVIII

CHINA

He hiked up a narrow stairwell to the motel room he'd secured earlier in the day and reclined on a mattress without springs affixed to a wobbly frame. Somewhat comfortable, he returned to reading Hemmingway's *The Sun Also Rises,* a tale of an American enjoying the high life in postwar France. He was nearing the end, the protagonist having had separated from the woman he loved in order to visit Spain and take in bullfighting, when the feeling came upon him that the time was right. He did not return the bookmark into the novel, closing the book without so much as glancing at the page number. There was no need for such things any longer. It was time.

He set the book atop a worn dresser and looked long and hard at himself in the mirror. He removed his shirt and trousers and took himself in. Certainly not muscular, even drooping in a few places but mostly firm. Definitely ready. He felt like a coiled spring and so he stretched this way and that, performing a few katas, bones creaking stubbornly as they rotated and sprung. A few minutes later, his body began to respond more fluidly and quietly. There was no room to practice kicking in the cramped room. A few sets of squats sufficed to bring his legs back into form. He leaned in close to his reflection and smiled faintly.

"It wasn't such a bad run, old boy."

He redressed, removed some items from his belongings, and knelt on an uncarpeted floor in need of a good sweeping, heels to buttocks as the Japanese kneel. He opened the bottle of fine scotch he had brought with him across the Pacific Ocean and took a slow, thin stream of quality liquor into his mouth, tasting it, feeling it course through his blood while taking care not to show it outwardly. Detached, dominant of self, he set down the bottle and refastened the lid with unhurried, steady twists, robotic in movement and demeanor.

Content with his positioning, he reached toward the other items he'd brought to the floor with him, a few pages of blank paper and a fine pen. There he remained motionless, thinking of his death poem. Time passed in which he ignored a growing pain that began flaring up at knees, heels, and thighs, pain that soon succumbed to numbness. More time passed. At last, he took up the pen, leaned over and wrote:

A great wave crashed upon me.
Stripped of everything I once held dear,
I set my feet upon a new path.

He folded the page into thirds as if it were to be inserted into an envelope -- as if anyone still did that sort of thing -- with the same reverence shown to the scotch. Setting this paper aside, he leaned to his left and retrieved the bottle, taking another slow, steady stream, enjoying the pungent aroma and taste. He focused on feeling the scotch in its entirety as it washed over his tongue, down his throat and into a newly warming stomach. He bowed low from a kneeling position, bowing to life: the good, the bad, the ugly, the beautiful, the foolish, the wise. He held his head low, forehead almost touching the floor, stomach muscles clasped tightly as his torso remained doubled over, frozen, still.

Ceremony completed, he returned upright to a kneeling position and then stood. Blood rushed into deprived leg muscles, tickling and stinging sharply. He shook his legs out to assist in this process and jogged in place in the minimal space available. Legs more or less back to normal, he took another pull from the scotch bottle, this one long and true, gulping a bit, letting the fire of the liquor overcome his senses: stinging his nose, watering eyes, and burning the throat. He pulled away happily, set the bottle aside and tucked the folded paper containing his poem underneath. He took a long look at himself in the mirror and made a funny face, chuckling merrily at his own fool-ishness.

"No sense hating life just because I'm leaving it. Much of it was precious and valuable," he spoke to his reflection. "In fact," he said, snatching up the bottle again, "there's no sense wasting the good stuff." He unscrewed the lid with a deft movement and downed another heavy, long stream of scotch before abruptly ejecting the lid from his outstretched hand. It flew as straight as any shuriken, bouncing off of the center of a spotted mirror in the unpartitioned far corner of the room that served as the bathroom. He nodded con-tentedly. *It is time.*

He took up the kitchen knife he'd purchased at the market, feel-ing its weight, finding the balancing point and testing the razor-sharp edge against his thumb before sliding it into the waistline of the small of his back. He practiced a few quickdraws to work out the ideal placement of the handle and understand just how far the blade extended within his reach. He leaped solidly across the room a few times and threw his knees up high while running in place testing the blade's commitment to stay positioned properly. Pleased with the re-sults, he turned his attention back to his reflection whereupon hap-piness dissipated but sorrow did not encroach. *It is time.*

As if in response, electronic bells began chiming in the distance, signaling the end of the school day and the beginning of the third and final step.

CHAPTER LXIX

CHINA

The sound of a thousand students romping about was plainly discernible from the lobby door of the motel though the school was still three blocks away. He strolled down the sidewalk, taking his time and remembering the good and bad times he'd experienced teaching over the past ten years eventually passing the poorly-manned security gate to his old apartment complex. He walked up familiar stairs and down the hallway that had connected to his apartment. There he ran his fingers along the frame of his old front door, remembering when he would throw it open and dash out into the night, chasing a mysterious culprit that had banged on his door before dashing off and into a neighboring flat. He put his ear to the door across the hall -- the bear's door -- and listened intently for quite some time. No one was inside.

He ascended the stairwell to the rooftop and sat on the edge of the roof, feet dangling over a fifty-foot drop. He thought back to the rooftop of the first apartment in downtown Guangzhou, of flashing passing aircraft SOS with a green laser pen, of the private planes that had buzzed by. *They were pointing me in the correct direction, after all,* Remy mused, recalling the memory.

He was fairly certain that completing step three would only deter such torture from afflicting another slightly if at all, that very little would actually change. His mind sought escape from what was to come and reimagined the next week, the next month, searching desperately for a hint of hope on the horizon. *There is only this,* he gently reminded himself. To shake the tendrils of sorrow, he thought of the temporary nature of life, like the petals of the cherry blossom tree, exquisite in blooming, dancing in the breeze as they fall, and then gone forever. He smiled to remember such beauty and leapt atop the edge. He leaned in and out, playing with the falling point before hopping back onto the safety of the main rooftop and strolling down the stairs.

He took his time in returning to the same open-air market where he had purchased the kitchen knife that rested snugly along his tailbone. The same market where he had shared lunch with Mary. There was nothing left to do and he was immediately impatient as he entered the vicinity, eyeing up wares he had no intention of buying, just making himself available. Before he reached the third shop, a familiar hulking brute emerged in the crowd and began barreling straight toward him.

"Oh good, you're here already. This has been such a per---"

"You want to kill me! You're going to kill me?!"

"Well, yes, that's the gist of it. You really seem to not be taking this well, though. Sort of embarrassing, really. Not very civilized of you."

"Civilized?! I don't know what the f&^% you're talking about." He muttered something incomprehensible and flourished a retractable baton in his left hand. From his right pocket he produced a tight fist bound up in a steel overlay. A weapon in each hand. From the tumult of milling shoppers, the shorter, more petite, athletic man materialized on Remy's right, much closer than he expected.

"Well done. Very professional. You almost got the drop on me, little sneak-thief," Remy retorted, sliding backward using the Water form of Ninjutsu, putting even distance between the giant and the little man. "I'd applaud, but I hate you both." He held his left hand up high and shook it about for no apparent reason, as if wielding an invisible tambourine. His enemies' eyes fell to the flashing hand while Remy's right slid behind his back and onto the handle of the knife. He smiled wide knowing he had the upper hand. The bear was dripping sweat already. They stood transfixed on the empty left hand flickering aimlessly. *This is too simple,* he thought, flashing the blade outward obviously, uncomfortable with such an unfair advantage.

"Watch out! He has a knife!" shouted the bear.

"Why yes, I think you're right. This is a knife. Seems fitting. You came at me with two weapons and with two people and all. One knife shouldn't scare you, right?" Remy adopted a comical, zombie-killer face, raised the blade high and walked hurriedly toward the opponent that had snuck up on his right. No form. No stance. Just playing with his food.

Obviously startled, the thin man jogged backward clumsily, turned and retreated along a wide arc far out of range. Remy laughed heartily.

"What the f^\$# are you guys doing? Are you serious right now? All that for this?"

The fleeing man eventually settled in behind John Smith who stood his ground, eyeing Remy evenly with a clear intent to do harm.

He looked him up and down, sizing the man up. The bear stood poised in a stance that displayed a bit of training, albeit not much. *What little experience he has is outweighed by weak knees and obesity, though heaviness could pose a problem if this turns to grappling,* he mused, hungry to engage. *He doesn't seem like he's in the mood to run, though*. He nodded approvingly and locked eyes with his only opponent, the thin man visibly shook and useless.

"You ready?"

In response, a bit of the bear's bravery ebbed. He turned his head to the thin man behind him.

"Go! Call the police. Bring the police." And with that, he was off and running.

"Are you f^*%ing kidding me right now?!" Remy -- about to pounce -- dissipated the Fire stance, threw up his arms in disappointment, and yelled at the sky. "Are you f*^%ing kidding me, right now?! You tortured me for months. Kept me sleepless. You didn't phone the police for any of that, did you? Threatened me with that Jimmy, bullshit. Openly mocked me. Harassed me over and over and here you are, desperate for the police to come and recue you." He lowered his blade further, the illusion of giving up. "It's like I came here to murder someone innocent. Only you aren't that at all, are you?" he asked, nestling in quite close to his opponent during the dialogue, something the bear only became aware of as the blade flashed upward toward his exposed neck.

He had pivoted himself so that the movement of his body would manifest through the blade's edge, through the newly slit throat of his tormentor, and then be positioned away from the arterial spray that would follow. For the second time in his life, however, his hand disobeyed his command, locked up awkwardly at the husky man's throat, leaving Remy frozen and off balance within a handsbreadth of his opponent, adjacent to a man he had meant to kill a second prior. He smiled awkwardly before dodging a baton blow to the side of his head. He fell into Water stance as he retreated.

"Wow. I mean, if your own hands don't obey, what do you have? Am I right?"

The bear didn't respond. He looked more shook up than ever but remained an unyielding presence.

They locked eyes again.

"Well, come on then. Here I am."

"I'm not going anywhere," he growled.

"Yeah, I see that."

Remy followed this up with a wide smile before closing his eyes and walking directly into the man. As he opened his eyes, a fist laced with metal knuckles was heading straight into his face. He side-stepped, spun the kitchen knife about in his hands and jabbed the man in the ribs with the handle of the knife. Fear -- not concern, but fear -- played out plainly across his face though he responded reasonably swiftly, lashing out in a wide, violent arc with the baton he held in his other hand, ultimately failing to connect. Remy circled his opponent, staying on the outer edge of the man's reach. Seizing an opportunity after another missed baton blow, he positioned himself behind Smith. He brought the blade up, gently grazing the point across his back and along a bit of the nape of his neck before needing to dance back to dodge another strike.

"Do you see how easy this is for me? Do you get it? You only live today because I will it to be so." He skittered the tip of the knife down the man's chest and abdomen painlessly as he Watered backward. The bear spun about attacking the air with both baton and weaponized fist but Remy out of range.

This is just murder, he thought, all joy dissipating. He slid the knife back into his beltline at the small of his back and held up two empty hands.

"Go home," Remy commanded, eyes locked on his opponent. "I'm not going to attack you. I can't end your life apparently so we're done here. I don't know what happens next, but I can't do this. You've undoubtedly tortured me by depriving me of sleep but

I can't kill you for that. Literally. My hands won't allow it. Just go. Get out of here."

"I'm not going anywhere."

"Yeah, okay, I get it. Look, I'm not going to attack you from behind. I wouldn't have sent that message through Mary if that were the case. I vowed to never strike first and needed you to attack me which you did." His voice oozed disappointment. "I thought this would end differently. Honestly, I don't know what to do now but you can go."

"I'm not goi---"

"Okay! For f^$*'s sake, I get it! Fine. I'll go."

Remy turned about and marched off toward the apartment complex. Dazed, he stopped at a convenient store along the way to purchase a pack of cigarettes and a lighter. Having already written his death poem, he had no idea what to do next. He knelt, heels to buttocks, just outside of that convenient shop and smoked one cigarette after another until the police arrived.

"Greetings, officer."

"What you do?"

"Me? I'm reserving my right to be silent. That anything I say may and probably will be used against me in a court of law." Remy looked up, smiling. "What're you doing, that's a more interesting question. How are you, by the way? I bet not many people ask you that in this line of work. How are you, sir?"

"I'm fine, thank you. And you?" he replied oddly, an instinctive response to an English lesson learned long ago.

"I'm just going to pretend that didn't happen."

"You need come with me."

"Oh, come on. Don't get snippy with me because you just sounded like Dora the Explorer. That's not my fault. Listen, you're here because of that little guy that pals around with the giant, and he has undoubtedly left ninety-percent out of the story he told you."

He smiled and began to stand. "There are legitimate concerns here that need to be addressed."

The officer stepped back defensively. "Do you have knife?"

"Well, that's a funny question to ask a man." He looked to the officer, peace in his eyes. "Yes, I do have a knife. But you know that already." He slid the blade from his waistline and set it on the sidewalk where he had been resting and smoking, laying it down gently with due reverence.

"Would you mind that I arresting you?"

Remy's laugh cut through the tension. "Man, it is so difficult to hate you guys sometimes." He upturned his wrists. "Book me, Danno." The officer did not handcuff Remy, though he was not gentle in escorting him into the backseat of a police car. "Just know that this was all self-defense. I reacted to someone drawing a weapon against me. Two weapons, actually. And two people attacking me. More than twenty people, the more that I think about it, if you count all the previous Guangzhou torment."

"Yes. I understand," he replied, lying. "Where are you stay?"

The disinterest in Remy's words was palpable. He had been made the enemy. There was no bypassing that. *Best to cooperate,* he thought. *What else is there to do anyway? None of what was supposed to happen happened.* "Oh, it's right down the road. I'll guide you in," he replied cheerfully, apparently ignorant of the severity of the situation as he pointed the driver back to the motel where he had been staying.

The officer followed Remy up steep and creaking steps leading to his room. Inside, he slowly gathered what few belongings had been unpacked, taking his time, knowing that what would follow would be worse than where he was and what he was currently doing. As another officer marched up the groaning stairwell, Remy lit a cigarette in the confusion and swiftly ignited his death poem. As it blazed into ash, he marched over to the corner of the room and tossed the burning mess into the bathroom sink. A metallic shine drew his attention downward. He crouched to examine the object which turned out to be the scotch lid he had hurled at the mirror a couple of hours ago, a lifetime ago. He rolled it about the palm of his hand as if it were the finest of jewels.

Igniting paper and examining a lid on the ground had caused the police to grow impatient. Remy consoled them as best he could, drinking heavily from the scotch bottle when they turned their attention to each other to discuss what to do with him. Thoroughly inebriated in short time and absolutely clueless what to do now that his plan fell flat, he soon found himself clambering down three flights of stairs hauling his suitcase. In the makeshift lobby of the decrepit motel, the owner was undergoing an interrogation of his own. Fear showed plainly on his face as he absorbed cutting words in Mandarin delivered by an angry officer.

"How is this guy to blame? It's me you want. It's me you have. Let him be." The officer swung a confused face Remy's way, unaccustomed to counterargument. In response, Remy received a sharp nudge from behind, propelling him out of the exit. He was then driven to a nearby police station where he was officially detained.

Locked in an empty room, he played a harmonica he had stowed away in his pocket, missing notes here and there but enjoying the melodies of Super Mario Bros., Zelda, the Superman theme, jazzy tunes, and impromptu blues songs played with varying degrees of skill. Youthful guards advised him to cease playing the instrument around smiles that plainly displayed they were enjoying the festivities. He roundly ignored their good-natured attempts to hush him. He had come to kill and then die and had done neither. Having already forfeited his own life, threat of imprisonment meant very little.

He was formally arrested later that day, manacled, and driven to a detainment center as evening stole the last of the daylight. By midnight, he had stored his luggage, stripped naked in a locker room, squatted, coughed, donned a prisoner uniform, and laid down on a portion of a cell floor marked with a faded number seven. Twelve men sprawled out side by side across a cell that stretched eight meters or so end to end, three meters wide. The back end served as a public toilet composed of little more than a small hole in the floor that connected to an open sewer. The sound of a dozen men snoring was an easy thing to overtake, however, and Remy soon collapsed into deep, restful sleep.

CHAPTER LXX

CHINA

He awoke early the next morning to a prison guard barking orders through vertical strips of iron bars extending from ceiling to floor. The inmates were surprised to see a foreign face when Remy awoke with them that first morning. Africans charged with overstaying their visas and/or selling illegal commodities were not uncommon inhabitants of the detainment site in which he woke. Caucasians were a rarity. He would later be told by a guard who had worked at the facility for close to twenty years that he was the second one he had overseen.

The English of Remy's cellmates was mostly limited to three words: *hello* and *good morning*. In short time they simply spoke to him in Mandarin and while Remy was only able to catch the meaning of a word or two in these limited exchanges, he appreciated the change. Most of the time, what was being said was fairly apparent based on the situation: *pass me that sliver of soap; move over; etc.* His cellmates were neither polite nor rude and Remy found them decent company. No one imposed themselves on him. They weren't violent. There was no blustering or puffing up or attempting to assert dominance. Quite a step up compared to the characters he had lived and worked with over the past couple of years in China and Florida. The atmosphere was horrid, the stench undeniable, but the company wasn't so bad.

Old school prison life. Tightly packed prisoners behind thick bars. A hallway patrolled by guards. The only portal leading out of or into the long cell full of men was a sliding gate held in place by a massive, corroded padlock. On the opposite end of the long cell, passed a floor striped with eroded yellow lines marking each man's section of cement that he was to sleep upon during his stay, passed a hand-size hole in the floor that fed into the sewers and served as a toilet, passed a dripping tap with a handle worn to a nub and an accompanying cracked plastic bucket the men used to bathe with and flush away their waste, were a series of firmly locked windows laced with more iron bars that looked out onto a dimly lit, unremarkable hallway periodically patrolled by guards. Cameras sat perched in corners all throughout the facility, a reminder that money had been spent on the place, just not to the prisoners' well-being.

Remy was given neither a comb nor a toothbrush. He learned from the more experienced cellmates to finger comb his hair and use a finger to rub away film from his teeth. He rinsed his mouth out each morning with the same water he drank throughout the day, water that smelled of many things, none of them healthy. The men shared one small bar of soap, which would quickly become a slivered, hairy disc. Guards would usually resupply a new, tiny bar of soap if asked nicely, but there were many times the cell went without, the men using water alone to bathe. Shampoo was not available. Razors were not available. Each prisoner was issued a single towel which also served as a pillow after being folded several times. A fresh towel and a newly laundered uniform were issued once a week. A single blanket -- used to soften the issue of sleeping on the cement floor or to keep warm, but not both -- was only taken in for cleaning upon the prisoner's release. A broom could be provided upon request. Mops were unavailable.

Each night, the men were required to take shifts watching over the other men while they slept. Like soldiers in battle, one man would be wakened and relieve the old watch. Most of the prisoners had taken their turn sitting on a rickety, wooden stool staring at snoring, farting, sleeping men by the time day broke. Late nights in the cells were uneventful and often the cellmate on guard duty would fall asleep on duty, later upsetting a passing guard. Angry barking in Mandarin in the middle of the night was not uncommon.

Once a week, the men would be marched outside single file directly down a flight of stairs to a paved courtyard that served as a basketball court that only prison guards were allowed to utilize properly. The prisoners were positioned onto a grid of dots that speckled the court from goal to goal and instructed to sit. Twelve columns. Twelve rows. Once situated, the head officer -- the equivalent of a warden -- would deliver a speech about the merits of obeying the law while standing upon a small, worn wooden box. Through the filter of limited Mandarin comprehension and a keen understanding of human interactions, Remy sensed encouragement from the warden to the prisoners who had gathered, reminding them that whatever incident had led to their incarcerations would not define their futures. Afterward, the men were marched around the perimeter of the basketball court several times before being sent back upstairs to their cells where they would remain for the next seven days until the cycle repeated itself.

Each morning the men were awakened at sunrise to a triumphant military tune blaring through worn speakers. Within five minutes, the inmates were required to be on their feet, standing at attention, blanket and towel/pillow folded at the head of each prisoner's corresponding number, a single digit often faded and peeled away into illegibility. A single guard was charged with manning the locked gate of several cells to bark commands to those slow to rise. The music would cut out and shift abruptly to the Chinese national anthem, a song Remy had had translated once, its content primarily focused on how China was alone and surrounded by enemies, so do your duty citizen and protect the good ol' Communist party. He had found it a rather paranoid song and didn't love that he was forced to quietly respect it each morning. Like on the tightly packed subway cars of Tokyo, his mind drew him to happier places while the anthem played each morning.

The final note would play out long and majestically before yet another militaristic tune cut the respectful stillness of the early morning. Then the men were commanded to march in place for four minutes, turning to the right, to the left, about-faces. Military stuff. While this was the only exercise allowed each day, half of the men in Remy's cell, himself included, disobeyed this rule routinely, doing push-ups and sit-ups throughout the day to pass the time. Some of the guards would bang angrily on the bars when they saw this infraction occurring but most looked the other way. Though against the rules, the practice continued, much like the playing of Chinese chess, the board made of memory, pieces composed of torn scraps of communist propaganda positioned about the dirty floor. Remy practiced Mandarin as the days dragged on, asking fellow inmates the meaning of characters though rarely making himself understood as the men were not keen on the notion of tutoring him. He practiced drawing characters by using his index finger as a pen and his palm as paper. In this way he would spend an hour each morning while some secretly played chess and others stared blankly through crumpled paper listing the party's doctrines and accomplishments.

The four hours after that consisted of nothing. The guards would retrieve the worn-out propaganda papers and tend to duties elsewhere. Left alone, some men exercised in what little open space existed. Some men conversed amiably with one another. Some men slept.

Breakfast, lunch, and dinner were served each day, though without a clock, it was difficult to tell if the timing was consistent or not. Each meal was the same: rice boiled way too long at far too high of a temperature. There were flecks of questionable, dark material: residue scraped from the bottom of the pot or possibly specks of vegetable or meat too small to taste or even feel in one's mouth. Whatever it was, the prisoners secretly cherished those dark flecks that peppered the rice boiled into a consistency similar to mashed potatoes. There was no salt, no butter, no seasoning, no garnish. Each day that ticked by was equally palatable.

CHAPTER LXXI

CHINA

At the end of the second day, a guard called Remy over and handed him a sheet of paper through a slit at the locked gate. Remy's name, written in alphabetic lettering, was typed neatly across the top of the document. Everything else was in Mandarin. He studied the thing for all of ten seconds before a man tore the paper from his hand. He wrestled with an immediate instinct to snatch the paper back but instead waited patiently while the cellmate perused what Remy had come to realize was his formal sentencing and punishment, issued without trial, judge, or lawyer. The prisoner, clucked his tongue and wagged his finger, smiling like a fool.

"You very bad boy, mister."

This aroused the attention of the other ten cellmates. Soon, eleven men huddled around the paper as it was eagerly ripped from one prisoner's grasp to the next. As the third man snatched at it, a corner ripped free. The men paying the destruction no mind, laughed at the newfound excitement. Remy had had enough, however, and voiced it.

"Okay. Enough," he responded calmly. No response. The men continued to cluck like excited chickens. "I said, *Enough!*" This echoed throughout the length of the elongated, narrow cell and down the hallway housing a dozen more of the same cells. He walked over, retrieved his sentencing sheet from the frozen men, and returned to his numbered slot on the floor. The moment passed and his cellmates soon dispersed, some into smaller groups, some back to sleeping. Remy studied the document carefully, not getting much out of it, just keywords here and there: *man, age, knife, outside, Huamei School, foreigner, fifteen days.*

"It say you stay here fifteen day."

Remy looked up to a well-built, clean prisoner standing over him. Remy returned a smile and offered his hand.

"Remy LeBeau."

"Giu Jing," he replied, shaking. Remy motioned for him to sit nearby but he continued to stand.

"It very bad. Longest time stay here. Any longer and go to prison."

"This isn't prison? There's a facility worse than this? How would that even work? What's worse than a hole in the floor as a toilet?"

The man shrugged, not understanding much of what was said.

"You try kill man? Why you want kill?"

"Well, it's a long story. And no one believes me anyway." He turned his attention to a distant sliver of window situated across the hallway in which one could almost envision a sky, and searched for the right words, completely overlooking a prisoner squatting over the toilet hole and the foul stench permeating throughout. In the end, he just shrugged. "I don't know how to say it. I was attacked first. That was important to me. I drew a knife only after weapons were drawn against me. I defended myself against two attackers. That doesn't sound like a crime to me. I don't feel especially guilty."

He repeated the bulk of this back to the man, speaking more slowly and using simpler words to get most of the point across.

"You good man," Giu Jing chuckled. "We all very good." They both shared a laugh.

"Actually, you lot seem fine to me. Except that one. He needs to bathe. He smells like he hasn't bathed in months. It's nauseating." Remy nodded across the floor to where an old man slept on his side, snoring loudly. Giu slowly nodded his agreement then held his index and middle finger across his nostrils, a gesture to block smell, showing he understood and agreed. "I know he's old and senile but we need to make sure he bathes tonight. Don't you think?"

Giu studied Remy before replying. "We talk him. It good idea."

"Xie xie." *Thank you.*

"Your Chinese very good."

"Better than your lying." They shared a last chuckle and Giu took a step back, looking for something else to do.

"Wait, before you go. What does this say my crime is? What do they say I did wrong?"

"You have knife. Knife bad."

"But it was a kitchen knife. Everyone has a kitchen knife at home, right? The knife itself can't be the illegal thing. Is there anything else?"

"You no have knife in kitchen. You have knife on road with bad men."

"Well, the knife has to get from the shop to the kitchen somehow. But yeah, I see the point. Still, I needed to protect myself. I was attacked first. Doesn't that count for something?"

Giu shrugged again, bored.

"Alright. Thank you. Have fun doing nothing over there, I guess." Remy waved as the man strolled into a chatting trio of men. He pointed to Remy and made exaggerated stabbing motions in the air while telling a story. The listeners turned to look at Remy with demeanors that had shifted from comfortable to concerned.

"Great," Remy muttered. "Now everyone thinks I'm a serial killer."

CHAPTER LXXII

CHINA

On the third day, Remy was called over to the locked gate at the head of the cell where a guard aggressively barked orders to him that he couldn't understand. He looked about, unsure how to proceed.

"He say, don't go." Giu called out from the back.

"He called me over here to tell me not to leave a locked cell?"

That was not the case. The massive padlock was soon unfastened and the iron gate slid to the side, revealing an opening just wide enough for Remy to slip through. He was then prodded downstairs, out of the holding cells, through an empty booking room, through a locker room for the prisoners, and then outside of the detainment building altogether. The door swung open to an outdoor walkway where he was met with fresh air and sunshine. The beauty of the moment lolled him into thinking he was to be released early for good behavior. Instead, he was nudged into an independent building near the main entrance of the facility.

The guard opened the door, motioned for Remy to step through, and closed it firmly behind him. Inside, a professionally dressed Caucasian woman in her early forties sat across from a solitary empty chair. To her right sat a Chinese official, presumably a guard based on his uniform, though Remy hadn't seen him around the facility. He was young and nervous and Remy immediately dismissed him, focusing solely on the woman.

"You're American." Remy presumed.

"I am. I work for the United States consulate of Guangzhou, China. I'm here to help you, Mr. LeBeau. Please take a seat."

"That's good news," he said, complying. "Let's get out of here. I could use a ride to the airport, too, if that doesn't put you out." A delicate grin emerged at the remark and he immediately took a shine to her. The Chinese official fidgeted disapprovingly in his chair.

"I'm afraid that's beyond my control, sir," she replied. The Chinese official fidgeted uncomfortably in his seat. "But I'm being rude. Allow me to introduce Mr. Chen. He's been assisting me in touring this facility."

Remy rose from his seat, leaned over and shook the man's sweaty hand.

"So, what do you think of the place?" he asked the American. "I mean, if I had known you were coming, I would've cleaned up a bit."

"I think our facilities in America are more humane," she replied curtly, sobering the mood. Mr. Chen visibly flinched in his seat.

"I'm sorry, but why is he here?"

"I'm here to assist America and Chinese relations," Chen replied.

"Good luck with that."

The consulate representative pressed on, in charge and owning it. "I cannot release you, Mr. LeBeau. You've been found guilty of a crime here according to their judicial system. There isn't much I can do about that."

"Their judicial system? Are you sure *judicial* is the right word? Pretty sure the captain of the police force was the sentencing judge. I was approached by two men with weapons and attacked and I'm the one in prison."

"I'm not arguing with you, Mr. LeBeau. I don't know the details but I've read the sentencing document. I know what you've been charged with."

"Guilty until proven innocent. I'm familiar with the concept."

"America doesn't recognize Chinese judicial verdicts." Her eyes shone a bit. *There's hope for you once this over,* her eyes seemed to speak. "But you'll be incarcerated for the next two weeks, I'm afraid. Now, we don't have much time together. So,---"

"Why don't we have much time?" No reply from the consulate rep. Remy turned to Mr. Chen who quickly looked away. "This has caused quite the international incident, hasn't it?" Remy asked through a smirk, connecting dots. His mind raced as he considered what might have been happening outside of his cramped cell since the incident transpired. China would have needed to notify America. America would have requested details of the arrest. High level players communicating with one another for the first time, probably awkwardly. Feathers were likely ruffled. Lines stepped over.

"What can I do for you, Mr. LeBeau?"

"What *can* you do for me? I don't understand what your powers are in this matter."

"Well, I can provide you with reading material. I brought these," she leaned over, flipped through a briefcase and came up with six magazines: *National Geographic, Time, Smithsonian,* and the like. Mr. Chen rose from his seat and approached the magazine stack, flipping through pages in search of contraband.

"They will need to be inspected first, of course," the rep stated.

"Thank you. That was very thoughtful. The waiting room of the U.S. consulate is now short on magazines, I bet. I doubt there is a protocol for this sort of thing." Her eyes confirmed his assumption. "I appreciate the sacrifice. If I may," he stated diplomatically, changing his tone, "be so bold as to inquire if accessing the novels in my suitcase would be allowed, as well. I haven't read Jonathan Livingston Seagull yet and this feels like the proper time for it."

"It's a very good story," she said, smiling cordially despite the formal environment. "I'm just surprised that you have that book with you. And you haven't read it yet? That was required reading for me in high school. Or was it middle school?" she pondered aloud, forgetting her environment for a moment or perhaps transcending it.

"It's on my to-do list and I do seem to have the time now."

"Almost as if you planned for this."

"I was prepared for something far different, actually."

She turned away and spoke swiftly in Mandarin to Chen, exhibiting fine control of the language.

"Just present the novels to an officer for inspection. You should be able to bring them back to your room."

"My room? Judicial system? You are an optimist. A glass half full kind of gal."

She stiffened.

"Look, I'm not trying to offend you or anything. I mean, the word *gal* doesn't sound demeaning to me, but whatever, if it makes you---"

"Food, Mr. LeBeau. I can help with the meals, too," she broke in.

"Okay." Remy took his cue and fell silent.

"How do you feel about the meals here?"

Chen was listening intently. For some reason, this was a hot topic.

"Well, I wouldn't call them meals. It's just rice mush. Over-boiled rice. That's it, except for the dark specks which I shouldn't look forward to but I do." Remy turned to face Chen, directing his words to the guard. "There's no calcium. No iron. No protein. No vitamin A through what is it now? K? And ten B's. What's that all about?" He turned back to the consulate rep who seemed to be suppressing mirth. "Seems like the B's should really have their own letters."

"You haven't lost your sense of humor, I see."

"It's all I have." A sorrow fell over him as he realized the truth of it. "It's really all I have now."

She sensed the gravity and straightened up in her seat, squaring her shoulders. "I can replace your meals. We've agreed to use a noodle shop nearby that the guards here often frequent. Your meals will change to---"

"Look, I'm sorry to interrupt you but will everyone incarcerated have their meals upgraded to noodles?"

"I think you know the answer to that, Mr. LeBeau. We cannot change the nutritional delivery system of this detainment facility. China is a sovereign nation and they serve food to their prisoners as they see fit. We can't change that." Chen nodded firmly, approving.

"Look at you nodding away like you're proud that your nation weakens and starves its prisoners. Is that something to be proud of? That your prisoners aren't fed properly? Come on, man. Wake up."

Chen stumbled through a reply about prisoners deserving punishment. Remy nodded politely until he finished talking, then turned back to the American representative.

"I appreciate the gesture and I would love to eat better food. But it just doesn't seem fair; me eating the good stuff while everyone else eats boiled mush. They're a decent bunch of guys in there. Not saints or anything but I'm beginning to think most of the decent people here are imprisoned. No. I couldn't dine on noodles and meat and veggies while they spooned mush into their mouths. It just wouldn't be right."

"Are you certain?"

"Stop tempting me. Please," he spoke around a soft smile. "Please. I want that. I very much want to eat better food, but it's wrong. It wouldn't be fair. No. I officially refuse."

He stood, bringing the meeting to a close. "I will take that reading material though." His mind drifted, imagining readings in the future sharing colorful magazine images with his cellmates.

"This is my card, Mr. LeBeau." She slid her consulate business card across the table. "I hope to hear from you later. When this is over, please call. Or send me an email." She locked eyes with him. "It was a pleasure meeting you."

"The pleasure was mine," he replied shaking her hand. "Thank you." He paused, looking down at the card, momentarily lost in thought. "I can't imagine what will happen next. None of this is part of the plan. Leaving here won't be much better than staying here. It's going to be hard for a while. A long while." He smirked playfully as was his way when faced with grave uncertainty, then turned about and walked to the exit in the back of the empty chamber. "It would be nice to speak with you again," he called over his shoulder as he exited. "Maybe one day I'll figure out how to tell this story."

CHAPTER LXXIII

CHINA

He returned to his cell balancing four novels and five magazines in his outstretched arms. A pretty good haul, all things considered. For the next twelve days, Remy read throughout most of the day, the exception being the morning marching routine, which he overdid dramatically for laughs, saluting each and every person in a goofy sort of protest. Some of the sterner guards, failing to understand the mocking that was going on, would often commend his apparent vigor and enthusiasm, humoring the cellmates all the more so. He brought a bit of happiness to them in the dungeon they shared, albeit fleeting, rekindling a vague echo of a sense of purpose in the man. He made a painful thing less unpleasant for the men who shared his long cell and for that he was pleased to have purpose.

Three hours or so after the ridiculous marching in place, national anthem, and one-hour indoctrination of the greatness of communism, the speakers would crackle on and the tune of *Yesterday, Once More* would muddle through the PA system signaling the coming of lunch. The ancient speaker system distorted the song to the point that the lyrics were practically unintelligible, and yet, the tune was enough to elicit hunger pangs and salivation, an unavoidable Pavlovian reaction which was likely the point in playing the song. Remy found the song choice odd given the environment, wondering why a soothing Chinese folk song didn't mark the lunch hour each day. Instead, the Carpenters crooned their famous tune each afternoon, looped for a half-hour or so while mush was distributed amongst the prisoners. Just as abruptly as the song crackled into existence, it would cut out as guards curtly collected and counted trays and chopsticks, leaving the men alone once again.

Remy's magazines were widely distributed among the cellmates for the first couple of days before the novelty of the imagery wore off. Finding the magazines casually discarded here and there, he brought them into his private domain -- two painted yellow lines on a concrete floor -- next to the stack of novels adjacent to his towel/pillow. Remy read every article in each magazine, finished Jonathan Livingston Seagull, reread Jonathan Livingston Seagull, reread his favorite articles, and finished two other novels, as Giu and others exited the facility and new stock entered in.

Female prisoners from the top floor were marched down for weekly pep talks on the basketball court eliciting a stirring among the men who would flock to the edge of the iron sliding gate that kept them locked in place, hooting and calling out, searching the distant stairwell for a glance of the ladies, finding only distant shadows against the stairwell walls at best. Many of these female prisoners would call back, laughing giddily from just beyond the edge of vision, disembodied voices that breathed hope of a normal existence one day. Remy couldn't follow what was said on either side of the distant exchange but the feeling seemed mutually appreciative, and so he guessed it wasn't overly lewd or sexual in nature. It felt like good-natured flirting on both sides. The guards hated this, but much like the exercising prisoners, they failed to quell the behavior.

It was not possible to tell a rainy day from a sunny one as only a sliver of sky was visible from a distant and mostly obscured window. Daylight glowed from afar but never truly touched the prisoners or penetrated the darkness of their cell. Fending off mold and mildew was a constant struggle, the only weapons barehanded rubbing, elbow grease, and splashed water from a broken and filthy bucket. Some new arrivals came in desperate need of cleanliness, most of which were senile and uncared for elderly men, others drunk and irate, needing to be calmed and as isolated as the cramped cell made possible. Immersed in a stench of feces, urine, stagnant water, mold, and body odor in the crowded dark cell, Remy caught up on all of the sleep stolen from him by the city of Guangzhou. It was boring and dank, but his last two apartments in Guangzhou had been much worse.

The days ticked by.

Having nothing opportune waiting for him outside of his cell, he wasn't exactly counting down the minutes until he would be released. While he had prepared himself for day one of freedom, day two and three and afterward held no promise. There was no realistic path to set himself upon. He wracked his mind between reading sessions searching for a way up and out once he returned to the states.

The math doesn't lie. I don't have enough money to keep myself aloft in a motel while I search for work, then wait two weeks for an undoubtedly small paycheck, if, and only if, I score a job soon after returning, which judging by the time I spent in Florida last year searching for employment, simply won't be the case. No matter how many different ways he approached the problem, it ended with him completely broke in America very soon.

Homeless shelters exceeding capacity equipped with a long wait list for entry. He'd checked on that grim possibility during those final days on Josh's couch. No one had answered his calls. No one had replied to email inquiries. Outdated websites had channeled a series of yes/no answers into an automated apology; there would be no room for him as he was not the head of a homeless family, nor a battered woman, elderly, or disabled.

He thought of the consulate representative, of explaining his tale to her, but was harkened back to relating the details to former friends and family, of the walls they had projected, of the shunning that had followed. The plan, such as it was, was to sleep in a cheap motel for a couple of nights, enjoy the last taste of whiskey he would experience for a long while and then call the police to surrender himself as homeless. From one cell to the next. The only alternative was theft: robbing vacant homes or places of business, but he found that repulsive and so prepared for a new stint in an American prison. Arrested for vagrancy.

As the final day of his confinement in the Chinese detainment center arrived, he was pleased but not ecstatic to hear his name called by a guard heading the gate. He gathered his reading materials and was soon surrounded by his cellmates, all grouped and clustered and shaking his hand awkwardly. He had not expected such a rousing farewell and was touched by it.

"Keep those chins up!" he called back to the prisoners that had shared his floor. He did not expect a reply, and yet, one voice thick in African accent replied, "Yes, brother." Remy smiled warmly as he descended the stairwell. The future, quite perilous. The recent past, not so bad.

CHAPTER LXXIV

CHINA

"Yeah, I hear what you're saying, I'm just not answering you."

"What?"

"I understand the questions you're asking. I just think they're none of your f*^%ing business so I'm ignoring you. Well, was ignoring you. Now, I'm engaging in conversation with you. The silence was better, right? You sure you want to be doing this?"

The officer was in his late-twenties and had grown a reasonably thick mustache. He was visibly stunned after Remy's rebuttal, having thought that his English was somehow the problem in the lack of communication. Remy meanwhile -- completely nude in a locker room while in the process of changing from the prison uniform into clean clothes gathered from his suitcase -- used the opportunity to graze his fingers along an envelope containing a wad of cash, and while in no position to open the envelope and count the bills, was heartened that the papery lump felt the same as when he tucked it away fifteen days ago.

Remy pressed on, "You going to keep yammering away, or can I dress myself? Back up, Sgt. Do-Right. I'm trying to put my clothes on over here." The other officers in the room almost openly laughed at this exchange. They seemed to be enjoying the show which puzzled Remy as he slipped on his briefs. Then it came to him.

"You're from out of town, aren't you?" He smiled as the words hit home, the young officer's slack expression all the proof he needed. "Tell me, do you live in Guangzhou?"

"I don't need to tell you that," he retorted, looking away, collecting himself. His English was quite good.

"Oh, really? Is that too personal a question for you? You just asked me for the phone numbers of my friends and family. Any friend. Any family member. Someone. Anyone. You sounded desperate and you lack couth. Why do you care if I contact them, pray tell? Is it because you're concerned for my emotional and physical wellbeing? You want to make sure I feel loved and cared for? Then improve this squalor. Put a toilet in each cell. Give a man a trial."

"Look, just don't speak down to me. Don't try to trick me. You look like a f*^#ing fool trying to deceive me and I just don't care enough to play the long con with you. Quite frankly, you won't be in my life long enough for it to be advantageous that you believe your deception is believed." Remy slipped on a clean undershirt atop proper trousers, feeling revitalized in properly fitting clothes. "Now, try again. Only speak to me like you're talking to a human being."

The officer collected himself and tried again. "Your family is very concerned for you. Your children. Call. Tell them you are okay. So sad, so scared for you, I think." He added a slight frown to the end of the statement, punctuating disappointment that Remy didn't care enough about his family to quench their worries.

Remy put on a mask of his own, showing a cracked exterior, an acceptance that he was in the wrong, a twinge of guilt he did not feel. "You're right," he said, staring down at his shoes. "I should at least speak to my kids. I mean, Joey, and Demetrius, little Nay-Nay... they must be wondering where I am right now. Joe-Joe, she's a dancer you know, so grown-up, but still so young, just a kid, really." He kept his face glued to the floor, unable to conceal a wide grin.

"They must miss their daddy."

At the word *daddy*, Remy burst out laughing. There was a wave of grumbling from the other officers as they began piecing together what had just happened, grumbles that swiftly turned to quiet chuckles as they slowly filed out, leaving the two men alone.

"Really didn't do your research with this one, Do-Right. How do you not know that I don't have children?" All false pretenses were gone, replaced by silent, smoldering hate mirroring Remy's obvious enjoyment. The mustached officer was in no rush to answer the question. "I've lived here for five years. No children. How is that not on file somewhere?"

Remy zipped his suitcase shut with false bravado, wishing little more than to be able to open up the envelope that he hoped still contained around $300 in cash. Instead, he looked up and focused solid eye contact with the furious police officer. "Look, I asked you if you really wanted me to engage in conversation with you and you pressed on. I asked you to be real with me after your insistence and you didn't. I don't feel bad for you, copper. You don't care about my family and friends. You just want me to call them so they'll send money and buy an airline ticket to take me back to the United States. Only you're going to do that, Do-Right. China's going to pay the bill, and let me tell you, this vile place owes me more than a single one-way ticket. But hey, it's a start." He opened his designated locker door and returned possessions from a metal shelf into his pockets. The officer eyed the items intently.

"No phone, officer." There was in fact a phone, with battery and SIM removed tucked away in the suitcase. "No friends or family, so no need for a phone, though that really isn't any of your business at all. I'm not going to ask a soul for money, Sgt. Do-Right. Not any-one. This was a one-way trip that was supposed to end very differently. I didn't bring return fare. I'm not going to ask for return fare. You are paying the cost of travel back to America. Get that through your head and stop acting like you give a shit about my life. You don't."

The officer muttered angrily to himself in Mandarin.

"Now, you're getting it. You're also going to drive me to the airport so let's get going. Or I'll stay at a motel nearby while you figure this all out. Are we leaving today or tomorrow? Talk to me. What's going on?"

"Now. We leaving now. Do you have money to pay for the ticket? How much money do you have with you?"

"I have zero dollars and zero cents that I will pass your way. Have I not made that clear to you? I'd burn it into ash before I hand it to you." Remy flicked a lighter, testing that it still sparked into flame, emphasizing his point. He pulled a cigarette from the pack and inhaled the aroma of unburnt tobacco through widened nostrils, savoring the scent before tucking the smoke behind his right ear. He slipped backpack straps over his shoulders, grabbed the handle of his suitcase, tilted it back on its wheels, and set out for the neighboring room, the booking station, where a friendly, thirty-something Chinese lady worked behind a counter.

Sgt. Do-Right caught up with him easily and grabbed Remy's shoulder, pulling him back. Remy abandoned the suitcase, the bulk slamming noisily on the tiled floor as he pivoted. With aligned posture, squared hips and shoulders, he pivoted.

"Do-Right, I'm losing my patience with you. Why are you touching me right now?"

"You must come with me. We are leaving now."

"No. We're leaving after I speak with that lady at the booking window. I'm obviously not a danger to anyone here. You're just being fussy that I schooled you in front of your peers. Now, please remove your hand from my shoulder like a civilized person would do and allow me to do something that will help this place before I leave."

Instead, the grip grew tighter. Remy raised his voice dramatically, prepared to act.

"Oy! What are you doing to me? Oy! Everyone see this?!" he shouted to a room full of police officers who were engaged in surrounding and intimidating a suspect being taken into custody and an accompanying saddened family sniffling amongst the perimeter.

Everyone froze. All attention shifted to Remy and the officer who held him back by the shoulder. Remy remained calm and gently pointed to the booking window, making his objective obvious to all, regardless of language barriers. "I just want to go there. To help, not hurt. This won't take long. Relax." With all eyes on the scene, he pivoted out of the weakened grasp, turned his back to his attacker, and walked calmly into a line that had developed nearby the new arrestee. Sgt. Do-Right detached himself and sat on a bench nearby while Remy waited patiently for his turn in line. One officer, tall and athletic, inserted himself next to Remy as he waited for the newcomer to be arrested, feeling him out, ensuring that the loud foreigner posed no danger. Remy made eye contact and they shared a forced, false smile. Remy tried a little English with him, but the officer spoke none. Not a little. None.

Remy nodded his head over to where Sgt. Do-Right was thumbing away on his mobile phone, wholly unaware. "Shanghai?" Remy guessed.

"Beijing," the officer replied.

Remy stuck out his bottom lip in respect and surprise. Beijing was a long way away. Similar to an FBI agent coming in alone to a local police station. *Such an agent would not be loved,* Remy thought, looking back to Sgt. Do-Right. *Yeah, that would explain it all. But it's not like I can trust anything in this place.*

Five minutes later, the shirtless soon-to-be prisoner was led away, leaving a tearful family sitting along plain, wooden benches, sobbing and conferring with one another about what to do next. Remy, now head of the line, approached the booking counter with a wide, true smile.

"Greetings, police woman. How are you? I bet no one asks you that question with this job? How are you?"

She smiled, understanding only half of the English, "I'm fine, thank you. And you?" And then realizing how tired such an answer was, she added, "I good. Today good. *Xie xie.*" *Thank you.*

"Good to hear. Listen, my driver is in a hurry to go and honestly, that doesn't sound half bad to me either, but I do have a quick thing I want to do first." He crouched and opened his suitcase, removing the novels and magazines that had been gifted to him by the consulate. "I want to give these to you. To the detainment center or prison or whatever this is. Whatever you call this place, it needs a library, ma'am. These men need something to read. Something positive, preferably. The forced reading of the communist party doctrines each morning doesn't make these guys love the system more." He slid over the magazines and novels. "I know there's an African gentleman in custody that would like to read these. That's a good start. Would you do that for me? Please. It would mean a lot to him. And me."

"I will take these," she answered, receiving the package.

"To the African. And then keep them here?"

"Yes."

"As a little library for other to use?"

"Others use this. Yes. I understand."

"Beautiful! That's what I wanted to hear. Thank you." Remy turned about and prepared to leave. "And feel free to add some more to that little stack. Plenty of good Chinese novels out there. These guys need good reading material in their lives, not just government propaganda. Point them in the right direction, you know? Help them."

"Okay," she called after him, doubtfully understanding the nuance of each word. "Goodbye."

"Such a nice prison. I mean, the conditions were abhorrent but the people were actually quite pleasant," he remarked to himself, wheeling his belongings toward Do-Right who stood upright at his approach and began ushering Remy to the exit. "Okay, okay. I'm coming. Chill out. Just lead the way. I'm hauling quite a bit of stuff here so I'm not going to give you the slip or anything." Do-Right kept pace while Remy exited, visibly upset at the need to slow his gait. In the parking lot a police van sat waiting, the driver dozing at the wheel. Do-Right jogged up, rousing the driver into wakefulness, barking commands at the man. Suddenly on his own, Remy looked left, then right, then slowly walked down the parking lot in another direction, strolling off while whistling innocently. The joke was completely lost on Do-Right, who jogged back, ready to apprehend.

Remy turned about with a smile, "You really need a hobby, Do-Right. Come on, man. Relax a little. If I can laugh about this, you certainly should."

But Do-Right did not laugh. Remy lit the cigarette he had stored behind his ear as he proceeded to the van. Do-Right sat alongside Remy in the backseat during the short ride to the airport. Remained as close as if they were handcuffed all throughout the airport, all the way through to the first security checkpoint. As Remy made his way to the head of the line, he broke a long silence.

"I've had fifteen days to think about today. Don't take it personally. You asking me and mine for money to pay for this airline ticket was totally predictable. You driving me to the airport, staying with me the whole way, also foreseen. You representing Beijing? That was different. I didn't think Beijing would get involved. Actually, the really interesting part was how little Guangzhou thinks of you, Beijing-man. There is a divide here that most people don't know about."

The officer said nothing. Fuming.

Remy pressed on. "Oh, you're so cute when you're angry. I would pinch those rosy cheeks of yours but I'm pretty sure you would break my arm."

"You go now. Don't come back to China."

Remy smiled sweetly. "Be good, Do-Right. Maybe I'll see you around one day."

<u>USA</u>

The flight across the Pacific had become a familiar commute. There was neither thrill nor fear as the landing gear clutched the runway. He hadn't arrived home. He wasn't on vacation. There was no business to be done. Limbo. Unavoidable limbo in every direction.

He snatched the suitcase off the looping conveyor belt of passenger luggage passionlessly, mind and body in two different places. Ignoring airport etiquette, he zipped open his suitcase on the floor nearby, combing through its contents until he reached the cash-filled envelope which turned out to be all present and accounted for. He found a cheap motel five miles from L.A.'s international airport, hopped on a bus, and spent half of the bundle securing a room for two nights.

He drank all of the scotch that remained in the bottle from the day in which he had intended to kill and die, passing out drunk while mumbling happily into clean bedsheets. He awoke late into the second day, devoured a loaded pizza, bought more scotch, drank excessively, and tried to develop a plan but there was nowhere to go and nothing to do. The only thing he knew as he slept that second night was that the third would be far less comfortable. He awoke later the next morning, drank the remainder of the second bottle of scotch -- just a few shots or so -- and moved his suitcase down to the checkout counter where a lobby attendant assured him that his belongings would be secure for twenty-four hours, after which they would be subject to search and removal. He nodded dully and stepped outside.

The idea was to walk northward across California to Oregon and then Washington. There was a vague notion of continuing through Canada and into Alaska to locate and join a tribe of native peoples, doing his part to contribute: hunting, fishing, farming, protecting. A long walk to surpass all the long walks before it. It didn't strike Remy as a realistic goal, but being the only one he had, he began putting it into action.

He passed the airport an hour later. Kept walking. Three hours after that, the township or district or whatever Torrance is, came and went on his right. He soldiered on: sweaty, hot, uncertain of direction. A familiar sense of unease. Backtracking so as to continue in a northern progression, he crossed a swath of undeveloped land alongside the interstate, ending up in an isolated neighborhood full of sharp hills and fine gated homes. Vast yards contained by high brick walls dotted the landscape. Beverly Hills. *This is definitely where the successful movie types live. No doubt about that.* Iron gates barred entry into the majority of driveways he passed. There was a distinct absence of sidewalks that very clearly stated: "We do not support pedestrians here."

Most of the homes seemed unoccupied. Thirsty and sore, he squinted into the setting sun, mulling over what to do next before settling on resting among the roots of a tree growing in a grassy patch of land between two single lane roads running parallel with one another. He surveyed his immediate surroundings, seriously considering scaling over a wall and sleeping under a tree in a private yard or alongside the outer wall of a vacant house for the night. In the end, concerns of trespassing won out. Not so much of the legal ramifications but mostly how his presence might frighten an innocent.

Coupled with the notion that traveling mostly by night would be the wiser way to hike he powered on, kneeling and resting for ten minutes periodically to gather his strength alongside neighborhood roads that oddly lacked sidewalks. He continued on for a few more hours before finally arriving at Santa Monica, a deserted stretch of beach in the midnight hour. He found no trouble finding an open bench to stretch out his cramping legs and soon his head grew heavy and he fell into a rough slumber, awakening with a start sometime later as a police car rolled by, slowed, and turned about. *Danger,* his mind flashed, and his body shot upward, suddenly awake. He was on his feet and walking away from the bench against the direction of the recently doubled-back police car before he had even fully awakened, instinct moving muscle rather than thought.

As the vehicle disappeared from sight, he turned and faced the ocean, continuing on until he reached the northernmost edge, the point where a pedestrian traveling north was forced to either turn east and return to wealthy neighborhoods or tromp through shin-high water in order to continue moving northward. Exhausted to the point of stumbling, he spied a public outdoor restroom on the beach and collapsed on a sandy floor smelling of antiseptic and human waste, legs cramping in protest of recent activities. Two hours of restlessness later, he abandoned the concept of walking to Oregon and began the long walk back to the cheap motel five miles south of the airport. He took a bus as dawn progressed into morning, arriving back at the motel in just enough time to retrieve his suitcase, which was almost sent away, twenty-three hours into a twenty-four-hour limitation.

He secured a room for one more night, collapsed onto soft bedding, and slept until late afternoon, sore and detached. Heavily burdened by life, he placed a call to the Los Angeles police force.

"Los Angeles police department. What is the nature of your emergency?"

"Yeah, it's not an emergency. I'm just broke. I have no money, no family, no friends. Even my dog's gone. This sounds like a country song now that I say it all aloud. Anyway, I have zero money and no place to sleep. I'm pretty sure that's illegal. So, I'm calling to tell you to pick me up. I have no money so come and put me in jail."

"Sir?"

"Yes?"

"It's not illegal to be poor, sir."

"Yeah, it sort of is. I don't have a place to sleep at night so I'll be loitering. Nobody wants homeless people sleeping in front of their houses and offices, right? Pretty sure, that's not acceptable."

Pause.

"You know, I thought I would just sort of walk until opportunity crossed my path or I died, but that didn't work out. I couldn't hack it. I sort of hate long walks now anyway, and it wasn't such a solid plan to begin with."

Long, awkward pause.

"So, come pick me up. My name is Remy LeBeau and this is where I'm located." He spouted out the motel's address.

"No officers will go there. I don't know what to tell you, sir."

"Tell me what to do. What can I do? I have no money."

"Call a homeless shelter, sir. This is the line for the police department of…"

"Yeah, I know what number I just dialed. I've called those shelter lines. No one picked up the phone. Nobody returned my voicemail. No replies to my emails."

A deep pause. "I don't know what to say." Another pause, and then the voice shifted into something humane. "I didn't know it was like that. I'm sorry."

"It's not your fault. Thank you, though. Feels like I'm talking to a human now."

A brittle laugh. "We are busy, you know."

"Yeah, I'm sure you are." Another pause, this one warm and comfortable. "What should I do next, ma'am? I've never been in this situation before. I don't know what to do."

"Go to Skid Row. You'll find something there."

"Go to where? Sounded like you named a late eighties rock group for a second there."

She chuckled. "I think you're going to be fine in Los Angeles, sir."

"Yeah, it's really not feeling that way right now."

"Go to downtown. Do you have bus fare?"

"Not much else, but yeah, I've ten dollars or so. Maybe twenty." He checked the contents of his wallet, stifling the urge to hyperventilate. "Not twenty."

"That's enough. Get on a bus and get to Skid Row. Just get there before sunset or you won't find a bed tonight."

"Downtown? Go to downtown L.A. and find Skid Row before five p.m.?"

She chuckled in a way that Remy found very comforting.

"Yes."

"Anything else you want to tell me?"

"Good luck." She replied with sincerity, and then she was gone, leaving Remy to figure out the details on his own.

CHAPTER LXXV

USA

"If you go down there, they gonna' chase you down the street."

He nodded casually to the remark, unable to pinpoint the exact source of the comment from the bustling sidewalk and too preoccupied to care. The advice went wholly unheeded as he continued onward through sidewalks pockmarked with loose papers and cellophane plastic, turning this way and that to avoid pools of bodily waste and general filth that covered the ground.

"They'll eat you up," the old woman continued as he walked past. *He don't belong here,* she thought to herself, slowly resuming her duties tending to a disheveled shop along Los Angeles' lower quarters. Skid Row. Official signs at intersections provided the names of streets that few vehicles utilized in lettering too faded to read. Sidewalks choked with tents and sleeping bags and huddles of the poverty-stricken. The young, the old, the sick, criminals and the innocent, Christians, Muslims, Atheists, blacks, whites, Hispanics, men, women, children, artists, laborers, introverts and extroverts, singers, dancers, do-nothings and did-it-alls, the hopeful and the hopeless, all coalesced seeking shelter and food.

The sun hovered low in the sky, illuminating a horizon choked with tenements and dilapidated motels with promising names. Paradise Inn. Fortune Hotel. Titles standing in stark contrast to reality. It was a clear day in L.A., the sky blue and boastful, the sidewalks predominantly filled with blacks and Latinos with just a sprinkling of white, the stereotypical American demographic turned on its head. Further in, a large group milled at the closed gates of a shelter, staring through the bars of an iron gate at the idea of warmth, a roof, hot water, and food within. Remy arrived with a worn suitcase in tow, wearing a mask of confidence. Around him, destitute men clustered and gossiped.

"A man got stabbed out here yesterday. Got'n an argument and that other man just opened him up. Then he done run away."

"Some guy walked up to me with a knife last week. Said he was paid to watch my back, to protect me. Can you believe that?! I don't even know the man. Just walks up to me and says, 'They pay me to watch your back.' I looked down and he has this little knife in his hand. I said, 'If you stab me, you better kill me 'cause I'll....'"

"I hope they serve somethin' good in there tonight. Last night's was disgustin'."

Smiles, nods. Compassionate grimaces over shared misfortune, laughter at a stranger's.

Others worked the north and south corners, hustling marijuana, cocaine, crack, and crank. "I got those boulders."

"I got that smoke."

"What you need? You good?"

A light-skinned black woman wearing a hot pink wig and a strained smile walked briskly through the scene, arm in arm with a dark-skinned man whose face showed only resolution. Emaciated and trying her best to look sexy, poorly clothed in shorts that covered too little leg and sagged at the waistline with a top that hung loosely off of the shoulders. The whole outfit jostled about her bony form, threatening to fall of completely with each step. She wore the ensemble with head held high as might a baroness, thoroughly stained though it was. The couple rounded the corner and was soon out of sight, leaving Remy with less interesting inhabitants of the city streets to study.

The homeless in downtown L.A. were generally quite familiar with one another and Remy was the freshest of fish. An inch-long, thick, curly, white beard situated about a face framed with high cheekbones and a prominent chin. His eyes, normally bright and on the greener side of hazel, were slightly sunken and far darker than normal. He looked tired and worn and he was. Observing the sights and sounds of the place, judging potential dangers, finding his bearings, life itself, had all taken their toll and while the promise of a dry bed and a hot shower inside was a lovely thing to focus on, he was as prepared as one can be to be refused and turned back onto unfriendly sidewalks to fend for himself, sleeping and living publicly. *If there is a God,* Remy thought, *he does not smile upon me and I have nothing to say to him.*

"Is this the line to the mission?" he asked, knowing the answer, attempting to initiate conversation with a trio of young men that had been eyeing him in the way that hungry wolves eye sheep. They didn't respond to the direct line of questioning and turned away, though they soon began sizing him up once again. "I, say," repeated Remy, "Is this the line to the mission?" using his hands to articulate the question, puffing up and demonstrating that he would not be easy game. Their eyes lowered. "Not even tryin' talk to you," one muttered. Remy accepted this and rolled his suitcase away. He had time to kill before the gates were scheduled to open and with the crowd tightening uncomfortably into a chaotic semi-circle of pushing, cutting, and pressing inward, he left and put some distance between himself and the shelter.

From Fifth Street over to Sixth, to Seventh, he walked in a casual stride, in no hurry, taking in the environment, breathing deeply through widened nostrils, taking in the scents of the street. Urine, perfume, incense, marijuana, human feces, tobacco, the odors of the washed and unwashed alike taken in without prejudice in cool detached absorption, analyzing, trying to make some sense of it all. The crowds thinned and the number of tents lessened as he approached the fishing district on Ninth Street, a region of warehouses where truckloads of seafood were sorted, labeled, and reshipped. Two vigilant seagulls perched along the edge of a rooftop transfixed a steely gaze upon the potential troublemaker until he turned the corner and was out of sight.

He looped his way back to the more densely populated region of Skid Row, circumnavigating those who inserted themselves into his path -- beggars, drug pushers, the inebriated, the fearful and the frightening, the sick and the old -- with disinterest, too exhausted to feel threatened or disrespected or compassionate.

Sweating in the newly setting sun as he hauled his luggage block after block, he stopped for a rest in the shade along the side of a building, unbuttoned his cuffs and folded up the long sleeves of his white and blue striped, button-up shirt. Leaving his belongings resting against a wall nearby, he approached the edge of the sidewalk and surveyed the scene. Shielding his eyes from the blazing sun slowly lowering in the western sky, he took in the surroundings of Skid Row: north to south, east to west. *This is my neighborhood now,* he thought to himself. *For better or worse.* Behind him, the downtown skyline sat poised in the distance as he surveyed the streets, providing the backdrop for a songbird that flitted by, a flash of feather and song.

END

Milton Keynes UK
Ingram Content Group UK Ltd.
UKHW040707120324
439192UK00001B/57